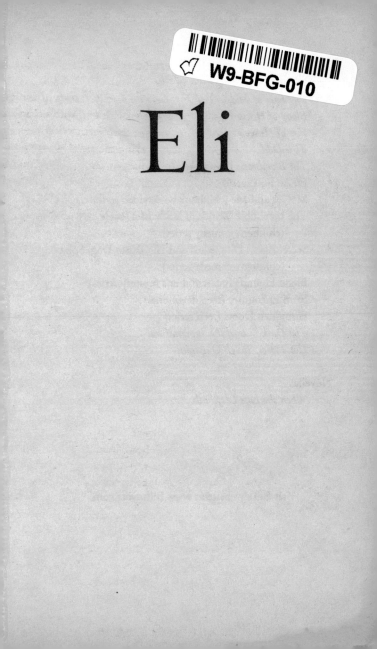

Eli

Other Books by Bill Myers

The Face of God
Blood of Heaven
Fire of Heaven
Threshold
The Bloodstone Chronicles
Eli Audio Pages®
McGee and Me (children's book/video series)
The Incredible Worlds of Wally McDoogle
    (children's comedy series)
Secret Agent Dingledorf and His Trusty Dog, Splat
    (children's comedy series)
Blood Hounds Inc. (children's mystery series)
Faith Encounter (teen devotional)
Forbidden Doors (teen series)
The Dark Side of the Supernatural
Hot Topics, Tough Questions

Novellas
When the Last Leaf Falls

visit Bill's website at www.Billmyers.com

Eli

BILL MYERS

ZONDERVAN™

GRAND RAPIDS, MICHIGAN 49530 USA

ZONDERVAN™

Eli
Copyright © 2000 by Bill Myers

This title is also available as a Zondervan ebook product. Visit
www.zondervan.com/ebooks for more information.

This title is also available as a Zondervan audio product. Visit
www.zondervan.com/audiopages for more information.

Requests for information should be addressed to:

Zondervan, *Grand Rapids, Michigan 49530*

ISBN: 0-310-25114-1

Published in association with the literary agency of Alive Commu-
nications, Inc., 7680 Goddard Street, Suite 200, Colorado Springs,
CO 80920.

Interior design by Tracey Moran

Printed in the United States of America

02 03 04 05 06 07 08 /❖ OP/ 10 9 8 7 6 5 4 3 2 1

For Eve Roberts,
who helped me understand the power of drama

This is fiction, nothing more. It's merely an attempt to examine some issues and to get us thinking about others. It is certainly no substitute for the real thing. Those familiar with my fiction know that I believe storytelling's greatest strength lies in its ability to stir up our thoughts. By putting the gospel in a contemporary setting, I've moved Christ out of my comfort zone and put him back in my face where he can test me, challenge me, and encourage me. By stripping away the historical and cultural trappings that I hide behind to insulate myself from his truths, I allow him to become more of the radical life-changer he was the first time I encountered him.

Unfortunately, the attempt also brings with it some failures. First, by removing the rich Jewish heritage of the gospel, I've deprived the story of much of its depth. There were times, for instance, when I wanted to elaborate on the hundreds of Old Testament prophecies and symbolism that speak of Christ, but this novel was not the forum for that.

Still, that failure and others only underline the fact that this is merely an appetizer. For those who haven't yet enjoyed the feast, don't waste time here—go to the real banquet. Read the book that most of antiquity and today's scholars still insist is the greatest piece of writing in human history. If it's been a while since you cracked open a Bible, or if you've never really explored it, start off with the gospel of John. In one sense, it's the easiest, in another, the most profound.

And since I'm in a confessional mood, there's another shortcoming you need to be aware of as you read this novel. To accurately portray a world in which Christ has not yet come would be to create a society so dark and ugly that it's doubtful any of us would recognize it, let alone relate to it. To do so would have again defeated my purposes. So, I didn't. If you're interested in the impact Jesus Christ has had upon our society, Kennedy and Newcombe's book, *What If Jesus Had Never Been Born,* gives interesting insights on how different our society would be today if Jesus had not come.

A final note. Scripture makes it clear that the Christ would come as a man born of woman only once. It states that his second coming will not be like his first. The first was the meek servant who washed our feet and died for our failures. According to Scripture, the second time he comes it will be as a conquering King. In fact, Jesus himself warned that if someone born into our world today claimed to be the Christ (even with accompanying miracles) he would be a counterfeit, the antichrist prophesied long ago. According to Jesus Christ, when he appears the next time it will be from the heavens, accompanied by the glory of God.

Now, to the thanks. Grateful appreciation goes to Debbie Setters, my research assistant Doug McIntosh, my agent Greg Johnson, Dave Lambert, Lori VandenBosch, Joel Carlson, Tony Myles, Tina Schuman, Sue Brower,

Sherry Guzy, Nancy Rue, Lissa Halls Johnson, Nancy Hargiss-Tatlock, Lynn Marzulli, Vincent Crunk, Craig and Sue Cameron, Dr. Di, and Janey DeMeo. A special thanks also to my children Nicole and Mackenzie who would indulge me in playing the "What If Jesus Were Here Today" game (a sneaky way for their dad to get ideas). And finally and always to my friend and partner in life, Brenda.

Bill Myers
www.Billmyers.com

"The thief comes only to steal and kill and destroy. I have come that you might have life, and have it to the full."

Jesus Christ

PART ONE

Monday was an inconvenient time to die. Come to think of it, Tuesday through Sunday weren't all that agreeable either. Conrad Davis had too many important things to do. Too many fires to put out. Too many producers to plead with, cajole, and, if necessary, circumvent.

Not interesting? Too cerebral? What were they talking about? Did they honestly think TV audiences were that stupid?

"Give us another multibirth story," they'd said. "Those McCaughey septuplets, don't they have a birthday coming up? Or how about another psychic piece—some mother visited by her dead daughter; those always work."

"Guys . . ." Conrad glanced around the table in the smoke-filled war room. He could already feel the back of his neck beginning to tighten. "We're talking about a major scientific breakthrough here."

But the other producers of the prime time news magazine, *Up Front,* continued without hearing. "Or how 'bout another cripple story," suggested Peggy Martin, one of the few females on staff. "Some guy in a wheelchair climbing Mount Everest or something."

"Guys . . ."

"We did that last November."

"Guys!"

"Listen, Connie." It was Phil Harrison, the show's exec. He took a drag off his cigarette and motioned to the monitor where they'd just viewed a rough cut of Conrad's segment. "All we're saying is that this piece is too cerebral. I mean, 'Parallel Universes'? Come on, who cares?"

Leo Singer, a rival producer, snickered. "Next time he'll be doing a piece on quantum physics."

The rest of the room chuckled. It was supposed to be good-natured, but Conrad knew that nothing in this dog-eat-dog world of TV journalism was good-natured. One or two missteps, like producing a worthless segment that no one cared about, could spell disaster—especially with five thousand kids half his age waiting in the wings for his job.

"Is that what you would have said about the Wright Brothers at Kitty Hawk?" Conrad argued. "Or the moon landing, or the invention of the light bulb—that it's too cerebral? What we're talking about is the existence of other realities right here beside our own, worlds identical to ours but with minor, or sometimes major, differences."

"Worlds we can't even see," another producer pointed out.

"How convenient," Singer sighed.

Peggy Martin added, "And worlds that have no effect upon the lives of our viewers."

Conrad glanced at the faces around the table. He was going down for the count, and his colleagues, better known as competitors, were doing their best to keep him there. But he'd been in this position a hundred times before, refusing to dish out pabulum for the masses, insisting upon truth and relevancy. That's how he'd earned the two Emmys and those countless other awards.

"Connie." It was Harrison again. "This professor that you interviewed . . . what's his name?"

"Endo."

"All this Professor Endo has is theory, right?"

"Plus support from top world physicists," Conrad corrected, "not to mention some staggering mathematical formulas."

"Oh, mathematics, that'll kick up the ratings," Singer scoffed. Others around the table agreed. The tension from Conrad's neck crept into the base of his skull.

Harrison continued. "If there was something tangible, something you could show on tape, then you'd have a story. But this . . ." Harrison shook his head and dropped his cigarette into the half-empty can of Diet Coke. It hissed quietly as he turned to the next producer. "Wolff, how's that toxic-waste segment coming?"

The meeting had been less than two hours ago, and Conrad was already back on the 101 heading north out of Los Angeles. Professor Endo lived an hour outside the city in the town of Camarillo. If they wanted something tangible, he'd get something tangible. Not because this story was a great passion of his, but because he needed it. Despite his twenty-five years in news, despite past accolades, a setback like this could seriously cripple a career. That's how the business was. There was no resting on your laurels. You were only as good as your last segment. And if your last segment was a failure . . .

It had started to rain, the first time since early April. Conrad reached over and turned on his wipers. The blades had rotted from last summer's sun, and their first few passes left dirty smears. How ironic. Here he was driving a $72,000 Jaguar but couldn't find the time to replace its wiper blades. But that's how it was with everything in his life—too busy winning the prizes to enjoy them. And he had won them, won them all, everything he'd ever wanted and more: great job, great pay, esteem from his peers, plenty of toys, beautiful wives (although a few more than he'd intended), and the list went on. Yet over the past several years, the list had begun to grow more and more meaningless. And, though he tried his best to ignore it, an empty hollowness had begun gnawing and eating away at him. He'd won the game, all right; the only problem was that neither the victory nor the prizes meant anything.

He pumped the washer fluid a few times and the smearing on the windshield thinned. Glancing at his speedometer, he eased back to 70. Besides the oil that had accumulated on the pavement these many rainless weeks, there was also the recurring amnesia Southern Californians suffer whenever it comes to remembering how to drive on wet roads. He'd been in several fender benders since moving to L.A., many of them thanks to the rain.

He rolled his head, trying to work out the tension in his neck. He pulled a bottle of Motrin from his coat pocket, popped another handful into his mouth, and glanced around for something to wash them down. Nothing. Just a couple empty Taco Bell bags, some wadded up Big Mac wrappers, and a stale bag of corn chips. Ah, the glamorous life of a TV reporter. He held the pills on his tongue until he accumulated enough saliva to swallow one. Then he repeated the process for the next, and the next, and the next—each one going down a little harder than the last.

A sign read *23 Freeway North*. Good. Just a couple more miles, then down the steep grade into Camarillo.

He'd already put in a call to his favorite cameraman, Ned Burton, as well as to the lighting and sound guys, to meet him there. And, before that, to Professor Endo, who was only too happy to oblige with another interview.

"Something tangible?" the doctor had asked in his faint Japanese accent.

"Exactly," Conrad said. "Your theories and formulas, they're all very interesting, but we need something we can show on tape, something the audience can grasp."

"Certainly, that will be no problem."

"Really? Like what? Eyewitnesses? People who have seen these—"

The old man chuckled. "I am afraid that if there are eyewitnesses to such universes, you would find them locked up in insane asylums, or involved in drug rehab programs."

"Then what?" Conrad asked. "How can you physically prove the existence of parallel universes if no one has seen them?"

"It is an old experiment, really. I am sorry I did not mention it to you before."

"What do you need to set it up?"

"I have all that is necessary at the lab. Just a board with two small slits cut into it and a low-powered laser."

"That's it?"

"That is all. We shine the laser onto the two slits and record how many slits of light appear on the wall behind it."

"I don't understand. Two slits in the board will cast two slits on the wall."

"Actually, they will cast several more than two."

"Several? That's impossible."

"You will see for yourself. And if we cut two more slits in the board how many will appear on the wall?"

Conrad frowned. "I'd say four, but you're going to tell me twice as many as whatever the two slits were."

"Actually, with four slits there will be half as many bands of light as if there were only two slits."

"That's crazy."

"Yes, if you are thinking in terms of a single universe. But ask today's best scientific minds, Stephen Hawking and others, and they will say invisible light beams from other worlds similar to ours that are involved in the very same experiment at the very same time are actually interfering with some of our beams."

"And you can prove this?"

"I shall be waiting for you in the lab."

Even as he thought over the conversation, Conrad shook his head. To think that there was another one of him traveling to another Camarillo to meet with another professor at this exact same moment—it was incomprehensible. And not just one of him, but millions, all identical. Well, not exactly identical, because according to Endo, each of his counterparts still had a free will to make different decisions along the way. One Conrad Davis could have waited to ride with his crew. Another could have agreed with his boss to cancel the segment. Or another could have decided to pursue philosophy in college instead of journalism. And on and on it went, the possibilities infinite.

Then there was the matter of time . . .

"It is my personal belief," Endo had said, "that these various realities may also be traveling at different velocities. For some, an entire lifetime of seventy to eighty years may be lived in just a few of our hours. For others, it may be just the opposite."

"You're telling me that there's someone exactly like me in another reality who's only living a few hours?"

"A few hours by our standards, yes. But by his, it will be the full eighty years."

No wonder Harrison and the others thought the story was over everyone's head. But if this sort of thing could be proven in the lab and actually captured on videotape . . .

The rain came down harder, and he turned the wiper speed to high. Conrad was nearly fifty years old, but the methodic *swish-swish, swish-swish* of the wiper blades still brought warm memories of his childhood in Washington State, where the sound of windshield wipers was a part of many a car trip.

He crested the ridge and started down the steep grade into Camarillo. Even shrouded by clouds, it was a beautiful sight. The coastal mountains rose on either side, giving one last burst of rock and cliff before dropping suddenly to the flat coastal plain seven hundred feet below. In the distance, the furrowed fields of onions and strawberries stretched all the way to the ocean, or at least as far as the newest housing development that encroached upon them.

Swish-swish, swish-swish . . .

The left lanes of traffic had slowed, so he threw a look over his shoulder and pulled into the far right where there was less congestion. He glanced up through the windshield. It was still there. Up to the left. The jagged rock formation that looked like the profile of a noble Indian surveying the valley. Being the first to spot it was a favorite pastime of Suzanne and little Julia whenever they took their Sunday drives up the coast.

Swish-swish, swish-swish . . .

Sunday drives up the coast—one of the few bribes that had actually worked in luring Suzanne away from church. She'd been a good woman. The best he'd had. Committed to her family at any cost. Granted, she may have been a little fanatical in the faith department, but her beliefs in God posed no real threat for them. He gave her her space, and she gave him his. And, truth be told, the older he got, the more wisdom he saw in some of her God talk.

God . . . if all this multi-world business was true, it would be interesting to see how the theologians would try and squeeze him into the picture. And what about the great religious leaders? What about Jesus Christ? If, as Suzanne had always insisted, this world needed to be "saved," then didn't all these similar worlds need to be saved as well? Again Conrad shook his head. The implications were staggering.

Swish-swish, swish-swish . . .

He could smell the mixture of dust and water that came with the first rain. Under that, the faint aroma of onions wafting up from the valley. He smiled, almost sadly, as he remembered little Julia holding her nose, complaining about the smell. Those had been good times. Some of the best. In fact, if he could pick one season in his life to freeze and forever live in, it would be—

The blast of an air horn jarred Conrad from his thoughts. He glanced up at his mirror and saw a big rig approaching from behind, flashing its high beams. *Come on,* he thought, *no one's in that big of a hurry.* Sure, he'd moved into the truck lane, but he was already exceeding the speed limit. Besides there was traffic directly ahead, so what was the big—

The horn blasted again. Longer, closer.

Conrad looked back into the mirror. The truck was rapidly approaching. In a matter of moments it would be on Conrad's tail, trying to intimidate him. But Conrad Davis was not so easy to intimidate.

More blasting.

"What's your problem?" Conrad mouthed the words into the mirror, raising his hands, motioning to the traffic around them. "What do you want me to do?"

And then he saw the driver. A kid. He wasn't looking at Conrad. Instead, he was fighting something in the cab. Perhaps stomping on foot pedals or wrestling with the gearshift—Conrad couldn't tell for certain. He didn't have to. Because when the young driver finally looked up, Conrad saw the terror in the boy's eyes.

Conrad quickly looked to the left, searching for a way to slip into the adjoining lane and out of the truck's path. There was none. All three lanes were packed.

The horn continued to blast. The truck was nearly on top of him—so close Conrad could no longer see the boy, only the big rig's aluminum grill.

Up ahead, about thirty feet, a cement truck lumbered its way down the grade. Conrad pushed back his panic, looking for some way out. He glanced to the right, to the emergency lane. Suddenly, the Jaguar shuddered and lunged forward. The rig had hit him, hard, throwing his head forward, then back. Instantly, the car began picking up speed.

Conrad hit the brakes. They did no good, only threw him into a screaming skid, making it harder to steer.

The cement truck lay twenty-five feet ahead now, rapidly drawing closer.

Again Conrad looked to the right. The lane was narrow, with a steep rock wall rising beside it—a wall that a more experienced big rig driver might have used to slide against and slow down. But this kid was not experienced.

They continued picking up speed.

The cement truck was fifteen feet away. If Conrad was to act, it had to be now. He cranked the wheel hard to the right. But as the Jaguar swerved to the right, the big rig followed. The kid had lost control. He was going into a skid, jackknifing. As he did, he continued shoving Conrad forward . . . but forward into the emergency lane and toward the rock wall.

Conrad fought the wheel.

Tires shrieked and smoked. The horn blasted.

He struggled with all of his strength to turn the car back onto the road. But it was too wet, the surface too slick. The Jaguar hit a small curb at the edge of the emergency lane. Suddenly it was airborne. The wheel turned easily now, but it made no difference. The rock wall loomed ahead, filling Conrad's vision. When he struck it, the explosion roared in his ears. He was thrown forward, metal crushing around him. The air bag deployed, but nothing would stop his headlong rush at the rock.

"My God!" he screamed, lifting his hands against the jagged wall as it crashed through his windshield. But he could not duck. He could not move.

And then there was nothing.

Twenty-seven-year-old Julia Davis-Preston woke with a start. It took several moments to get her bearings as she glanced around the dimly lit 757 cabin. She'd just had another dream about her father. The hallway dream. It didn't come often, but when it did it always left her a little weak and shaken. In the dream she was a girl of five dressed in a chiffon party gown. She wore flowers in her hair, and in the more vivid dreams she could actually smell them. They were magnolias—from the tree at their home in Pasadena.

As always, she had been groping her way down the long, dimly lit hallway. As always, her father's dark walnut door waited at the far end. And, as always, it was closed.

"Daddy," she called, *"Daddy, I'm scared."*

She knew he was there. He had to be. She could hear the muffled voices, the wisps of conversation.

"Daddy ... please ..."

And the laughter. There was always laughter.

"Daddy." She ran her hand along the wood paneling. The laughter grew louder.

"Daddy?" She could barely see the door for the frightened tears welling up in her eyes. *"Daddy!"*

Then she arrived. With trembling fingers she reached for the doorknob. She could feel the cold brass in her hands as she began turning it. Further and further it turned until—

Julia awoke. Sometimes she opened the door, sometimes she even entered the room. But not tonight. Tonight she had remained outside in the hallway. She never knew if the details of the dream were based on actual fact or if they were something her subconscious had manufactured. It didn't matter. Regardless of whether the details were fact or fantasy, the substance was just as true.

She looked down and smoothed her tweed skirt. The cabin had grown a little chilly, and she thought of rising and grabbing her matching jacket from the overhead compartment. But the old gentleman in the aisle seat beside her was sleeping too peacefully to disturb. Besides, the jacket wrinkled easily, and it might be better to give it a head start on what could be a very long day.

Julia turned and looked out the window. In the darkness, the lights of a small Nebraska town twinkled up at her. As she stared, her thoughts drifted back to her father. She hated it when they did that. Not because she hated the thoughts, but because she hated him. It wasn't something she was proud of, but it was the truth. And if there was one thing her father had instilled in her, it was the value of truth. "A reporter's stock in trade," he was so fond of saying. "A person is only as good as his word, never any better, never any worse." It was perhaps this fact more than any other that had helped make Julia Davis-Preston one of the fastest-rising prosecutors in Atlanta's D.A. office. She was tough, uncompromising, and, above all else, a woman of integrity. Everyone knew it. And in this age of corrupt politics and voter cynicism, some folks were already considering the possibility of grooming her for office.

She glanced at her watch. It was 4:40 A.M. She closed her eyes, hoping sleep would return. They'd be landing in L.A. in two hours. Then it would be a matter of renting a car and heading up the coast to the Conejo Valley Medical Center, a hospital in Thousand Oaks not far from Camarillo where three, now four days earlier, her father had been in a serious car accident. "Critical head trauma," they'd said. "Extensive internal injuries." Initially they hadn't expected him to live through that first night. Somehow he had, but no one gave any hope for his recovery. Today, this evening, sometime very soon he would die.

But that's not why Julia was heading back to California. She'd barely spoken to the man in five years, and she was in no hurry to race to his side for some sort of artificial reconciliation. She was in no mood for a teary-eyed forgiveness scene with a comatose patient who couldn't hear and wasn't interested. No, that's not why she was headed home. If she had her way, she wouldn't show up until the funeral, if then. Julia was heading home because, a few years earlier, when she'd graduated from law school, her father had had the bright idea of giving her power of attorney. It was an honor she had immediately declined, but one that his most recently divorced wife (Rosy, Rosette, Rosa, whatever her name was) had said he'd continued to assign to her anyway. An honor that, among other things, made Julia the sole person responsible for deciding whether her father should remain on life support systems or die. According to the State of California, if a person is unable to make that decision himself, then it falls solely and completely upon the one to whom he has assigned the power of attorney.

So—entirely against her wishes, but living by the code her father had instilled, Julia was traveling cross-country to view his condition firsthand before giving the doctors permission to pull the plug. She sighed wearily. Even in death he remained an intrusion upon her life.

Minutes passed, and the dull roar of the plane once again lulled her into semisleep. And another dream. But this one was based upon the clear, vivid memories of her seventh birthday. It was a typical Southern California day, bright and clear. They were in a park with rolling hills and a hundred trees. Wind blew against her face and through her hair. And she was flying, soaring . . .

"Daddy," she half laughed, half screamed, *"don't let go!"* She gripped the shiny handlebars of her new bicycle with all of her might. *"Don't let go! Don't let go of me!"*

He ran behind her, hand on the seat, keeping her upright. She could hear his panting. *"I won't let go of you,"* he laughed. *"I won't let go."*

They hit a bump and she wobbled. *"Daddy!"*

"I'm right here," he laughed.

"Don't let go!" she shrieked.

"I'm right here, Sweetheart. Trust me, I won't let go!"

She was sailing, zooming, never traveling so fast in her life. The blades of grass blurred under her wheels. Her heart pounded with thrill and fear until—

Suddenly, Julia awoke again. She took a deep breath and brought her seat upright. There would be no more sleeping. Not for her. And there would be no more dreams. Especially of her father. She'd see to that. Even if she stayed up the rest of the night, there would be no more dreaming about the man.

He didn't deserve it.

Conrad Davis awoke standing. Time had passed, he knew that. But he didn't know how much. It was still raining, but now it was night. It was night and he was standing in the middle of a city street. There was no Jaguar, no big rig, and no sheer rock wall. Instead, a horn honked as a car raced past, missing him by inches. He spun around and was met by another vehicle coming from the opposite direction. The driver swerved hard and tires squealed. A moment later there was a sickening thud followed by tinkling glass and a stuck horn that began to blare. The car had slid into another parked at the curb. Conrad frantically looked about, trying to get his bearings. Some of the shops and buildings appeared familiar, like those in Santa Monica, a beach city he frequented just west of L.A. But many of the others—

A siren blasted. He twirled around and was blinded by a pair of high beams coming directly at him. For the briefest moment he froze, unsure what to do. The vehicle jerked to a halt fifteen feet away. Doors opened. Dark figures emerged, starting toward him. That's when Conrad found his legs. He turned, darting to the right, heading for the sidewalk. An oncoming car hit its brakes, swerved hard, and barely missed him—before plowing into the other two disabled vehicles.

Voices shouted, others cursed, and the dark figures began pursuit. The blaring horn made it impossible for Conrad to hear what was being yelled, but he knew they were not happy. He hit the curb, stumbling slightly, before turning to his right and racing down the sidewalk. The voices continued, no doubt demanding he stop. But he was not stopping. Not for them. Not for anybody. Where was he? What was going on?

Up ahead and across the street he saw Santa Monica's Mayfair Theater. So he was in Santa Monica. But how? And what of these other buildings and shops he didn't recognize? He continued running, passing two or three pedestrians, kids walking in the rain—long stringy hair, beads, embroidered bell-bottoms, looked like they'd stepped right out of the sixties.

The footsteps behind him were gaining. To his left was an alley; he turned so hard his feet nearly slipped, but he caught his balance and continued running.

"Stop!" the voices behind him shouted. "We order you to stop!"

Conrad bore down. He wasn't sure how much farther he could go. It had been a long time since he'd sprinted like this. His lungs were already crying out for air.

Headlights swept in and bounced behind him, illuminating the alley. He heard a car accelerate, knew he couldn't outrun it. It would be over in seconds. He'd be struck from behind, knocked to the ground, maybe run over. The car roared closer. Then, out of the corner of his left eye, he could see the headlights. Instead of hitting him, it was pulling beside him.

"Get in!" another voice shouted.

He turned to see an old Volkswagen bus, hand-painted with fluorescent flowers. The passenger's window was rolled down, and a black kid with a full-blown Afro was shouting, "Get in!"

Now he heard other voices, younger. "Come on! Jump in! Hurry!" The bus pulled ahead to reveal two more kids, a guy and a girl, dressed in hippie garb similar to the pedestrians he'd seen. They leaned out the open side door, reaching for him. "Take my hand!" they shouted. "Come on, man! They're right behind you!"

There was a loud thump on the back of the bus. Then another. The kids looked past Conrad in wide-eyed fear.

"Stop!" a voice behind him shouted. It was less than two yards away. "I order you to stop!"

Another thump, this time followed by the shattering of glass.

"Oh, man," the girl moaned. She turned to the driver, shouting, "The pigs just busted your taillight, man."

"Take my hand!" her companion reached out further to Conrad. "Take it now!"

Conrad had no choice. Whoever pursued him had bats or rocks or something equally as painful, and these kids—well, at least they wanted to help. He threw them another glance.

"Take my hand, man! Take my hand!"

It was now or never. He veered toward the VW bus, then tried leaping inside. Unfortunately, *tried* was the operative word. It wasn't as easy as it looked. He barely caught his left knee on the edge, before the weight of the rest of his body began twisting him away, pulling him off. There was nothing he could do except hope he'd roll free of the wheels and not fall under them. That's when each kid grabbed him by an arm and pulled with all of their might. He wasn't a heavy man, but heavy enough. At last they succeeded, and he flew into the bus, landing face first into green shag carpeting, gasping for air.

"We got him!" the kids shouted. "Step on it, man! Let's go, let's go!"

The bus accelerated as they shut the door.

"You okay, mister?" The young woman leaned over him. "You all right?"

Conrad wanted to answer, but at the moment he had more important things to do—like breathe. The bus continued to bounce and sway as the young man from the back shouted directions. "Right up there! Turn right up there, man!"

When he'd finally caught his breath, Conrad attempted to sit up.

"Here, let me help," the girl said. She was a sweet thing, seventeen, eighteen, straight blond hair, peasant blouse pulled off the shoulders, and bracelets. Lots of jangling bracelets.

There were no seats in the back, just the green shag carpeting, a mattress with a coarse Mexican blanket pulled across it, and eight-track tapes—a half-dozen eight-track tapes scattered along the side. Beads swayed back and forth over the windows, and a sweet pungent odor filled the air. Although Conrad hadn't smelled it in years, he immediately recognized it as pot.

"Where am I?" he asked.

"You don't know where you are?" the blond said.

"Am I . . . dead? Am I in Heaven?"

The group broke into laughter.

"That's a good one, man," the kid up front chuckled. "No, mister, you ain't dead, at least not yet."

"But we could definitely show you some Heaven," the young man beside him said as he pulled out a few pills from his leather vest.

Conrad recognized them for what they were. "No, uh, thanks. I don't, uh . . ."

"Not your thing?" The kid smiled.

"No . . ."

He shrugged. "Tha's cool."

Conrad's head swam. What was going on? A dream? A hallucination? No, this was too real. He glanced out the window. And the buildings. Some looked so familiar. He'd spent lots of time in Santa Monica. In fact, weren't they on . . . yes, they were on Arizona Street, heading east. He turned back to the blond. "Is this Santa Monica?"

"Sure is," she smiled. Her eyes were bloodshot and watery. She either had a bad case of allergies or was stoned. Conrad guessed the latter.

The kid beside her called up to the driver, "Turn right up here at Third."

Conrad looked back out the window. "Actually"—he cleared his throat—"you can't turn right at Third. It's the mall."

"The what?"

"The outdoor mall. It's been there since the eighties."

"Nice pants," the girl said. Suddenly Conrad was distracted by a playful hand on his leg. "What are they?"

"These?" Conrad glanced down. "Just some, uh, Dockers."

"What-ers?"

"Dockers."

"Never heard of 'em."

The leather-vested youth wrapped his arm around the girl's shoulders just in case there was any miscommunication. "Crystal here, she wants to be a clothes designer. Pretty good, too. Made me this vest." He reached down and lifted the beaded tassels along its edge.

Conrad nodded and looked back out the window. They were at Third Street and to his astonishment, making a right. There was no mall, just the continuation of the street.

"So what were the pigs after you for?" the driver called back.

"Pigs?"

"Our esteemed law enforcement officers."

"I'm not sure."

"Could be anything these days," the kid with the Afro said. "They're so jumpy with the protesters and all."

"Maybe they saw those UFO things, too," the girl offered.

"UFOs?" Conrad asked.

"If that's what they were," her boyfriend interjected. He looked through the windshield and suddenly called, "Hold on—that's it up there." He pointed ahead. "Right there, man. Pull up right there."

"Got it," the driver answered as he slowed the van and pulled it to a stop.

They were in front of a rundown, seedy building— blue cinderblock walls, front steps covered in green Astro- turf, bright pink doors. Overhead, a neon sign, partially burned out, blinked: *MOT L . . . MOT L . . . MOT L.*

"All right," the kid with the Afro announced as he opened the door and stepped outside. "Everyone stay cool till I find out what's happening." He headed up the steps into the lobby.

Conrad glanced down the street. He was sure this is where the mall had been. In fact, some evenings, just to unwind, he'd come down here to hit the bookshop, listen to the musicians, and sip a café latte while watching the street entertainers.

Where was he? What was going on? And who were these kids? These throwbacks to the sixties?

Up on a billboard just down the street, a woman stood in a black, one-piece bathing suit drinking a bottle of cola. Above her, the slogan read: "Keep tab with Tab." Conrad closed his eyes and reopened them. That's what it said. "Keep tab with Tab." And the bottle she was drink- ing from had "Tab" written on it. Tab? Wasn't that a diet soft drink of the sixties?

He glanced down the street at the passing autos, and those parked along the curb. As far as he could tell, there wasn't a late model in the bunch. Nothing past 1970. And the license plates? He squinted at the license tab of a nearby American Rambler. It read: *April 1970*.

What was going on? Was someone playing a joke? Was he losing his mind? Or had he . . . no, he pushed the thought out of his head. Again he found himself looking back up at the billboard. It was crazy, and he was embarrassed even thinking it, but these kids, their van, the disappearance of the mall, the cars, this billboard. Was it possible? No, it was just a dream, an elaborate hallucination. No way could he have possibly traveled back in—

"All right," the kid with the Afro called to them as he stepped out of the lobby. "They say they're in the back. In the service room where they do the laundry."

"Laundry?" the blond asked.

"That's what they said. All the rooms are booked, so they gave them a cot and a couple blankets in the laundry room. Just leave the bus there. It's cool."

The driver nodded, turned off the ignition, and the group piled out. Conrad joined them, unsure what to do, what questions to ask. They walked past the lobby and down the crumbling sidewalk beside the rooms. There was the faint tinkling of bells on someone's shoes, the jangling of the girl's bracelets. Conrad turned to the kid in the leather vest and asked, "You said you saw a UFO?"

"Not one," the boy corrected. "Hundreds of 'em. They lit up the sky."

"No kidding."

"But they really weren't spaceships," the blond explained. "More like people. Big, glowing people, filling the whole sky."

"Like angels or something," her boyfriend agreed. "Really blew our minds."

Conrad nodded. "Did they say something?"

"Yeah," the boy answered. "We were out on the beach, groovin' with the sunset, when this big, glowing giant, he's like suddenly standing in front of us."

"Giant?" Conrad repeated.

The blond nodded. "And we're like really scared, big time."

Her boyfriend agreed. "Bad scene."

"Then what happened?"

"Then he starts speaking," the boyfriend said. "He tells us not to be afraid and that he's bringing good news for everyone in the world."

"Good news?"

"Yeah. He says that here, right here at this motel, some sort of ruler is being born and he's gonna save us. Said we'd recognize him 'cause he'd be wrapped up in a bunch of bath towels."

Conrad frowned. "Did he have a name? Did he give this ruler a name?"

The boyfriend shrugged. "Don't remember. But suddenly, the whole sky, it like lights up with thousands, maybe a million of these glowing guys. And they all start saying, 'Glory to God, glory to God . . . and to those that please him, major peace.'"

The story was starting to have an eerie ring of familiarity. "And then what?" Conrad asked.

"Then nothing." The boy shrugged. "Then they were gone."

The girl nodded. "Pretty trippy, huh?"

"Here we are," the kid with the Afro announced.

The group slowed to a stop outside the very last door in the back. It was marked: Employees Only. The kid with the Afro reached out and gave a knock. Nothing. He tried again. A moment later the door cracked open. A young man in his early twenties stuck out his head.

"We've, uh ..." The kid in the Afro cleared his throat. "We've come to see the baby."

The young man peered at him suspiciously, then to the group behind him. He looked worn, tired, and very frightened. "Who told you?" he asked.

"The, uh ... um ..." The kid was hard-pressed to find the words. "The glowing guys down at the beach. They said that he was here."

A girl's voice came faintly from inside. Conrad couldn't make out what she said, but a moment later the young man opened the door wider. He took a half step outside and glanced around the parking lot to make sure there were no others. When he was satisfied, he stepped back and pushed the door wider.

Silently, almost reverently, the young people shuffled in, Conrad bringing up the rear.

And there, under the flickering light of a fluorescent bulb, was a young girl, about the same age as the blond. She lay on a cot wedged between several dirty laundry carts and a beat-up washer and dryer. Her raven hair was damp and plastered against her face, and she looked even more exhausted than the young man. But, despite the exhaustion, her deep sapphire eyes held a look of triumph, an indefinable peace. Because there in her arms, wrapped in worn bath towels, was her newborn baby boy.

CHAPTER TWO

Conrad fought his way through the empty blackness. Everything was gone. The city, the laundry room. Nothing was there. Only darkness. And the murmur of voices—distant conversations, past and present, snippets of sound. He tried clinging to them, using them to pull himself out of the void.

"Has he had any purposeful movement since surgery?"

The sound of screaming tires filled his head. So loud he winced.

"What was that?" the voice asked.

"Where?"

"His eyes."

"Probably nystagmus."

The voice grew louder, closer. "Mr. Davis, can you hear me? Mr. Dav—"

The air horn of a truck blasted again, drowning out the voice.

" —can you hear me at all?"

Conrad tried to answer, mustering all of his strength and will. But it was futile. His body would not respond.

The sound of crushing metal filled his ears . . . exploding glass shattered around him. Flits and flurries of a crash strobed through his mind but in no particular order. A sheer rock wall. *Swish-swish, swish-swish.* More squealing tires. Rain. As he fought the darkness, he tried connecting the fragments together, one way then another. *Swish-swish, swish-swish.* The deafening horn. The frightened young face of the driver. More glass shattering, metal crushing.

He'd been in an accident—

"We ran the Glasgow Coma a second time en route to the hospital before the surgery."

—and, apparently, hospitalized.

But what of the baby . . . the laundry room? Where had they been? Where had they gone? They were so vivid. The entire scene had been as real as any bits he remembered from the accident. Even now he could smell the penetrating odor of marijuana, hear the jingling of beads and bells.

". . . worlds we can't even see . . ."

Where had he been? And when had he been there? Before the accident? After?

"No, Mister, you ain't dead . . . at least not yet."

More shattering glass.

Swish-swish, swish-swish . . .

"We've come to see the baby."

It seemed so real. Santa Monica, 1970—the flower children, the cars, "Keep tab with Tab," the mother and baby . . . he remembered them down to the tiniest detail.

". . . we're talking the existence of other realities . . ."

". . . you can prove this?"

"He shouldn't be having any residual chemical paralysis at this point."

Maybe it was one of those out-of-body experiences somehow connected to the accident. Or a hallucination from all the drugs they were no doubt pumping into him, or . . .

". . . eyewitnesses, people have seen these . . ."

"I am afraid eyewitnesses would be locked up in insane asylums, or in drug rehab programs."

Swish-swish, swish-swish . . .

". . . worlds identical . . . but with differences."

The idea of a savior born in a laundry room was intriguing—and he'd be a fool not to recognize the similarities between what he saw and the Christmas story Suzanne insisted upon reading every Christmas morning . . . although he suspected that "Away in the Laundry Basket" might not carry the same poetic charm as the original.

Swish-swish, swish-swish . . .

". . . worlds identical . . . but with minor differences . . ."

A heavier darkness began to wash over him.

Was it possible? He didn't know. Then again, maybe even these thoughts were a hallucination. How could he be thinking so clearly and yet be so . . . so . . .

He fought the dullness as it started to swallow him.

Maybe . . . from the trauma, the drugs, his imagination, or some combination, maybe he *had* entered another world. And if that was true, hadn't Endo said there were others? Millions? Traveling at different speeds?

The darkness was nearly complete and still he fought it.

And if he had entered it once, wouldn't it be possible to . . . to . . . couldn't he . . .

Conrad's thoughts collapsed upon themselves as he fell back into the silent void.

Julia was so lost in thought that she nearly missed the Janss Road Exit off Freeway 23 into Thousand Oaks. Fortunately the early Sunday morning traffic was light, and she was able to swerve sharply, crossing two lanes and barely catching the exit ramp in time. As a girl, she remembered Thousand Oaks being a backwoods hick town with cowboys and horses. Well, all of that had changed. The expansive, grass-covered hills with their occasional dual-wheel ruts leading up to the summits had now been transformed into wave after wave of red-tile-roofed homes. She could still spot a few fields here and there, even catch the faint odor of dried grass and horse, but it was just a matter of time before that, too, would be swallowed up by L.A. sprawl.

She turned onto Janss and followed the four-lane road to the hospital. To her left was a Methodist church with a blood donation banner hung across the reader board. To her right a sign posted the speed limit and the words, "Welcome Home. Relax and Slow Down." Everywhere she looked there were houses and trees. Not a billboard in sight. Even the strip mall she passed was signless and surrounded by so much greenery that it was nearly impossible to catch a glimpse of the local McDonald's.

She'd read recently that the city had been voted the safest in America. She could see why. It appeared to be the quintessential American town. Quiet, peaceful, an occasional morning jogger, an elderly couple on bicycles. Water from a front-yard sprinkler sparkling in the sun. Everything about the city looked safe, quiet, secure . . . in many ways it reminded Julia of her own childhood.

But looks can be deceiving. Julia, of all people, knew that.

She crossed a major intersection—still no billboards or signs—and continued through another residential area until finally a small lit sign came into view. It read: The Conejo Valley Medical Center. She slowed, took a deep breath, and turned into the tree-lined drive. Eventually she found the visitor's section and pulled into a stall. She turned off the ignition and was surprised at how hard her heart was pounding.

She opened the car door, was reminded to remove the keys by the chiming bell, and stepped out into the warm sunlight.

Everything was deathly still. Not a hint of breeze. Not a sound of traffic. Directly ahead lay the three-story, white-and-beige hospital. On the pole beside its entrance was the American flag and the California flag with its brown bear on white background. Both hung lifeless. Overhead, in one of the dozens of pine trees, a crow clicked and cawed, and in the distance she could hear the dull roar of someone using a leaf blower.

Everything else was silent, except for her own breathing and the pounding of her heart. Julia closed her eyes and lifted her face to the warm California sun, feeling it soak into her skin. She took another breath, smelling the morning heat and sun-softened asphalt.

Then she opened her eyes and started toward the hospital.

"So do you want to move in for close-ups?"

A disoriented Conrad turned from the glaring sun. He looked down to see he was standing on a small ridge of sand and bunchgrass about twenty yards from a river. The river was good sized, broad and flat, surrounded sparsely by cottonwoods. Beyond it lay rolling hills, tan and gold, sprinkled with clumps of olive green trees. And beyond those were dark, navy blue mountains shaded by ominous black clouds.

"Connie?"

Still trying to get his bearings, he turned toward the voice. It was Ned Burton, his favorite cameraman—late thirties, short, scraggly red hair, and a moth-eaten goatee. As a member of the old school who insisted upon producing his own segments, Conrad tried to work with those he trusted most. And Ned, with his experience and dogged tenacity, was always his first choice. At the moment, his eye was glued to the viewfinder of JVC's latest digital camera—a mere $11,673 (list price before tax), top of the line . . . until next year's model came out.

"We got enough on this clown," Ned said, opening his other eye to look at Conrad. "Let's get some cutaways of the audience and get outa here 'fore that storm hits."

Conrad turned back toward the mountains. Thunderheads darkened the sky above them. He could smell the moisture in the air. Already a breeze had kicked up. "Yeah," he cleared his throat, "uh, cutaways, that would be good."

Without a word, Ned pulled his eye away from the camera, wiped his face with his sleeve, and motioned to the nearby sound man, Mike Horton. They'd only used Mike once or twice before. He was skinny, eager, and Ned's junior by ten years. As always he was wearing earphones, holding a boom with a shotgun mike at the end, and doing his best to stay out of Ned's picture. Together the two half-walked, half-slid down the sandy knoll to join the outside fringes of the crowd—a crowd that listened to a half-naked young man whose skin was red from the sun and whose sandy blond dreadlocks fell to the tops of his shoulders. He stood in a waist-deep eddy of the river, shouting at them:

"You snakes! You vipers! Like frightened reptiles you slither from the desert's wildfire, hoping this river can save you. Do you honestly think there's something magical about this water, or about any water, that can save your souls? In your wildest dreams do you really believe that all you need to do is be baptized?"

Some of the crowd murmured in resentment. Most simply listened. Conrad carefully surveyed them. He estimated there to be between five and six hundred. Five to six hundred people standing on the bank of a river in the middle of nowhere, baking in the sun, listening to someone browbeat them. Now he at least understood why he was out here covering the story—wherever "here" was. But why were these people here?

As best as he could tell, they came from every background—the rich in their shorts and polo shirts, the poor in jeans and cutoffs, teens in halter tops and swimsuits. He noticed a large number of Hispanics, and by their dress and leathered faces he guessed many of them to be migrant workers. He guessed something else as well. He had not returned to the seventies. There were no painted VW vans, no flower children. Just contemporary people with contemporary cars, soccer mom vans, and the occasional RV.

In the distance he heard thunder rumble.

"You say, 'I'm religious, I believe in God, I'll be saved from the coming wrath.' Who are you kidding?" the young man shouted. "God can raise up religious people from these very stones! And saying you believe in God isn't going to save you! It's what you *do*, not what you say!

Standing in a garage screaming, 'I'm a BMW!' does not make you a BMW! You've got to prove it! You've got to bear the fruit!"

Someone in the crowd started to shout, but he cut him off. "Save me your doctrines, your pious theologies. Walk the walk! Bear the fruit! Do not be like our esteemed leaders. Those who go to religious services Sunday, then continue their adulterous affairs throughout the week. Turn! Change! Do an about-face, or you'll be good for nothing but firewood!"

Thunder again rumbled in the background. Conrad glanced up. The storm was quickly approaching. He still wasn't sure where he was, though the desolate hills, the mountains, and the smell of sage made it clear he was out West. Central California, he guessed, maybe Eastern Washington.

The people had heard the thunder as well. Some were stooping down, gathering their things. Others had already started toward the makeshift parking lot—a flat area just off a single-lane ribbon of blacktop that snaked its way into the hills. For every intent and purpose, it appeared that Conrad was back in his own world. But he knew better. He remembered the accident. Vividly. He still suspected that his own world consisted of doctors, drugs, and hospitals. He suspected it. But for whatever reason, he was no longer experiencing it.

"Who exactly do you claim to be?" an angry man shouted from the crowd. Conrad turned to Ned, who was already zooming in for a close-up as Horton repositioned his mike. The speaker was a distinguished gentleman with gray hair and a neatly trimmed beard. "Where do you come from? What is your training?"

"I am nothing!" cried the young man. "Just a voice shouting in the middle of nowhere!"

"Are you the Messiah?" a young mother with a baby called. "The one we've been waiting for?"

"No! I'm not even worthy to mow his lawn or empty his garbage. I'm only baptizing you with water, but when He comes, He'll baptize you with fire and with the Spirit of God! He will look into your hearts and read them. He will separate you, saving the good and throwing the rest into the fire that burns forever!"

As if on cue, lightning lit up the sky, followed by clapping thunder that echoed through the hills. The wind grew stronger. The storm was arriving. More people turned and gathered their things, preparing to leave.

"Hey, Connie!"

Conrad looked down and saw Gerald McFarland, a heavyset, balding man with soft, pudding jowls. He was a news producer/reporter for the Eternal Broadcasting Network, the country's largest religious network. As usual, he was all grins and good ol' boy charm.

Conrad felt relieved to see someone else he recognized. They'd both entered the profession at about the same time and, over the years, had become friendly rivals—McFarland reporting with his religious bias and Conrad with his hopefully more objective outlook (though he knew there was no such thing as perfect objectivity in their business). McFarland had always struck Conrad as a strange mixture of grace and ruthless ambition. One moment the man was all care and compassion, like he was your best friend, the next he'd be stealing a story right from under your nose. Conrad knew that the man's beliefs were sincere. In fact, one teary night at a bar, when Conrad and his first wife were separating, McFarland had almost gotten him to consider God.

Almost.

But there was something about McFarland's "schizophrenia" that made Conrad nervous. He knew the rules when dealing with other competitors . . . there were none. In TV journalism, it was every person for himself and that was okay, because everyone understood it. Everyone but McFarland. Was he your friend or your rival? Was he interested in your soul or your story? No one knew. And, as near as Conrad could tell, sometimes neither did McFarland.

McFarland shouted up to him. "Don't tell me . . ." The wind had picked up, whipping and snapping Conrad's clothes, drowning out some of McFarland's words. ". . . is of secular interest, too?"

Conrad yelled. "What?"

"You here on business or pleasure?" McFarland shouted.

"Pleasure?" Conrad yelled.

"Didn't you see her?"

"What?"

"Suzanne's here . . . thought maybe you came because of Suzanne."

Conrad's heart quickened. He hadn't seen her in five, maybe six years, not since Julia's wedding. "Suzanne?" he shouted. "Here?"

"Yeah, got some nice shots of her being baptized."

Conrad blinked. What was she doing here? Sure, she'd always been the religious type, but—

There was a brilliant flash of lightning, followed by an explosion of thunder.

"Listen," McFarland shouted, "I'm no rocket scientist, but I wouldn't be standing on top of that knoll in this storm!"

"Yeah." Conrad nodded. "Thanks!" He slid down the hill to join McFarland. Giant drops of rain began plopping as he zipped up his nylon windbreaker.

"I'm heading out of Sea-Tac tomorrow morning," McFarland said. "Any chance of getting together and sharing notes on this guy?"

Conrad didn't know how to respond. Tell him he had no idea who the kid was? That he hadn't the slightest clue where they were or how he got there? No, somehow he suspected that might be a bit more sharing than McFarland had in mind. He settled for something a little more vague. "Let me check what Ned has first."

McFarland nodded. "Right." He turned and shouted over his shoulder, "I'm staying at the Plaza."

Conrad nodded. "Got it."

The storm had arrived in full force. Now everyone was racing for their cars. Well, almost everyone. When Conrad looked back out to the river, he saw the young man still standing there. He was no longer shouting and he barely noticed the weather. Instead, his eyes were glued to another fellow about his age wading toward him from the opposite bank. The young man had left his shirt on the shore, revealing an upper torso that was lean and somewhat muscular. His features were dark, his hair casual. As he approached he appeared to be a good three, maybe four inches taller than the first young man.

Conrad watched as the two met and exchanged words. Then the new arrival slowly knelt until he was chest deep in the water. He was obviously preparing to be baptized. Not that it appeared necessary. Thanks to the rain, both were already soaked and dripping. The first young man knelt beside him, put his hand behind the newcomer's head, and lowered him backwards into the river.

More lightning strobed across the sky—directly overhead this time, followed by loud, ominous thunder. And, as the young man rose from the water, coughing and wiping his eyes, a most remarkable thing occurred. A bird—Conrad guessed it to be a dove by its brown and white markings—appeared in the sky against the black clouds. It descended, flapping its wings, struggling against the wind. Both men saw it and rose silently to watch. Another gust of wind pushed the bird back, but it would not be deterred. It pressed harder, working the currents this way and that, until, at last, with fluttering wings it landed gently upon the second youth's bare shoulder.

In surprise, Conrad wiped the rain from his eyes. But when he looked back, the bird was gone, as if it had never been there. More lightning lit the scene, immediately followed by an explosion of thunder, loud and long. At least Conrad thought it was thunder. But in the midst of the pounding roar, there were what almost sounded like . . . words. Phrases, really. Three of them. Booming, reverberating, as if part of the thunder. He was sure it was an illusion, just the way the thunder echoed off the gullies and river. Still, they were so clear, so distinct:

YOU ARE MY . . . BELOVED SON AND . . .
I AM PLEASED . . .

Conrad glanced back at the crowd. Several of them had heard something as well. Many had stopped and were looking back.

Conrad turned toward the river. The two men now stood, locked in an embrace. When they finally separated, the new arrival took the other's shoulders, spoke something, and then without another word turned and headed for the opposite bank, away from the parking lot, away from the crowd. The rain fell harder—blowing and slanting. But through the sheets of water and thick grayness Conrad saw the young man arrive on the opposite shore, stoop to pick up his shirt, and start toward the distant hills.

Julia stepped into the ICU visitor's area. It appeared modern and comfortable. The burgundy carpet with its gray, geometric designs was cheery without being obnoxious. The abstract paintings of mountains and rolling hills on the wall were soothing. Not far away sat the room's only occupant, an attractive brunette—long, carefully styled hair, high cheekbones, full lips, a figure that was slim where fashion dictated it to be slim and voluptuous where it was to be voluptuous. She looked to be in her thirties . . . but recognizing the tight, shiny skin and other signs of cosmetic surgery, Julia guessed her closer to mid-forty. At the moment she was immersed in the latest Danielle Steel novel.

"Roseanne?" Julia asked.

The woman looked up, then broke into a smile that was the perfect mixture of pleasure and sympathy. As she rose she extended her hand and spoke. "Julia . . ."

She sounded Latin, and why not. Julia's mother was mostly Irish, her first stepmother had been Italian, and the woman after that was Swedish. It was about time her father broaden his tastes to the Southern Hemisphere.

"I am so sorry," the woman said as they shook hands.

Julia gave a tight smile and nodded. She couldn't help noticing the carefully applied mascara that showed absolutely no trace of running or smearing from tears. Not that it should. After all, they'd been divorced for nearly twelve weeks.

"How is he?" Julia asked.

"From when we spoke last night, no difference I am afraid."

Julia nodded as she took note of the woman's wardrobe—her silk blouse, diamond necklace, jade earrings, calfskin pumps. She obviously knew how to spend money . . . which may explain why she was willing to travel all the way out here from L.A. on a Sunday morning. Of course, Julia immediately felt guilty for the thought. She knew nothing of this woman, nor of her relationship with her father. Besides, they'd barely divorced. And knowing her father, it was doubtful that he'd yet taken the time to cut the woman out of his will . . . which could be the very reason she'd gone to all this effort to—*Stop it!* Julia chided herself. *Stop it this instant!*

"Ernesto and Beatrice, they will be here soon."

Julia frowned. "Who?"

"My children."

"Ah, yes. Of course."

"They loved your father very much. He had been such a good man to them."

Julia wasn't sure how much of the response was sincere and how much was performance—though she didn't appreciate hearing her father already spoken of in past tense. Still she felt herself nodding. "Yes," she said, "everybody loves him."

Roseanne continued to nod. "Yes, we loved him, very, very much."

Julia prepared to sit on the sofa across from her when the woman asked, "Do you not wish to see him?"

She glanced up. "Pardon me?"

"Your father. You want to see him, don't you?"

Halfway between sitting and standing, Julia rose. "Well, yes. Certainly."

"Just go to that phone, over there." Roseanne pointed to a white phone on the wall.

"Right," Julia nodded. "Of course." She walked toward the phone.

"Dial 423," Roseanne explained. "Tell them you want to see Conrad Davis and that you are one of his children."

Actually, she was his only child, but Julia let it go as she reached for the receiver. She dialed the number and explained to the voice on the other end who she was. A moment later there was a soft buzz. She pushed open the door, turned to thank Roseanne, and stepped inside.

Just ahead and to her right stretched a long nurses' station. To her left were the patients' rooms, each separate and cordoned off from the hall by sliding glass doors, most of which were open. Nearly all contained sleeping or unconscious patients hooked up to various life supports. Julia resisted the temptation to look in on them, partially out of respect for their privacy and partially because she was afraid one of them might be her father.

As she approached the nurse behind the counter she noticed her head was feeling a bit light. "Excuse . . ." Julia cleared the raspiness from her throat and tried again. "Excuse me?"

The nurse looked up from a chart.

"I'm Conrad Davis's . . . I'm his daughter."

The woman nodded and pointed toward the far end. "Mr. Davis is over in number four."

"Thanks. Do I just, uh . . ." Her mouth was unusually dry. "Do I just go in and see him, then?"

The nurse nodded.

Julia felt perspiration breaking out on her forehead. "I mean, I don't have to wear a mask or anything like that?"

The nurse shook her head, then looked at her quizzically. "Are you all right?"

"Yeah, I'm fine."

The nurse rose and rounded the counter to join her. She was a plump woman, several years older than Julia. "Here, let me show you."

The room directly across from the station had the number eight painted in the upper right corner of the glass.

"You say you're his daughter?" the nurse asked as they started down the row, passing room seven.

"Yes. I just flew in from Atlanta this morning."

"I met your mother earlier. A charming lady."

There was room six.

"Well actually, she's not, uh—" The place seemed to be growing warmer, Julia's head much lighter. "She's not my mother."

"Of course, I understand." Again she felt the nurse looking at her. "Are you certain you're all right?"

Room five. It wasn't intentional, but Julia's pace was slowing, her legs growing heavier.

"Yes, I'm just a little . . ." The door to room number four came into view. "I didn't have anything to eat on the plane, and—" There was the foot of the bed, *his* bed. Then the form under the blanket, then the stainless steel IV stands. "—and my head's a little . . ." Then she saw a pale arm taped with tubes and wires, and finally she saw the face. But it wasn't a face, not really—just a mass of bandages with plastic tubes and hoses and wires and—

Julia's legs turned to rubber, but she barely felt it. All she was aware of were the bandages and the tubes in the nose and hoses down the throat and the wires and more bandages and the *hiss-click* of the respirator and the—

"Ma'am, here, let me get you a chair." The voice sounded far away.

"No, that's okay," she heard herself say. "I'm just a little . . ."

No way could that be her father.

"Here, take my arm."

He was so strong, so vital.

"Ma'am, take my arm." The command was firm but growing more distant. "Take my arm."

And now, now he looked so lifeless, so—

Her legs gave out.

"Whoa, hang on," the distant voice cried.

She heard the faint scraping of metal legs across linoleum, felt the woman gripping both arms—"Just ease back now"—until she was sitting in a chair . . . a chair not three feet away from a mass of bandages, wires, tubes, and hoses that was supposed to be her father.

"The Kingdom of Heaven is more than just some place you go when you die. It's a way of life. It's the way God had intended life to be lived. And the good news is, you can become citizens of that life right now, while you're still on earth."

Conrad discovered himself standing amidst a small crowd in the parking lot of a community baseball field. It felt like summer, maybe late spring, with just the slightest trace of a breeze to keep things cooled. Once again, Ned Burton was at his side with his eye to the camera viewfinder. Beside him stood Mike Horton, the same sound man as before. To their immediate right lay a baseball diamond with a sagging backstop in need of repair. The infield grass could have used more water, and the outfield was encircled by a shoulder-high fence displaying several sponsors' names—Pizza Hut, Barton Auto Repair, Blue Bird Cafe— some recently painted, most in various stages of fading and peeling. Beyond the fence stretched flat farmland where, off in the distance, a cloud of dust rolled across a field behind a tractor. As before, everything seemed strikingly real. As real as the world Conrad had left behind.

"This earthly kingdom has one way of doing things, but it's all backwards, it's all upside down."

Conrad focused his attention upon the speaker. He was a young man, just under six foot, late twenties, maybe early thirties, Mediterranean look, possibly Jewish, and not a bad build. In fact, his features were much like those of the youth who had been baptized back at the river, whenever that had been. He stood on the rear bumper of a beat-up, gray and white RV, speaking pleasantly but loud enough for everyone to hear. The audience of a hundred or so were dressed casually—cutoffs, shorts, tank tops, mostly families, moms, dads, kids. Several of the men and children carried gloves, making it clear that an informal softball game was soon to begin.

"In *this* kingdom, if you want, you take. If you want to be great, you conquer people. But in the Kingdom of Heaven, it's just the opposite. If you want, you give; if you want to rule, you serve."

"So how do we enter this other Kingdom?" a heavy-set, middle-aged man shouted, then added with humor, "I mean without dying?"

The group chuckled. So did the young man. It was interesting that he wasn't haranguing the crowd or preaching at them, as the man back at the river had. Instead, he appeared to be enjoying the easy, give-and-take banter. "That's a good question, and you may not like my answer." He grew more earnest, carefully looking over the audience. "You do have to die."

The crowd began to react, but he continued. "Not physically, no, I'm not saying that. But in order to enter the Kingdom of God you have to die spiritually. You have to die to yourself and come alive in me."

The stirring increased, and he held out his hands good-naturedly.

"I know, I know, to most of you that sounds incredibly egotistical and arrogant. And I'm sorry, I can't do much about that. But what I can do is tell you the truth, and this is truth: I am the way to that Kingdom. I am the door." More folks shifted and exchanged glances. But he continued. "There's no other entrance, there's absolutely no other way to reach God and His Kingdom, but through me."

The restlessness grew. A few began to murmur.

"I know," the young man nodded in agreement. "I told you you wouldn't like the answer. But if you stay open, if you drop your pride and humble your hearts, I guarantee you my words will take root inside you and bear fruit." He paused a moment, looking at the ballfield, then lifted his eyes and seemed to be gazing beyond, at the distant tractor kicking up dust. When he turned back to the group, he had a mischievous smile. "I think I feel another story coming on."

"Oh, no," the middle-aged man teased, "another one."

A few chuckled. An old-timer called out, "Tell us your story, son, tell your story."

The young man grinned and prepared to start. He seemed to genuinely enjoy the crowd, and Conrad could tell that, despite his off-the-wall claims, they enjoyed him.

Conrad glanced at Ned, who was looking back at him with his free eye. Unsure what to do or even where he was, Conrad nodded to him, indicating that he should continue taping. Ned repositioned himself, relayed the nod to Horton, and zoomed in.

The young man began. "A farmer went out to plant seed. When he was near the road, some of that seed blew onto the pavement. What do you suppose happened to it?"

"It got squished by a semi!" a boy volunteered.

The group chuckled quietly.

"All right," the young man smiled, "that's one possibility. Any others?"

"Maybe some animals ate it," the child's father offered.

"Or the birds got it," another added.

The young man nodded. "Good. Now other seed fell, but it landed off to the side where the soil was thin and rocky. What would happen to it?"

The group gave no response.

"Come on," the young man encouraged, "one or two of you are farmers—what happens when seed lands in thin soil?"

"It still germinates," a heavy woman ventured. "It still grows."

The young man nodded. "At first, yes. But what happens when the days get hot, when August rolls around and the sun begins beating down on it?"

The old-timer spoke up. "The plant shrivels and dies."

"It has no roots," the woman agreed.

"Exactly." The young man stooped down closer to the audience, growing more intimate. He seemed to enjoy prodding and urging them to think. "Other seed fell along the roadside where the weeds and thistles grew. What do you suppose—"

"You can kiss them goodbye," a good-looking father in his thirties called from the back.

"Why?" The young man rose to his feet to better see him.

"The weeds are going to steal the nutrients. They're going to choke out the seeds before they ever get started."

The young man slowly nodded as he surveyed the crowd. "Yes . . ." And then, for the first time, his eyes connected with Conrad's. They seemed to sparkle, yet were filled with compassion. Though the two of them were nearly fifty feet apart, the experience left Conrad a little disarmed. It was as if he was an old friend who knew exactly what Conrad was thinking.

"What about the good seed?" someone shouted.

The young man turned from him to face the question, and Conrad felt a slight wave of relief. "That, my friend," the young man grinned, "is the good news. Unlike the seed that lands on hearts of hard pavement where the enemy quickly snatches it away, or on the thin soil where it sprouts until the hot sun of hard times dries it up, or in the weeds of riches and worries that choke it with concern ... the seed that lands in soft, fertile hearts will yield an incredible harvest, a crop a hundred times greater than what was originally planted."

He said no more but watched in silence as the audience slowly digested the story, several beginning to nod in understanding. Conrad looked on, marveling at the man's ability to weave a story so simple, yet so full of meaning that it held everyone's attention. And his style—Conrad could think of no other description except *casual dignity*. He obviously had the crowd's respect, but at the same time he was totally accessible.

"Now I don't know about you folks"—the young man grinned—"but I came to watch a ball game." The group voiced their approval, and he hopped down from the vehicle's dented bumper. "Jake?" he shouted.

A burly moose of a man who had already started for the ballfield turned. "Yeah?"

"Thanks for the use of the RV."

"No prob," he replied, then turned and continued toward the field.

Those who weren't playing started toward their cars or walked to the shaded picnic tables or the bleachers. Unsure what to do next, Conrad glanced back to his cameraman. "Uh, Ned ..."

"I know, I know," Ned sighed. "Get cutaways of him interacting with the crowd."

It sounded like a good idea and Conrad nodded. "Go to it."

The man shrugged, nodded to Horton, and the two moved into the group.

"Connie? Connie, is that you?"

Conrad turned to see Suzanne approaching through the crowd. As always, she was all grace and smiles. Granted, there were a few more lines around the mouth than he had remembered and her eyes looked a touch sadder, but it was still the same smile that had captured his heart so many years earlier. The same smile that he had turned to tears more times than he cared to remember.

"Suzanne . . ."

They embraced. She felt warm and good. Most important, she felt real. He held her longer than he should, but he needed to. She'd always been an anchor for him, even after the divorce. And now, wherever he was, whatever he was going through, he needed to feel her support, he needed to feel the familiarity of her presence.

When they finally separated, the words tumbled out before he could stop them. It was one thing to exercise restraint around Ned and Horton, but this was Suzanne. Despite the years, there was still a connection. There would always be some part of them that others could not share. "Where are we?" he blurted. "Do you know what's going on?"

She tilted her head at him quizzically. "What?"

"All of this . . . it all seems so . . . real!"

She continued looking at him, still not understanding.

He swallowed and regrouped, trying to explain. "What about the hospital? What about my accident?"

Her expression clouded. "You were in an accident?"

"Well, yeah . . . I mean . . ."

"Were you hurt?"

"I, uh . . ." His hand shot self-consciously to his face, feeling for wounds, for stitches, for some evidence of the exploding windshield, the rock, the crushing metal. But of course there was nothing. At least not in this whatever or wherever he was.

Suzanne continued searching him. "Connie . . . are you all right?"

He took a deep breath. How could he explain it, what he suspected? How could he explain to someone that they may be only his hallucination? Or that he really wasn't a part of their world? How could he explain that he was just dropping in from one of a million different realities that were almost like theirs but not quite?

"If there are eyewitnesses to such universes they would be locked up in insane asylums . . ."

He opened his mouth, but there were no words. He looked at her, seeing her concern. How could he tell her? *What* could he tell her? How could he explain something he didn't understand? He couldn't. No, right now, he needed the reality of who she was. Hallucination or not. Parallel world or not. He needed the simple assurance of her presence.

"Connie?"

It took more effort than he anticipated, but somehow he managed to force a smile, then give a shrugging answer. "It's a long story."

She didn't buy it, not entirely. She continued searching his face. "But you're okay now?"

He nodded and turned up the smile. "Yeah, better than ever." And it wasn't a lie. Because whatever reality he was experiencing, for however long he would experience it, whether it was real or not, had to be better than the one he'd left behind.

Suzanne's expression relaxed, but only slightly. "You sure?"

He nodded.

She seemed a bit more convinced as she pushed the graying hair behind her ears. The woman was in her late forties now, but underneath, she was still that same sensitive and compassionate eighteen-year-old he'd run off with so many lifetimes before.

He did his best to change the subject, to try for small talk. "You look . . . you look good," he said.

"You too."

He shrugged. "A little grayer and thinner on top."

"It gives you that wise, distinguished look."

"Yeah, well, we both know better than that, don't we?"

Her smile broadened.

Refusing to let the uneasiness between them return and intrigued at how real everything appeared, he continued to play along. "So, how's Julia? And Cody—he's almost four now, right?"

"Five," she corrected. "And the perfect angel . . . when he's not being the devil. You knew she and Ken separated, didn't you?"

Conrad frowned. "No, I didn't know that."

"Almost six months now."

A familiar sorrow crept in. Even in this world, Julia was having her problems. And with his sorrow came the guilt. Not because he hadn't known of the separation.

How could he? He'd not spoken to his daughter in years, had never even seen his grandson. No, it was from something much deeper. "You think they'll work it out?" he asked.

"With our bullheaded daughter?" Suzanne almost laughed. "I've got my doubts. If there's any working out, I'm afraid it will all have to be at Ken's end. But I'm praying."

Conrad nodded. "Good ... good." Looking for another change in subject he motioned toward the young man. "So you found another guru, I see."

Suzanne took the barb graciously and turned to the group of people encircling the man. "Not another one, Connie. This one's the real thing." There was no missing the quiet admiration in her voice. "What Eli has been doing these past several months, his teachings, the miracles ... I think we've finally found him, Connie. I think we've finally found the Messiah we've been waiting so long for."

Her words surprised him. After all, she'd been a devout Christian since her twenties. "What about Jesus?" he asked. "Don't tell me you're throwing all that away?"

Her response was an even greater surprise. "Who?" she asked.

"You know," he repeated, "Jesus?"

She frowned as if not recognizing the name. "I'm sorry, I'm not sure who you—"

She was interrupted by a loud commotion. They turned to see excitement rippling through the crowd surrounding the young man.

"What's going on?" Conrad asked.

Suzanne's face brightened. "Probably another healing." Before he could respond, she took his hand. "Come and see." As she led him through the group, Conrad instinctively searched for Ned and Horton. Just as he suspected, his crew was right where the action was, capturing it all on tape.

The young man was speaking to an older, scruffy-looking fellow in a plaid shirt and slightly dirty jeans. His face was leathery and his neck was crosshatched from years of work in the sun. His right arm was covered in shiny, uneven scar tissue. Below it, his right hand hung shriveled and useless.

"That's Brian Tuffts," Suzanne half-whispered. "A farmer from here in Oregon. Lost the use of his arm in some sort of fire."

The crowd had grown very quiet as the young man—what had Suzanne called him? Eli—wrapped both of his hands around the old-timer's elbow. He was smiling at Tuffts, encouraging him not to be afraid. But it did little good. The man's eyes were as big as saucers.

"It's okay," Eli said. "The heat you're feeling is only natural."

Tuffts tried to nod. But what was not natural was seeing the healed muscle and new pink skin appearing directly under Eli's hand. The old man began to tremble. Sweat appeared on his forehead. But Eli continued speaking words of encouragement while slowly moving his hand along the arm. As he did, more and more new skin appeared . . . everything, down to the tiniest detail, down to the bulging blue veins and new hair follicles.

The crowd watched in silent awe.

Conrad glanced over to Ned. Good, he was getting it all. If this was some sort of parlor trick they'd be able to examine it more closely in the editing.

Eli was down to the hand now, holding it in both of his own. After several seconds he slowly released it. The crowd gasped. Like his arm, Tuffts's hand was perfect ... though as pink as a newborn's. Eli finally looked up to the man with a grin.

Tuffts could only stare, speechless, his eyes brimming with tears. He looked from his hand to Eli, then back to his hand, then to Eli again.

"Sorry about the color." Eli shrugged. "Guess you'll have to work on the tan yourself."

The group chuckled, both at the comment and as a way of releasing tension. Then, suddenly, the man came to life. He threw his arms around Eli and hoarsely cried, "Thank you! "Thank you, thank you!"

Eli smiled, doing his best to endure the fierce bear hug, and trying to return it.

Suzanne turned to Conrad and asked quietly, "So what do you think?" Her voice was thick with compassion, her own eyes glistening with emotion.

"Amazing." Conrad cleared his throat. "I mean if that's real, it's incredible."

Suzanne smiled. "Oh, it's real," she said. "He does this sort of thing three, four times a day. Sometimes it's the blind, sometimes the deaf. Yesterday he healed a quadriplegic."

Conrad looked on, his reporter's instincts telling him to reserve judgment.

"And it's not just physical healings," Suzanne said. "See that guy over there?" She motioned to a huge man— a biker type complete with shaved head, black leather vest, and chains. A large gold swastika dangled from his neck. Tattoos covered his forearms and shoulders, so dense that it was impossible to see any detail, except a paisley print of blues, greens, and an occasional red. "Will Patton," she said. "Member of the Aryan Brotherhood. He followed us down from Tacoma. Sweetest man you'll ever meet."

"I bet."

"He is."

"As long as you're not black or gay or Jewish."

"Oh, really?" She smiled that smile of hers and motioned to the crowd. "They don't exactly look like your blond, blue-eyed Germans to me."

Conrad looked out across the ball field. He had to agree. There seemed to be a fair number of blacks, Hispanics, and other minorities. For the most part everyone appeared to be middle to lower middle class. He turned back to Suzanne. "And Eli?" he asked. "I suppose you're going to tell me he's Jewish, right?"

Suzanne's smile brightened. "Why don't you ask him yourself?"

"Hey." A pleasant voice spoke from behind. Conrad turned to see Eli approaching—his coal-black eyes sparkling with pleasure, while at the same time gently probing. "My name's Eli," he said. "You're a friend of Suzanne's?"

"Uh, yes, we, that is—"

"We used to be married," Suzanne explained, "a long time ago. Conrad Davis, meet Eli Shepherd."

The two shook. Eli's grip was firm, his hands somewhat rough and callused.

"That was quite a stunt you pulled over there," Conrad said.

Eli's sparkle did not disappear. "By the looks of things you and your crew have it all on tape."

"Probably."

"And if I'm lucky I might be able to make some late-night filler piece."

Conrad smiled at his candidness. "If you're lucky."

Eli grinned and pretended to quote a headline. "'Con Artist Fools Hundreds, film at eleven.'" There was no malice in his eyes, just good-natured bantering.

Conrad couldn't help smiling back. "That's how it works. Of course if you're the real deal, well, now, I'd have myself quite a story, wouldn't I?"

"At least worthy of Jerry Springer."

Again Conrad smiled. Despite himself, he was beginning to like this kid. "Suzanne says you do that sort of thing all the time."

Eli said nothing, but looked over to the crowd and the game that was just starting. "The world's full of sickness, Conrad." The sparkle faded slightly from his eyes. "Unfortunately, most of it is not physical."

"And you think you can change that?"

Eli turned back to him. "I came into the world *to* change that." He held his gaze. For the briefest moment Conrad wasn't sure he could look away, even if he wanted. Sensing his discomfort, Eli's smile reappeared. "It was good talking with you, Conrad." He patted him on the shoulder and started to pass. "But my team's up to bat and ol' Jake's at the plate." He motioned to the burly man he'd thanked earlier for the use of the RV. "The poor guy's about zero for forty right now, so I think he could stand a little coaching. I hope we can talk again."

"Me, too," Conrad said. "Oh, and about that tape." Eli turned. "If what you're doing is the real McCoy, I could get you some quality exposure."

"Thanks." Eli grinned. "Don't need it." Then on second thought he added, "But if it's good for you, feel free. In fact, the sooner, the better."

The response surprised Conrad. "Why? What's the hurry?"

"I'm afraid neither you nor I have that much time left, Conrad Davis." With that, Eli turned and headed toward the backstop.

The comment left Conrad uneasy, as uneasy as when their eyes had first connected. He couldn't put his finger on it, but if there was the slightest possibility that this Eli was who he thought he might be . . . considering Endo's theory, considering what he'd seen and heard at the river baptism, considering what he'd experienced in that seventies motel laundry room . . . then was there also a chance that Eli knew who *he* was, and where he'd come from? No. Conrad shook his head. Such things were not possible.

"Hey, Jake," Eli called as he approached the backstop.

"'Sup?" Jake shouted, throwing a look over his shoulder, then taking a few practice swings.

"If I were you, I'd keep my eye open for a high lob, outside corner."

The big man turned to him. He coughed then spit. "What?"

"The next one's going to be on the outside corner."

"Come on, Eli!" It was the pitcher. He was about the same age as Jake, with the same ruddy features, but with a good fifty pounds less bulk. "That ain't fair."

Eli chuckled. "Throw what you want, Robert. I'm just trying to even the odds a little for big brother here."

Turning back to Jake he repeated, "Watch for the high lob, outside corner."

Jake scowled and took a couple more practice swings. "But he knows you told me."

Eli shrugged. "It's your choice. I'm just making a suggestion."

Jake looked back at Eli again, obviously sizing him up. Then, turning, he gripped the bat, crouched down, and got ready to swing.

Up on the mound Robert turned the ball around and around in his glove. Then he rolled his head and squinted at the plate. Apparently this was all part of his pitching ritual—more for superstition and luck than expertise and concentration.

"Come on, Jake!" one of the kids from his team cried. "Lay into it! Rip a good one!"

Conrad watched. Obviously, no one knew for certain what Robert would throw to his brother. Still, given Jake's batting average and the amount of muscle and flesh that he had to move, the big guy needed all the help he could get. But the fact that Eli had broadcast it for everyone to hear made an outside lob anything but likely. Or did it?

After finishing his ritual, Robert finally tossed the first pitch of the game.

Anticipating an outside corner lob, Jake stepped forward. He guessed correctly. He took a hefty swing, grunting like a wounded beast, and to everyone's astonishment, he connected.

The bat cracked and the ball sailed high into the sun.

His teammates clapped and cheered. So did those in the bleachers. So did Eli.

And Jake? Jake stood, absolutely mesmerized, watching the ball slowly arch over the right field fence and roll to a stop in the farmer's field.

"Run, Jake!" a boy on his team cried. Others joined in. "Run, Jake! Run!"

But Jake did not run. Instead, he turned to Eli who continued to watch and grin from behind the backstop.

"Run!" By now his entire team was shouting. "Run, Jake!"

Realizing he still held the bat, Jake dropped it to the ground. It rang with a metallic clunk. But instead of heading for first, he started toward the backstop.

"Run, Jake!" By now the crowd had taken up the cheer. "Run!"

But Jake did not hear. Instead, the big man lumbered around the backstop. Eli met him, laughing and slapping him on the back—until Jake threw his arms around him in a monstrous, life-threatening hug. By now everyone was laughing and cheering. Even the other team. Even Conrad. Because, whatever gift Eli may or may not have, and regardless of his seriousness of purpose . . . there was a playfulness about him. A love that was contagious.

"Dad, you promised. Daddy . . ."

The nurse had been kind enough to track down something for Julia to eat . . . a little toast and some orange juice. Her head had quit spinning, and now she sat all alone in the room, just her and her father. Eventually, she knew, they would ask her permission to pull the plug. What legal procedure they would follow, she hadn't the foggiest. But that was okay. Right now there was only the rhythmic hiss of the respirator, the green glow of the monitors above him . . . and her memories.

"Sweetheart, not now, I'm expecting a very important guest to be coming over."

"But you said I could. You promised."

He looked so small in the bed with its crisp, white sheets. So lost and vulnerable. The thick, hairy arms—"ape-man" arms she used to tease him—the ones that had carried her, had wrapped around her in the backyard hammock, protected her during scary movies . . . now they lay unmoving with IV needles stuck in and taped like he was some lifeless object. His four-day beard had not been shaved, and there were still a few tufts of graying hair on the back of his neck that the ER had missed when prepping him for the operation.

It was that hair that now had her attention.

"I know I promised, but I forgot."

"A promise is a promise. 'You're only as good as your word,' isn't that what you always say?"

"Jules . . ."

"Isn't it?"

"Julia, dear." It was her mother's voice. *"Daddy's got a very important visitor."*

"But he promised. And you're only as good as your word. Right? Right!"

"She's right," he sighed.

The memory continued flickering through her mind. He was much younger, in his twenties. He sat on the sofa, and she stood behind him. She held his thick, curly hair in her fingers and carefully snapped in another bright red barrette. There were at least a dozen scattered through his hair. Some red, others green or purple—plus a handful of plastic daisies, along with two pink rollers from Mom's collection.

"How much longer?" Dad asked, squirming to glance at his watch.

"Hold still," Julia ordered. *"Just a few more to go."*

"Jules . . ."

"Okay, okay, at least let me finish this one." He held still as she clipped in the final barrette. *"There. Perfect!"*

He rose and turned to her—tufts of hair sticking out in all directions, held in place by the bright hair clips. He was a masterpiece of the absurd, and she broke out laughing. It got no better when he began making monster faces at her and started to chase her around the room . . . until the doorbell rang.

Suddenly the monster face froze. It glanced to its watch. *"He's early!"*

Instantly his hands shot up to his hair, yanking at the barrettes, trying to undo the clips. Some he managed to remove, most he did not.

The doorbell rang again.

"Want me to get it?" Mom called from the other room.

"No, I, uh. . . I've got it." He gave Julia a look. She tried to cover her laughter but it did no good.

The bell rang a third time. With resignation and a heavy sigh, Dad headed for the door. Julia turned and started for cover, but he grabbed her hand. *"Oh, no, you're in on this, too."*

"Daddy," she squealed, protesting in delight. *"Let me go, let me go!"*

But he did not let go. He reached for the handle and opened it. Before them stood a tall, distinguished gentleman. A gentleman Julia had seen a hundred times on television. Yet she had never seen him with such a surprised look as he had that morning when seeing her father.

He cleared his throat and in a deep resonating voice asked, *"Do I have the right time?"*

Dad grinned sheepishly. *"Yes, sir, I'm afraid you do."* Then glancing down at Julia, he said, *"I'd like you to meet my new hairdresser. Julia Davis, this is Walter Cronkite. Mr. Cronkite, my daughter, Julia Davis."*

CHAPTER THREE

S tand by to roll tape," the director ordered.

The technical director, a thin, nervous fellow with glasses, punched an illuminated button on the console before him and repeated the order into his headset. "Intro tape, stand by."

Conrad and Suzanne stood behind the two men at the board. A third, the effects operator, a pudgy individual with an embarrassing comb-over, sat to their right, while two college-aged production assistants, male and female, hovered near the back doing their best to appear cool and nonchalant. The room was dim, lit by a single row of track lights running along a low, black ceiling. The only other illumination came from the TV monitors forming a wall in front of them. Most were black and white. Two were somewhat larger and in color—the program monitor, which displayed what would be on the show, and the preview monitor, displaying what the director planned to cut to next.

Up on the program monitor, Charlene Marshal, host of her own TV talk show, looked directly into the camera and read the prompter mounted in front of it. She was an attractive redhead, early thirties, with just enough compassion and charm to woo her guests into revealing intimate secrets, but enough grit and determination to steadily rise in the ratings. At the moment, her TV-Q was a solid 65 percent. She wasn't at the top of the heap yet, but as the network continued to promote and send stories down to her, it wouldn't be long.

"—a young man who has been creating quite a stir these past several months," she said to the camera, "and who we are honored to have as our next guest. But before we bring him out, let's take just a moment to show him in action."

The director dropped his index finger and the technical director gave the command. "Roll tape."

In the room behind them, the VTR operator hit play, and the footage that Ned had taped at the softball field began to roll. Eli had been right—network didn't consider him worthy of hard news, but he was definite fodder for afternoon talk shows. Conrad wasn't crazy about passing the segment down to this level, but after his debacle with the parallel universe story, he thought it best to lay low and be a team player.

The parallel universe story . . . as far as he could tell, that had been about the only major difference between this new world he was living in and his old one. Apparently, in this new world, he had decided *not* to pursue the story any further, he had *not* gone up to Camarillo, and he had *not* been involved in a serious car accident. In fact, upon his return from the Oregon softball game just ten days ago, he'd found the Jaguar, complete with sun-rotten wiper blades, unscathed and sitting in the same LAX parking lot that he always parked in when he flew out of town on his trips. He even had the parking stub in his wallet.

The same was true with every other area of his life. Everything was exactly as it had been—the same messy divorce with Roseanne, the same dirty dishes in the sink, the same shark-infested waters at work. It was remarkable. Uncanny. And in some ways, almost comforting. Because gradually, as Conrad remained in this new world, as the minutes turned to hours and now to days, it grew more and more difficult to believe there actually had been another one, one of automobile accidents and hospitalization. Granted, the idea still haunted him, forcing him to question if he was living out some elaborate fantasy or self-generated hallucination. In fact during those first few days he had even tried to jerk or startle himself back into his old world. But he'd met no success. Then there were those calls to the California State Patrol as well as to the hospitals surrounding the Camarillo area—Saint John's, Conejo Valley Medical Center, and others. But the information was always the same. There had been no accident involving a Conrad Davis, and no patient by that name had been admitted. So, gradually, as the days unfolded, he found himself wondering more and more which reality was the real world and which one was the fantasy.

Apparently, whatever reality he'd experienced before, if it was a reality, no longer existed. At least not in this world. Because in this world, except for the auto accident and hospitalization, everything was exactly as it had been.

Well, almost exactly . . .

There were two other differences. First, Suzanne's change of faith. She'd always been a devout Christian. But now, she'd suddenly jumped ship and embraced a new Messiah. Not only that, but she kept denying that she'd ever heard the name of Jesus Christ. It was more than a little surprising. But not as surprising as the reason . . .

Conrad had had his suspicions ever since the baptism scene in Eastern Washington—actually ever since he'd seen (or imagined he'd seen) the baby in the laundry room of that earlier, 1970 Santa Monica. He'd barely returned to his home in Pasadena and unpacked before he headed to a bookshelf and dug out an old Bible—an old Bible that, to his surprise, appeared to have never included the New Testament. A Bible that simply ended with the book of Malachi—no Matthew, Mark, Luke or whatever, no mention of Jesus Christ and his disciples, and no epistles. And it wasn't just his Bible. Every Bible he ran across, from hotel rooms to bookstores, had the same omissions. It was as if the gospel had never occurred.

Charlene's voice came up over the speaker. It was the audio piece he'd written and that she'd recorded earlier that morning. Over the taped footage from the softball field she spoke of Eli Shepherd, of his rising popularity and fame, and of his supposed gift of healing.

"Supposed?" Suzanne nudged Conrad.

He smiled. "Got to maintain some objectivity."

She cut him a glance.

"Just keep watching," he said.

Suzanne had come down from San Jose yesterday afternoon with Eli and his band of rag-tag followers. They weren't organized—just an assortment of campers, RVs, and cars, about a dozen and a half, that had slowly been making their way down the coast. When Conrad heard of their arrival he swung by and tried to convince Suzanne to stay at the house. That way she wouldn't have to pay for a motel or sleep in some RV. She could stay in Julia's old room.

Of course she declined. And he certainly understood, what with Roseanne gone and just the two of them alone.

But he also understood something else. Felt it, really. That connection. Yes, he needed her presence up at the softball game, back when he was getting his bearings. But, even after he had returned home, even after he'd grown used to the situation and had settled back into his routine, he found himself thinking about her. Often, several times a day.

He'd heard that could be the case with first loves. And they were each other's first loves—high-school sweethearts. Of course he'd thought about her from time to time throughout the years. But this was different. More frequent. More . . . distracting. And now that he was single again and since she had never remarried, maybe they could—

Stop it, he scolded himself. *What are you doing? She's too good for you, you know that. And so does she.* It was a painful truth, but one he'd forced himself to accept. As difficult as it was, he knew there were simply some things that could not be changed.

Still, it felt good to have her standing beside him, almost like old times, back when he'd produced his very first stories. He remembered how they had sat together on that second-hand sofa, the one with the awful striped pattern, waiting breathlessly for his first segment to appear on TV. Those were good times. Back when their life was new and exciting and full of possibility. Back before he'd ruined it.

Up on the monitor, the taped Eli was completing his story about the seeds and the soil. Conrad knew Suzanne would be happy with the way he'd edited it. He'd put in plenty of audience reaction shots of folks listening and contemplating. It was an old TV trick that would assure viewers that Eli was to be taken seriously. Not that Eli needed tricks. To be honest, he didn't need much fixing at all. The only substantial part Conrad had to cut was that unfortunate comment he'd made about being the only way to God. There was no reason to needlessly antagonize the audience.

Now the healing segment began. Conrad had made only two or three cuts to speed up the process. As they watched, he could practically hear Suzanne beam. And he was pleased when she gave his arm a squeeze of excitement. The segment came to an end on a freeze-frame where the weeping Brian Tuffts threw his arms around Eli in gratitude.

The studio audience applauded as Charlene came back on the program monitor. "And now, if you'll join me in welcoming ... Mr. Eli Shepherd." The audience clapped louder as Eli appeared and joined Charlene on the platform. He looked anything but religious, wearing jeans, a forest-green T-shirt, and a tweed sports coat.

The two greeted one another and, as the applause faded, they took their seats up on the carpeted platform. It was a homey set, with a floral sofa, love seat, matching coffee and end tables, a bookshelf on the back wall with plenty of pictures, and, of course, the obligatory gas fireplace.

Once they were seated, Charlene began. "Eli, thanks for joining us."

"My pleasure." And the smile on his face made it clear that it really was his pleasure. They began talking about his birth in Santa Monica (a fact not lost on Conrad), his uneventful childhood in the Pacific Northwest, the early death of his father, an education that took him only as far as high school, and the past dozen years that he'd been working as a general contractor building homes in the Seattle area.

Although Conrad did his best to maintain a reporter's objectivity, he was pleased to see how well the cameras captured Eli's warmth and openness. Charlene must have sensed it too for she was turning up her charm to an all-time high, half-flirting, half-cross-examining. "Seriously, though"—she threw him a mischievous grin— "you don't expect me to believe you can just walk around healing whoever you want?"

"You can believe whatever you like." He smiled back. "That choice is up to you."

"And if I don't?"

"Hey," he teased back, "everybody is wrong once in a while."

The audience ate it up. His honesty, his sense of humor, the obvious ease and joy he had in talking with her—it was all there, as the two continued the playful banter. But Conrad knew it wouldn't last forever. Charlene Marshal did not get where she was through good-natured chitchat. And, true to form, once she'd put her guest at ease, she brought out the big guns.

"So, you're telling me you can heal any physical ailment you want?"

"Physical sickness is of minor concern."

"Pardon me?"

"It's the sickness of the soul that I've really come to heal."

For the briefest second Charlene was unsure how to respond. Conrad had to chuckle. The girl had no idea who she was up against. But this was her show and she would not be put off. "I see." She cleared her throat.

"Well, the reason I was asking was we have a production assistant . . ." She turned to the audience. "Keith? Keith Anderson, would you come out here, please?"

A young man on crutches emerged from behind the audience seating area. He wore a blue polo shirt and a pair of beige shorts that clearly displayed a left leg shriveled to a stump just below the knee.

Back in the control room, Suzanne turned to Conrad. "You never said this would happen."

"I didn't know, not until the read-through this morning."

"Connie—"

"Relax." He gave her a reassuring smile. "This guy can take care of himself."

"But—"

"If he's who I think he is, he'll do just fine." Conrad turned back to the monitor and watched with interest as Keith made his way toward the platform.

Charlene continued. "Keith has been physically challenged like this since birth, so . . ." She turned to Eli. "We figured if you really can heal whoever you want whenever you want, what better candidate than our young friend here?" She turned to the audience for confirmation. "Wouldn't you agree?"

The audience clapped in approval. Eli rose to shake Keith's hand. They spoke briefly, but it was impossible to hear what was said over the applause.

When they finally sat, Charlene motioned to Eli. "So what do you say?" She was still smiling, but there was no missing the challenge underneath. "Can you deliver? Right here, right now, in front of a national TV audience?"

Eli did not answer. Instead, he continued to watch Keith, who shifted uncomfortably under his gaze.

"Well?" Charlene smiled.

The audience waited patiently.

When Eli finally spoke, his voice was softer than before. And a little sadder. "I'm sorry, Keith." He slowly shook his head.

Charlene's smile began to fade.

"I'm sorry they pressured you into this."

The boy's eyes shot up to Eli's. A nerve had been hit.

"Is your prosthesis backstage, or did they make you leave it at home?"

The boy's eyes faltered.

That's when Eli turned to Charlene. "I expected you to turn this into a circus and try to make me jump through hoops . . . but you should never have forced the boy."

"Actually," Charlene countered, "I believe it was Keith's request. Isn't that right, Keith?"

Keith swallowed, staring hard at the carpet.

Charlene fidgeted slightly. Once again she was caught off balance and once again she recovered. "So . . . Is that a no, then? Are you telling us you can't heal our friend here?"

Eli turned his eyes from Keith to Charlene. The look was so powerful that the woman actually caught her breath. But before she could respond, a howling scream filled the studio.

"What's that?" the director demanded inside the control room.

"Somebody from the audience!" the technical director shouted as he searched the monitors. "There!" He pointed to the black-and-white monitor used for audience reactions. "Third row up, next to the center aisle."

Conrad's eyes darted to the monitor. It was a young girl, a teenager. Long blond hair. She was squirming in the seat as she took a breath and let out another scream, more tortured than the first.

"Looks like a seizure," the technical director said.

Instinctively, Conrad glanced to the program monitor, the one still showing Charlene. If she was shaken before, she was definitely unnerved now.

The director swore and ripped off his headphones. "All right, stop tape! Stop tape!"

But Conrad had spotted something else. On Eli's monitor. An expression he hadn't seen on the young man before—a quiet resolve, almost anger. "No," Conrad said. He hadn't worked in TV this long without having some instincts to trust. "Keep rolling."

"What?" the director turned to him.

"Keep rolling!"

"Connie, it's ruined!" The director swore again. "We've got to stop the show and call the paramedics. We'll go back and reset when they're through."

Up on the monitor, the teen threw herself onto the aisle steps where she rolled and writhed, shrieking out of control. An older gentleman, most likely her father, dropped to her side, trying to restrain her, trying to keep her from hurting herself, waving off others who tried to help.

"Stop tape!" the director ordered.

"Look at Eli!" Conrad pointed to the monitor where they saw him stepping off the platform. "Follow your guest! Follow your guest!"

He felt Suzanne take his arm in concern. "Connie . . ."

But he knew what he was doing. "Keep it rolling! Keep rolling!"

The director stared at the monitor, then shouted over his shoulder to one of the production assistants, "Get the paramedics here."

The boy reached for a phone as the director turned back to Eli's monitor. "Camera two, follow him. Follow him!" He looked back to the program monitor. Charlene remained standing with her mouth open.

"Camera one, get off her, go to the guest, reverse angle!"

Images on the monitors swished as they turned and zoomed toward Eli, passing them and approaching the girl. Her writhing eased as her father continued to hold her. Eventually he tried sitting her up. She relaxed some, but her mouth continued to twitch and distort.

Eli arrived and the father looked up at him. "I'm ..." The man said something inaudible.

"Get me sound!" the director cried. "Get a mike in there!"

The father continued. "She's been like this since she was a child." He leaned his cheek against her sweating face, whispering something soothing into her ear. But the girl was again growing agitated. The father looked back up to Eli. "We've tried everything, but—"

Suddenly, she threw her head back and cried, howling like a wounded animal.

"Give me close-ups!" the director yelled. "Three, tight on the girl! One, tight on Eli!"

Another cry. Then a voice began to rumble up from deep inside her. It came from her chest. Thick, raspy.

Guttural. She tried to sound fierce, but there was no missing the fear on her face, and in her eyes. "Why have you come to torment us before our time?" she demanded.

Eli said nothing. He simply watched.

A sneer flickered across her face. "We know who you are." She gasped, sucking in air. Then she spit out the words, "You . . . Chosen One! You son of the most—"

"Be quiet." Eli's voice was soft, but commanded absolute authority.

The girl's mouth clamped shut. She tried to open it but could not. Her lips curled, then snarled. She hissed and growled, but her mouth remained clinched. She began rolling her head back and forth in frustration, saliva slipping out of the corners of her mouth, glistening on her chin.

But Eli was unfazed. Instead, ever so gently, he knelt beside her. Her eyes widened as she recoiled, pulling back and cowering against the steps, trying to get as far from him as possible. Seeing her fear, Eli drew no closer. Instead, he spoke two words. Just two. They were barely above a whisper:

"Leave her."

Suddenly the body convulsed. Her head jerked to the left, then to the right, back and forth, back and forth, sweat and hair and spittle flying.

"Now!"

At the command she threw her head back, her eyes bulging at the ceiling, her mouth exploding open. But there were no words, just a low, guttural gasp, a hissing from the back of the throat. It started deep and quiet, growing in intensity, resonating through her entire body, until it broke into a shrill scream. Anguished. Chilling. So eerie that Conrad felt the hairs on his arms rise, a coldness sweep across his shoulders. Finally the cry faded, ending in a ragged, raspy wheeze. And then the girl went limp, falling unconscious into her father.

"There's your break," Conrad said. "Go to commercial."

The director nodded. "Got it. Camera two, go back to Charlene."

The camera turned and focused upon the host. Unfortunately, she remained standing, mouth still agape.

"Go to commercial," the director shouted. "Tell her to go to commercial."

The technical director hit the intercom. "Charlene." His voice echoed through the studio. "Char, go to break." She still didn't hear. "Charlene!"

At last she turned toward the camera, struggling to crank up just the right look of wisdom and knowing. It was only one sentence, but it seemed to take forever to get out the words. "And we'll . . . be back, right after this."

I do not want heroic efforts made to prolong my life, and I do not want life-sustaining treatment to be provided or continued: (1) if I am in an irreversible coma or persistent vegetative state; or (2) if I am terminally ill and the use of life-sustaining procedures would serve only to artificially delay the moment of my death; or (3) under any other circumstances where the burdens of the treatment outweigh the expected benefits. In making decisions about life-sustaining treatment under provision (3) above, I want my agent to consider the relief of suffering and the quality of my life, as well as the extent of the possible prolongation of my life.

Julia stared at the California Durable Power of Attorney for Health Care document she'd brought from home. The one her father had sent several years earlier. The one she'd protested and refused, but that he had sent anyway. And the one she'd kept because it was the responsible thing to do—until he found someone else, which of course he never had.

She looked back at the words:

I do not want heroic efforts made to prolong my life, and I do not want life-sustaining treatment to be provided or continued: (1) if I am in an irreversible coma or persistent vegetative state ...

Legally, it was cut and dried. If there was no chance of him living without life-sustaining treatment such as the respirator or feeding tube, or if they had to perform "heroic" efforts to keep him alive such as resuscitation or CPR, then as his "agent" she had the power, no, she had the *obligation* to prevent those efforts and let him die.

But what if there was a chance? What if by applying those efforts or continuing those treatments a few more hours, a few more days or weeks or months, what if he eventually started to live on his own? Such things were possible. It happened all the time, though with far less critical patients. How was she to be certain, *absolutely certain*, that it could not happen with him? And if it could happen, and if she ordered the treatments to be removed prematurely, wouldn't that simply mean that she'd murdered her father?

She continued staring at the paper.

I want my agent to consider the relief of suffering and the quality of my life ... I want my agent to consider ... I want my agent to consider ... I want my agent ...

She noticed the paper shaking in her hands. *Why?* She seethed. *Why am I always the responsible one?* She lowered the trembling paper and glared at the unmoving form in front of her. How dare he put her through this! How dare he make it *her* decision!

I want my agent to consider . . .

Tears welled up in her eyes. Tears of rage and hate and a hundred other conflicting emotions.

"Daddy, it's not fair!"

"Just answer me, did you or did you not beat up Willard Hayes?"

"But all the kids—"

"Julia, answer me."

She was in her room, sitting on her bed beside him. A dozen stuffed animals surrounded her, but each and every one remained silent. She was on her own.

She turned up the tears, increased the pout. It worked with her friends and their parents, it worked with Mom. Why wouldn't it work with him?

"Jules, I'm asking you for the final time . . . did you beat up Willard Hayes?"

"It's not fair," she wailed. *"All the other kids—"*

"We're not talking about the other kids."

She folded her arms in defiance. If it was a test of wills, she would win. This time she would win.

"All right." Her father took a deep breath. *"If you refuse to take responsibility and answer my question, you will stay in your room."*

She held out, saying nothing.

"You will stay in your room and, if necessary, you will miss dinner."

"DAD!" she exploded.

"All I want from you is the truth, Sweetheart." He rose from her bed and headed for the door. *"And when you're ready to tell me the truth, when you're ready to be responsible for your actions, we can talk."*

She saw the pain in his eyes, knew he hated for all the world to punish her, so she gave it one last try. *"Oh, Daddy . . ."* It was the most helpless, pitiful whimper she could muster, and she completed the effect by looking up to him with a trembling chin.

"When you're ready, Jules," he said, reaching for the door, *"just let me know."* And with that, he closed it.

She let out another mournful wail, but even as it escaped, she knew he would not bend. He would not bend, and even more importantly, at the tender age of eight . . . she knew he was right not to.

Dr. Thomas J. Kerston looked directly into the camera and furrowed his thick, graying brows. "I just want to make sure you're not part of this whole New Age nonsense," he said.

"What nonsense is that?" Charlene Marshal asked.

"You know, all this silliness about angels, spirit guides, and 'connecting to some great cosmic force,' whatever that is." He finished the phrase with a chuckle that sent ripples through both double chins.

Conrad stared at the monitor in the control room. He never understood why men so heavy insisted on wearing shirts so tight that their flesh literally spilled over their collars. Still, Dr. Kerston was powerful enough to wear whatever he wanted and get away with it. During the commercial break Charlene had regained her composure. They had removed the girl and had shuffled

Keith Anderson backstage. Now she was hosting the final segment, a satellite link with Dr. Thomas J. Kerston down in Georgia. As leader of one of the largest denominations in America, host of his own talk show on his own network, EBN, he'd been steadily rising in popularity, even becoming a serious political force. All Southern charm and good ol' boy on the outside, he was steel and grit underneath. Both Republicans and Democrats had been courting his favor, and by never committing too strongly to either side, he managed to hold everyone's feet to the fire.

Besides being a shrewd politician, he was also a remarkable salesman. In the first sixty seconds that he'd been on the show he'd already managed to work in the opening of his new facility, the City of God. "The world's largest worship center, complete with a giant food court with food from all around the world, an elaborate water park for the kiddies, plus workout facilities, tennis courts, and shoot, we even got our own dating service. There's something here for the entire family, just a short two-hour drive from Atlanta, right in beautiful Salem County, Georgia."

It had been a remarkable piece of salesmanship, but with Charlene's gentle prodding, they had managed to return to Eli and to bring up the gentleman's concern regarding any affiliation he may have with the New Age movement.

"So," Charlene said, turning back to Eli. "How would you address that question?"

"I think the doctor is right to be concerned about these issues," Eli said. "Most of today's supernatural experiences—channeling, spirit guides, and the like, are cheap counterfeits of the real thing. And they can prove to be quite dangerous. But, the question we have to ask ourselves, Doctor, is why? If people are so starved to find God, why aren't they coming to us? What are we doing wrong that causes a person to look to counterfeit experiences instead of—"

"—instead of the Word of God," the doctor interrupted, nodding in agreement. "Which, of course, is the real source of life."

Eli shook his head. "No, that's not correct."

"Pardon me?"

"The Bible is not the source of life. Although it does point to that life."

Once again a scowl crept over the Doctor's face. "And that life is . . ."

"Me."

The studio audience stirred.

"Oh brother," Conrad sighed from the control room. "Here we go again."

Eli continued. "You see, Doctor, I am the ultimate truth. I am the life."

"Wait a minute." Charlene smelled blood and went in for the kill. "Are you telling us that you are the only truth, that none of these other religions matter?"

Eli turned to her, his gaze riveting. "I am the way, Charlene. No one comes to my Father, but through Me."

"Your . . . *Father*?" Charlene pretended to cough in surprise.

Dr. Kerston's image chuckled. "I see. So tell me, Eli, how does that make you any different from, say, the David Koreshes of the world, or any other half-baked delusionist with a Messiah complex?"

"It doesn't. Except for one minor detail."

"And what is that?"

"I'm telling you the truth."

Back in the control room, Conrad turned to Suzanne. "What's he doing? He had them, they were on his side."

"Give me audience reactions," the director ordered.

The program monitor cut to an audience growing more and more unsettled.

"I am the door, Dr. Kerston. It is impossible to enter the Kingdom of Heaven without entering through me."

There was another good-natured chortle from Dr. Kerston. "Don't you find that, oh, I don't know, just a little bit 'exclusive'—being the only way to Heaven, I mean?"

Eli turned directly to Kerston's video-link image and spoke. "You know nothing about the Kingdom of Heaven, Doctor. My Father's Kingdom is not about food courts, dating services, or water parks. It has nothing to do with day planners or becoming the CEO of a great, flourishing congregation."

"Go split screen," the director ordered. Immediately both faces were side by side on the monitor—Eli, speaking earnestly, Dr. Kerston striving to maintain his smile.

"The Kingdom of God is about dying. It is about pouring your life into others, regardless of the cost. It is about laying down your life so that you can receive Mine. Bigger is not better, Doctor." Eli leaned closer into the camera. "The Kingdom is not part of the American dream. Hear Me carefully. In the Kingdom of Heaven, there is no greater temptation, no quicker road to ruin . . . than worldly success."

"Tell her we've got thirty seconds," the director ordered. Then turning to the sound booth he said, "Give me closing music."

Charlene took her cue and turned toward her camera. "Well, guys, that was more than a little enlightening. We have just a few seconds left. Any closing comments?"

Dr. Kerston cleared his throat and smiled. "Well, despite our differences, I want Eli there to understand he's still welcome to come on down to Salem County when we open this Fourth of July. And that same invitation goes to all of your audience, Charlene. Come on down to the City of God, just a short two-hour drive from Atlanta, and let us offer you a little old-fashioned, godly hospitality."

"This guy doesn't miss a beat," Conrad mused out loud.

The director nodded. "Your friend could take a few lessons."

"And if you don't want to eat at our food court"— Dr. Kerston gave another chuckle—"shoot, you don't have to. But if any of you are thinking about a vacation or just wanting to see what great and mighty things our God is doing here, well, come on down, our door is always open."

"Eli?" Charlene asked.

Eli swallowed quietly. Finally he answered, "I think the doctor has said it all."

"Come on," Charlene prodded. "What does that mean?"

"It means Dr. Kerston is not building my Father's Kingdom ... but his own. On the outside it's a beautiful complex with good and decent things. But on the inside it is exactly like the doctor ... full of death and stench and decay."

The director let out a whoop.

Dr. Kerston's smile quivered.

And Conrad shook his head mumbling. "Oh boy."

"Give her fifteen seconds," the director ordered. "Wrap it up."

Conrad turned and motioned Suzanne toward the exit. "Let's get in there and get him out before the audience goes after him."

Suzanne nodded and they headed for the door. Conrad could tell she was just as embarrassed over the performance as he was. Too bad. It had been going so well. But now . . . now when the show was aired, folks across the country would begin cutting him up and serving him for lunch. You don't lash out at one of the most respected religious icons in America (not to mention the most powerful) without major repercussions. And you certainly don't go around claiming to be the only way to God.

They headed down the thickly carpeted hallway until they reached the studio door. He tugged it open. It was thick and heavily padded to dampen the sound. Once inside, he spotted Eli off to the right. The audience had already started shuffling out while Charlene talked to the floor director. It was obvious she was avoiding Eli like the plague. The same was true for the rest of the crew. And who could blame them?

"Eli." Suzanne walked across the black, concrete floor and gave him a brief hug. Conrad was right behind.

"So, how did I do?" Eli asked with his trademark twinkle.

"Well . . ." Conrad gave a little grimace.

Eli chuckled, "That good, huh?"

Conrad shrugged, pleased to see Eli wasn't taking it too badly. "Let's just say a few more lessons in diplomacy wouldn't hurt."

Eli smiled. "But it's truth, Conrad. You of all people know the value of truth. 'A person is only as good as their word,' remember?"

Conrad opened his mouth, but for a second no words would come. How did he know? Had Suzanne— no, that was too personal, too private. Finally the question formed. "Who . . . who exactly are you?"

Eli's smile broadened. "I think you know, Connie."

Again Conrad was speechless.

After a moment, Suzanne stepped in. "It's too bad about that Keith boy," she said.

Eli turned to her. "What do you mean?"

"I mean it's too bad you didn't heal him."

"I didn't?"

Before Suzanne could respond there was a loud cry backstage. All three turned to see a small crowd gathering. In its center stood Keith Anderson. "I've got it!" he shouted. "I've got my leg! I've got a leg!"

Eli turned and started toward the exit. "Come on," he said. "We should be going."

Suzanne nodded and started to follow. But Conrad could only stand staring.

"Conrad?" Eli turned back to him. "Connie, you all right?"

Conrad slowly turned toward him, still stunned, still amazed.

Eli waited patiently until Conrad could finally find the words. "You . . . you really are him, aren't you?"

"Who's that?" Eli asked, his eyes sparkling.

"Jesus . . ." Conrad's voice caught in his throat and he tried again. "Jesus Christ."

Julia jerked awake and looked toward her father's unconscious body. Impossible. The respirator hose was taped to his mouth, making it impossible for him to speak. But she heard it. Clearly. Unmistakably.

"Jesus . . . Jesus Christ."

It had been his voice, there was no denying it. She rose from the yellow fiberglass chair and leaned toward him, looking down at the swollen, bandaged head. "Dad . . . Dad, did you say something?"

No response.

"Dad, it's me, Jules. Did you try to speak?"

There was no movement, no indication he'd heard. How could he answer even if he had? But he had said something, she was certain of it.

Or had he? In her half-asleep state, had she only thought she'd heard his voice? No. She shook her head. She'd heard it. Somehow, someway. As clear as a bell. It was her father's voice.

"Jesus . . . Jesus Christ."

She suspected it to be an oath that he'd mumbled through his pain. Then again it could have been some sort of prayer, who knows. But she'd heard something.

And if it was something, that meant part of him was still there. His brain hadn't been entirely destroyed. There was some consciousness left. And if that was true—she felt herself growing uncomfortably cold—then if she gave permission for them to take him off life support . . . there was something, some part of her father's consciousness, she would be killing.

"Dad ... Dad, if you can hear me, let me know. Dad?"
Nothing.

"Dad ..." She felt her voice filling with emotion.
"Dad ..."

The more she looked at the taped mouth, the more
she knew how impossible it was for him to have spoken.
Maybe it was just a grunt or a groan. But why had she
heard a name ... much less that one? Whether he was
swearing or praying or groaning, she did not know. But
she did know this: her dad was still there. Under the bandages, under the wires and hoses and hardware, some part
of him was still there. He'd found a way to tell her. And as
long as he was there, she would not, she could not let
them take him.

CHAPTER FOUR

Alone in his Jaguar a frustrated Conrad negotiated the snaking twists and turns up Brooke Street as he headed high into the Hollywood Hills. What was Eli doing now? What had he blundered into this time? It seemed that whenever the guy turned around, he was making a wrong move. And if Suzanne was right, this could be the worst one of all.

After Charlene Marshal's program aired—receiving impressive ratings along with sound bites on many of the softer news shows—word of Eli began to spread. Not that he was a major topic of conversation, but people across the country were beginning to take notice. As far as Conrad could tell, opinions fell into three camps. One group looked upon him as a potential Jim Jones or David Koresh, some guy with a Messiah complex who used parlor tricks to woo the masses. Then there were the masses, those who admired his testosterone level for publicly challenging a powerful religious figure like Dr. Kerston. And finally there were the religious leaders. Some considered him an embarrassing annoyance that would self-destruct; others looked upon his words as blasphemous, his miracles as works of the devil.

All of the attention over the piece and over Eli had been good for Conrad. It more than made up for his failed parallel-universe story, and it had put him back in good standing with Phil Harrison and the *Up Front* team. But at the moment, that didn't much matter. At least not tonight. Tonight he was being a friend. He liked Eli. He appreciated his honesty and his no-nonsense approach. Then, of course, there was the other matter ... the question of his true identity. For if Conrad had indeed entered another world, one in which Jesus had not yet appeared ... well, the similarity to Eli and his actions was growing more apparent every day. Now if he could just stop the guy from being so naive and self-destructive.

A white Corvette convertible rounded the corner directly in front of Conrad, taking its half out of the middle of the road. Conrad swerved to the far side, nearly snapping off a row of mail boxes. He could honk his horn in anger, but what good would it do? The guy would just flip him off and continue on his merry, *I've-got-more-money-than-brains-and-if-I-break-this-toy-I'll-just-buy-another-one* way.

Conrad pulled back onto the narrow road and refocused his attention to Eli's current problem. If you're trying to be taken seriously as a religious figure, you don't go into the Hollywood Hills and party with Leon Brewster; it was as simple as that. Leon Brewster was the leading porn producer on the West Coast. It was an absurd move. What could Eli possibly be thinking?

A half hour ago, Conrad had swung by the Motel 6 on La Brea where Suzanne and the others were staying. He'd said it was just to say hi. Granted it had been his fourth visit since they'd come into town last week, but she didn't seem to mind. Nor did he. Maybe it was those fleeting memories of the accident, of realizing how close he'd come to death. He wasn't sure, but it felt good to catch up on old times, and to reconnect with the one person in his life who'd ever mattered. Of course there was another truth, though he was careful to hide it from her, and was doing his best to hide it from himself. He was falling for her. Again. Not that he'd ever stopped. She'd always been there, in the back of his mind, even during the other marriages. And, though he constantly reminded himself that he had no right to be having such thoughts, the feelings were returning, growing stronger every day.

Still, that would be his secret. Always. Because, despite the swelling he felt inside his chest whenever they were together, the warmth that filled his body, and the way his mind continually drifted to her whenever they were apart, he would not tell her. He had destroyed her life once. He cared too deeply for the lady to do it again.

He'd only seen Eli one time during his visits. They'd spoken briefly, but it was nothing of substance, just chitchat, good-natured ribbing over Eli's talent for saying such wrong things at such wrong times. The subject of Jesus Christ had not returned.

But, earlier that week, Conrad had swung by Santa Monica. It was only a thirty-minute drive from the office, and he had a little time to kill. Of course, just as he had expected; there were no hippies, the mall had returned to its rightful place, and there was no run-down motel, at least not where he remembered it. And he did remember it. Vividly. So vividly that earlier he'd even called up Dr. Endo in Camarillo. He mentioned nothing of his experience, he had no way to prove it was real, and no need to foster rumors that he was an overimpressionable fruitcake. *"If there are eyewitnesses to such universes they would be locked up in insane asylums . . .* " Still, he did ask one question.

"If a person were to actually slip into another reality, and if the conditions that allowed him to do that remained, would it be possible for him to do it again, maybe at a different time?"

The doctor's answer was clear and unmistakable. "Yes. Remember, I said that time in another universe may not travel at our velocity or be bound by our restrictions?"

Conrad had remembered it. And as best he figured, that's what had happened. If—*if*—the Santa Monica experience had been real, then somehow he had entered this world at an earlier time, then managed to skip ahead and re-enter it thirty years later. It was an absurd theory, impossible to prove, but in those uncertain, middle-of-the-night moments, it gave him something to hang on to.

The hill grew steeper, the switchbacks sharper and more treacherous as Conrad dropped the Jaguar into second. Already he could see cars parked off to the side. Mercedes, Beamers, off-road utility vehicles . . . the preferred mode of transportation by the rich and chic. And the rich and chic were the only guests Leon Brewster ever invited. There was good money in his line of work, and he attracted only the best, or the worst, depending upon your point of view. Actually, the porn itself didn't bother Conrad much—after all, he was in L.A., the land of tolerant thinking. It was the Internet stuff with the kiddies that made him uneasy. That's why he was heading up to the mansion. That's why, after Suzanne had mentioned Leon's name, Conrad had hopped into the car and was racing to Eli's rescue.

He took another hairpin curve, and the mansion appeared to the right. It was cut out of the hillside, its marble facade glowing in the milky moonlight. Just ahead, a pair of car jockeys waited to park his car. They were dressed in black-and-white French maid costumes, complete with fishnet stockings and garter belts. The fact that they were young men was a clear indication of what awaited Conrad inside.

What could Eli possibly be thinking?

Conrad stopped his car, climbed out, and gave his key to one of the attendants. The night air felt warm and pleasant. And the sweet smell of jasmine lay heavy along the hillside. He turned toward the mansion. It loomed fifty yards ahead. With a sigh, he started up the brick driveway toward the open, wrought-iron gate. But before he'd even entered, he heard a voice call from the side, "Conrad! Hey, Connie!"

He peered to the left, toward a large group of oleander bushes, eight to ten feet high, covered with white and pink flowers. "Who's there?"

Two forms cautiously stepped from the shadows.

"Jake?" Conrad asked. It was the burly softball player Eli had helped to hit the home run. Beside him was the racist biker, the one with the shaved head and tattoos. "Will?" The men slunk out into the moonlight. "What are you guys doing here?"

"Waiting for Eli," Jake said, throwing a glance up to the house.

"They wouldn't let you in?" Conrad asked.

"You crazy?" Will answered. "There ain't nothin' up there but Jews and blacks and perverts. No way we're going up there."

"But Eli's there," Conrad said.

Will said nothing and looked down. Jake nodded sullenly.

Conrad glanced back up at the house. It was obvious these two country bumpkins had more sense than their leader. He turned back to them. "I'm going up to get him now. Just stay put; we'll be back in a couple of minutes."

Relief flooded their faces, and Conrad had to smile as he turned and started up the driveway. Anywhere else, somebody like Will would have chewed up and spit out Leon Brewster in a second—a black porno king infesting the world, particularly God's "chosen race," with his poison. But put some money around him, a fancy mansion, fancy cars . . . and suddenly Will is cowering in the bushes. Funny how money can turn the tables.

The house up ahead was Greco-Roman and anything but understated. Marble pillars, marble steps, and of course marble statues. Lots and lots of statues, each separately lit and each anatomically correct. A dozen in the yard, at least that many surrounding the entrance. Once he reached the porch he was greeted by two slave girls, blond twins, dressed in leather and chains. Their perfume rivaled the jasmine as they pushed open the large brass doors. When he entered, the one to his right was careful to brush against him, just in case he was interested.

Inside, it was no better. An explosion of bad taste and vulgarity. Turquoise soap bubbles drifted down from bubble machines up in the balcony. Alternating floodlights of blue, yellow, and red lit men of every persuasion, scantily dressed and impossibly endowed women, transvestites, adults with children's bodies, children with adult's bodies.

Many were drunk or loaded or both, and several sported more body-piercing rivets than a Navy battleship.

Conrad worked his way through the crowd, waving aside the drinks and a silver tray of cocaine that floated past. He entered a large archway and stepped down into the main room. It was encircled by marble pillars and more statues. A large fountain set directly in the middle and bubbled a pink liquid, most likely champagne. And there, sitting on the edge of the fountain, the focus of the room's attention, was Eli. He wore the same jeans, T-shirt, and sports coat that he'd worn on Charlene's show. At least fifty guests surrounded him. Several stood; others were stretched out on the floor. All appeared to be listening, enraptured by the story he was telling.

Conrad moved closer to hear. Eli spotted him and gave a slight nod. He was speaking with the same enthusiasm and joy he'd had when talking to the group at the softball field.

"... but the younger son, he wanted to get out there and live. He wanted to leave the farm and taste everything the world had to offer. Everything and then some."

"You go, boy," an anorexic model shouted in approval. Others chuckled.

Eli continued. "So he asked his father for his half of the inheritance now. And his father said—"

"No way, child," a platinum blond transvestite shouted. "You gotta stay on this farm, shoveling horse pucky, till you croak."

More chuckles.

Eli grinned and shook his head. "No, not with this father. Even though he knew what was on his son's mind, he honored and respected him enough to let him go. He gave him the entire portion of inheritance and bid him farewell."

"Why, that's just plain ignorant," scoffed a handsome black man in his thirties. Conrad recognized him immediately: Leon Brewster, host of the party.

Eli shot him a smile. "No, not for this father. You see, he loved him, Leon. He loved him so much that he was willing to let him go."

Even though Leon looked away, shaking his head in disapproval, it was obvious Eli had hit some sort of nerve. The two had connected about something.

"What about the kid?" a buff male guest asked.

Eli continued. "The son had the time of his life. I mean, with his daddy's money he tried everything, every drug, every club, every party, fast cars, fast women. Until one day it was all gone. The poor kid had run out of cash and he'd completely maxed out his credit cards. Eventually he was evicted and thrown onto the streets."

"What about his friends?" a pretty teenager asked.

"Without the money, honey, he ain't got friends," the platinum blond said.

Others agreed knowingly.

"So what could he do?" Eli asked.

"There's always Jack in the Box," someone quipped.

"No way," a woman in her late thirties answered. She had the worn and haggard look of someone living too long on the edge. "If he's been doin' drugs and the party scene, he's got himself a habit to feed." She turned to Eli. "Am I right?"

Eli slowly nodded, holding her gaze just a fraction longer than necessary. She gave a nervous smile, then glanced away.

"Maybe he gets discovered by ol' Leon here," another suggested.

"No way," Leon scoffed, "I only hang out with the beautiful people." A few guests applauded. He turned to the group and played for more. "Am I right?" More applause and some cheers. "Well, am I right?"

The group clapped and voiced their approval.

"So what happened?" the teen girl called over the applause. "What happened to the boy?"

The crowd settled and turned their attention back to Eli.

"I'm afraid you're right," he said. "The kid had no friends, he had no trade, and he had himself a major habit to support. One thing led to another, and, well, eventually he had to start working the streets, turning tricks on the Boulevard."

"You gotta start somewhere," Leon quipped. A few chuckled, but the focus remained on Eli.

"So what happened?" the platinum blond called out. "Did he ever break away and get out?"

Eli answered. "He worked the streets night after night. Month after month. Eventually he became so skinny and riddled with disease that nobody would touch him. And then, one day, standing in line at the free clinic, he suddenly came to his senses. *Why am I here?* he thought. *Why don't I just go home and throw myself at my father's feet?*"

"'Cause he'll kick your sweet butt back onto the streets and call the cops after you," Leon answered. There was no humor in his voice this time.

Eli nodded. "That's what he figured. So he thought maybe, just maybe he could go back and become one of his father's field hands. He wouldn't even stay in the house; he'd just live like the other migrant workers. He'd do anything, just as long as he could come back."

"Fat chance, Jack," someone muttered.

The blond agreed. "As far as my old man's concerned, I'm dead."

"And buried," Leon added, "dead and buried."

Others nodded.

Eli turned to Leon and shook his head. "No . . . this father was different. Every day the boy was gone, this father had hoped for a phone call; every day when he went to the mailbox, he prayed for a letter."

"That's some father," the teen girl said.

"Yes, he is," Eli agreed. "And, though it took a while to save the money, the young man eventually got a bus ticket and headed back home."

"And you're telling me the old man took him back?" Leon asked skeptically. "Just like that?"

Eli nodded. "He got the call from the Greyhound station and raced into town to pick him up. And right there, in the middle of the terminal in front of everyone, he threw his arms around his child, embracing him, kissing him, and weeping over him. And the boy cried, 'Dad, I'm sorry, I'm so very sorry.'" There was no missing the emotion growing in Eli's voice. "'If you'll just have me back, if you'll just let me be a field worker for you, I'll do anything, but please, *please* take me back.'"

Except for the fountain, the room had grown silent. Conrad glanced around the group. Everyone was lost in the story. Some eyes were even shining with moisture.

Once again Eli's gaze landed on Leon. Only this time it did not leave. "But instead of punishing him or making him pay, the father took him back into his home. He gave him everything he'd originally had and more." Eli slowly rose from the edge of the fountain. "He even called up his family, his friends, his neighbors, and he threw a tremendous party, all in honor of the boy."

"Why?" Leon's voice was softer, thicker.

Eli held his gaze. Something powerful was happening between the two. Everyone saw it. "'Because,' his loving father said . . ." Slowly, Eli started toward him. People scooted aside so he could pass. "'This son of mine, who was dead, has come back to life again.'"

Leon was breathing a little heavier.

Eli continued, his voice growing hoarse with emotion. "He was lost, given up by everyone as dead. But now . . ." Eli finally arrived, stopping directly in front of Leon. The producer's gaze faltered, then dropped to the floor. Eli gently set a hand upon his shoulder. The man looked up, his eyes filling with moisture. "But now, at long last, after all these years . . . he has been found."

Tears spilled onto Leon's cheeks. His body shuddered once, then twice. Eli wrapped an arm around him. Leon responded, awkwardly at first, then clutching him fiercely.

The crowd murmured approval as the two continued to hold one another, both clenching their eyes against their tears. Eli whispered something into Leon's ear. No one heard what was said, but they all watched as Leon's body continued shuddering in quiet sobs. Others were crying now, too. Obviously their own lives were being touched. Even Conrad's eyes began to burn as he recalled all that he'd destroyed, all that he'd left behind.

But the moment was short-lived. Suddenly, one of the slave girls ran into the room shouting, "It's the police! The police are here!"

Panic filled the mansion as people began to scatter. Minors were hustled toward exits; silver drug trays quickly disappeared. But the warning came too late. Within seconds the blue-clad vice squad poured into the room. And behind them came the glaring lights of a news crew. McFarland's news crew—two cameramen and a sound man from EBN.

Conrad spun back to Eli, who remained standing at Leon's side, watching. Conrad wanted to separate them, to pull Eli away and try to run for it, but he knew it would be useless. There was no place to go. Besides, the real damage was already being done. Because, off to the side, one of the cameramen had spotted them together and was zooming in for a tight two shot.

"Connie . . ."

He turned to see McFarland approach.

"What are you doing here?"

Making sure his voice dripped with sarcasm, Conrad answered, "Just like you, I guess I can smell a good story."

"Yeah." McFarland grinned.

"What a coincidence that you just happened to arrive the same time as the police."

McFarland's grin broadened. "Just lucky I guess. But that's how it usually is with Dr. Kerston. When you know the right people, it's easy to be lucky."

Conrad nodded, knowing full well what had just been said.

"Well, if you'll excuse me, I've got a story to cover." McFarland started forward, then turned back and nodded toward the police. "If they give you any trouble, just let 'em know you're with me."

"You *what?*"

"I'm, uh." Julia cleared her throat. "I'm not prepared to order that life support systems be removed. Not yet."

"That's absurd!" Ernesto stood up in the ICU lobby beside his mother and sister. He was a handsome fellow, a year or two younger than Julia with strong Latin features. His sister, Beatrice, who had ridden to the hospital with him, was equally attractive—a twenty-year-old version of her mother before the trips to the Beverly Hills' surgeons.

Ernesto continued to sputter. "You've seen his condition? You know what the doctors say?"

"Actually, I haven't spoken to a doctor yet."

"Well, we'll see to it that you do." He turned to his mother. "What did they tell you?"

Roseanne shook her head, bringing a tissue to her face. For the first time since they'd met, Julia almost thought the woman's sorrow was sincere.

Almost.

"They say . . . he will not survive." Roseanne took a trembling breath and forced herself to continue. "That his brain, most of it is . . . they say it is gone." Tears rolled down her sculptured cheeks, and Beatrice moved in to wrap a comforting arm around her. It was quite a performance, and Julia almost felt guilty for being too jaded to believe it.

Almost.

"Doctors can be wrong," Julia replied.

"What, you're suddenly a medical expert?"

"Ernesto," Beatrice chided.

The man ran his hands through his short dark hair. "I'm sorry, Julia, I know this isn't any easier for you than it is for us." For the briefest second Julia wanted to punch him in the gut. How dare he put their feelings on the same level as hers? He continued, "But you must understand, we need to start thinking about what is best for him."

"He's the one I *am* thinking of. Who are you?"

His eyes widened a fraction, making it clear he understood the barb. Julia had taken off the gloves. She was too tired and spent to play the game. But not Ernesto. Once he'd caught himself, he continued, smooth and gentle in his understanding. "I just don't want your love to cloud your judgment. Let's face it." He looked to his mother and sister for affirmation. "You are his only child. Of course this is hardest on you."

The two nodded in agreement.

It was a nice recovery, but a bit late. Julia waited, expecting to hear more. She was not disappointed.

"You want him to stay alive and remain with us. We all want him to stay. But not like . . . not like that." He motioned toward the ICU door. "It's just not fair to him, Julia. You've read his directive." Ernesto reached into the pocket of his sports coat and pulled out a paper. It was a copy of the same living will Julia had been reading minutes before. She watched as he unfolded the paper. *How convenient for him to have it,* she thought. *And efficient.*

He found the appropriate spot and began to read:

"'I do not want heroic efforts made to prolong my life, and I do not want life-sustaining treatment to be provided or continued (1) if I am in an irreversible coma or persistent vegetative state; or (2) if I—'"

"I know the document." Julia cut him off. "I know what it says."

"Then you must put aside selfish emotion and do what is best for your father."

If Julia had wanted to punch Ernesto before, she wanted to beat the tar out of him now. But she managed restraint and maintained her composure. After all she was the responsible one, the professional. And, as a professional, it was important she put aside her emotion and act in the best interest of her client. "I am not yet convinced that the coma is irreversible or that he will remain in a persistent vegetative state," she said.

"Julia," Roseanne tried to reason, "how can you say that?"

"I heard him speak."

All three caught their breath.

"You what?" Ernesto said.

"You heard Connie speak?" Roseanne asked.

Julia nodded. "Not words . . . I mean, maybe they were words, it was hard to tell with the respirator in his mouth. But I believe he was trying to communicate."

"You're not serious?" Ernesto said.

Julia nodded.

"It was a gasp," he argued, "an involuntary reflex."

"Perhaps. But until I know for certain, I believe it would be premature to discontinue the life supports."

"You know what the doctors say. The man's brain is gone, it's scrambled. There's nothing left in his skull."

"Ernesto," his mother admonished.

Again Ernesto's hand was in his hair. "You can't deny the medical facts."

"And I can't deny my client his rights."

"Your client?"

Julia closed her eyes, trying to remain calm. She'd been awake nearly twenty-eight hours with virtually no sleep. "He is my father. He has given me power of attorney. And as long as I have that power, I say we need to wait and see."

"How long? Another day?" Ernesto argued. "A week? If he gasps again do we give him a month? Just because you say so?"

"As long as I have power of attorney, we give him whatever I say we give him."

Ernesto held her gaze and began to nod. She knew exactly what he was thinking: Two thousand dollars a day times seven days or thirty days or 180 days ... once her father's insurance had maxed out, nothing eats up an estate's money like ICU bills. And if Ernesto and Mom and Sis, there, were still in the will and if Julia decided to feed their inheritance to hospital bills—well, she knew that the loyal, grieving Ernesto would soon be thinking of something else. If Julia was the only one with the power to pull the plug ... then there had to be some way to replace her.

And, of course, there was. It was just a matter of time before he found it.

"So you haven't seen him since yesterday morning?" Conrad asked.

Suzanne took another sip of her Dr. Pepper and answered. "He said he was going off to Griffith Park for the night. Wanted to spend some time in prayer."

"Griffith Park?" Conrad asked in concern.

Suzanne nodded.

"By himself? For the entire night?"

"He does that once in a while."

"Suzanne, this is Los Angeles."

"He'll be okay." She glanced out the Burger King window toward the Motel 6 across the street. Jake and a slight, skinny kid were in the parking lot working under the hood of a beater Toyota. The rest of the group were either in their motel rooms, out shopping, or catching some of the Southern California sights.

"Did he say when he'd return?" Conrad asked.

Suzanne pushed her hair back, smiling that smile of hers, the one that always made his heart swell. "Never stop being the reporter, do you?" she teased. "Always have to be asking questions."

He glanced at the uneaten burger before him and shrugged. "I guess old habits are hard to break."

She reached out and patted his arm in understanding. "I know."

His eyes darted to hers. She knew? What did she know? Surely, she wasn't talking about his feelings. Surely he was better at hiding them than that.

"He'll be okay," she repeated. "He does this from time to time, especially when he has important decisions to make."

She withdrew her hand. Conrad glanced out the window, both relieved and saddened. His panic had been unwarranted; she had thought he was still talking about Eli. And why not? After all, that's the excuse he always used when visiting her. It was a small lie, but one worth the telling if it gave him an opportunity to be near her.

Then there was the matter of his posting bail for the man. Of course, he'd told himself that putting up the money was to help balance out the injustice of the raid. But deep inside he knew it was for Suzanne. She'd finally found her knight in shining armor. He could see it in her eyes every time she looked at Eli, every time she spoke his name. And, although he could not deny the jealousy, his logic dictated that if he couldn't be the one to be with her, what better person was there for her than Eli Shepherd.

Of course he'd hinted to her about the love he saw, and of course she'd denied it.

"Connie," she had laughed, "I'm fifteen years his senior. What possible romance could there be between us?"

Maybe he was wrong. Part of him hoped so. But Conrad had put up the bond money just the same. Romance or no romance, the knight would not rust in jail, not if he could do anything about it.

There was, however, something he could not do: Stop EBN's broadcast of the story . . . and their selling of it to any news organization showing interest. And there were plenty. The arrest had been forty-eight hours ago, and by now hundreds of local stations had picked it up as a softer, people-in-the-news piece. If Eli Shepherd hadn't become a household word yet, he was certainly on his way.

"There he is now." Suzanne motioned out the window. Conrad leaned past an advertisement painted on the glass and saw the young man making his way down the sidewalk. "Let's see what's up," she said, finishing her soft drink and rising from the table. He nodded and crawled out of the booth.

"You okay?" she asked as they swung past the drink dispenser so she could refill her drink.

"Sure, why?"

"I don't know, you just seem a little ... sullen, that's all."

Conrad cranked up a grin, doing his best to hide the sadness. Because, despite the warm rush he felt whenever she was near, there was also the hollow aching when he realized that they could never be together. "Just got a lot on my mind," he lied.

She nodded. But as they walked across the orange tiled floor, sticky from a recently spilled drink, and he pushed open the glass door for her, he could tell she wasn't entirely convinced. He'd just have to work harder, that's all.

The outside air was hot and raw with exhaust fumes. A metro bus eased to the curb in front of them, its brakes screeching as impatient cars accelerated around it. Conrad started for the crosswalk, but Suzanne grabbed his arm and dragged him behind the bus and out into the street. Fortunately, cars were stopped for the light so the couple could safely thread their way between bumpers until they made it to the other side.

"Eli?" Suzanne called as they approached the curb. "Eli?"

The young man looked up from his thoughts and broke into a smile as they joined him. Despite the fatigue in his eyes, the pleasure at seeing the two of them showed through. "Hey." He grinned.

"You had us worried," Conrad said.

Eli gave a brief nod as they continued walking toward the parking lot. "I'm glad you're here, Connie. I've got some good news."

"What's that?"

"Can you stick around a few minutes?"

"Sure."

"Great." As they arrived at the parking lot, Eli called over to the Toyota where the two men were working. "Jake? Trevor?"

Two heads emerged from under the hood.

"Would you mind rounding up the folks, tell them we've got a meeting out here? I have an important announcement to make."

The men nodded and closed the Toyota's hood. It gave a creaking groan of resistance.

"Suzanne, Connie—would you bang on the Carlsons' and Barnicks' RVs, see if anyone's home? I'll check on Maggie, the Browns, and Scott and Brent."

"Sure," Suzanne agreed.

Twenty minutes later two dozen people were gathered in the broiling parking lot of the Motel 6. Most of them Conrad recognized from the softball game or from his visits with Suzanne. A few he did not.

"All right, everybody," Eli called from the partial shade cast by Jake's RV, "listen up." The group quieted. "We've got some new marching orders. Looks like my Father wants me to go to Salem County, Georgia."

Some in the group murmured in surprise.

"He wants me to be there in time for the grand opening of Dr. Kerston's new facility."

"What?" Big Jake cried from the back of the group. "You're not serious?"

Others voiced similar objections.

Eli grinned and raised his hands. "I know, I know. It's crazy, but it's not the first crazy thing I've been asked to do, is it?" There was little reaction. "Well, is it?"

Reluctantly, a few agreed.

"Okay. Now since we've got plenty of time and since there are so many people across our land who are clueless about the Kingdom of Heaven, I've decided not to take a plane. Instead, I want to turn it into a road trip . . . which in a sense we've already begun. So, first thing tomorrow I'm heading out, and I'd love for all of you who are interested to join me."

There was more murmuring—some of it positive, some of it concerned.

"Eli," an older gentleman in shorts called out, "what about our families?" Others nodded as the man continued. "I've been away from them for nearly three weeks now."

Eli answered, "I understand, Jeff. And if your family's more important to you than me, you're right, you need to get back to them."

The man gave a nod followed by a frown . . . as if he wasn't entirely sure he'd received the answer he'd wanted.

"What about school?" a young brunette in shortly cropped hair asked. "Summer classes start in a week."

"Another good point," Eli said. "If school's more important to you, then by all means, head back to it."

"And work?" asked Brian Tuffts, the man whose arm Eli had healed at the softball park.

"What about it, Brian?"

"Most of us have jobs we've got to get back to." Eli remained silent. The man continued. "I mean, we've got to eat, right? We've got bills to pay, kids to put through college, mortgages."

Eli slowly nodded. He looked across the parking lot as he chewed on the statement. Something near the motel's office caught his eye, and he turned back to Tuffts. "Tell me, Brian." He motioned toward the brick planter next to the motel's glass doors. "Check out those birch trees over there, and the geraniums." The group turned to look. "You don't see them fretting and worrying, do you? They're not concerned about paying bills, or meeting mortgages. But look how my Father takes care of them. And look at those birds." He nodded toward a handful of pigeons sitting on the electrical wires running to the office. "Have you ever seen them starve?"

"But Eli," he protested, "they're pigeons."

"Exactly. And aren't you more important to my Father than pigeons? If He takes care of their needs, as insignificant as they are, don't you think He'll take care of yours?"

Brian held his gaze a moment, then glanced away, unable to find an answer.

Eli turned to the rest of the group. "If you can't come with me, I'll understand. But there is not one of you who, if you give up your family, or work, or career, will not receive a hundred times that much back—not only in this lifetime, but later, with me in Heaven." The group shifted slightly and he continued. "Listen very carefully now. If you pursue God's Kingdom before anything else, all of these other things that you're worrying about, they will be given to you. Automatically. No strings attached. I give you my word. That's how my Father works. That's how His Kingdom works."

The group grew quiet, obviously pondering the truthfulness of the statement, working through its relevance in each of their lives.

Eli waited a moment, then continued. "Now, there are only twelve of you that my Father has clearly pointed out to me. The rest of you are more than welcome to come, and as I said, you will certainly be happier if you do. But I know for a fact that God has called these twelve men to be by my side."

"*Men?*" a heavyset woman asked.

"It's nothing against you, Maggie. Your dedication and hard work has outshone these goofballs more times than I can count." He nodded to the men with a teasing grin. A few of the guys responded in mock protest. He continued. "It's just going to be easier if they're the ones breaking down the traditions and religious barriers."

"Because?" Maggie demanded.

"Because those traditions and barriers are controlled by some very rigid men."

Maggie began to nod. She didn't like the answer, but she understood.

Eli turned to the group. "So everyone is invited, both men and women, but I specifically want these twelve to follow me." He glanced over at Jake, his eyes once again sparkling. "So what do you say, big guy? You interested?"

Jake nodded. "You can count on me, Eli, you know that."

Eli grinned. "And your brother, Robert? Where is he?"

"He's over with Rachel and her mom checking out them movie star footprints. I'll tell him when he gets back."

"Good." Next Eli turned to the bald-headed biker with the racist tattoos. "Will?"

The man looked up, more than a little surprised.

"You with me?"

He shuffled slightly then gave a stiff, self-conscious nod.

Conrad looked around the group and smiled at the number of people exchanging raised eyebrows.

"Terry, are you here?" Eli asked. "Carl?"

"They're down at Disneyland," Maggie volunteered.

"Hector?"

"The same."

"You'll tell them?" he asked.

"Of course," she sighed.

Eli nodded and turned to the skinny kid who had been working with Jake on the Toyota. "Trevor?"

The kid blinked in surprise, then nodded slightly before looking at the ground in painful shyness.

"Scott? Brent?"

Two good-looking brothers about Eli's age exchanged glances with one another, then turned to their mother who stood not far away. She gave a solemn, almost imperceptible nod, which the boys duplicated and returned to Eli.

Eli smiled and turned to Keith Anderson, the production assistant from Charlene Marshal's show. The kid wore the same shorts he had worn on the broadcast, only this time they revealed two strong, healthy legs. "What do you say, Keith?"

"You bet." The kid beamed, obviously eager for the adventure. But the moment was short-lived.

"Eli! Yo, Eli?" The group turned to see Leon Brewster strutting forward, having just arrived. "You wanted to see me, man?"

Eli broke into his trademark grin. "I was just going down the list."

"And I'm on it, right? Just like we said?"

"You're on it, Leon . . . just like we said."

This time the crowd made no effort to hide their surprise. And concern. Conrad threw an amused look over at Will, who appeared anything but excited. And for good reason. The two men's lives couldn't be any more different, or their hatred toward each other any stronger. Eli would definitely have his hands full with those two.

"And finally," Eli said, as his eyes turned to Conrad, "Davis."

If Conrad had been surprised at the mention of Leon's name, he was dumbstruck at the sound of his own. He felt Suzanne give his arm a squeeze, but could barely hear what she said. In fact, he barely remembered responding. But he must have said something, because Eli had eventually turned back to the group, spoken some final words, and brought the meeting to a close. It was only then, after Eli had started for his motel room, that Conrad finally found his voice ... and his legs.

He quickly crossed the parking lot toward him. "Eli? Eli ..."

Eli turned to him with his usual delight.

"What ... what are you saying?" Conrad stammered. "You can't be serious?"

"About what?"

"About me!"

"Why not?"

"Why not? *Why not?*"

Eli waited for an answer.

"Because ... why not? Because I'm not the ... I mean ..." He regrouped, trying to put his thoughts into a coherent string of words. "Why me? I'm not ready for anything like this."

There was that sparkle again, and then the answer. "Of course you're ready, Connie. You've been waiting for this your entire life."

"The Life Flight crew was on the ground beside him at 16:25, approximately twenty minutes after the accident. He was found to be unconscious, with traumatic head wounds to his forehead and the right side of his skull. His clavicle was shattered, both legs broken, and there appeared to be severe internal injuries. He was intubated, immobilized with cervical collar and backboard, and . . ."

Julia sat impatiently in the ICU lobby, practically knee to knee with Dr. Martin, head of neurosurgery. In his mid-sixties with short gray hair, the gentleman exhibited a quiet wisdom that could come only from years of similar scenarios. Carefully, he ran down the minute-by-minute details of the care given to her father. The itemized account was of little interest to her, but she understood how important it was to the doctor. As an experienced physician, he obviously knew all the realities and possibilities of malpractice suits.

"We ran a Glasgow Coma Scale on him at the site to measure the seriousness of the trauma."

This was getting closer to what she needed to hear. "What all does that entail?" she asked.

"We do various tests to measure the response of his eyes, his motor skills, and his verbal ability. Possible scores range from three to fifteen points. A score of thirteen to fifteen indicates relatively minor damage. A score of eight and below indicates serious brain damage."

"And what was his reading?" Ernesto asked from the sofa beside them. Julia glanced up, almost forgetting the family was there.

"We ran the test twice. Once at the scene of the accident and once en route."

"And the readings?" Julia asked.

The doctor glanced down and checked the chart on his lap. "At the accident we had a reading of four."

"And en route?" Ernesto asked.

"Three."

The silence was interminable.

The doctor looked down and continued to read. "Once in the air we started intravenous mannitol to reduce swelling. He arrived here at 16:58. We immediately ran a CT scan—"

"Which is?" Ernesto interrupted.

"A three-dimensional picture of the brain. It allows us to pinpoint any operable lesions, hematomas, and bone fragments."

"Do you have that on file?" Julia heard herself ask. It was the lawyer Julia again. The last thing the daughter Julia wanted was to see a 3-D image of her father's destroyed brain, but the question still had to be asked.

The doctor glanced up from the chart and looked directly into her eyes. "Yes, it's on file, and if you insist we will show it to you. But it would be better for you if we did not."

The words put a cold knot in Julia's stomach, but she pushed herself ahead. "Why's that?"

Dr. Martin removed his glasses. "The human brain is a very delicate organ. It has the strength and consistency of Jell-O. It takes very little to disrupt it even when the injuries are closed, but if they are penetrating as is the case with your father—"

"I'm sorry ... '*penetrating*'?"

For the first time he seemed to hesitate. "The front half of your father's skull was shattered. Between the bone fragments, the multiple lesions, and massive blood clots, I'm afraid there's little of his brain left unaffected."

Whatever strength Julia had managed to muster rapidly drained.

The doctor continued, gently yet professionally. "If I had been on the site, I would not have intubated him. If I had been the surgeon on call, most likely I would not have operated."

"Meaning?"

"We have a young and ambitious staff, Ms. Preston. From time to time, their zeal and commitment to save lives blinds them to the realities."

"You would have declared him dead," Ernesto stated.

"In many ways your father is already dead."

"But he spoke!" The words came before Julia could stop them. "I heard him speak."

The doctor turned to her, carefully choosing his words. "I don't think that is likely."

"But he said something, he was making some sort of sound."

"Possibly. With traumatic brain injury there's always room for the unexplained, but . . ." He let the sentence trail off.

"Doctor." It was Ernesto again. "We have a signed advanced directive from the patient."

The doctor nodded. "What does he ask?"

"He asks that no life-sustaining treatment be administered or continued if he's in an irreversible coma or persistent vegetative state."

The doctor remained silent.

"So . . ." Ernesto raised his hand, waiting for a response. "I mean, if you had to make a call here, what would be your recommendation?"

"Recommendation?" he asked.

Julia looked on, watching the doctor work. She knew these could be treacherous legal waters for him, and it was obvious he was not anxious to negotiate them.

Ernesto pressed in. "If he were your father, what would you do?"

"I'm sorry, I am not in a position to make that type of—"

"All right, all right, I hear what you're saying, but we need to make a decision here, and you're the expert."

The doctor began slowly, carefully. "As I have said, traumatic brain injuries can be very unpredictable. Sometimes patients with a Glasgow Coma Score below eight have surprised us all with—"

"Right," Ernesto cut him off. "I hear you. But from your experience, I mean what type of odds would you give him?"

"Odds?"

"For his survival."

The doctor looked back down at the chart on his lap. Then he carefully placed each fingertip of one hand against the fingertip of the other. Soon all were touching. Julia stopped breathing. The world had stopped moving. Then, after a slow deliberate breath, he answered. "It is my opinion . . . and only an opinion to which I would urge you to seek a second or third—"

"Right, right, but what is *your* opinion?"

"It is my opinion that your father's coma is irreversible."

CHAPTER FIVE

H i, Mom."

"Hello, Sweetheart. Are you being good for Daddy?"

"Me and Danny and Kevin, we built this real cool fort in the tree, you know the one that's in Kevin's yard? I didn't build it really, but I got to bring them stuff to eat and drink and stuff. It was so cool."

"Uh-huh." Julia adjusted the phone to her other ear and glanced at her watch.

"I brought them that drink, you know that powder stuff you mix with water, it's kinda sweet and sour at the same time? Me and Dad, we found some at Wal-Mart and we brought a big jar home and we made some up and oh, they got these coolest swimming pools, you know like at Jodi's? He said he'd get me one but only if you said I could, but I can, can't I? I mean it's so—"

"Sweetheart," Julia interrupted, "I really don't think there's room in the townhouse."

"That's what he said you'd say, but if we moved back with him, he's got all sorts of space in the backyard and Danny and Kevin they got a swing in their backyard. We swing really high on it and then we let go and go shooting off until we . . ."

Julia let Cody rattle on. At four they said he had terrific verbal skills. At five they called it hyperactivity. To say he was energetic was an understatement, and they were still experimenting with just the right drugs and dosage. But they assured her in time everything would work out.

Well, everything may work out with him, but it sure wasn't working out with Julia, or with Julia and her husband. She and Ken had been separated for just over six months now. Initially, she had believed it would be temporary, just enough to catch her breath and get some focus. But six months had come and gone, and now the truth was beginning to emerge. She was not designed to be a wife ... or a mother. One of Atlanta's top attorneys, absolutely. Defender of truth, justice, and the American way. No doubt. But dinner fixer, nose wiper, boo-boo kisser? Not in this lifetime. How can you be there for a husband or a little boy when the rest of the world is being torn asunder by liars, thieves, and serial killers?

Bottom line: When it came to having a family, Julia was a failure. Like her father, she was a one-trick pony, and that trick had nothing to do with domestic life or, even more sadly, lasting relationships. That's why she'd not been completely resistant to Ken's hints about his taking over full custody. She knew that her own mother, who put family above all else, would hit the ceiling, and that friends would sprain their eyebrows arching them. But to her the truth was painful and obvious. Little Cody was better off with his daddy than with his mommy.

"Mom, when you coming home? I miss you."

"I know, Sweetheart, and I miss you."

"So come home."

"I can't, not right now."

"Please . . ."

"Grandpa is real sick, Sweetheart, and he needs me to help him."

"Can't somebody else do that? I really, really miss you. Please . . ."

The sound of his voice tugged at her heart. She may be a lousy mother, but she still loved her baby.

"Sweetheart . . ." She took a breath. "I sort of gave your grandpa my word a long, long time ago. And you know what I always say?"

"I know, I know," the little voice wearily quoted. "You're only as good as your word."

"That's right. You're only as good as your word."

"Dad wants to talk to you some more. Bye."

"Sweetheart, don't—"

But he was gone. Just like that. Julia knew he was angry and disappointed, but there was nothing she could do. As with so many other things, there was nothing she could do.

"Hey, Jules." It was Ken again. The two had been friends since her junior year in college. They'd met during winter break, on one of those rare occasions when she'd let her mother drag her to church. For him it was love at first sight. For her . . . well, she'd liked him. Good looking, thoughtful, sensitive—what's not to like? And after the wedding, he had become the adoring, supportive husband. Later, the dedicated father. If anybody deserved to be happy and to be loved, it was this man. And if she would ever be capable of loving somebody, he would be the one.

But slowly, sadly, the truth had become evident. She was not capable.

"Are you sure you don't want me out there?" he asked.

"No. This is something I have to do myself."

"I understand." He always understood. Even when she was a monster, he understood—another reason she had no right being married to him. "Listen," he continued, "you don't want to hear this, but you need to know: Suzanne has already bought a ticket and is flying out there tomorrow."

"Mom? She's coming out here? Why?"

"They were married, Jules."

"Yeah, but . . ." She shifted uncomfortably. "He treated her like dirt."

"He treated you both like dirt, but—"

"So what's her purpose in coming out? I don't understand. That's just plain ignorant."

"I told her you wouldn't be happy, but sometimes she can be almost as stubborn as you."

Almost, Julia thought.

Motion in the ICU lounge attracted her attention, and she glanced up from the phone cubicle. Two men in suits had arrived—an older one and a younger one holding a leather brief satchel. The first greeted Roseanne and was expressing his sympathies. The second shook Ernesto's hand. Julia didn't have to be a nuclear scientist to know what was happening. Doctors and visitors don't come wearing suits and carrying brief satchels.

"Listen, Ken, I need to be going. Tell Cody I love him and that I'll call again tomorrow."

"Right. Anything you want me to tell your mom?"

"What good would it do?"

She heard a soft chuckle. "Listen, Jules, I just want you to know . . ." He hesitated.

"Yes?"

"Just that I'll be praying for you. That you make the right decision."

She took a deep breath and let it out. "Thanks. We'll talk tomorrow." She didn't know what his reply was. Didn't care. Because over in the ICU lounge the two lawyers were making themselves comfortable, glancing in her direction and clearly waiting. Just as she had anticipated, Ernesto had wasted little time in discovering the way he could challenge her decision.

"Eli, we're just asking that you play it smart, that's all."

"Conrad's right," Keith Anderson agreed. "You don't have to tell everybody all the truth all the time."

Eli looked at them and asked, "And by telling half the truth, how is that different from telling half a lie?" Conrad and Keith exchanged glances. Neither had an answer. But Eli wasn't finished. "Connie, you of all people know the importance of truth. Hasn't that been your standard since you were in college?"

Conrad blinked, taken aback at Eli's insight . . . and at his accusation. They'd been on the road a little over a week, and this was the fourth or fifth correction he'd received from him. Eli's comments were never harsh or critical—in fact they were often simple observations spoken in a gentle tease or with that twinkle of his. Still, they were spoken.

As a mature adult, nearly fifty, Conrad took Eli's admonitions a bit harder than the younger ones in the group. After all, he was twenty years Eli's senior and he already knew a few things about life, thank you very much. And let's not forget the sacrifice he was making in taking a sabbatical from *Up Front* magazine—something every colleague and friend had cautioned him against. Something that, if he wasn't careful, could become the death knell to his career. Because, regardless of past success, a few months out of the public eye and who would remember him? Certainly not the twenty-five-year-old network execs with MBAs. And yet, despite the risks, despite the gentle humblings, there was something about Eli's truth, about his penetrating insight, that made it worthwhile. Maybe it was because Conrad was getting older, maybe it was because the prestige and toys of his life no longer had their appeal. He wasn't sure. But as each day led to the next, Conrad Davis found himself listening to Eli more earnestly and realizing that there was far more to this young man than miracles and charisma.

Unfortunately, there were also these other issues . . .

Conrad sighed heavily and looked down at the cluttered table inside Jake's swaying RV. Once again it had become obvious that they weren't getting through to Eli. Unlike the others in the group, he and Keith understood the media—Conrad more than Keith, though the kid was an ambitious and eager learner. And, by default, they had become Eli's publicists . . . well, at least they tried. But the job grew more difficult every time Eli spoke, which he did nightly, hitting every podunk congregation between here and Georgia. Still, it wasn't the number of speaking engagements that caused the problem; it was the content of those speeches.

Once again the three of them sat around the table inside Jake's rattling RV—a table covered with a dozen press clippings, a Toshiba laptop, two half-scribbled legal pads, various pencils all sporting new rubber triangular grips so as not to roll off the table (Jake's driving could be somewhat aggressive), an open Day Runner, a handful of dirty coffee mugs, crumpled Equal packets, and expired Coke cans.

Trying his best to exercise patience, Conrad finally gave his answer. "You're right, Eli, nobody believes in telling the truth more than I do. A man is only as good as his word. My point is that the media can be your friend or they can be your enemy, depending on how you use them. I mean, they certainly have no qualms about using *you*."

Keith nodded. "All we're asking is that you don't hit the crowds with the hard stuff all the time."

"Hard stuff?" Eli asked.

Conrad reached for the newspaper on the seat, the one they'd kept from Eli's recent appearance in Indio, California: "'You can't follow me if you love your parents and wife and children or even yourself more than me.'" He skimmed down a few lines and continued. "'If you love your life, you'll lose it. If you lose your life for me, you'll find it.'" He looked up at Eli, tapping the paper with the back of his hand. "This has 'cult' written all over it. The media will kill you with this kind of stuff." He waited for Eli's response, but there was none. He continued, a little kinder. "Look, you talk about God's love and coming to save a lost and dying world all the time, right?"

"Because it's true," Eli said.

"Precisely. So focus on those truths. No one's asking you to deny these others, but in the hands of the wrong people . . ." Conrad shook his head. "I'm telling you, they'll kill you. They'll either label you a David Koresh fruitcake, or some sort of con artist, or—"

"—exactly who I say I am."

Conrad took another breath. That was the other thing that bothered him. How someone so compassionate for others and with such keen insights could turn right around and sound like a raving egotist, claiming to be the *only* way to God. Maybe the Messiah the religious folks have been clamoring about, sure—maybe some great prophet or teacher, no problem. But the *only* way? In this age of religious tolerance? It was another one of Eli's blind spots that they were constantly trying to correct.

Conrad chose his words carefully. "If you want people to believe those things about you, fine—but let *them* make the decision, not the media."

Keith agreed. "Because once the media's got you pigeonholed, there's nothing more either of us can do to sell you."

"Who's interested in being sold?"

Conrad's impatience grew. "If you're not interested in reaching people, why bother with this trip, why have us book you into all these congregations?"

"To speak to those who have ears to hear."

"Exactly, and the broader your message, the better your odds of reaching those ears."

"Except," Eli said, "God doesn't play the odds."

Conrad had had enough. He was about to rise and cross to the other side of the RV to cool down, when Eli leaned across the table and rested his hand on his arm. "Listen, you two. I appreciate your efforts. I know you're trying to help, but hear me carefully—your very strengths will become your weakness." Conrad simply stared at him. "Don't be offended by that. That's how it is with most people. Where they are the strongest, they are actually the weakest. You two handle public opinion like bankers handle money. And that's a great gift, but the Kingdom doesn't need it. Fame, power, money—these are the riches of the world. And they can be so seductive, gentlemen, so terribly dangerous. Without even knowing it, you will find yourself starting to serve them instead of God. And you cannot serve both. Hear me on this. You cannot serve the riches of this world and God. You'll wind up hating one and loving the other. You cannot serve both; it is simply not possible."

Eli held Conrad's gaze a long moment, as if making sure the words were planted deep. Then he turned to Keith. As he did, Conrad lowered his eyes to the rattling table, partly in anger, partly in thought. Eli was doing it to him again. Once again, he was being corrected and challenged.

He stared at the yellow legal pad with the notes he'd jotted down from yesterday's phone calls. It had taken him three days and a dozen calls to finally convince the people at the Cathedral of God to consider allowing Eli to speak. Located in Aurora, Colorado, the Cathedral was one of the fastest-growing fellowships in America. It had an estimated membership of twelve thousand and a Sunday morning, coast-to-coast TV and radio audience with the potential to reach over fifty million homes. It had taken hours on the phone to spin Eli's statements to their liking, to insist he was a victim of the press who were taking quotes out of context.

The fact that the founder and senior pastor, Reverend Frederick Snyder, was a fierce rival of Dr. Kerston had made Conrad's work a little easier. After all, it was Dr. Kerston who had on national TV invited Eli to come down and visit his facility in Georgia opening day. And the only possible way for Snyder to top that was to bring Eli to his congregation first. It was dueling egos with Eli in the middle—a publicist's dream come true. Eli could talk about God not playing the odds all he wanted, but the three days Conrad had spent nudging those odds in Eli's favor certainly hadn't hurt.

Not that they would stop booking the smaller congregations. They were Eli's passion. But if they could also schedule some bigger events, so much the better. Events that might include—and this was where Conrad had called in all of his favors and then some—swinging up to Chicago and appearing on Oprah. If Conrad's math was correct, the number of people reached in one appearance on her television show equaled the same as a hundred thousand appearances in those smaller congregations. Not bad for a single event—an event that Conrad was virtually one or, at the most, two phone calls away from securing.

And Keith's observations were also correct. Since the media hadn't yet quite figured out how to label Eli, he had to be extremely careful. Some had focused upon his attacks on established religion, others highlighted his miracles, and some, unfortunately, were zeroing in on his self-proclamations. Of course, Dr. Kerston had gotten into the act there as well. Although his news organization never officially branded Eli a huckster or madman (after all, Eli was gaining a large following, and large followings could mean large voting blocks), Conrad had found a disturbing amount of disinformation being released to other groups through Kerston's organization.

Finally, there was the rising interest of the tabloids. The most outrageous suggested that Eli was the offspring of an extraterrestrial father and an earthling mother. Another wondered if he was the spawn of the devil. And what rumor mill would be complete without suggesting that he might be a direct descendant of Elvis?

"Stop the van."

Conrad looked up, startled. "What?"

Eli rose and called out to the driver. "Jake, pull over."

"What, here?" the big man asked.

"Yes, here. Right here."

Jake nodded and reached for the CB to alert the rest of the convoy—a group of anywhere from eight to fifteen vehicles, depending on the number of press and curious onlookers. Lately, they had started announcing each day's destination ahead of time so that the various groups could travel at their own leisure, arriving whenever they wished. But Eli was not known to be a slave to timetables. "I've come to serve the people," he would say, "not their schedules." From time to time, he would alter their course or bring it to a momentary halt. This looked like it might be one of those times.

Conrad looked out the dusty side window as the RV slowed. They were just outside Salome, Arizona, passing a small cemetery. Up on the ridge, under a navy blue canopy to stave off the hot desert sun, a funeral was getting underway. "What's up?" he asked.

Eli turned to him. Instead of the trademark sparkle, his eyes were filled with gentle sorrow. "I want everybody to stay by the vehicles," he said. "I don't want this to be a circus. She's been through enough already."

"Who?"

Eli motioned toward the ridge. "The mother."

Conrad nodded. He caught Keith's attention and motioned toward the video camera on the seat cushion beside him. Part of his agreement in taking a leave of absence from *Up Front* was to tape anything that proved newsworthy. Nothing hardcore professional, just a home video camera in case something came up. Of course that meant saying goodbye to his videographer, Ned Burton, but Keith, with his overabundance of ambition, was only too happy to fill in.

The van had barely stopped when Eli threw open the door and stepped outside. Once again he instructed Conrad, calling over his shoulder, "Keep the people back."

"We've got some reporters with us today," Conrad shouted from the open doorway.

"You know how to deal with them," Eli replied. He was already a dozen yards away. "I want her to have her privacy." Without another word, he continued up the ridge.

Conrad ducked his head back into the RV. "Jake . . ."

"I heard, I heard," the big man grumbled as he reached for the CB mike. He keyed it and spoke, "Will, get the guys out. We got media with us today, and Eli don't want 'em in his hair."

"Ten–four," came the reply.

Conrad almost smiled as he stepped out of the van. He didn't know how many news people were with them this morning. But he'd seen Will, Robert, and some of the guys in action a couple of times earlier. When Eli didn't want to be disturbed or videotaped, he was not disturbed or videotaped.

He looked down the road behind them. Other campers, vans, and cars were easing to a stop—about a dozen, their dust catching up and rolling over them. But it was the last vehicle that caught his attention. A gray, late-model Taurus. It slowed with the others, but instead of stopping, it pulled back out onto the road and continued past. Conrad stepped back from the RV to get a better look. As it sped by, he saw the driver and passenger, both wearing suits. Instinctively his eyes dropped to the license plate. Just as he suspected. Federal agents. Yes sir, everyone was beginning to keep an eye on Eli.

Car and camper doors opened. He turned to see Will, Hector, and some of the larger men emerging from their rigs. They glanced about, spotted the white news van near the back of the convoy, and quickly headed for it. As the big fellows approached, the van's occupants were no doubt having second thoughts about getting out. Eli never condoned violence, and to date there had not been any. But, as Conrad had seen before, there could certainly be a fair share of intimidating body language.

He turned back to the ridge. Eli arrived at the top as the last of the mourners stepped from their cars. Most had already seated themselves under the canopy in front of the grave.

Keith stepped from the RV, camera in hand. "Here, let me have that," Conrad said as he reached for it. He popped off the lens cap, raised the camera to his eye, and pressed the record button. He zoomed in as tightly as possible until Eli practically filled the frame. He was kneeling down beside a woman seated in the front row, dead center. Conrad guessed her to be the mother. Others on both sides appeared surprised, then alarmed as Eli continued speaking to her. But she didn't seem upset. Instead, she listened carefully, occasionally dabbing her nose with a white handkerchief.

When Eli had finished speaking, he waited patiently for a reply. The woman nodded, almost imperceptibly. He quietly smiled and rose. People on both sides of the mother shook their heads. One was reaching out to her arm, but Conrad kept the camera trained on Eli. He followed him as he took four or five steps to the casket, which rested above the grave on a shiny brass catafalque. A short man with a clerical collar moved to intercept him. They spoke a few words, then turned back toward the mother. Conrad was too tight on Eli to see her response, but it disturbed the cleric enough for him to leave Eli's side and join her. As he did, Eli turned back to the coffin, reached out his hand, and rested it on top.

"What's he doing, Connie?" It was Suzanne's voice.

Conrad glanced up from the viewfinder. The morning sun shown directly behind her, making her hair glow radiantly. "Hang on." He smiled. "I'll know in a second."

By the time he returned to the viewfinder, two of the funeral's guests were on their feet confronting Eli. No doubt they were insisting that he step away from the casket, asking him to leave.

And, true to form, Eli did not resist. Instead, he slowly removed his hand from the coffin. Then, giving the slightest nod to the mother, he turned and started back down the hill.

"What happened?" Suzanne repeated. "What did he do?"

Conrad shook his head. "Nothing." He followed Eli a few more steps down the ridge, then pushed the record button to off and pulled his eye away from the viewfinder.

"Nothing?" she repeated.

"He went up to the graveside, talked to a woman there, and then he just—"

They were interrupted by a cry and turned back to the ridge. There was some sort of commotion. The mother had risen to her feet, people were scrambling. Conrad brought the camera back up and zoomed in for a better look.

To his astonishment, the casket lid had opened. And inside, a young man, in his late teens, was sitting up! The boy looked around, confused, disoriented. Many of the guests were stepping back. Others, more brave, stood their ground. A moment later two or three began to approach. The young man reached out to them, speaking something. They moved closer. He continued reaching out until slowly, cautiously, they arrived at his side. Finally they began to help him out of the casket.

Conrad zoomed out wider to include the mother. A handful of people had helped her rise to her feet. They supported her as she took a tentative, unsteady step toward her son. Then another. Both groups approached each other now, those helping the mother, those with the son—until, at last, the two met. Finally mother and son fell into each other's arms . . . weeping, crying, separating to look at each other, then falling back into one another and crying some more.

"Connie . . ." Suzanne's voice was full of awe and disbelief. "Did he just do what I think he did?"

Refusing to miss the slightest detail, Conrad kept his eye to the viewfinder. "Yes," he answered, his voice barely above a whisper.

"This is unbelievable." Suzanne could hardly contain her excitement. "He always said he had authority over death . . . but this? This is incredible; no one will believe it."

"Oh, they'll believe it, kiddo," Conrad spoke confidently. "They've got to. We've got it all on tape."

"Yes, but—"

"One look at this footage and they'll have to believe it."

"But, Connie?"

His mind raced with possibilities. Eli could say all he wanted about not selling to the masses, about fame and popularity, but this would skyrocket him to the top.

"Connie?"

He turned to her smiling, his face flush with victory. "Yeah?"

"When you record, isn't that red light on the front supposed to be on?"

His smile froze. His eyes shot to the light. It was unlit. He quickly brought the camera back to his face, checking for the "REC" display in the bottom of the viewfinder. It was not on. A sinking feeling filled his stomach. In his haste, he'd forgotten to re-press the *record* button. His footage only continued up to the point where Eli was escorted away from the casket. The rest, the opening lid, the rising boy, the mother and child reunion . . . all were left unrecorded.

And as the sinking feeling spread through the rest of his body, Conrad realized another important fact. Eli's wishes had been followed. *"And who is interested in being sold . . . "* And what had he said about the mother? *"I want her to have her privacy."* As he looked up from the viewfinder and saw Eli approach, grinning from ear to ear, he realized that once again it had happened. Once again Eli's wishes had been followed. To the letter.

"Look at the odds," the younger of the two lawyers said as he paced back and forth in the ICU lobby. "Of patients entering the best trauma centers in our country and who register an eight or lower on the Glasgow Coma Scale, only sixty percent survive. Your father registered a three. A three!"

Julia had no answer as she watched the lawyer pace, his dark hair falling casually into his eyes. He was Julia's age, perhaps a year or two younger, with a studied *GQ* look. A sophisticated ambulance chaser. One she would normally have shredded to pieces, if she just wasn't so tired, if the client in the other room was not her father, if—No, those were excuses, and Julia Davis-Preston did not make excuses.

To her left sat the older lawyer, a distinguished, balding gentleman with a kind, fatherly expression.

It was the good cop, bad cop scenario. She recognized it immediately. The younger one would come off tough and ruthless. The older one would step in and be her friend, the sympathetic ear, the calm voice of reason. Julia was almost offended at the obvious tactic. But then, considering their level on the legal food chain, and looking across the room at who they represented, maybe this was a new strategy for them.

Brushing the hair from his eyes, the younger one continued. "Another study conducted showed that after six months, there was only a 14.3 percent survival rate of patients in a persistent vegetative state."

"That's still fourteen out of a hundred," Julia argued.

The young man came to a stop. "Yes, but are you aware of what persistent vegetative state, what 'pvs' really is?"

Julia didn't answer, figuring she'd find out soon enough.

"It means they're alive, but not alive. Their organs may function; they may breathe, even open their eyes. But their minds are gone. They lack any ability to think, to feel, any ability to ever interact with another."

"But it's still life," she countered.

"Is it? A recent poll of Americans showed that ninety percent would rather die than live such a life."

"And the cost," Ernesto interjected from across the room. "Explain to her the cost."

Julia turned to him, marveling at how transparent the man had become in so few hours.

"Here, see for yourself." The lawyer crossed to his brief satchel, pulled out a paper, and handed it to her. She was too exhausted to focus on the numbers but pretended to look as he continued. "Acute care hospitals such as this can run between $1,000 and $2,000 a day. It's not unusual for those suffering severe injures, such as your father, to remain several months. After that, should he miraculously survive, there comes post-acute care which, as you can see, runs between $350 and $1,000 a day. And finally there will come the nursing facilities, unless of course you plan to take care of him yourself. For the brain-damaged, they will run between $7,500 and $18,000 per month. I'll save you the math, Ms. Preston. Bottom line is it will cost 4.6 million dollars to keep alive a man who will never be able to think, feel, or communicate. Over four million dollars simply to keep the organs of a dead man's body functioning!"

"Norman," the older gentleman admonished.

The young lawyer turned on him, his voice impassioned. "That's what we're talking about here. With so much brain missing, her father will always be in pvs. Even if he survives, he'll be a vegetable—no more alive than some radish or cucumber or—"

"Norman, please."

Even though she'd seen it coming, the blow left Julia weakened.

The older gentleman stepped in, right on cue. "Listen, Julia. May I call you Julia?" He didn't wait for her answer. "All these numbers, these statistics . . . we know they are not your father. Your father was a vital, living human being. A great man. To reduce him to percentages, to dollars and cents, is an insult. That's not how his life should be measured."

Julia turned to him, grateful in spite of herself.

"His life was about living . . . about living without compromise."

The words were soothing, comforting, and for the most part true.

"He was a man of honesty and integrity who insisted upon exposing falseness in our society . . . at least that's who I saw on TV. Am I right about this?"

He had her. There was nothing she could do but nod.

"Honesty was his life's creed. And now we have to ask ourselves, is this how he would want to continue? A life that isn't life . . . living that really isn't living . . . something that is in essence masquerading itself as a lie? Wouldn't we be forcing him to live the very falseness that he'd spent a lifetime fighting?"

He was good. Better than she'd anticipated. Already she could feel her eyes burning with moisture.

"And finally"—he let out a sigh—"there's the matter of his advance directive." She looked on numbly as the young lawyer reached into his satchel and pulled out the papers. "Could he have made himself any clearer? It's right there in black and white, Julia."

The young man cleared his throat, preparing to read his copy, but the older gentleman raised a hand and cut him off. "Ms. Preston knows what it says."

Julia blinked as a tear spilled onto her cheek. Her hand shot up, hoping to wipe it away before it was seen.

The gentleman continued. "Please, Julia, tell me if I'm missing something. Here we have a man who will never be able to think, who will never be able to feel, who is virtually—"

"But he spoke," Julia blurted out before she could stop herself. "I distinctly heard words."

The two men exchanged glances, then looked over at Ernesto who watched soberly.

"So I've been told," the older gentleman softly answered. "But what type of words? What exactly did you hear?"

"He said ... well, I mean I thought I heard him say ..." She swallowed. "I thought I heard him say 'Jesus Christ.'"

Another pause.

"You thought he said Jesus Christ?" the gentleman repeated.

Julia nodded, brushing away another tear. "Or something like that."

The younger lawyer stepped in, incredulous. "With the respirator hose shoved down his throat, with it taped to his mouth ... you heard words?"

Julia tried to hold her ground. "It may not have been those exact words, but I heard something."

Another moment of silence hung over them. The older gentleman resumed. "Ms. Preston, Julia, are you a religious person?"

"No, not at all."

"Is your father?"

"Are you kidding?"

"Well, then, why would he—"

"I don't know—maybe he was swearing. How should I know? But he said something."

Ernesto spoke from across the room. "The doctor thinks it was just a grunt or spasm."

The young lawyer nodded. "Some sort of reflex."

"Exactly."

"Julia . . ." It was the older gentleman again. "Can you look at me a moment? Julia?"

Reluctantly, she raised her eyes to meet his.

"You're under a lot of stress here. That's apparent to everybody. And rightfully so. May I ask, when was the last time you slept?"

"It's been—" She cleared her voice. "It's been a while."

He nodded in quiet understanding. She glanced away. If she had more strength she would have risen to the defense. But any strength she'd had was already gone.

"Julia . . ." His voice was gentle, sincere. "I don't know what you heard, but I must tell you it could not have been words. That is physically impossible."

She scowled, but he was not affected.

"My suggestion is this. Find a hotel. Get some sleep. And then in the morning, when you're fresh and rested, we'll talk again."

"I know what I heard."

He nodded. "I know you think you heard it. But I also know what is physically possible and impossible, and I know what the doctors have stated. Even more importantly, I know what your father ordered in his advance directive." The gentleman paused one last time. "And if for whatever reason you are incapable of carrying out his order, Julia, then it is your responsibility to relinquish your power of attorney."

"And if I don't?"

She knew the answer before it came.

"Then you will be legally removed and replaced by someone who can."

"Where did all these people come from?" Kristi Burke, the high-strung, somewhat anorexic producer of *Cathedral Time* cried. She and Conrad had just entered through one of the side doors of the Cathedral of God, a massive auditorium of honey oak, gleaming chrome, sunlight, and people—lots and lots of people.

"I told you to expect a crowd," Conrad chuckled.

"Yes, but not this, not . . . *these.*"

He looked out over the audience, not entirely sure what she meant. The doors to the Cathedral had been open less than twenty-five minutes, and the 5800-seat auditorium was rapidly filling. He turned back to her and asked, "What do you mean?"

"What do I mean? What do I mean?" She waved her hand toward the front rows. "Look at them!"

Conrad turned his attention to the front. These were usually the rows that filled up the fastest whenever Eli spoke. It was here that the neediest often sat, the ones who'd lined up for hours waiting for his appearance—

hoping for a word, a prophecy, a healing. Conrad shook his head. "I'm sorry, I still don't—"

"Look at them. Right there. And there. And there!"

Now he saw it. Scattered among the clean and smartly dressed congregation were pockets of others who were—well—not so clean and smartly dressed. Some sported frayed collars or matted sweaters. Others wore torn and dirty trousers. A handful appeared unshaven. For many, it was obvious that soap and shampoo were not always an attainable luxury. Conrad was not surprised. The caravan had been on the road fifteen days now. And lately, the poor and homeless were showing up more and more often—partially because they needed Eli's message of hope more than others, and partially because Eli often sent Suzanne, Maggie, and members of the group ahead as an advance team specifically to invite them, often using the group's own cars and vans to bus them in.

"No." The producer shook her head while motioning to the head usher near the back doors. "This will not do, this will not do at all."

"You've got a problem with the poor being here?" Conrad asked.

"Of course not." She snapped her fingers discreetly, insisting the usher hurry. "Everyone's welcome here. But not in the front rows. I've got an estimated fifty million potential households who are watching nationwide. It would be unfortunate to give the impression that these people are the primary attendees of our service."

Although Conrad didn't think it was possible, his dislike for the woman increased. Part of that was due to his natural sense of justice, but he also suspected part of it had to do with Eli. Of course, he still had problems with Eli's operating procedures, and it looked like he always would. Yet there was something so true and uncompromising about him. And it didn't stop there. Because the more Conrad remained in his presence, the more he found *himself* changing. It wasn't intentional, but gradually, day after day, *he* was starting to see things differently. He was starting to *act* differently.

"Well . . ." Conrad glanced at his watch. "The service starts in less than ten minutes. There's not much you can do now."

"We'll see about that," she responded.

The head usher finally arrived. He was a bald, intimidating man who could just as easily have passed for a bouncer, were it not for the perma-grin attached to his face.

"Listen," she ordered, "I need you to move these people in the front here, you see them? I need them to trade places with our regulars. Put them in the back, out of the lights."

He nodded.

"And do it fast. We're on the air in eight minutes."

The usher signaled for two of his colleagues to join him. Immediately all three headed for the front.

Without a word, Kristi Burke spun on her heels, dashed up the steps, and was out of the sanctuary doors. Conrad followed, catching up to her in the hallway. "Listen," he said, "I don't know if that's such a good idea."

"Relax, our ushers are professional." They arrived at the elevators and she pressed the *up* button. "They'll have everyone reseated in plenty of time."

The doors opened and they stepped in. "Actually," Conrad answered, "I meant moving the people toward the back like that." She pressed the third floor button and the doors slid shut. "Eli's kind of partial to the poor. In fact, I think if he had a preference, he'd——"

"Well, then, he'll just have to be a good guest and play by our rules, won't he?"

The elevator had started to rise.

"My point is——"

"I know what your point is, Mr. Davis. And when your friend has his own ministry to support, especially one this large, then he'll understand the importance of maintaining a sizable *and influential* donor base."

"Meaning . . ."

"Success breeds success. People won't support us if they tune in and think they're giving people like your friends in the front row a free ride."

The elevator doors opened, and she headed down the hall toward the director's booth, her heels clicking on the expensive, tumbled marble tile. Conrad followed and said nothing more. They arrived at the door to the back of the booth and entered. It was an adequate room, located dead center on the third balcony. In some ways it reminded Conrad of the press club seats at Dodger Stadium. He stayed against the side wall, moving past the director and switching board until he arrived at the tinted glass that looked down upon the auditorium.

"Okay, we're at two minutes," the director spoke into his headset. Conrad turned to survey the equipment. It was a smaller operation than the Charlene Marshal Show, but definitely state of the art. They had everything they needed . . . and then some. The director, a seasoned pro in his fifties, continued, "Let's place Reverend Snyder and his guest, please."

Conrad looked back out the glass as, down on the stage, two opposite doors opened. Reverend Snyder, a trim, distinguished man with coal-black hair, was ushered in and seated on the left by one stagehand while Eli was ushered in and seated on the right by another. They were separated by a good thirty feet of plush burgundy carpet, and a large oak altar with two man-sized candelabras on either side—each supporting a dozen white, lit candles.

Down below, the team of ushers was just finishing their replacement of people—escorting the poorer ones to the back, bringing the more affluent ones to the front.

"How's the reverend's wireless?" the director asked.

"Up and running," the pudgy sound man to his right answered.

"And the guest's?"

"Checked."

"Okay, gentlemen, we're at one minute. Stand by pre-roll intro."

"Standing by."

Conrad was impressed at how clean and professional the operation was run. There seemed little difference between it and any secular broadcast.

"Hold it." The director pointed to one of the monitors before him. "What's he doing?" He spoke into his headset. "Larry, tell our guest he has to be seated, we're about to go on the air."

Conrad turned back toward the window. His stomach tightened as he saw that Eli had risen to his feet and was walking to the front of the stage. The floor director scrambled over to intercept him. Conrad watched as they spoke.

"What's going on?" Kristi Burke's nervous voice demanded from the back of the room. "What's he saying?"

The director shouted back into his headset, *"What do you mean he's leaving?"*

Conrad watched numbly as Eli patted the floor director on the shoulder, then started down the steps toward the audience.

"Get him back up there!" the director shouted. "We're on in thirty!"

Once again the floor director scurried to Eli's side and once again they spoke.

"Larry? Larry!" The director turned to the sound technician and barked, "Open up the guest's mike, I want to hear what they're saying!"

But the conversation had already finished. Eli had already turned and started up the aisle toward the exit.

"What's he doing? Bring him back! Bring him back!"

But Eli was not coming back. Instead, he continued moving up the aisle.

"Where's he going?"

Eli traveled some twenty-five paces before he finally came to a stop. Then he began motioning to specific people in the audience. They were directly below Conrad, and he had to press his face against the glass to look down. Now he could see. They were the homeless people, the ones who had been relocated to the back. Eli was motioning for them to stand. He was directing them to come out into the aisle and join him.

"What is he doing?" the director shouted. Turning to Conrad, he practically roared. "Tell me what is going on!"

And then, through the audio monitor, Eli's voice was heard—gentle but full of authority. "Come with me," he said, as he began ushering the group toward the exit. "That's right, there we go. Come with me."

"What's he doing? What's he saying?"

The sound man increased the volume.

"Come with me. Let's go someplace where we all belong."

CHAPTER SIX

Conrad looked up from the laptop and removed his glasses. He rubbed his eyes and surveyed the passing countryside of southeastern Montana. The "Big Open," they called it. And for good reason. As far as he could see, there was only grass and wind and sky. At first the scenery had intimidated him. He was a man who felt far more at home surrounded by buildings and people and frenzied activity. But out here, with a ratio of one person for every three square miles, where the only drama was the way the beige earth collided with the sapphire blue sky, and where the only activity was the undulating waves of blowing grass . . . well, Conrad was slowly gaining a new perspective. Here he could breathe. Here he could appreciate the grandness of eternity versus the—well, versus the futility of man. He wasn't willing to believe in God yet, at least not as Eli defined him. But he was beginning to believe in something.

Then there was the silence. Often when the caravan stopped, he found himself strolling away from the group just to listen to the absolute stillness . . . and the occasional meadowlark whose sharp, melodic song so startled him the first time he heard it, that it literally took his breath away.

In a place like this it was easy for perspectives to shift, for belief to begin. It was even easy to toy with the idea of walking away from the harried world of TV news altogether, from the very thing that had been his life for twenty-five years. But Conrad knew it was more than just the landscape. It was also Eli. And all his talk about the Kingdom of God and its upside-down principles.

Just yesterday, at lunch, he had called them together and reviewed the major points in what the guys had jokingly called, "The Sermon at Denny's." "If you want to receive," he had said, "then you have to give. Whether it's time, money, mercy, or whatever the case may be, the more you give of anything in life, the more of life you receive." It was a strange paradox, but also a truth that resonated deep inside Conrad's heart—one that he recognized from his own successes and failures.

Other points were equally as strange . . . and true. The idea that if you really want to be the ruler of men, then you need to become their servant . . . or that in matters of the spirit, the poor were far more rich than the wealthy . . . or that you're blessed if people attack you for doing good . . . or that if you cling to your life, you'll lose it.

They were unusual contradictions, their logic entirely backwards from the way the world operated. And yet, they had a logic that rang with such clarity and truth that Conrad frequently found himself making mental notes— not as a reporter, but as a person. And, on more than one late evening or quiet afternoon, he found himself pausing to consider the depth of what he'd heard.

They'd been on the road just over three weeks now. Nearly two months had passed since he'd first dropped into Eli's world up in Eastern Washington and later in Oregon. Two months since he'd left his old world of automobile accidents and hospitalization (if there really had been such a world). Memories of the glitch, which is all it really felt like, were rapidly dulling, fading. This was his world now. Identical to the old one. Well—it was and it wasn't. Because almost daily, Eli turned it upside down just a little bit more. And, almost daily, Conrad was amazed at how startlingly clear everything looked from this new perspective.

But new perspective or not, there were still some facts that could not be ignored. He sighed heavily, replaced his glasses, and turned back to the computer. Once again, Eli had placed himself in jeopardy, and once again Conrad appeared to be the only one who could bail him out. At the moment he was composing an e-mail, a press release he planned to send to all of the major news organizations and producers—a preemptive strike that he hoped to get out before the press and cameras caught Eli's arrival at the Liberty Compound of America in less than—he glanced at his watch—in less than three hours. Because the news crews would all be waiting for this one. CBN, MSNBC, most definitely EBN. Not to mention the local affiliates of the majors. Yes sir, as many as could be there would be there. It was too good a story to pass up.

"You okay?" Suzanne asked, scooting on the bench seat beside him.

He glanced at her and smiled. He couldn't help it. Even in times like these, her warmth and concern had that effect upon him. Their friendship had grown. Over the past weeks, it had become more genuine than at any time he could remember during their marriage. He supposed part of it was because they were the oldest in the group, the designated chaperones on this grown-up field trip. On more than one occasion, they found themselves becoming the voice of reason in putting out petty disputes. You couldn't throw this many people together with this many backgrounds and not expect some turbulence. There were the expected tensions like those between Leon, the black porn producer, and Will, a member of the Aryan Brotherhood. But there were also a dozen smaller fires to be put out on a daily basis. In fact, just this morning there had been a huge blowup regarding Scott and Brent's mom pressuring Eli into making her boys his right-hand men.

But Conrad and Suzanne's friendship was based on more than being peacekeepers. The truth is, they'd never really stopped liking each other, even during the fights, even during the tears, even during divorce. Then, of course, there was the other bond they shared: Julia. The fact that she'd not spoken to her father in nearly five years meant there was plenty Suzanne could tell him about his daughter. How she was doing with her new job in Atlanta, how she was adjusting to the separation from Ken, and finally little Cody, the grandson he had never seen. The list was endless, though bittersweet in that he had to learn it all secondhand.

There was, however, one more factor in their friendship, at least for Conrad. And it was stronger than all the others combined. He had fallen for her. Again. And no amount of rationalization or common sense could change that. He'd tried. He'd taken the long solitary walks, he'd gone the sleepless nights, he'd beaten himself up every way he could think of. He'd even tried praying. But nothing worked. He could not get her out of his head . . . or his heart.

It was love. But a different type of love. A love he'd never experienced before. It wasn't the sexually charged,

worship-me-the-conqueror-of-the-world love of his twenties and thirties. Nor was it the old-shoe-comfortable love
of his forties. No, this was different. This had nothing to
do with sex, or conquering, or habit. Instead, it had everything to do with giving—with simply wanting to make
her happy, with wanting to protect her, and to help her
smile that smile of hers . . . at any cost.

Even if that cost meant keeping those feelings to
himself. Even if it meant simply being a friend when she
needed one.

That was the most painful of all. That's what brought
the warmth to his chest whenever they were together, and
the empty yearning whenever they were apart. But she must
never know. He'd taken every precaution to make sure she
wouldn't. He'd even gone out of his way to pretend to ignore
her, to be irritated with her, to flirt with other women. No,
she would never know. But he wasn't so certain of Eli. On
more than one occasion Eli had caught him staring after her,
and at least once he had flashed Conrad that knowing smile
of his. Well, if Eli knew, there was nothing Conrad could
do about it. But it would stay their secret. Conrad would
make sure of that much. Suzanne deserved that much.

"What's wrong?" Suzanne repeated.

He shrugged and continued staring at the computer.

"You're still worried about this meeting?" she asked.

Again he took off his glasses and rubbed his eyes. "I
don't know why he won't listen."

"Maybe he's right."

Conrad shook his head. "Not with this guy." He
pointed at the screen. "He's a walking booby trap, a political

land mine. For crying out loud, the U.S. government has warrants out on him!"

She said nothing.

"He's a racist, Suzanne. A hate monger. There isn't a thinking soul in this country who doesn't despise him or at least think he's psycho. Neil Ralston is the role model for every paramilitary, neo-Nazi survivalist in North America."

"He's also the father of a very sick little girl."

Conrad sighed in exasperation and sat back in his seat. He looked across the rattling RV to sleeping Will Patton, the tattooed follower through whom Ralston had made the request two days earlier. A request that had forced Conrad to cancel and rework much of their itinerary. A request that, if fulfilled, would bring them directly to the headquarters of Liberty America, the largest and most outspoken separatist cult in the United States. Located just forty miles east of Ashland and nestled within a 340-acre valley, the Liberty Compound of America had once been a prosperous horse ranch. Now it had become a mecca for every white-power fanatic and separatist in the country.

"I just don't know what he's thinking," Conrad said, sadly shaking his head.

"Maybe you don't have to," Suzanne offered.

He tried hiding his irritation. "Do you have any inkling how this is going to look to the rest of the nation?"

"That one person with no respect for creed or philosophy has come to help another."

Conrad shook his head. "No, that's just it. By going there he'll be endorsing those philosophies. Ralston is hated by every rational individual in our country. And by appearing to be his friend, Eli will also be hated. It's as simple as that. And once that happens, no amount of spinning or damage control on my part will help. He's already alienated a sizable portion of the religious establishment. Is his next step to antagonize the rest of the country?"

"Connie . . ." It was Suzanne's turn to let out a heavy sigh.

"What?"

"Maybe—I don't know."

"What? Tell me."

"Maybe you're trying too hard."

"Meaning?"

"Maybe you should just let go. Maybe, instead of all this spinning and damage control . . . maybe you should just let him be who he is."

"But they'll kill him. They'll eat him alive."

Suzanne looked at him a long moment. And then, ever so slowly, she began to nod. "Maybe you're right. Maybe they will."

"Daddy!" Five-year-old Julia cried, *"Daddy, I'm scared."* She reached out to the wall, groping her way through the darkness. She could smell the magnolias again. Out in the yard. Up ahead in the shadows loomed the immense walnut door to her father's study.

"Daddy . . ."

There were the muffled voices. Then the laughter. She continued forward, running her hand along the cold, paneled wall.

"Please . . ."

She could barely see the door through the darkness, much less through her tears.

There was more laughter. Louder.

Her heart pounded. Her chest heaved in frightened sobs but she would not let them escape. A moment later she was standing in front of the door, feeling its presence more than seeing it. She took her hand from the paneled wall and with trembling fingers reached toward the brass knob. It felt cold, like ice. She began turning it until there was a loud *click*. It had unlatched.

"*Daddy* . . ." Her voice was a breathless whisper.

There was no answer.

Cautiously, she pushed the heavy door, afraid of what she would see, knowing from past dreams what waited inside.

The end of a towering bookshelf came into view. A dim light caught the reds, the browns, the blacks of a thousand books. "Keys to life's mysteries," he had told her. "The ones who read are the ones who hold the knowledge."

And they did read. Almost every night. Right here. He, in his big leather chair, she on the floor beside him or up on his lap. This was their room. Their sanctuary. She loved it more than any place on earth.

On the floor a stack of magazines came into view. Then another. Then a pile of newspapers. They had been there in one form or another for as long as she could remember.

The door continued to open. Now the window came into view, its dusty oak shutters closed. On the shelf below sat his trophies, sparkling dully in the incandescent light. He always won trophies. She was proud of his trophies. And she often played with them on the floor, using them as dollies, having them talk to one another.

The laughter was louder. The words discernible.

The edge of the desk came into view. More stacks of papers, piles of books. Then his typewriter, whose rhythmic clicking would echo down the hall, lulling her to sleep at night.

"Daddy . . ."

And finally, just past the desk was—

Julia forced herself awake. Her heart was racing and she was breathing hard as she glanced around the ICU, trying to get her bearings. Why she was still there, this late in the afternoon, was beyond her. She had an important decision to make. A decision that should be made only after she'd gotten some much-needed rest and could think more clearly. Maybe she was staying there out of some misguided duty or obligation. Maybe it was in hopes that she'd hear him speak again. She didn't know. All she knew was that she didn't want to be there, not for one second. And yet she remained.

So, for whatever reason, Julia continued to sit in the tiny ICU cubicle, staring at her father's near lifeless form. And there she would continue to wait.

"Hi, Bill." Eli grinned as he reached out to shake the man's hand. "I'm Eli Shepherd."

For a moment Bill Johnson hesitated. He stroked his large handlebar mustache, staring at the outstretched hand. He wore black army boots, olive-green khakis, and had a Winchester 30–30 complete with scope slung over his shoulder. Eli continued to grin and continued to hold out his hand until the man reluctantly reached out and shook it. His two escorts were dressed similarly and armed with Colt .45 automatic handguns in their hip holsters. Both looked the other way, pretending to eye the press who were stationed just outside the compound's gate some fifty yards beyond.

"You're not really thrilled that I'm here, are you?" Eli asked.

"This is Ralston's show, not mine," Johnson replied. "I've been against it from the start."

"Because?"

"You're a Jew, ain't you?"

"Yes, I am, Bill. Born and raised. And these are my friends." Eli turned to the three companions he'd asked to accompany him. The three who had walked from the RV, past the mob of reporters, and through the gates of the compound to meet at Bill Johnson's Jeep.

"This is Leon Brewster," Eli said. "He used to be a porn producer, now he's part of the team." Although neither Leon nor Johnson bothered to remove their sunglasses, the icy glare between them was impossible to miss. Eli turned to his left, motioning to his second companion. "And this is Trevor Walters; he used to sell his body on Hollywood Boulevard." Johnson noticeably stiffened, and it was a stroke of wisdom that Trevor didn't bother extending his hand. "And finally—" Eli reached over and rested a palm on Conrad's shoulder. "Conrad Davis— maybe you've seen his work on TV. He's a member of the liberal media."

If Johnson's look had been icy before, it was downright murderous now. Conrad cut a glance around the property. Unlike the flat grasslands further west, this 340-acre ranch was nestled among hills, bluffs, and a small canyon cut by Elk Creek. There were also plenty of pine trees. Trees any number of paranoid militiamen could be hiding behind, taking aim, waiting for a signal to fire.

Conrad was certain he'd been equally frightened sometime during his life, although, at the moment, he was hard pressed to remember when. Consequently, he responded the way the reporter in him always responded when afraid: by putting his opponent on the defense with questions. "Where's Ralston?" he asked.

Johnson looked at him, then glanced down, mumbling something. It was so quiet that it was doubtful even the media, with their rifle mikes and parabolic reflectors, could pick it up.

"I'm sorry," Eli asked, "what was that?"

Johnson looked up, holding Eli's gaze. "He didn't want to embarrass you by coming out. Said it would be a media circus and that you were already jeopardizing your reputation by doing this much."

Conrad glanced over his shoulder at the cameras and reporters recording every second, most in telephoto close-up. Ralston might be a gun-toting fanatic, but he had more media sense than Eli.

Leon, who Conrad suspected had more bravado than brains, confirmed that suspicion by asking, "So you're telling me we come all the way out here and your boss, he isn't even going to meet us?"

Refusing to look at Leon, Johnson spoke to Eli. "He said it would be best for *you,* if he didn't come out and if you didn't come in."

Eli nodded, then asked, "What does he want me to do for him, Bill?"

"He said"—Johnson cleared his throat—"and these are his words not mine. He said if you'd just give the order, his daughter would be healed."

Eli looked on, saying nothing.

Johnson shifted uneasily, then continued. "He said he understands authority. When he gives a command, he knows it will be obeyed. He says it's the same with you. That all you have to do is give the order, and it'll be done."

Conrad was both surprised and relieved. Maybe this public relations nightmare would end before it went any further. Maybe they wouldn't even meet Neil Ralston. If Eli could simply heal long distance, and Conrad suspected he could, then maybe there was a way to seal this rupture of immense political incorrectness before they drowned in negative opinion.

At least that's what he hoped . . . until he looked over and saw Eli. Once again he was smiling. Only it wasn't Eli's usual smile of enjoying another's company. This was a smile of amazement. And wonder. Without another word, he turned to the crowd of reporters behind him and called out, "This is incredible!" He raised his hand and pointed down the dirt road toward the canyon where Ralston's headquarters were hidden. "I tell you this—in all of America, I have not run into a man of such great faith!"

Cameras clicked. Videotapes whirred. And Conrad lowered his head in despair. Any hope of repairing the blunder had instantly vanished. If there had been any way for Eli to make the situation worse, he had just found it. The image of him pointing down the road, proclaiming Ralston's great faith—well, there wasn't a newspaper in the country that could resist printing it, not a television news show that wouldn't broadcast the sound bite. How long had it taken Eli to speak the sentence? Five, six seconds? In those brief seconds, Conrad had known it was over. All of his hard work, all of his weeks of shaping and packaging and positioning had been destroyed. Completely. So quickly and with so little effort.

Further comments were shared, but Conrad barely heard. Goodbyes were exchanged, and to everyone's relief, except perhaps Eli's, the meeting came to an end. The four of them turned and headed back toward the RV as Johnson and his men climbed back up into the Jeep. Of course, the press was already swarming outside the gate, repositioning themselves for the onslaught of questions they would fire at Eli, for the accusations and conclusions they would imply. Conrad scanned the crowd for familiar faces and caught a glimpse of McFarland and his crew from EBN. No surprise there. This would be child's play for them. The last word to discredit Eli, the final nail in his coffin.

Conrad glanced up the road and spotted the gray Taurus, the one with the government plates. Not only would the press eat them alive, but Eli's words of praise for Ralston wouldn't exactly endear them to the U.S. government, either.

Six seconds and it was over. One simple sentence. That was all it took.

They exited through the gate and entered the swarm of reporters. There was nothing Conrad could do to stop them now. The feeding frenzy had begun:

"Eli, how long have you been a racist and does that—"

"Are you going to use your gifts to defend Ralston should federal troops decide to—"

"Are you renouncing your Jewish heritage and—"

Conrad glanced to Jake's RV. It was only ten feet away. But ten feet with this crowd was as good as a mile.

"How long have you and Ralston been—"

"Does this confirm your hatred of the American govern—"

And yet Eli seemed virtually unfazed, even stopping to ask one reporter about his ailing wife. Then suddenly, over the noise and commotion, Johnson's voice cut through. "Eli . . . Eli!"

The crowd quieted, and Eli turned.

Johnson stood in the Jeep holding out his cell phone. "It's Ralston!"

The reporters grew silent. Now there was only the sound of wind through the grass and trees.

"He says his daughter is well. Says she's up and walking around, as good as—" He cupped his hands and shouted to make certain he was heard. "He says she's as good as new!"

Eli smiled. And during the momentary surprise of the crowd, he turned and disappeared into the RV.

"All I'm saying is that it's time to start fighting fire with fire."

"Connie, I can appreciate your frustration, but—"

"No! You cannot appreciate it. You cannot appreciate it, because you don't understand it! You don't know a thing about how corporations are run in this world."

The dozen men standing inside Eli's cramped room at the Holiday Inn grew very quiet. To Conrad's recollection this was the first time anybody in the group had openly challenged Eli. But it was time. Yes, his message was revolutionary, his truths penetrating, but for his own good, for the good of the group, it was time to make him see.

Suzanne was out in Jake's RV tidying it up. Although she and Maggie traveled and slept in their own vehicle, she also spent several hours a week in the RV. And after four weeks on the road enduring the men's version of cleanliness, she had said that it was time to reintroduce to them the concept of health and hygiene. Other members outside the inner circle were doing the same with their own cars, RVs, and campers. Some had rented rooms, hoping for a couple good nights of rest before heading back out on the road. For most, it was a welcome time of rest and relaxation. For Conrad it was time to refocus, to evaluate, and to insist that Eli make some serious midcourse corrections.

"Look." Conrad reached over to the stack of newspapers on the dimly lit counter behind him. He read the headlines of each, while dropping them one by one on the table in front of Eli. *"'Cult Leader Embraces Racism,' 'Miracle Worker Opposes Religion,' 'Is This a Traveling Jonestown?'"* Conrad pointed to the pile. "And these are the reputable papers. You don't even want to know what the tabloids are saying."

Eli looked up at him and answered quietly, "I don't suppose it would help if they printed that Neil Ralston and I talked by phone for a good hour last night?"

"He called you?" Keith asked.

Eli nodded. "Told me he's starting to read the Bible—that he's considering renouncing his activities, maybe even turn himself in to the authorities."

The news caught Conrad off guard, but only for a second. "Great, now every racist in the country will hate us as well." He leaned over the table, trying to make the man see reason. "Eli, no one is interested in those types of details."

"I know, I know." Eli smiled, making it clear he'd heard the lecture before. "All they're interested in is selling papers."

Conrad shook his head. "Not anymore. You've made too many enemies. Now they're looking for ways to stop you."

"Or destroy you," Keith added.

"Oh, that's rich," Leon scoffed. "The man, he's healing souls everywhere we go, and they're trying to destroy him?"

"It has nothing to do with souls," Conrad said. "It's about attacking spheres of power and influence. You can't strike out at these guys without being struck back in return."

Eli raised his deep, dark eyes to Conrad's. "I'm only speaking the truth, Connie."

Once again the honest simplicity caught Conrad off balance. It took a moment to find his anger and tap back into it. "We've been over that before. There's nothing wrong with telling the truth." He reached for a file folder on the counter. "There is, however, a problem with attacking someone's ministry." He opened the folder to reveal three legal complaints. "Or being sued for defamation of character."

Eli stared at the papers in disbelief. "Those are ministries suing me?"

"Of course. You don't smack Dr. Kerston on national TV or humiliate organizations like the Cathedral of God without expecting repercussions." He motioned to the documents. "And it doesn't stop here. These people's influence goes deeper than simply using the courts to drain you with legal fees." He turned to Keith who stood at the other end of the cluttered table. "Tell him about the cancellations."

Keith produced a handful of slips. "We're getting these every day now. Some saying you're too controversial. Others that you're a heretic or crazy or a tool of the devil."

Will Patton sighed heavily. "We've heard all them complaints before."

"Yes," Keith agreed, "but now even the ministers who used to support you are denouncing you. Partially because of the negative media coverage—"

"And partially because of their superiors," Conrad added. "You have no idea the influence such powers can have inside *and outside* the religious community. You know that Dr. Kerston's people are in the midst of creating a third political party."

Eli nodded. "But what's that got to do with—"

"Maybe nothing," Conrad answered. "But didn't you find that raid at Leon's party just a little suspicious? Or how about the IRS audit that's suddenly been slapped on you."

Eli said nothing, quietly absorbing the information.

"And now," Conrad said, pointing at the cancellation slips in Keith's hand, "now they're cutting you off from the very people you've been trying to reach."

Again Eli had no answer. Silence stole over the group. Travis coughed. Scott and Brent shifted uncomfortably. Everyone waited for a response. Finally Eli cleared his throat. His voice was soft and a little sad. "If the worship centers won't have me, then we'll go directly to the people."

"How?" Conrad asked. "Oprah's already canceled. After the Liberty America debacle, there isn't a legitimate news or talk show in the country that will take you seriously."

Conrad pressed in. "It was okay back when you were bashing organized religion. Then you were the rebel, the underdog. But now you're seen as one of the bad guys."

"You're just a wealth of cheery information tonight, ain't you?" Jake growled.

Conrad turned to him. "I'm simply giving you their understanding of the truth."

"Then let's take the real truth out to the streets," Jake said, "or to the parks, or wherever people will listen." He turned to the other men in the group. "No way are we gonna be stopped by a bunch of religious bigwigs or . . ." He turned back to Conrad. "The media."

Many of the group nodded.

"That's exactly my point," Conrad argued. "That's what I'm saying. Instead of taking these attacks lying down, let's stand up and fight back."

"That's what you been saying?" Jake asked.

"Yes," Conrad said, doing his best to hide his frustration. "That's exactly what I've been saying."

"Well, why didn't you say so?"

Others in the group nodded.

"Sounds good to me," Will said.

"Me, too," Leon added. "But how?"

Conrad explained. "The bigwigs sue us, we turn right around and countersue them. They attack us with slander and libel, then we fight fire with fire. We dig up dirt on them, and believe me there's plenty, and we fling it right back into their faces."

"An eye for an eye," Jake exclaimed.

"Exactly," Conrad said. "We'll make it so miserable for our opponents that they'll think twice before even trying to—"

"No."

Conrad came to a stop. He looked at Eli. "What?"

"You're doing it again, Connie. You're using the weapons of this world to fight this world."

"What's wrong with that?" Jake asked.

"If you fight with the world's weapons, you'll die by those weapons." Eli turned to the others. "Don't you get it? How long do I have to travel with you until you see? In the Kingdom of Heaven you don't return evil for evil. You overcome evil with good. You return acts of hatred with acts of love."

Jake shook his head. "I don't know, Eli. Somebody hits me in the gut, believe me they're going to know about it in a big way."

"No." Eli shook his head. "Somebody hits you, you let them hit you again and again and again. You don't resist them."

"But . . . that's crazy," Leon protested.

"It all depends upon what battle you're fighting," Eli explained. "If you're trying to win worldly battles, then you're right, it can be absurd. But like I've told you from the beginning, I'm not here to fight worldly battles. I'm not interested in obtaining earthly spoils that rust and rot. Mine's a different battle. As Leon said, it's a battle for people's souls. And those victories, those spoils of war . . . they will last for eternity. If you want to win eternal treasures, then fight with eternal weapons. If you want to win worldly treasures, then fight with worldly weapons."

"But these people, this world," Conrad tried to reason, "it will destroy you."

"Of course it will, Connie. That's all part of the plan. I will be destroyed. Count on it. But that destruction is only the beginning of something far bigger and vaster than you can even begin to—"

Conrad saw the flash of light a split second before the windows exploded. Flying glass filled the room with a concussion so powerful that it knocked him to the floor. The roar was deafening as debris rained all around them. It lasted several seconds then ended as quickly as it had begun. The roar and raining glass was replaced by quiet moaning and coughing, then the cursing of stunned men who lay on the floor inside the darkened room.

"What was that?" Jake coughed.

"Is everybody all right?" Will asked.

"Yeah," someone else coughed. It sounded like Hector.

"I'm all right," Leon volunteered. He was spitting something from his mouth. "Eli, you okay? Eli?"

"Yeah." The leader's voice was faint. And sad.

Others in the group began coughing and stirring. Conrad rose stiffly to his knees, feeling the broken glass under them and under his palms. He turned his head. And that's when he spotted the orange glow outside, the red flickering through the shredded drapes. Panic surged through his body. He pushed himself from the floor, a shard of glass slicing into his right hand. But it didn't matter. He staggered to his feet, stumbling through the debris, making his way toward the door. He could feel warm liquid running down his forehead, but he didn't care.

"Connie?" Eli called.

But Conrad didn't stop. If the explosion had done this much damage inside the room, who knew what type of damage it had done to those outside? He threw open the door—and stopped breathing. Out in the parking lot, the center of Jake's RV had been ripped open. A huge gash started from the bottom and yawned all the way up through the roof as flames leaped and rolled through the twisted metal.

"Suzanne!"

He sprinted toward it. Familiar faces passed, Maggie, men, other women, some wide-eyed with fear, others stained with smoke and tears. Will shouted from the motel's door, but Conrad paid no attention. Suzanne had been in that RV. Not twenty minutes before the meeting, he'd seen her working inside.

"Suzanne!"

He felt the heat before he arrived. Flames and black smoke boiled from the opening. It was impossible to enter from this side. Shielding his face from the heat with his arm, he raced around the RV to the back door. He grabbed the door's handle. The metal blistered his flesh, but he continued to pull and twist until it finally gave way and flew open.

Heat blasted out, burning his eyes, forcing them to close. But he shoved his head inside and shouted, "Suzanne! Su—" Suddenly his throat constricted, his lungs felt as if they were on fire. But he still managed to choke out the name, "Suzanne . . ." He began to cough. The smoke was too thick, the heat too intense. He pulled back a few steps to catch his breath, breathing in the cooler air, feeling it against his raw throat. A thought came to mind, and he ripped open his shirt, buttons flying. He peeled it off and covered his mouth. The heat burned against his bare chest and arms, but now at least he could breathe.

"Connie . . . Conrad!"

He turned to see Jake lumbering toward him.

"Suzanne's in there!" Conrad shouted. "I've got to get her!"

"No!" Jake bellowed.

Ignoring him, Conrad took a deep breath, turned, and headed up the steps into the inferno.

"Connie, don't! Conn—"

His voice was lost in Conrad's pain. Conrad's skin screamed with such anguish that he expected it to ignite. He bent down, trying to protect himself as well as he could, trying to keep his eyes open against the smoke and heat. "Suzanne! Su—" He began to cough.

"Connie!"

He inched forward. The coughing grew so bad he could barely speak. The air so hot it was impossible to breathe, even through his shirt. He coughed and gagged; his lungs felt as if they were imploding for lack of air. Still, he pushed himself forward, barely managing to gasp, "Su . . . zanne . . ."

He felt a grip around his arm and spun around to see Jake grabbing him. "No, Connie!" Jake coughed.

Conrad twisted. "Let . . . go!" He continued gagging, feeling the heat and smoke sear his lungs. But the big man did not let go. Instead, he began to pull. Conrad fought like a crazy person. Suzanne was in there! Didn't he understand? Suzanne!

Jake grabbed Conrad's other arm. "No," he coughed. "No!" Then he physically began to drag him out.

"Let . . . go!" Conrad squirmed and choked and fought.

But Jake continued, half pulling, half stumbling as he dragged Conrad to the door. With one last tug, they both tumbled out, falling down the metal steps and hitting the asphalt below.

But Conrad was not finished. With a final burst of adrenaline, he staggered to his feet.

"No!" Jake reached up and caught his waist. Then pulling himself up, he grabbed Conrad by both shoulders and spun him around. "Stop it!" He shouted into his face. He shook Conrad like a rag doll, trying to make him understand. "It's no use! Stop it, now!"

Tears streamed down Conrad's face. "Suzanne!"

"Stop it! Stop—"

"Connie?"

They both froze. It was her voice!

"Connie!"

He spun around. She was running to him. Not from the burning RV, but from the motel lobby.

"Suzanne!" He broke from Jake's grip and raced toward her. They fell into each other's arms and he held her with all of his might. "I thought you were . . ." He couldn't say the words. "I thought . . . I thought I'd lost . . ."

"I know," she whispered fiercely, "I know."

"I couldn't lose you." His face was wet with tears. "Not again, not—" He could no longer speak; he could only hold her.

"I'm here," she whispered. "I'm right here."

They pulled apart, and he kissed the top of her head, again and again, before drawing her back into an embrace. And that's when he saw it: the gray Taurus slowly driving up the road, the occupants calmly surveying the damage.

Only this time there was a third passenger. He sat in the back, smoking a cigarette. And, as he inhaled, the glowing embers revealed a large handlebar mustache—exactly like Bill Johnson's.

"Connie . . . Conrad, you all right?" He turned to see Eli quickly approaching with the others. "Are you okay?"

Rage surfaced. It boiled up inside Conrad, white-hot. He released Suzanne and turned on him. "No!" he shouted. "I'm not all right! None of us are all right!"

Eli said nothing.

"Don't you see what's happening? Don't you get it?" He wiped his face with his shirt. "We could have all been in that RV! We could all be dead!"

"Connie . . ." Suzanne cautioned.

But Conrad barely heard. He took a menacing step toward Eli. "This is not a game! People in very high places are playing for keeps! Do you hear me?" He continued to shout. "We've got more enemies than we can count! Do you hear me? *Do you hear me?*"

Eli answered with a quiet nod. "I know."

"No, you don't! You don't understand a thing! You're endangering our lives. All of ours!" He turned to the others. "This isn't what we signed up for! This isn't what we wanted!"

Again Eli nodded. "I know. But I've never lied to you, Connie. I never promised you this would be easy."

"Easy?" Conrad breathed heavily, wiping more sweat and blood from his face. "Easy! Somebody just tried to kill you!"

"I know."

"You know? That's all you've got to say? You know?"

Eli's face filled with compassion. "Connie, if you want to leave, you can. I'll completely understand."

Conrad snorted in frustration.

"And my love for you will not diminish. Whatever you choose, I'll still count it a privilege for us to have spent these weeks together."

Conrad felt his throat tighten, his eyes fill with moisture. Why, he wasn't sure.

Eli turned to the rest of the group and spoke with the same earnest compassion. "That goes for all of you. If you choose to leave, I'll understand. I mean that. Whatever you choose, I will understand."

An uneasy silence followed. Some of the group glanced at each other. Many looked at the ground. But no one ventured a word. The tears continued filling Conrad's eyes until they spilled onto his cheeks. Tears of anger, tears of confusion . . . and tears of love. He knew that now. He knew it, and there was nothing he could do about it. Finally raising his eyes to Eli, his voice still quivering in rage, he croaked, "Where would we go?"

Eli turned back to him.

Conrad continued, struggling to put his emotions into words. "Who else . . . who else has such words . . . of life?"

Suddenly Eli's own eyes glistened in moisture. Without a word, he crossed to Conrad and threw his arms around him in a powerful embrace. Conrad returned it. He couldn't help himself. More tears streamed down his face as he clung to him. Part of him wanted to beat Eli, to pound on him until the man saw reason. The other part wanted to hold him and never, never let him go.

"Daddy, don't let go!" Julia gripped the handlebars tighter as the wind blew into her face and through her hair. She was flying. *"Don't let go of me!"*

"I'm right here," he laughed. She could hear him running beside her, panting to keep up. *"I'm right here."*

They hit a bump and she shrieked, *"Don't let go!"*

"Trust me, Sweetheart, I won't let go!"

The sun was hot, the wind cool, and everything was a blur, a thrilling blur of grass and trees and sky. *"Daddy?"*

This time there was no answer.

"Daddy?"

Still nothing.

Panic seized her. She turned. No one was there. *"Dad—"* The bicycle wobbled once to the left and then she lost control. The handlebars spun from her hands, forcing the front wheel to veer sharply and throw her forward, over the front end, screaming as she flew through the air until she landed hard on the grass.

She felt no real pain, not really. Just shock. And betrayal. A betrayal like she had never experienced before. *"Daddy,"* she sobbed.

"I'm coming, Sweetheart!" Through her tears she saw his approach, heard the concern in his voice. *"I'm coming!"*

"You let go!" she wailed. *"You promised, but you let go!"* She pounded her fist into the mattress. *"You promised ... you promised."* Julia Davis-Preston sat hunched forward, her head on her father's mattress, quietly sobbing. She felt the sheet wet against her face from her tears. As the dream dissolved, she bit her lip, trying to hold back the emotion. She knew where she was. Back in ICU. Back in her father's hospital room.

She raised her head and glanced around. Fortunately no one had seen or heard her. She wiped her eyes and looked down at her watch. It was nearly 8:00 P.M. She took a deep breath, shoved the remaining fragments of the memory from her mind, and rose. It was time to go. Time to get some rest. She gathered her things and started for the door. She hesitated a moment, thinking of turning back to him, of saying something. But she didn't. Instead, she kept on walking, down the long corridor, through the lobby, and out into the night.

PART TWO

CHAPTER SEVEN

I sn't this incredible?" Conrad shouted over the wind.

Suzanne stood a dozen feet from him looking down at the river and the vast farmland stretching beyond. It was nearly dusk. The two had just arrived at the top of a bluff overlooking the Smokey Hill River in Kansas. The view was spectacular. But it was more than just the land and the river. It was also the sky. Violet-black thunderheads hung heavy over the landscape. They swirled and churned as a dozen shades of blue and black and gray broiled, mixing and remixing into each other. Their insides glowed and pulsated with flashes of light, as occasional forks snaked to the ground.

There was majesty here. Conrad could feel it. In the land, the river, the sky. Everywhere. He stood in reverent awe, drinking it in . . . the raw, terrible, frightening power. Any strength man possessed paled in comparison to this breathtaking display of grandeur.

He glanced to Suzanne who watched, equally moved. He'd known she would be. That's why he'd invited her. The rest of the group were camped down at the Sommer's farm, a small piece of land owned by Scott and Brent's aunt, thirty miles southwest of Abilene. Conrad could have invited the others up here as well, but he'd sensed they wouldn't appreciate it like Suzanne . . . or need it as much.

Three days ago she'd received a letter from her sister in Lebanon, Tennessee, saying that their brother, Michael, had been in a serious construction accident and would she please come down at once. Conrad was well aware of Suzanne's strong dedication to family, and he could only imagine how difficult it had been for her when she had finally made up her mind and refused. But she had. She had decided to stay on and continue with Eli. Of course this had brought all kinds of outrage from her loved ones. Even daughter Julia had gotten into the act, hinting at taking some sort of legal action against Eli. And why not? Everyone else seemed to be.

It had been eight days since the bombing up in Montana—that's what the officials called it: a bombing—though they claimed to have no clues or suspects. Conrad's list, however, was just a little bit longer. Between angry religious leaders, the millions who had been inflamed by the media coverage, and the hundreds of angry white separatists whose beloved leader had just turned himself in, the possibilities seemed endless. Then there was that image of the gray Taurus with the government officials, and Bill Johnson watching from the backseat. The thought of that collaboration still made him shudder. How deep did it all go?

He pushed the thought from his mind and turned his attention back to Suzanne. The wind had increased, blowing back her salt-and-pepper hair, pressing her printed summer dress against her body. She still had a nice figure, though nothing compared to the way she'd looked in her twenties. Then again, who did? And yet, almost to his surprise, he had come to realize that looks really didn't matter that much. Not when it came to Suzanne. Not when it came to someone he so deeply cared for. Not when it came to someone he so . . . he so . . . well, any word he thought of rang like a hollow cliché in comparison to the frightening depth of his feeling for her.

He continued to watch her, trying to understand where his feelings came from. He remembered when they were in their twenties, working so hard to refurbish the house in Pasadena. She had worn sweats and Conrad's old work shirts, nothing to complement her beauty, and yet somehow that had made her all the more attractive. Or when she was pregnant with Julia. Definitely not material for the *Sports Illustrated* swimsuit edition, but underneath the weight and the puffiness, she had literally glowed. It was the same now. Despite the gradual loss of her figure and the lines etching their way into her face—that was only the outside covering, like wearing the sweats and his work shirt at the house. Somehow, this exterior only accentuated her interior beauty, making her all the more graceful and peaceful and lovely. It was amazing. He'd had some of the most beautiful women in the world, and yet none of them held a candle to what he saw now. To what he felt now.

She turned and caught him staring. "Are you okay?" she asked, stepping over to join him.

He glanced away, a little embarrassed. "Yeah, I'm fine." And it was true, he was fine. Finer than he had been in a very long while. He looked out at the approaching storm. "Have you ever seen anything so . . . majestic?"

She shook her head and looked back up at him.

"What?" he asked.

She tried unsuccessfully to hide her amusement.

"What is it?"

She looked back out to the storm. "You're changing, Conrad Davis."

"Me?"

She nodded. "In the old days I couldn't get you to look at anything except the latest TV news. Then all you would do is complain about how somebody had botched up a report, or how you should have been there, or how you could have done it better. It was all Julia and I could do to get you to take vacations. Even then you really weren't with us. But this?" She motioned toward the storm. "You dragged me all the way up here just to look at . . . clouds?"

He smiled, again embarrassed. Then he turned and looked back at the storm.

"What's happening?" she quietly asked.

He gave a shrug and watched. Another blinding jag of lightning forked its way to the ground.

"Connie?" she gently pressed him.

He took a deep breath and let it out. "All of my life I've been looking for the truth. And now . . ." He took another breath. "And now, I'm finally finding it." She kept watching as he struggled to put his thoughts into words. "You know how he keeps talking about letting go, about giving up our life so we can find it?"

She nodded.

Finally he was able to look at her. "I think that's happening. I'm giving up my life—not all at once, but a little at a time—and I'm finding it. And the amazing thing is that the truth I've been searching for . . . it's not in facts and figures and stories. It's in a man."

Suzanne reached out and quietly took his hand. He continued. "And if we can get the rest of the world to see that truth . . ." He searched for the words.

She finished his thought. "Then it will never be the same."

"Yes." He nodded. "That's it. Exactly. Now if we could just get Eli to sign up for that program."

"Oh, I think he has, Connie," Suzanne said. "It's just the way he goes about it that you can't accept. Doesn't it seem odd—we say we trust him with the big things, with all his theories, but when it comes to the actual details of our lives, to the areas we're the experts in, we can barely give him an inch."

"You, too?" he asked in surprise.

"All of us."

Conrad said nothing and looked back out at the storm. She was right, of course. But what about common sense? You wouldn't jump off this cliff without expecting to fall. You wouldn't stand in the middle of that field during this storm. And once you're in the public eye you surely wouldn't act without considering all of the possible public reactions. It was common sense, just another law of nature.

The wind blew harder now, and it had started to rain. But Conrad felt no compulsion to leave. Apparently, neither did Suzanne, and for that he was grateful. Once again he thought of the changes in his life. So many wasted years, so many damaged lives. Then, of course, there was his daughter. "Any news from Julia?" he asked.

Suzanne shook her head. "Just the latest accusation that I've been brainwashed by a religious cult."

"Good ol' Julia. You told her I was here?"

"Oh, yeah."

"And?"

"Let's just say it didn't improve her outlook on my situation."

He nodded sadly. The wind whipped at their clothes as the rain fell harder. He slipped his arm from the sleeve of his parka and offered her half his jacket. She gratefully accepted, moving in as he wrapped it about her. Immediately, he recognized his mistake. They were together now, pressed side by side, closer than he had ever intended. What had he done? He had been so careful, promised himself never to let something like this happen. Granted, there was that emotional outburst at the bombing, but this, this was entirely different.

He tried to concentrate on the storm. But it was no contest. The warmth of her body, the smell of her hair, the gentle rhythm of her breathing pressing against his side, it was more than he could endure.

She took a deeper breath and quietly sighed. "You ever wonder if it's true?" she said.

He'd forgotten the thread of the conversation. "What's that?" he asked huskily.

"That we're part of some religious cult?"

"Sure, in the beginning." Grateful to find his voice, he continued. "But the teaching, it's so pure. And the miracles . . . It's been a while since I've seen a cult leader raise someone from the dead."

"Or transform lives," she added. "Taking cold hearts of stone and changing them into loving, caring hearts of flesh."

At first Conrad was unsure what she meant, until she turned and gazed up at him, and he saw those compassionate, engaging eyes. Despite their age, the years had not dimmed them. But he saw something else in them as well. Something searching . . . and something very, very compelling. She held his gaze, refusing to look away. Then, before he knew it, he pulled her closer. She did not resist. A moment later he was dropping his head and lowering his mouth to hers. He found her lips and they gently kissed. It was a tender kiss, soft and delicate, until he felt his passion begin to grow. That's when, with every ounce of self-control, he pulled away. Shuddering, he caught his breath, looking everywhere but to her.

"I'm sorry," he apologized. "I don't know what I was thinking. That was totally insensi—"

Her arms reached around his neck and she pulled his mouth back to hers. Their lips met and they kissed again, longer, slower. Somewhere in the back of his mind he was aware of the pounding rain, the whipping wind . . . and of the tears forming in his eyes. But it didn't matter. How long they kissed, he wasn't sure. But when they finally parted, he saw that her own eyes were as wet as his, from both the rain and the tears. She continued looking at him, refusing to take those eyes from his. And then she spoke. It was soft, barely audible in the blowing wind. But audible, nonetheless. "What took you so long, Conrad Davis?" she whispered. "What took you?"

Julia eased her rental car to a stop alongside the curb. She put it into park and sat for a long moment. The drive had taken over an hour. Initially she had thought of staying at one of the motels in Thousand Oaks, or even along the 118 Freeway as she headed through Simi Valley. But one missed exit followed another, until for whatever reason, she found herself here in the old section of Pasadena. Here, at her childhood home.

She ducked her head to look out the passenger window. The house was an old two-and-a-half-story affair, with a large wraparound porch. No lights were on inside.

Five years. It had been five years since the last time she'd been back. And then it had been only briefly . . . just long enough to get into another fight with him before she was off again. Her father could be so stubborn sometimes, so bullheaded. And, of course, hypocritical. She supposed he could make the same claims about her—except for the hypocrisy. That was one thing she could never be accused of.

She still wasn't sure why she was there. Maybe it was because this house had been such a part of her life. And his. After all, the man had lived here thirty years. You don't live in a place that long without it becoming a part of you. Maybe that was it. Maybe staying here was her way of staying close to him.

The thought gave her little solace.

She reached for the car door and opened it. The evening was still, almost balmy. The old-fashioned lights with their large, acorn-shaped lamps glowed yellow-white along the street. The smell of cut grass filled the air. And, of course, the smell of magnolia—rich and sweet, the doorway to a thousand childhood memories. Julia closed her eyes and took a long, deep breath. She'd read once that the smell center of the brain was closest to the memory center . . . which would explain why certain aromas can touch off long-forgotten memories.

That was certainly the case here. So many memories . . . sweet, tender, loving, bitter. Maybe that was why her father had fought so hard to keep the place through all the divorces, because of the memories. Sometimes he was quite the sentimentalist.

She popped the trunk, stepped outside the car, and walked to the back where she pulled out her suit bag. She closed the lid with her free hand and turned to face the darkened house. She took a long moment to prepare herself. Finally she started up the sidewalk, her pumps clicking softly against the worn concrete. The cracks were the same, except for one or two new ones. Just ahead was where she'd skinned her knee double Dutching with Katie Green. Up there was where she and Kevin Thomas had started a fire with his father's magnifying glass. And there, right near the porch was where the two of them had dripped melted wax on wayward ants, embalming them for posterity.

She arrived at the porch steps and started up them. The white paint had peeled slightly and they could definitely stand for another coat. Once she reached the top she headed for the door. She stooped down to the geranium pot, the same geranium pot that had been there forever, the one her father had promised would always have a key under it. She tilted it back. It was difficult to see in the dark, but there it was, coated with years of corrosion and dirt.

She scooped it into her hand, rose, and reached for the screen door. It gave a quiet groan as she opened it. It was only then, when she tried to put the key into the lock, that she noticed how violently her hand trembled. It shook so badly that she could not insert the key. The sight angered her, making her all the more determined until finally she succeeded. Once the key was in place, she turned the lock. It gave a dull click. Then, with the same trembling hand, she grabbed the knob, turned it, and pushed open the door.

"Jake?" Conrad yelled into the camper. "Trevor?"

There was no answer, only the howling wind outside.

"Anybody in here?"

Still nothing. He pulled his head from the camper and shut the door.

"Nobody?" Suzanne shouted.

"No," he yelled back.

She turned to look down the row of deserted RVs and campers. "Where could they be?"

He shook his head and glanced back at the farmhouse. It also looked deserted.

Twenty minutes had passed since they'd kissed. Just long enough to climb back down the ridge . . . and just long enough to find themselves caught in the middle of the growing storm. Now wind tore and tugged at their clothes as rain pelted their faces.

"What's that sound?" Suzanne yelled as she pulled back her hair, trying to keep it from slapping her eyes.

"What?"

"That roar, where's it coming from?"

Conrad heard it now, too. But it was more than hearing it. He could feel it—in his body, vibrating through the air, through the ground. An earthquake? No, not here. But it had that same ominous rumble. He looked toward the barn, then out to the pasture, squinting into the wind.

"Connie! Over there!"

He turned to see Suzanne pointing at the storm cellar by the pump house. The door was open, and Jake stood down in the steps, waving and shouting at them.

Conrad grabbed Suzanne's hand and yelled, "Come on!" They started forward, tucking their heads down, fighting to keep their balance against the wind. Conrad stole a glance to Jake. The man stood half in and half out of the cellar waving and shouting, though it was impossible to hear him over the wind and growing roar.

A loud *CRACK* exploded above their heads. Conrad looked to see a giant tree limb tearing from its trunk. "Look out!" He pushed Suzanne to the ground, instinctively throwing himself over her. The limb slammed down with a powerful *WHOMP*, its smaller branches slapping their bodies, the main limb barely missing them.

Conrad scrambled back to his feet, pulling Suzanne with him. "Let's go!" Branches whipped and scratched as they crawled over and through them. The wind grew louder, the roar deafening.

They were close enough to hear Jake's voice now, as he continued shouting and waving. "Hurry! Hurry!"

They stumbled out of the remaining branches, half falling, then running as fast as they could across the wet grass. The rain was turning to hail. It began clicking and clattering about them.

"Hurry!"

Finally they arrived, breathless and soaked to the skin.

"You guys all right?" Jake yelled.

They nodded. "Where is everybody?" Conrad shouted.

"Down here!" a voice called from below.

He looked down the steep wooden steps to see a Coleman lantern glowing on a table. Familiar faces of the group were huddled around it. At least a dozen. More in the shadows.

He turned back to Jake as they helped Suzanne down the slippery steps. "What's that noise?" he shouted.

Jake motioned to his left. Conrad turned and sucked in his breath. Out in the field, a hundred yards from the lane and two hundred yards up it, was a swirling vortex of wind and cloud and debris. A tornado. He'd seen enough of them on TV and in the movies, but it took a moment to register that this was the real thing.

"Where's Eli?" Jake shouted.

"Isn't he here?"

Jake shook his head. "I thought he was with you! Must have gone on one of those prayer walks of his!"

"You mean he's out there?" Conrad yelled.

"Everyone else is accounted for!"

Conrad fought back his panic. He saw Jake doing the same. Neither said a word. They turned and resumed looking across the pastures, the outbuildings, down the lane. From time to time Conrad would steal a peek over at the funnel cloud as it continued to approach. What awesome power.

There was another crack, then a tearing sound.

"Look out!"

Conrad turned just in time to see a handful of shingles from the barn's roof heading for them. They ducked, dropping to the stairs, as several crashed around them, striking the door, knocking it out of Jake's hand. The wind threw it backwards, snapping off one of its hinges. The people below cried out in fear.

"Get down here!" Robert's voice shouted. "Get down here where it's safe!"

Conrad turned to Jake and yelled over the wind, "We better get below!"

"You go! I'm staying!"

"Jake!"

The big guy shook his head and continued to scan the fields.

It was useless to debate. Jake may not be the brightest bulb in the pack, and there were times Conrad could barely stand his good ol' boy mentality, but there was something about his commitment and unswerving dedication to Eli—like a bulldog refusing to leave his master—that told him it would do no good to argue.

"Connie!" Robert yelled. He'd taken a tentative step up the stairs. "Jake! Get down here!" Others from the group joined in, demanding they come down and join them where it was safe.

Conrad hesitated. He turned back toward the twister. It had closed its distance to them by half. It was now fifty yards to the left of the lane, a hundred yards ahead. The air pressure began dropping so quickly that he suddenly found it difficult to catch his breath.

"Connie!" Suzanne's voice had joined the chorus from below. "Please come down!"

Then, without warning, Jake scrambled out into the wind.

"Jake!"

He grabbed the door and tried to pull it back down. Realizing he needed help, Conrad joined him. The wind shrieked, its force so powerful, it was difficult to stand. Hail and flying mud stung his face. Jake had hold of the door's metal handle, so Conrad grabbed the rough wooden edge. Together they pulled, digging in, tugging with all of their might. But the wind was too strong. The door bucked and banged but refused to cooperate.

"Get behind it!" Jake yelled. "We gotta push!"

Conrad nodded and joined Jake as they scrambled behind the door. The roar filled his ears; water and mud spattered into his eyes and mouth. He spat as, together, they shoved against the door, arms and shoulders pushing, feet slipping on muddy wet grass. It took three tries until they finally managed to lift it up. Hanging on, they scurried to the other side and began pulling it down. For a moment they nearly had it, until a gust caught the door, ripping it out of their hands and off the remaining hinges. It tumbled and cartwheeled away. The people below screamed.

Conrad dropped back into the cellar three or four steps, catching his breath, wiping the mud from his eyes with one hand while holding the wet concrete wall for support with the other. Jake followed him by one or two steps. But, despite the yelling and pleading from below, both continued standing, squinting into the wind and hail and mud.

Suddenly Jake shouted, "There he is!"

"Where?"

"Coming down the lane!"

Conrad took another step higher and then another until he could see past Jake. Sure enough, there was Eli, strolling down the gravel road. *Strolling!* The towering funnel loomed behind him and the man was strolling! Except for his flapping clothes and flying hair, he seemed completely untouched. And instead of panicking for his life, he appeared to be enjoying the experience. Amidst the wind and rain and hail and debris it almost looked as if he was laughing!

"Eli!" Jake took a step higher up the stairs and waved. "Eli!"

Eli spotted him and waved back.

"Get in here!" Jake yelled.

But Eli only grinned, motioning to the spectacle around him. And then he did something even more incredible. He motioned for the two of them to come out and join him!

Conrad stared, dumbfounded.

The black, shrieking funnel suddenly shifted direction. It no longer approached the lane. Instead it began running parallel to Eli, less than sixty yards from his right. Fence posts near him shuddered. Some ripped out, exploding into splinters, flipping and whipping barbed wire. Yet Eli was completely unaffected . . . not only unaffected, but enjoying the experience!

Once again he waved to them. Down below, his followers were screaming in terror, and Eli was waving for them to join him? Things could not have been any more absurd. Well, actually, they could.

Suddenly Jake turned to Conrad and shouted, "I'm going!"

"*What?*" Conrad yelled. "Are you crazy?"

Again Eli waved.

Jake hesitated, obviously frightened, and yet . . .

"Jake, don't be—"

Eli waved again.

"Jake, don't—"

And then Jake stepped out of the cellar and into the storm. Conrad lunged for him, but he was too late. "Jake, come back! Jake!"

But Jake was not coming back. Instead, he started walking toward Eli.

It was a nightmare. Down below people were screaming in fear. Up above, the approaching tornado thundered and roared—pieces of building, branches, debris, everything was flying, swirling around the periphery of the funnel. And there, in the midst of all the chaos and confusion, two men walked toward each other.

A chunk of corrugated metal banged and rattled, barely giving Conrad enough warning to duck as it flew overhead. He inched back up, keeping his eyes just high enough above the ground to see.

Jake continued walking, his eyes riveted to Eli. The wind seemed to have no serious effect upon him either. Except for the blowing of his clothes and hair, it was as if the storm didn't exist. Eli kept right on grinning at him in encouragement, and Jake kept right on walking.

Again, the cloud shifted course. Now it was heading directly toward the two.

"LOOK OUT!" Conrad shouted. But they couldn't hear. He staggered up another step, shouting into the wind. "LOOK OUT!"

To Jake's left, a rusting cultivator creaked loudly, then groaned, then exploded into a cloud of flying metal. Jake spun around to see the pieces of iron and steel lifting into the air. That's when he panicked. Instead of turning back to Eli, he looked to the cloud, to the giant black snake whipping and roaring toward him. He could not look away. Despite Eli's shouting, he could not look back. His steps began to falter, then stumble. The wind pulled at him harder, nearly dragging him from his feet.

Eli continued to shout, trying to get his attention. But it did no good. By now they were only a few yards apart. But Jake did not hear.

The funnel approached, drawing so close that its outer edges began to engulf them. Jake fought it, staggering, using all of his strength to stay on his feet. But it did no good. The two were so close they could practically touch, but Jake would not take his eyes off the wind and look at Eli. Suddenly his feet lifted from the ground and he cried out. It was as if he had jumped or skipped. He came back down hard, stumbling, nearly falling before he was lifted up again—only this time he continued to rise.

He twisted toward Eli, desperately reaching for him, screaming in horror. But he was too late. Jake's hand was just out of reach. Eli lunged for him and at the last second he managed to catch his waist, the back of his belt. He pulled down hard, and the big man fell backwards onto the ground. Eli stooped down and helped him up. And a moment later, the two stood facing each other in the howling gale.

Conrad continued to watch, huddled on the steps, peering into the black wind. He could see Jake staring straight into Eli's face now, obviously afraid to look anywhere else. Eli said something to him, then turned to face the funnel cloud. Slowly raising his hand, he shouted. It was impossible for Conrad to make out the words. Whatever they were, they were brief . . . but their impact, astonishing.

Instantly the wind started to die. The howling faded. Conrad watched in amazement as the black wall of wind and water began to dissolve. Items started falling back to earth, raining around Eli and Jake, raining around Conrad and the storm cellar. The cloud turned light gray. In a matter of seconds, it dissipated into nothing but a rainstorm, the final wisps of black vapor disappearing even as he watched. Now there was only rain and falling debris.

Eli and Jake turned and started back toward the cellar. Cautiously, Conrad rose, staring in unbelief, glancing up to make sure he wouldn't be hit by falling objects. At last he stepped out of the cellar.

Others followed, carefully emerging, looking as baffled and as astonished as Conrad. Several moments passed before Eli arrived. He wasn't angry, but the joy in his eyes was missing. Instead, it was replaced by a type of sadness . . . and disappointment.

"Where is your faith?" he called out. Then, shaking his head, he added, "When will you stop doubting me?"

The group exchanged guilty glances. Most would not look at Eli. But Conrad did. And when their eyes connected he saw no condemnation, just that sad disappointment. Eli repeated the question. Although it was for everyone, Conrad knew that for that particular moment, it was mostly for him.

"When will you stop doubting?"

CHAPTER EIGHT

"McFarland, do I look that stupid?"

"Do I have to answer that?" the balding news reporter from EBN fired back. It was supposed to be in jest, but the way the overweight man was huffing and puffing as they moved up the terraced hillside, it looked like he was having anything but fun.

Not that Conrad blamed him. After all, the only way he'd agreed to talk with McFarland was by pressing him into service alongside Keith and himself as they handed out food to the crowd. The big man had reluctantly joined them less than five minutes ago, and the poor guy was already working up a sweat in the hot Oklahoma sun. Conrad knew it galled him helping out like this, which was probably why he insisted he do it. Still, with this large of a crowd, they needed all the help they could get.

What had started out as a scheduled event at the Woodward Memorial Park in Tulsa, this Saturday, had turned into an all-day marathon. Although the group had rented the bandstand from 9 to 12, the officials and assigned police were so captivated by what they saw and heard that they allowed Eli to continue. The crowd was equally caught up, and noontime came and went with most not even caring that they'd missed lunch.

Eli was in great form, sharing one story after another, explaining how absolutely holy God expected His children to be, yet how loving and forgiving He was if they failed. And, despite the crowd's size, Eli remained as intimate as if it were a handful of his closest friends. More often than not he was off the stage with the park department's wireless mike, casually strolling through the crowd, occasionally chatting with individuals, sometimes healing them.

But by three o'clock Jake and Robert, along with Scott and Brent, had pulled Eli into the backstage shade and suggested he call it quits. If not for himself, than at least for the crowd.

"The folks haven't eaten since morning," Robert insisted, handing Eli a Styrofoam glass with ice water. "Lots of them got kids. They must be starved."

"I know I am," grumbled Jake as he slumped onto the wooden steps leading to the stage. He popped open another of the dozen Diet Cokes he consumed daily and began to guzzle.

Eli nodded, slowly thinking it over. He grabbed the towel Maggie had brought from her camper and wiped off his sweating face. Then he scooped ice out of his cup, lowered his head, and pressed it against the back of his neck. The summer heat was taking a lot out of him, but he never complained. Not as long as there was a need. Not as long as people were willing to listen.

"All right," Eli finally answered, his voice hoarse from the lengthening day. "Why don't you guys go ahead and feed them."

"With what?" Scott asked. "All we've got are a couple burgers and a side of fries some kid brought you."

Eli raised his head and gave his face another swipe while catching the stray ice water dribbling down his chest. "Then give that to them."

"Right," Brent scoffed, "we've got how many thousands of people out there, and you want us to feed them with two burgers and a side of fries?"

"Give it a shot," Eli said as he stepped over Jake to head back onstage. Then with that infectious twinkle he called over his shoulder, "You might be surprised."

That had been forty-five minutes ago. And now Conrad and the guys were *definitely* surprised. So far they'd fed about half the crowd with more hamburgers and fries than they could count. No one had bought more. No one had donated more. Instead, Scott had simply poured the contents of the kid's bag into a grocery sack Suzanne had provided . . . until her sack literally overflowed with wrapped burgers and loose fries. More sacks and bags were scrounged up. They, too, were filled to the brim. And, still, it didn't stop. When the sacks were distributed to Eli's followers and they moved through the crowd passing out the burgers and fries, their sacks never seemed to empty either. All Conrad and the others had to do was reach into their bags and pull out one burger after another after another, or pour out one helping of fries after another. Now, Conrad was no math whiz, but he knew this defied logic by any standard. Of course, McFarland, who had just joined the serving committee, hadn't a clue as to what was happening. But he would.

"Look, we just need a link to him," the big man gasped as he trudged up the grassy hillside passing out the food. "An unofficial diplomatic channel."

"And the reason it has to be unofficial?" Keith asked.

"You don't need me to tell you that."

"Try us," Conrad said.

McFarland lowered his voice, making sure those in the crowd were not following the conversation. "Let's just say it would be a great source of embarrassment if the public knew he and my boss were talking."

"But he hasn't withdrawn his invitation to the City of God, has he?" Conrad asked.

"Of course not. That would be a breach of Southern hospitality."

"Of course," Conrad said. "But you wouldn't be opposed if Eli backed out."

"Not in the slightest. But of course he won't."

"Not in the slightest."

"Well . . ." McFarland sighed heavily, motioning to his bag. "I'm about out." He wiped the sweat from his face. "Maybe we can go someplace a little cooler to talk."

"Here," Conrad said, reaching over and dumping his sack of burgers into McFarland's . . . until it was full.

McFarland looked on, astonished. "Where'd you get all those?"

Conrad smiled and continued the conversation. "What else do you want from me? Besides being this liaison?"

"Is it that obvious?" McFarland asked.

"With you, always."

McFarland tried to chuckle, though it came out more of a wheezing cough. Again he lowered his voice. "Look, you know how the religious community has been looking for a Messiah. How our country's been going down the drain and how we need someone to kick a little sinners' heinie to get this nation back on track with God."

"And you think Eli might be the one?" Keith asked.

Conrad threw a glance at his ambitious young partner. No doubt the kid felt cocky thinking he was on equal footing with such seasoned pros.

"That's just it," McFarland answered. "We don't know."

Conrad replied, "After his arrest at Leon's party, the lawsuits you've slapped on him, the disinformation you're spreading through the media and Internet . . . sounds to me like your boss has more than made up his mind."

"He just doesn't fit the prophecies, that's all."

"What do you mean?"

"There are hundreds of prophecies in the Bible that talk of a man who will rally the people for God. A great leader who will straighten things out and get people to start doing things God's way."

"Someone like . . . Dr. Thomas J. Kerston?"

McFarland gave him a look. "That's always a possibility."

Conrad shook his head, quietly musing.

McFarland continued. "My point is, your boy here is not fulfilling any of those prophecies. He's not fitting the profile."

"Except for the miracles, the healings, and raising people from the dead," Conrad said. He couldn't resist the temptation of pouring more burgers into McFarland's bag to underscore the point.

"Yes," McFarland said, numbly watching the burgers pour in, "except for the miracles."

"And you want us to . . ."

It took a moment for McFarland to recover. "Help us. Help us force him to play his hand. I mean, if he's the guy we're all waiting for, Dr. Kerston would be the first to admit that he's been wrong."

"I bet."

"He would. Not only that, but he'd be the first to put his sizable muscle behind him. Think what that could do for Eli, for his cause. Who knows, with Dr. Kerston's political clout, we might even be able to get your boy into office somewhere."

"And if he's not the one?" Keith asked.

For a moment, McFarland did not answer.

Conrad repeated the question, "And if he's not the one you're waiting for?"

"Then he needs to be stopped. Before he leads any more people astray."

"I see."

"We just want him to be straight with us, that's all. One minute he says he's God's son, then a good teacher, then he performs miracles, then he doesn't . . . either this man is the Messiah we've been waiting for, or he isn't. It's as simple as that. We just need to know the truth. Help us find the truth, Connie. You've been a proponent of truth all your life; it's your greatest strength."

Conrad said nothing. He was grateful that Keith decided to follow his example.

"For the good of these people, for the good of the country . . . help us find the truth."

It was an obvious ploy that Conrad saw through immediately. But still . . . now that Eli had polarized everyone anyway, now that people either loved him or hated him, what would be so terribly wrong with encouraging him to take the next step, to go public with the identity that many suspected of him anyway? And if, as McFarland suggested, they could get the religious establishment behind him . . . well, his impact upon the country would be enormous. Hadn't that been Eli's purpose all along?

Granted, it was just a thought, a cleverly planted one whose source he didn't entirely trust, but it was a thought.

The phone rang as Julia opened the front door to the house. She pulled the key from the lock and fumbled for the hall switch, clicking both it and the porch light on at the same time. The screen door slammed behind her, and she elbowed the front door shut. Straight ahead lay the paneled hallway leading to her father's office. To her right was the arched entrance into the living room.

She chose the arched entrance.

The phone rang a second time. She dumped her suit bag onto a chair already covered in books and magazines. She reached over to the end table and snapped on the lamp. The place looked no better in the light. Magazines, newspapers, and stacks and stacks of videotapes lay on the floor in front of a big-screen TV. It's not that her father was a slob, it's just that he was always working. And now that he had the house to himself, his work space had naturally invaded his living space. Then there was the stale smell of cigars. He was never much of a smoker, but from time to time he pretended to be.

The phone rang a third time. She ignored it as she crossed through the dining room, snapping on more lights, seeing more books and papers piled on the old cherry table. She headed for the kitchen as much out of hunger as habit—a habit that started in elementary school and continued later when she visited from college.

She arrived and turned on the light. Another table, another pile of papers. Over at the sink rose a mound of dirty dishes, mostly coffee mugs, precariously balanced. To the right, near the refrigerator, was a garbage bag overflowing with used microwave food cartons and containers. The phone made its fourth and final ring before the answering machine kicked in.

It was her father's voice, direct and to the point. "Hi. Leave a message at the tone. Thanks."

Beep.

And then another voice followed.

"Hi, Julia . . . this is Mom. If you're there, will you pick up?"

What on earth? How did she know she'd be there?

"Julia?"

Julia dashed out of the kitchen and back into the living room. She brushed the papers off the end table, but the phone wasn't there.

"I don't know if you'll get this or not, but Ken said he told you I'd be out in the morning."

She zeroed in on the voice. It came from the stacks of books piled in front of the fireplace.

"My plane's boarding now. I think it's the same flight you were on last night."

She raced to the stacks, searching for the machine, for anything plastic amidst the pile of paper.

"It's a terrible decision you're having to make and, I know, I know, you can handle it by yourself and you probably want me to keep my nose out of it. But I just don't think you should be there alone."

"Mom?" She pushed the books aside, digging more frantically until she spotted the answering machine. The phone had to be nearby. She grabbed the line and physically followed it through the books.

"Anyway, I guess it was stupid, thinking you'd be there. I also left word at the hospital. One way or another, I'll see you soon, Sweetheart."

No, that line led to the wall jack. She had to follow the other one, the one to the phone. "Mom!" Backtracking to the answering machine, she dropped to her knees.

"I love you, Jules. And I'll be praying."

There it was, on the hearth. She lunged for the receiver and scooped it up.

"Bye-bye."

"Mom?" she shouted into the receiver. There was a click. "Mom, are you there? Mom?"

Nothing. Just silence . . . and then the dial tone.

"Mom . . ." Her voice wearily faded. She was so drained, so exhausted . . . and so very much alone. She closed her eyes. Every inch of her head throbbed. She lowered it, letting out a long, slow sigh. Eventually the phone began to beep, a reminder to hang up. She reached over and replaced the receiver. There, still on her knees, amidst the piles of books, she thought how easy it would be to stretch out, to just use a book or two for a pillow and catch a little sleep right there, right now.

But of course, she wouldn't. That wasn't her style. Julia Davis-Preston was stronger than that. She had to be. So with another heavy sigh, she rose to her feet and once again did what she had to do.

The park officials shut the meeting down a little before eight. Just as well. There's no telling how long Eli would have gone on if they hadn't. With so many people in need of healing and teaching and explanations regarding the Kingdom of Heaven, he would have stayed there all night. On three separate occasions Conrad and the guys had tried to convince him to quit. But his argument was always the same: "These are the people I've come to help . . . and my time is so short."

Yet, as dusk approached, it was obvious that even the great Eli Shepherd was reaching his limit. By five o'clock his voice was going. By seven o'clock it was barely above a whisper. And still he was reluctant to stop, and still the crowd was reluctant to leave. "There's so much pain here," he had croaked to the guys. "So much need."

Conrad was pleased that McFarland had chosen to stay. He was pleased for Eli's sake, he was pleased for McFarland's sake, and he was pleased for his own. Truth be told, he enjoyed watching Eli's logic scramble McFarland's religious self-righteousness. There were times the man listened with his mouth agape, times he nearly scoffed out loud, and times he could only shake his head in wonder. It was amusing, to say the least.

What was not amusing was the way McFarland, after the crowd had been dismissed and was heading home, suddenly produced a tape recorder and confronted Eli. Conrad, Jake, and Will had been trying to get him through the mass of people to Maggie's camper parked backstage when McFarland suddenly appeared, calling and pushing his way toward the front. "Eli? Eli, Gerald McFarland from EBN News. Eli!"

If Eli heard, he did not respond. Instead he turned and suddenly came to a stop. "Who touched me?" he croaked.

Conrad exchanged glances with Jake and Will. What was he talking about?

"Somebody touched me," Eli's voice cracked. "Who was it?"

"Eli." Jake leaned closer. "We've got a whole crowd pushing in here, what do you mean, who touched you?"

Eli tried to speak louder, his ruined voice croaking and skipping. "Somebody touched me. I felt power leave. Where are you?"

The small crowd murmured, glancing at one another.

McFarland took advantage of the moment to try again. "Eli? Gerald McFarland from EBN News."

Eli held out his hand, motioning for silence. "It's important that you tell me," he tried to shout. He waited, continuing to search the crowd. "It's important for you."

Jake coughed slightly. "Eli, I don't think he'll—"

"Shh," Eli said. "Give her time."

The crowd grew restless. Now there was only the sound of crickets and the nearby highway. Nearly a half minute passed before a slight disturbance began toward the back. People stepped aside, making room for someone to pass. Finally, an embarrassed woman in shorts and frizzy red hair came into view. She was in her late twenties, perspiring heavily, and very, very frightened. But she continued forward. As she approached, her gaze dropped to the ground, and when she arrived she was breathing so hard she could not speak.

"It's you," Eli croaked.

She looked up, but only for a moment. "I . . . I've . . ." Her voice trembled as she looked back down. She swallowed and tried again, this time in a low whisper. "I've had this problem . . . for years."

"Go on," Eli said.

She swallowed again. "They keep operating and stuff . . . but nobody is able to fix it."

Eli nodded but remained silent, forcing her to continue.

She stared at the ground, struggling with each phrase. "I knew . . . if I could just touch you . . . or your clothing . . . I knew I'd get well."

"And?" Eli's wrecked voice whispered back.

Finally she looked up, tears spilling onto her cheeks. "I am!" she blurted. "I can feel it! I'm completely well!"

At last Eli broke into a grin. He reached out to embrace her, and she threw herself into his arms. They remained hugging like that for a long moment. When they finally separated, Eli's face was as wet as her own.

"Thank you," she whispered fiercely. "Thank you, thank you, thank you."

He tried to answer, though it was growing harder for him to talk. "Your faith," he finally croaked, "that's what has made you well."

She hugged him again. Then, abruptly turning, she started back through the crowd. Although she was still embarrassed, she did not look back at the ground. Instead, she kept her head up, beaming.

Eli watched after her, also grinning . . . until he was again interrupted by McFarland. "Eli? Eli, Dr. Kerston has a question for you."

Conrad tensed as he saw Eli slowly turn toward him.

"Sir, Dr. Kerston has a question."

"You're Connie's friend," Eli said.

"Uh, yes, sir."

"Helped us . . ." His voice quit and he tried again. "Helped us to serve lunch."

"Well, yes, a little, that's right."

"Did you get anything out of my talk?"

"Me?" McFarland asked, caught off guard.

Eli nodded. "What do you . . . think?"

"What do *I* think?"

That's when Conrad moved in. "Come on, Eli, you two can talk another time."

"No," Eli croaked quietly, "I'd like to hear what your friend thinks."

The crowd focused their attention on McFarland.

"Well, I, uh . . . as far as the teaching, you mean?"

Eli nodded.

"Well," he cleared his throat, "it makes for some very interesting theory. I mean this business of giving to receive, of servants becoming leaders, of praying for your enemies. But that's all it is, just theory, right?"

"Why do you say that?"

"Why? Why? Well, let's face it, no one can possibly live by those standards."

"On their own, no. But with God's power, absolutely. In fact God *expects* us to." Eli's voice was again giving out, but he pushed himself. "Listen to me carefully, Gerald McFarland. My Father expects you to be holy just as He is holy."

McFarland blinked, trying to gather his wits. Finally he responded. "And yet you pick followers who"—he motioned across the crowd toward Will, then Leon—"no offense, but who are at the bottom of the moral and social food chain."

"Hey!" Leon countered.

"Yes." Eli quietly nodded. "But the Will Pattons and Leon Brewsters of the world . . . they know they need my help. They know they need God's forgiveness. Whereas men like you and Dr. Kerston—you are sadly oblivious to that fact."

"Men like Dr. Kerston are worth a hundred Leon Brewsters!"

Eli smiled sadly, then quietly answered, "To whom?"

McFarland's anger continued to rise. "Listen, you can't have it both ways. You can't talk about God's holiness and perfection one minute, then His love and forgiveness the next."

"Why not?"

"It's . . ." McFarland's frustration grew. "Because it's impossible, that's why." Eli was about to respond, but McFarland wasn't through. "That's exactly what I mean about theory versus reality. You can't have it both ways. Holiness and forgiveness. Justice and mercy. In theory, you can say anything you want. But when it comes down to practical, day-to-day living, the two are incompatible."

"Why?"

Conrad watched uneasily as McFarland's wheels turned. Over the years, he'd seen this man spin and weave traps for many a prey. He was quite good at it, and this would be no exception. "Take Ellen Perkins," McFarland finally said. "The little girl they're getting ready to execute in Texas for the murder of her boyfriend?"

Eli nodded.

"Says she was doped up out of her mind, didn't know what she was doing when she hacked him to pieces. And now she claims to be all sorrow and repentance over her actions, says she's—"

Eli finished his sentence. "—given her life to God. I know," he croaked, "I've been following her story."

Conrad moved in to clarify, "He means we've been following the story along with the rest of the nation."

Eli continued. "And now she's counseling with drug addicts, speaking to schools over the Internet, and—"

"So what's your position?" McFarland interrupted.

"About?"

"About whether or not she should be executed."

Suddenly Conrad saw it. McFarland was setting Eli up, putting him in a no-win situation. If Eli took the pro-death position, he'd be nullifying everything he'd said about God's mercy. If he took the anti-death position, he'd be nullifying everything he'd said about God's justice. McFarland had asked him the perfect lose/lose question. Once again Conrad moved in to the rescue. "Listen, it's been a long day for Eli, maybe—"

"So you're telling me you don't have a position?" McFarland asked.

Eli tried to answer, but again Conrad interrupted. "I'm just saying he's tired and there might be a better time to—"

"See what I mean?" McFarland forced a grin. "Your words are fine as long as they remain theory and conjecture. As long as they remain high and lofty ideals. But when you get down to practical application, well, I'm afraid they really don't hold water, do they?"

"They don't?"

"The facts speak for themselves. If you went down to Texas, what would you do—talk Milquetoast mercy and forgiveness to the family of the boy this woman brutally butchered, or do you tell her and all the kids she's helped that God is a holy tyrant who demands justice and expects blood for blood?"

Eli paused a moment and began to nod. "That's a good idea, Mr. McFarland."

"What?" McFarland frowned. "What's a good idea?"

"You're right," Eli croaked. "I should talk to them. Both of them."

"Eli!" The protest came from Conrad before he could stop it.

Eli turned to him. "Your friend has a point. I'd be happy to meet with Ellen. Didn't she e-mail us?"

"Well, yes, once, but—"

"And the boy's family. I'd be happy to talk with them also, if they'd let me."

Now it was Conrad's turn to stand openmouthed.

Eli turned back to McFarland. "Can you help us set that up?"

Instinctively, McFarland glanced to Conrad, then back to Eli. This was too good to be true. "Well"—he cleared his throat—"certainly"—he coughed again—"certainly, I could arrange that. That would be no problem at all."

Eli smiled. "Good. Then maybe you and Connie could work on the schedule."

Conrad stared as McFarland tried unsuccessfully to hide the smile spreading across his face. And why not? He'd set the perfect trap, and Eli had blindly strolled into it. No, he hadn't strolled in; he'd helped build it and purposely leaped into it! A sinking feeling filled Conrad's gut and spread through his limbs.

"I'd love to help," McFarland repeated, throwing another grin over at Conrad. "Anything I can do to help clarify this matter, you can count on me."

Julia did not relish heading down the paneled corridor to her father's office. It wasn't only because of the recurring dream, it was also because of the memories—sweet and bitter, tender and horrible. Still, that was where he kept his filing cabinets, and that was where she might find something, anything, to better enable her to make the correct decision. Because, despite what *she* thought of his current situation, as his attorney, it was more important to know what *he* thought. If there was something he'd saved in a file, something to further define his understanding of living wills or that all-elusive phrase, "heroic efforts," then it might help her better understand his wishes on the matter.

At least that's what she told herself as she made her way down the hall, as she took hold of the metal knob, opened the door, and headed for the filing cabinets. But no matter how many files she reviewed, no matter how she kept herself occupied flipping through them, she could not completely detach herself from this place or its past.

It was nearly midnight when she pushed the last of the heavy drawers shut and leaned against the cabinets with a sigh. There had been nothing. Just old articles, press releases, bios, contracts, and scripts from past segments—nothing to shed any light on his feelings or her decision. She hesitated a moment before finally allowing herself to look around the room.

So many memories.

She glanced over at the trophies on the shelf under the window. There were several more since the last time she'd been there. But something other than the trophies caught her attention. Amidst all of the dust and brass and Plexiglas set a yellowing baseball atop a child's teacup. She hadn't seen the ball in years, but recognized it immediately.

Slowly, almost cautiously, she stepped toward it. She reached out and carefully took it into her hands.

"Daddy? What happened, what's going on?"

"*It's a home run, Sweetheart!*" He grinned down at her as he clapped his hands with the other fans. "*He just hit a home run.*"

"*A home run!*" she cried. "*A home run?*"

"*Yes.*" He laughed at her excitement. "*Now he gets to run all around the bases and score a run.*"

"*A home run!*" little Julia shouted. "*He hit a home run!*"

Excitement overwhelmed her. She'd heard of home runs all of her life, but now to actually see one! Tears sprang to her eyes as she began to cry. "*A home run! He hit a home run!*"

Her father continued to laugh as he reached down to give her a hug. "*Are you okay?*"

"*Yes!*" she cried, watching the runner in awe. Then turning to her mother she shouted, "*Did you see it? He hit a home run!*"

"*Yes.*" Her mother grinned.

"*I mean just now . . . a real home run!*"

"*Yes.*" Her mother laughed as she glanced over to her father. "*I saw it, I saw it.*"

Then, suddenly, without a word, Dad turned and started to leave.

"*Daddy . . . Daddy, where are you going?*"

"*I'll be right back,*" he called as he stepped into the aisle and started up the concrete steps to the exit.

"*Daddy!*"

"*I'll be back in a minute.*"

And he was. Well, actually several minutes. And when he returned it was with a white, shiny baseball.

"*What is it?*" she asked.

"*It's the home-run ball. I bought it off the guy who caught it.*"

Her eyes widened in astonishment.

"Go ahead, take it."

At first, she was afraid to touch it.

"Go ahead, Jules, it's yours."

She looked up nervously to him. He nodded.

Then, ever so slowly, almost reverently, she reached out. He placed it in her hands and she turned it over and over. Once again tears leaped to her eyes. It was the home-run ball. Her daddy had gone out and brought her back the home-run baseball. The tears streamed down her cheeks, she was so overcome with joy, so overwhelmed by his love. She buried her face into his shirt and felt his big arms wrap around her. There was nothing this man wouldn't do for her. Nothing in the world.

Julia stared at the old, dusty ball for a long moment. What on earth was this doing with his awards, with the things that he'd fought and worked for his whole life? She glanced down at the faded teacup—a child's teacup from her old tea set. The toy tea set she and her father used to drink imaginary tea from—right here, right in the office. She glanced over at the desk—right under that desk.

Still holding the ball, she moved to the desk, pulled back the chair, and gently knelt down. The place underneath was impossibly small. It's a wonder they'd both been able to fit. But they had, on several occasions.

"Daddy, will we always be best friends?"

"Yes, Jules." He had smiled. *"We'll always be best friends."*

"And you'll never let anything bad happen to me?"

"I'll never ever let anything bad happen to you."

She smiled. *"Good. And I'll never let anything bad happen to you."*

"Good." He grinned. Then reaching out his hand the way she had taught him, with his little finger raised, he asked, *"Pinkie swear?"*

She giggled, delighted that he remembered, and reached out her own little finger to wrap it around his. *"Pinkie swear."*

Julia took a deep breath and slowly rose from the desk. "Pinkie swear," she murmured almost distastefully. Still holding the baseball, she walked round the desk and started for the door. Not once had she looked over at the leather couch. And not until this moment had she paused to consider the destruction performed on it. Rachel Thomas was her name. Some student intern. At least that's the one little Julia had caught him with. The one her mother had shouted and screamed and wept over. The one who had destroyed their—no, that wasn't right—the one *he* had destroyed their family with. How many more there had been, she didn't know. Two, three, a dozen, it didn't matter. Once a liar, always a liar. *A man is only as good as his word.* How many times had he told her that? Drilled it into her head? Made it her life's code? While, all that time, he was carrying out his destructive lies right in their own home. Right in their own room. *Their* room!

A man is only as good as his word. How right he was.

Arriving at the door, she turned back to the desk and tossed the ball onto it. It rolled across the papers, fell onto the floor, and disappeared into the shadows. It didn't matter where. She turned her back on the room, snapped off the light, and closed the door. She would not return.

CHAPTER NINE

The celebration outside Lewiston Community Fellowship was in full swing. What was supposed to be an after-service potluck had turned into quite a party. And for good reason. Of the forty or so members of the small, impoverished, black congregation, over half had been cured of some ailment—everything from diabetes to athlete's foot, breast cancer to canker sores. Then there was the Emerson boy whose hand had been missing since birth. Had been missing. Not anymore.

It had been several weeks since Conrad had seen such a concentration of miracles. Maybe it was because these people really believed. Or maybe it was because so few congregations were inviting Eli to speak that when he did he found it difficult to contain his enthusiasm and his love. Whatever the reason, the morning had been quite an event, and this afternoon was proving to be quite a celebration.

"Come on, brother!" The pastor slapped his big, meaty hand on Conrad's shoulder. "You ain't hardly touched that food." He was a large man, always chuckling and grinning, with a gold tooth that often caught the sunlight. And he was sweating, always sweating. Not that he could be blamed in this Texas heat. They'd been in the state three days now, and every day the temperature had easily hit the nineties.

Conrad glanced down at his paper plate. Most everything was fried. Some of it he recognized, some of it he was afraid to ask.

"An' if you're hankerin' for somethin' a little more substantial than lemonade . . ." The pastor lowered his voice slightly. "There's a cooler back of Ronnie Hendrick's pickup that don't seem to be runnin' out of beer."

Conrad glanced up at the grinning face.

"Tha's right." The big man chuckled as he dabbed the sweat off his forehead with a handkerchief. "Ronnie, he claims he only bought a couple six packs, but dang if I ain't already counted two, maybe three dozen empties. And they say it's better than anything they ever tasted!"

Conrad stole a look at Eli, who sat on the blistered front steps of the fellowship hall, chatting with several of the congregation. Somehow he suspected healings weren't the only miracles he'd performed that day.

"You call these clothes?" An old woman's voice rose from several lawn chairs over. "These ain't clothes—least not for men." Conrad turned to see Leon enduring a lecture from some white-haired grandmother. "Makes you look like a peacock. Or one of them foo-foo boys." Leon tried to shrug her off with a smile, but she was relentless. "You don't want people to be gettin' the wrong impression 'bout you, do you, son?"

"No, ma'am," he mumbled.

"What?"

"No, ma'am."

"Then what you wearin' girlie things like this for?"

Again he shrugged, and for the first time Conrad could remember, Leon Brewster didn't use his razor wit to fire off a snappy put-down—not that he could find space between her nonstop stream of words. Still, Conrad suspected that Leon's restraint had more to do with the day-to-day maturing taking place in him. Slowly but very surely, he could see Leon growing less concerned about drawing attention to himself and more concerned about others. This was no exception. Instead of shutting down the old woman, he glanced sheepishly about, until he connected with Will Patton, who smiled in both amusement and sympathy.

Will Patton—there was another. Like Leon, he was also changing. In fact, he almost seemed comfortable surrounded by these forty black people. Almost. Conrad was further impressed by Will's wisdom in trading in his muscle shirt for one whose sleeves were long enough to cover his racist tattoos.

But it wasn't just Leon and Will who were changing. It was everyone in the group. Each seemed to be undergoing their own maturing process. Jake was getting a handle on his temper and impetuousness; Brent and Scott (along with their mother) were slowly grasping the cost of real leadership; even shy, retiring Trevor seemed to be coming more and more out of his shell.

And then there was Suzanne, dear sweet Suzanne. What an incredible gift it was to have a second chance with her. But even she was being stretched. Just as Eli had said that Keith's and Conrad's greatest strength was their weakness, so he had said that Suzanne's greatest strength, the intense love she had for family, was hers.

On two separate occasions she had approached Eli, asking if he would fly back to Lebanon, Tennessee, at her family's expense, to heal her brother. And both times she had asked, he had declined. His response frustrated her, even made her angry. After all that she'd sacrificed for him, couldn't he at least do this for her? Even more frustrating was that, when she pressed him on the issue, his only explanation was, "It is for God's glory." *God's glory?* Her little brother was sick and dying . . . for *God's glory?* The answer made no sense. And with each e-mail from her sister describing his worsening condition, Suzanne's faith was being stretched to the limit.

Finally, there was Conrad's own growth—from curious doubter, to reluctant believer, to . . . well, he wasn't sure what he was now. But, for the first time in his life, that gnawing hunger, that haunting emptiness, was being filled. And it had nothing to do with becoming the best in his field, or owning the most toys, or bedding the most beauties. The last thought caused him to wince. Was that what all those affairs and marriages had been about? Trying to fill the void?

The stretching and growing were painful, there was no doubt about it—particularly the continual battle to give up everything that made sense and do it Eli's way. It was one thing to hear his profound teachings, but quite another to try and incorporate them in day-to-day living. And when Conrad wasn't frustrated at Eli's behavior (this current detour to Texas's death row being the most recent example), he was discouraged at his own lack of growth.

"Eli?" Suzanne emerged from the fellowship hall with the pastor's wife, a big-hipped woman who sweated almost as much as her husband. "Your mother's on the phone. She's down at the Imperial Motor Lodge."

Eli turned from the porch steps and looked up to her. "Is everything okay?"

Suzanne nodded. "She and your brothers just want to say hi."

"Great. Have them come on up."

"Already tried that," the pastor's wife answered. "Told her we had plenty a food and to bring the boys up and make herself at home."

"And . . ."

"I think . . ." Suzanne cleared her throat. "I think she just wants some time alone with the family. You know, just you and your brothers."

Eli turned and motioned to the group sitting on the brown lawn before him. "Tell her these here are my mother and brothers."

Silence stole over the group. The abruptness of the reply made some of the folks uneasy. He turned back to Suzanne, fixing her a look. He spoke clearly and evenly, making sure she understood the depth of his statement. "Tell her that the ones who hear what I have to say, and do it—tell her they are closer to me than any mother or brother. Tell her *they* are my family."

Conrad watched as Suzanne hesitated a moment. He knew full well what Eli meant, and he could see her weighing the implications in her own life. Finally she asked, "Is that really what you want me to tell her, Eli? Are you sure?"

Still holding her gaze, he nodded. "Yes, Suzanne. I'm sure."

"All right, then." She turned hesitantly, then nodded to the pastor's wife. The two of them reentered the building.

They'd barely disappeared before the pastor called out, "Say, Eli—Eli, I want ya ta meet a couple friends a mine." Eli turned to see him resting his big, meaty hands on two gentlemen's shoulders—one, an older white man with distinguished gray hair, the other a slender black man with thin, wiry wrists. Both wore suits, and they looked as uncomfortable in the hot sun as they did out of place with the casually dressed group. The pastor nodded to the white gentleman first. "This here is Reverend Caldwell from the First Assembly of Lewiston." He turned to the second. "And this is Brother Hudson from God's Holy Sanctuary."

"Hi, fellows." Eli nodded.

"Both of 'em are on Lewiston's Board of Clergy. They heard you were in town, and they take, how shall I put it, a rather dim view of your visit to our fine community." There was no missing the mischief in the pastor's eyes.

"I see," Eli said. "Well, please, gentlemen, make yourselves comfortable. I was just about to tell a story, one that you might find interesting."

"Thank you," Brother Hudson answered stiffly.

Both men looked for a place to sit. The grass was certainly inappropriate for their dress, and the people lounging in the lawn furniture and folding chairs felt no compulsion to volunteer their seats.

"Actually," Reverend Caldwell gave an awkward smile, "it might be better if we just stand."

"Suit yourself," Eli said. "But maybe off to the back so the folks behind you can see?"

"Oh, certainly," Brother Hudson coughed self-consciously. "Certainly."

The two slunk toward the back under the amused smiles of the group.

"Now, where were we?" Eli asked.

"You was gonna tell us 'bout some company," a teen in a sleeveless T-shirt replied.

"But you hadn't decided what type," a heavyset mother added.

An elder in a frayed sports coat spoke up. "Make it an insurance company."

"How 'bout a beautician school?"

"Or a—"

"Thanks," Eli grinned, "I think I've got one." He took a brief moment to gather his thoughts. Conrad scanned the group. He estimated there were nearly thirty people there. Thirty Southern black folks sitting in the hot, Texas sun waiting to hear some West Coast Jewish kid weave a story. He shook his head in amusement. The miracles just kept coming.

Eli began. "Once there was a computer software company."

"That will work," the elder agreed.

"The owner was a genius. I mean, this guy created the absolute, top-of-the-line software. He invested wisely, hired the best managers, the best employees—"

"Had great health care benefits?" the mother asked.

The group chuckled, and Eli agreed. "Had great health care benefits, plus a retirement plan, plus a day-care center, plus profit sharing. I mean this guy had it all. Plus money—lots and lots of money."

"All right, Bill Gates."

"I'm talking bigger than Bill Gates."

Someone whistled. Eli grinned. Once again his ease and camaraderie with the group were obvious. But it was more than camaraderie. It was a joy and a love that he had for them, for each of them. And it was a love they sensed and readily returned.

Eli continued. "Eventually he goes off on a long trip. Spends the summer in Switzerland."

"How 'bout Bermuda?" a younger woman called out.

"Let the man speak," the elder insisted.

"Sorry."

"Anyway, when he logs on to check how things are going, he realizes that the managers have locked him out. They've built a firewall he can't go around. So he calls up one of his corporate vice presidents and asks him to visit the plant to find out what's happening. But the guy—"

"Or gal," the younger woman corrected.

Eli nodded. "Or gal, shows up, and the managers won't let her in. Not only won't they let her in, but they slap a restraining order on her, refusing to let her anywhere near the place."

"They can do that?"

"Let the man speak."

"So the owner, he tries again with another corporate V.P. Only this time they beat him and throw him out with all kinds of threats on his life."

"So he finally comes back himself?" the mother asked.

Eli shook his head. "No, not yet."

Conrad watched as Eli grew more and more involved, almost as if he were taking the story personally.

"He sends yet another V.P., and he too is beaten and thrown out. So finally, finally, he decides to send his own son, his heir who will one day inherit the company. I mean, surely they'll respect his own son, right?"

The group listened, unsure how to respond. They had also noticed Eli's growing intensity.

"But they don't. Not in the slightest. Instead, when the owner's son finally arrives and enters the building, they grab him. Then they beat him. Worse than that . . ." He took a deep breath. "Worse than that, they eventually decide to kill him." Eli's eyes faltered, then dropped to the cracked sidewalk in front of him. Silence stole over the group.

Finally Brother Hudson, one of the visiting clergy, spoke up. "Why's that?"

Eli turned to him, then quietly answered, "You tell me."

The visitor stiffened under his gaze.

"So they can have all the profits," the young woman suggested.

Eli turned to her and nodded.

"Or maybe so they can stay in power," another offered.

"What happens next?" the elder asked.

Eli looked at him a moment, then continued. "Finally the owner has had enough. He comes back home. With the sheriff and a truckload of deputies, he enters the building. And what do you think he does?"

"Fires 'em all," the teen in the sleeveless T-shirt shouted.

"And tries the managers for murder," another said. "That's his son we're talkin' about."

Eli nodded. "Yes, he fires everyone on payroll, and he presses charges against all of the department heads for murder."

"What happens to the company?" the young woman asked.

"Ah . . ." Ever so slightly the sadness lifted from Eli's eyes. "This is where it gets interesting. The owner then goes out into the streets and hires anyone who wants to work for him."

"Anyone?" the teen asked.

"That's right," Eli smiled. "Anyone at all. It doesn't matter how unqualified they are—how bad their work record has been. Not only does he make them his new employees with even greater benefits, he also allows them to become co-owners of the company."

The group approved. A few clapped.

"And the moral to all this is . . ." It was Brother Hudson again. "What exactly are you trying to say?"

A large man sitting with his wife and kids answered, "The owner, he's supposed to be like God, right?"

Eli looked at him, his smile broadening. "That's right."

"And the company," the teen added, "that's like the whole world."

"No, fool," his buddy chided. "It's like the religious establishment or somethin', ain't that right, Eli?"

"Right again."

"And those vice presidents?" the young woman asked.

It was the pastor's turn to answer. "I believe those are the prophets of God, the ones who kept trying to turn the people back to Him."

"Oooh," an older woman teased. "Very good, Pastor."

He chuckled, flashing his gold tooth. "Why thank you, Sister Benson."

"And the managers?" Reverend Caldwell's voice came from the back. It was brittle and cool.

Eli turned to him but did not answer.

Caldwell cleared his throat and repeated a little louder. "And the managers that were thrown out, who exactly did you intend them to be?"

Eli's smile slowly faded. "It sounds to me like you already have your answer," he said.

"Why don't you enlighten us?" Reverend Hudson replied.

"The answer lies in the Scriptures you are so fond of quoting." Slowly, Eli rose to his feet. The group exchanged glances, unsure what was about to happen. Eli began to quote, "'The foundation which the builders rejected, the very cornerstone, is the chief cornerstone for the entire building.'"

The two visitors remained unmoving, staring hard at Eli. He took a step closer, his voice growing more quiet, even more intense. "And every person, regardless of their education, regardless of their wealth, regardless of their high religious position . . . every person who falls upon this stone will be broken to pieces." The group remained silent. Only the clatter of dry leaves stirring in the afternoon breeze could be heard.

Eli continued, speaking directly to the two men. "And whoever this stone falls upon will be smashed and ground into dust."

The silence grew as the entire group digested what had been said. But Conrad already understood. And he was already lowering his eyes, already shaking his head. Eli had done it again.

"Maybe I wouldn't have to go other places if my needs were met here!"

"How dare you!"

"Daddy, don't leave!" Julia was between them, in the living room.

"Maybe if I got the respect I deserve I wouldn't have to—"

"Respect! Don't you dare talk to me about respect!"

"Please, Daddy . . ."

"You with your bimbos, your—"

"Rachel is twice the woman you'll ever be. She's—"

"Get out!"

"At least she knows how to treat a man."

"Get out!"

"Mommy!"

"She knows how to be a real woman!"

"Get out!" Her mother's voice was breaking. *"Get out!"*

"My pleasure!" He spun around and headed for the door. She started after him. *"Daddy!"*

But he was outside and slamming it before she arrived. The windows in the old house shuddered.

"DADDY!"

But Daddy was gone. Daddy was gone and only her mother remained, sobbing.

"Don't cry, Mommy." She raced to her mother and threw her arms around her legs, clinging tightly, burying her wet face into her skirt. *"Don't cry, Mommy, don't cry."* Her mother's hand reached down, absentmindedly stroking the top of her head. Julia looked up at her through the tears. *"He'll be back,"* she choked. *"He promised. He'll never leave me. He promised . . ."*

But he did not come back. Never again. At least to them.

Now, twenty years later, Julia leaned against the doorway of her old room, staring out into the living room, lost in the memory. It had been a long, excruciating day. Too long. She turned and headed into her bedroom, suspecting that tomorrow would be no different.

"Why didn't you tell me sooner?"

"I wasn't sure until last night. Trevor's waiting outside to take me to the bus station now."

Conrad remained standing near the door. He watched as Suzanne flitted about the camper she'd been sharing with Maggie. The place always smelled of scented candles, a mixture of orange and cinnamon, he thought. And it always contained a certain warmth and hominess. A peace. Except this morning. This morning Suzanne scurried about, busying herself with last-minute preparations to leave. He knew she was upset. He could tell by the way she kept her back to him, the way she wouldn't let their eyes meet.

"Did you talk to Eli?" he asked. "Does he know?"

He caught a moment's hesitation before she answered. "Yes."

"What did he say?"

"He said what he always says, 'Michael's sickness is for the glory of God.'"

"I mean about your leaving, what did he say about your leaving?"

Suzanne slowed to a stop, her back still to him. She took a trembling, uneven breath. Conrad immediately spotted it and crossed to her. He wrapped his arms around her. "It's okay," he whispered, "it's okay."

She sniffed softly.

"What did he say?" Conrad repeated more gently.

She took another breath, steadying herself. "You know how he's always saying our life is made of choices?"

Conrad nodded.

"He said if I choose to follow him, if that's my decision, then I must hate my life. I must hate my mother and father, I must hate my sister . . . and I must hate my brother."

"He said *that*? To *you*?"

She looked down and nodded.

Conrad grew cold with anger. This was too much. "Where is he?"

"At the overpass. There's a homeless woman there that lives in the cemetery. People think she's possessed."

Conrad knew the place. It was a quarter mile away, easy walking distance from the campground where they'd spent the night. He released her and turned toward the door. "I'll talk to him. Don't leave until I—"

She grabbed his arm. "Connie, no."

He turned back to her. "Why?"

"Because . . . he's right."

"What?" She still would not look at him. He continued. "Telling you that you're supposed to hate yourself, that you're supposed to hate your brother?" There was no holding back his indignation. He wanted to pace, but there was little room in the camper. "What about all this talk of love, all of this—"

"No." She finally looked up to him. "He's not saying I shouldn't love my family."

"Then what is he—"

"He's talking about comparison. He's saying my love for him should be so great that by comparison it's like I hate my family."

"That's crazy. They're your family. Michael's your brother. And Eli's just your . . . your . . ."

"My what?" she asked.

Conrad looked at her but said nothing.

"He claims to be the Lord, Connie, the only way to his Father."

Now it was Conrad's turn to avoid Suzanne's eyes. It was one of the incongruities he still struggled with.

"And I believe he is."

His eyes raised to hers.

She nodded. "I do. But . . ." She took a ragged breath. "But he's not *my* Lord, not if I put my family ahead of him. Not if I love them more."

"What are you saying?"

"I love them more than him, Connie. I love my family more than the Lord. And if that's the case . . ." She swallowed hard. "If that's the case, then I can no longer follow him." She turned, looking for something to busy herself.

Conrad stared, dumbfounded. Then suddenly he declared, "I'm going too."

"No."

Her response surprised him. "Why not? Listen, if you're not good enough for him, then I'm certainly not—"

She turned back to him. "But you are, Connie."

"What?"

"Following Eli has nothing to do with how good you are. It's about how much you love him. And you love him, Connie. Look where you are, how far you've come. You've even walked away from your work, something I could never have dragged you from."

"I'm on a sabbatical."

She shook her head. "No. You love him more than your work, Connie. You love him more than your friends, your family. In truth, you love him more than—"

"No." He shook his head. "I do not love him more than you!"

She looked up into his eyes, holding his gaze. "Yes, you do," she whispered softly.

He shook his head, but before he could continue, she gently pressed her finger to his lips. "And you should."

He stood, searching her face. A moment passed before she suddenly reached over and scooped up a large, black gym bag from the counter. "He needs you, Connie. And you need him. More than you'll ever need me." She threw the bag over her shoulder and started for the door.

"Suzanne . . ." He moved to block her, his voice growing hoarse. "I lost you once . . ." He struggled against the emotion. "Please, I don't want to lose you again."

She looked sadly at him. "What is it Eli says? In order to find your life, you have to lose it? To keep something, we have to let it go?"

He searched her eyes. They were as shiny with tears as his. But he had no argument. And she knew it. Ever so gently, she raised up on her toes and gave him a kiss on the cheek. Then, without a word, she moved past him, opened the door, and stepped out into the morning sun.

He remained standing, head spinning, putting his hand on the counter for support.

"That all you taking?" Trevor called. Conrad turned and looked out to see her approach the boy's beat-up Toyota.

"It's all I need," she said. She opened the passenger door and tossed the gym bag into the back. Then, before ducking inside, she turned to Conrad and spoke one last time. "Everybody has priorities. Everybody has to make a choice. This is mine."

"Suzanne . . ." But he stopped, having no idea what he could say.

She paused, giving a sad sort of smile. Finally she turned, entered the car, and shut the door.

"Suzanne . . ." He eased down the aluminum steps.

Trevor dropped the Toyota into gear. The car lurched slightly, then pulled forward. Sun briefly glinted off her window, and when the glare disappeared she was still looking at him. She gave a final wave, then brought her hand to her mouth and turned away. Conrad knew she was crying, though it was hard to see through the moisture in his own eyes. He continued watching as the car bounced along the gravel surface, raising a small cloud of dust, before it pulled out onto the main road and disappeared.

Not two minutes later, Conrad was storming toward the overpass, ready to give Eli a piece of his mind. Suzanne was the best there was, worth all of the others put together. And the best still wasn't good enough? Then who was? "For the glory of God," he'd said. Yeah, right. More like for his own egotistical pleasures. "Hate others and love him." It was definitely time for a wake-up call.

Hot humidity already saturated the Texas morning air, and as he walked, there was no missing the smell of sage and mesquite. He'd barely crested the rise to the over-pass when he saw the police cars. Two of them. And a third down on the highway below. He picked up his pace, breaking into a stiff jog. As he approached, he moved closer to the steel railing for a better look. Down below was a red-and-white tow truck with the name Sorbet Towing painted across its door. The driver was busy hoisting up a white Dodge Caravan, its windshield shattered in two, maybe three places, the rest covered with spiderwebbing. Not far away, another tow truck had just pulled beside a burgundy Lexus. Its front end had been completely demolished, and its windshield was as shattered as the Dodge's. Directly below, scattered across the pavement, were the bodies of several dead animals. A dozen, maybe more. Cats, from what he could tell.

He glanced up and spotted Jake and Leon heading his way. "Hey," he shouted, then slowed to catch his breath. "What happened?"

Eli was about thirty yards behind them, talking to one of the officers. By his side stood what must have been the homeless woman, the demoniac. But instead of rolling around or writhing and screaming, she remained calm, listening as Eli spoke.

"What happened?" Conrad repeated as the men arrived.

"The cat lady back there—" Jake jerked his thumb over his shoulder. "She had a bunch of those demon things inside her. Some of the locals wanted Eli to come over and help her."

"It's the same old thing," Leon said, pretending to be bored. "The usual screamin' and swearin'. But finally their leader or whatever it was inside her, he begs Eli to throw them into a bunch of the woman's cats. She has like a hundred or so."

"And Eli does," Jake explained. "But the cats, they suddenly start leaping off the road like a bunch of lemmings, right down onto the highway, hitting some of the cars. None of the people were hurt, but there were definitely a few fender benders."

Conrad glanced over the railing at the dead cats below, then up at Eli who had just shaken the officer's hand and was turning to leave with the woman. "Is she okay?" he asked.

"Oh, sure," Jake said.

"But here's the thing," Leon added. "Soon as the local police get word, they come up here and threaten to throw our rear ends in jail if we don't leave."

"Why?"

"Seems Eli has caused too much damage."

"But," Conrad stammered, "he just healed that woman, he just gave her back her life."

"That's what I mean," Leon said, shaking his head. "One life completely healed in exchange for a couple accidents. Now you tell me what's more important."

Jake shrugged. "Guess everybody's got their priorities."

The similiarity of the phrase to Suzanne's caught Conrad off guard. "What did you say?"

"I said they had a choice between Eli and some busted autos—so they voted for the autos. Go figure." Jake shook his head, and the two moved past, heading toward the campsite, leaving a bewildered Conrad behind, trying to digest what he'd just heard.

"Connie!"

He glanced up as Eli and the woman approached. Though it was the end of June, she was dressed in the usual multilayered clothing and heavy, worn coat of the homeless. Something about seeing the two of them together, their smiles and friendliness, increased his resentment. And the closer they approached, the greater that resentment grew.

"Connie," Eli called again, grinning. "I want you to meet Elizabeth Warden."

Conrad did not return the smile. His mind was still back with Suzanne, still back with her tear-filled departure. And Eli's words to her still rang in his ears. Before he knew it, his own words came. Before he could stop himself, he demanded, "How much more do you want from us?" The intensity in his voice surprised even himself.

The joy in Eli's eyes faded.

"How much more?" Conrad was practically seething.

"To follow me?" Eli asked.

"How much more do we have to give up?"

"You already know that answer, Connie."

"How much!"

Eli paused a moment, searching Conrad's eyes. But Conrad would not back down. Finally, ever so gently, Eli gave his answer. It was very mild and yet absolutely firm:

"Everything."

CHAPTER TEN

"I f you ask me, this whole discussion is a waste of time."

"Why do you say that, Mr. Lazlo?" EBN anchor-person Karen Deutsch asked. She looked directly into the camera's prompter where she could see the video image of Herbert Lazlo, the father whose son had been murdered eight years earlier by Ellen Perkins. He and his wife sat in their darkly paneled living room some three hundred miles away in the tiny community of Kirby, while here at the Women's Correctional Facility in Gatesville, Texas, Karen Deutsch sat with Ellen Perkins, Eli Shepherd, and the rest of the EBN remote video crew. It was the video conference that Gerald McFarland had agreed to set up—the interview that Conrad had pleaded, had begged Eli to avoid at any cost.

Lazlo's answer was husky and to the point. "There weren't no fancy TV people and preachers around when she was butchering my boy. I don't recall nobody here discussing whether or not he should get to live. And there weren't nobody offerin' to give *him* a second chance when she was hacking off pieces of his body and he was screamin' for mercy!"

Conrad stood just out of camera range, watching as Ellen Perkins closed her eyes and quietly lowered her head. At twenty-five, she looked like the girl next door: shortly cropped auburn hair, freckles across the bridge of her nose, and a smile full of personality. But she was not smiling now. Nor was Eli, who sat beside her.

It had taken most of the afternoon for the EBN crew to set up in this large conference room of beige cinderblock walls, yellowed linoleum, and white acoustical ceiling. It was at least a four-camera setup—three stationed around the newly finished oak table here at the Correctional Facility, and one, maybe two, over at the Lazlos' home in Kirby. One hundred yards outside the barred windows and wire-meshed glass sat the network's finest remote—a semitrailer full of state-of-the-art audio and video equipment. It hummed quietly, pumping electricity through thick black cables to a half dozen glaring quartz lights strategically placed around the table. In exchange, another set of cables carrying the meeting's sounds and images snaked their way back to the truck's control room, where the director called the angles and beamed them across the country for the live telecast. EBN had spared no expense on this shoot, and Conrad certainly understood why. A trap this elaborate and thorough called for only the best equipment and crew.

Karen Deutsch responded gently to the father's accusation. "Your son's murder was eight years ago, Mr. Lazlo. People change. You can see that Ms. Perkins is a different person. Look at all the good she's done. Would demanding justice by putting an end to that goodness make things any better?"

Suddenly Mrs. Lazlo blurted out, "How much good would my son have done if *he'd* been allowed to live?" She was a frail, bony woman who, until now, had been able to keep her emotions in check. "He was a God-fearing boy, always helping others and wanting to do good. But we'll never know how much good he could have done, will we?" Her voice began to tremble. "Will we!"

It was the perfect dramatic moment, and Karen Deutsch used it to its fullest potential. Slowly, she turned to the young woman sitting across the table. "Mrs. Lazlo has an excellent point, Ellen. If you showed no mercy to their son, why should you expect any in return?"

Ellen remained staring at the table. "I can't," she answered hoarsely. "Not if people are looking for justice." She began to slowly shake her head. "I can't."

Conrad cringed as Eli reached over and discretely took her hand. It might have been the right thing to do, but not with twenty million viewers watching.

Karen Deutsch turned to her camera. "That's really the question, isn't it? Justice or mercy. That's the dilemma in a nutshell."

Conrad glanced across the room at McFarland. Those were the exact words he'd used on Eli at the park in Tulsa, back when he'd first presented the challenge. Obviously, Deutsch had been thoroughly briefed and carefully coached.

She continued as if thinking through these observations for the very first time. "Does one embrace justice and capital punishment ... or oppose justice and plead for mercy? The two really are incompatible; they cannot exist side by side." Then, turning to Eli, she asked, "I was wondering, Eli—I mean, it's never really been clear. Which of the two positions do you hold?"

There it was. Subtle, smooth. Perfect in its simplicity. The entire interview, the video link, the millions of dollars of equipment, it had all been positioned for this one question.

Conrad knew that the answer didn't matter. It was the perfect no-win setup that would expose Eli's inconsistency. One that Dr. Kerston and the boys back in Georgia must already be celebrating over. Since the beginning of his public ministry, Eli had stressed these two opposites: holiness and mercy, holiness and mercy. McFarland had been right. It was a paradox; the two could not possibly coexist. And now, finally, he would have the opportunity to discredit Eli in front of the entire nation.

"Eli?" Deutsch repeated.

Eli smiled quietly. "I'm afraid you're asking the wrong question."

"What do you mean?"

"You're giving me two options, 'A' or 'B.'"

"Is there a problem with that?"

"Not unless the answer happens to be 'Three.'"

"What?" Deutsch asked. "I'm sorry, I don't understand."

"I've come to heal souls, Karen, to save lives. I'm not here to play politics."

"But surely this is a valid ques—"

"Let the person who is holy, the one with no sin, be the one to give Ellen the lethal injection."

Silence stole over the room. "I take it that means you're opposed to capital punishment then?" Deutsch asked.

Eli shook his head. "The issue is not capital punishment." He turned to Ellen. "The issue is whether you have sincerely turned from your sins and have earnestly asked for God's forgiveness."

Ellen looked deeply into his eyes and swallowed. "I have, Mr. Shepherd, with all my heart." Her voice grew thicker as she continued. "I have turned from my sin, and a day doesn't go by that I don't ask God Almighty to somehow forgive me."

"Then"—Eli broke into his famous grin—"you are forgiven."

"And what about our son?" Mr. Lazlo demanded over the video link. "What about the Scriptures demanding blood to be shed for blood! What about God's justice?"

Deutsch nodded, and being the calm voice of reason, asked, "That's true, Eli. Doesn't the Bible clearly state that, except for the shedding of blood, there is no forgiveness?"

"Yes, it does," Eli agreed. "And the Bible is always correct."

"But you just said she was forgiven."

"Yes."

"You can't have it both ways."

Eli nodded, "Yes."

The anchorperson shook her head. "'Yes' is no answer. If Ellen here is forgiven, then where's God's justice? Whose blood is going to be shed for her crime?"

"Mine."

"Pardon me?"

"The blood of God will be shed, instead of hers."

"The blood of—what are you saying?"

"I've forgiven Ellen's sins."

"You? You can't do that."

"Why not?"

"What about the Law of Moses? The Scriptures?"

"They are being fulfilled."

"How?"

"Through me."

Karen Deutsch hesitated, unsure how to continue. "Eli, only God can forgive sin."

"That's right."

"Are you ... are you claiming to be God?"

He leaned toward her slightly. "Listen to me very carefully, Karen. Before the Scriptures were written, before the Law was given, before Moses or anyone else existed ... I am."

"Eli ... are you saying you're God?"

Eli paused just long enough to make sure his answer was clearly understood. And then he repeated the words: "I am."

Conrad, Karen Deutsch, Ellen, McFarland, the crew, the entire room stared in absolute astonishment and stunned shock.

Julia's eyes had barely closed before the early morning sun was blazing into the room. Disoriented, she bolted up and looked around as reality slowly filtered in. She was back in the bedroom of her childhood—that warm, safe place that had been the center of the universe for so many years. It had gone through several transformations since she'd left ... sewing room, TV room, rec room, and depending on whom her father was married to at the time, the bedroom of various stepsiblings. But, first and foremost, it was hers. It would always be hers.

She eased herself back down onto the pillow, snuggling between the sheets, hoping for a few more moments of peace. But peace did not come. Instead, she remembered that today was the day. Today was the day she would decide if her father lived or died.

Wearily, she rose from the bed. In record time she showered and slipped into the same business suit she'd worn the day before. She shuffled into the kitchen and rummaged around the cupboards until she found a box of snack bars. She took two.

"I'll do the dishes when I get back."

"You'll do no such thing, young lady."

"Mom . . . they're waiting."

"Then they'll have to wait just a little bit longer."

"I'll do them when I get back."

"Julia . . ."

Ignoring her, Julia started out of the kitchen.

"Julia!" Her mother grabbed her arm.

"Let go!"

"You will not leave this house until you do those dishes!"

She whirled around at her. *"You can't tell me what to do! You don't own me!"*

There was no missing the surprise on her mother's face. *"Julia!"*

"You're not my boss!"

"Jul—"

"That's why Daddy left! Isn't it? All you did was boss him around! Well, I'm not being bossed around. Not by you. Not by some stupid old cow who—"

Her mother's slap came so fast that both of them were shocked.

Julia was the first to recover, her eyes brimming with tears. *"It's you!"* she blurted. *"You're why he left! It's not me, it's you! You're why he doesn't want to come home!"*

Suddenly her mother's face filled with understanding. *"Oh, Julia . . ."*

Julia took a step back. *"It's not me, it's you! You made him leave. You're why he doesn't love us!"*

"Julia . . ." Her mother was reaching out.

She pushed her hands away. *"It's you, it's you, it's—"*

"Julia . . ."

"It's you, it's you—"

At last her mother grabbed her hands, pulling them down, wrapping her arms around her. *"Oh, Julia . . . Julia, Sweetheart . . ."*

The fight had drained from her, and she melted into her mother's embrace, sobbing.

"It's okay, Sweetheart," her mother soothed, *"it's okay."*

"Why, Momma?" she wailed. *"Why did he leave us?"*

"Shhh, baby. It's okay."

"How could he leave—" She took a shuddering breath. *"How could he leave and make memories with someone else!"*

"I don't know." Her mother was crying too.

"How could he—"

"I don't know, baby."

"How could he . . . how could he . . ."

Julia leaned against the kitchen counter a moment longer, lost in the memory. Then, cursing herself for her softness, she straightened and headed out of the kitchen to gather her things.

It was time to leave. Time to make a decision. And the sooner the better.

"I just think you made a mistake when you asked me to come along."

"Why's that?" Eli asked.

"Every time you turn around, I'm disagreeing with you."

"That's all part of the process, Connie."

"Process?"

"The dying process. You heard me say that the first day we met. Unless a seed falls to the ground and dies, it cannot bear fruit."

"But does it always . . ." Conrad took a weary breath. "Does it always have to be so difficult?"

Eli chuckled as they continued traipsing up the Arkansas mountain. Actually, to call it a mountain might be an exaggeration; it was more like a very large hill near the base of the Ozarks, not far from Fort Smith. Once again, the air hung heavy with humidity, causing Conrad to drip in perspiration while struggling to catch his breath. Then, of course, there were the insects. A recent bout with chiggers had left his ankles raw and itching. Today's specialties seemed to be flies and mosquitoes. But Conrad was not complaining. He was glad to be here. Jake and his brother, Robert, followed several steps behind. They were the only ones from the group who had been invited. For whatever reason, Eli had felt the need to spend special time with the three of them this afternoon.

Eli continued. "All your life, you've been taught to think with fleshly logic. And, admittedly, you've become quite good at it. But you're more than flesh, Connie. You're spirit. And to understand things of the Spirit, you must die and be reborn in spirit."

"You're not suggesting that I crawl back in my mother's womb and start at the beginning, are you?"

Eli smiled. "Not physically. But in many ways you *have* had to start at the beginning."

"Learning these 'Kingdom of God' principles," Conrad said.

Eli nodded.

"That's what I'm talking about. It seems I no sooner get a handle on one of those principles than you turn around and raise the stakes on me. I mean, first there's this business of you being the only way to the Father. Then that our method of doing things is all backwards compared to yours, then this business of losing our lives to find it. And now your claims of actually being God?"

"It's not so easy to accept, is it?"

"Or to live. But when I finally make the leap and try to embrace these things, you raise the bar again . . . and then again."

There was a moment of silence before Eli finally spoke. "Connie, when I left Heaven and took on your humanity, it was to cleanse you and draw you closer to my Divinity. I don't want you reborn but then walking around like a baby the rest of your life. I want you reborn so you can become a mature man of God. I want you to be led by the Spirit, not your flesh. I want you to become like me."

Conrad snorted in disbelief. "There's no way I'll ever be like you."

"If you keep saying yes to me, that's exactly what you'll become."

Conrad looked at him.

"Those are your options," Eli said. "You can become more and more like me, or you can continue crawling around like a baby, reborn but never maturing. The choice is yours."

"Choices," Conrad mused, as he grabbed a twig from a rhododendron and began to methodically snap it. "You're always forcing us to make choices."

"That's the game plan, my friend—encouraging you to choose my way over your way, to choose my wisdom over the world's wisdom . . . to choose my Spirit over your flesh. It's all a matter of choice."

"You sound like a professor friend of mine back in California."

"Dr. Endo?"

Conrad's mouth opened. "You know him?"

"Of course I know him."

"About his theories? You're familiar with parallel universes?"

"Familiar with them?" Eli grinned. "I created them."

Conrad slowed to a stop. "Then you know . . ." He fought to keep his voice level. "You know about the car accident?"

Eli smiled warmly. "I was there when you cried out to me, Connie. I was there when you *chose* to seek my help."

Conrad remained staring, slack jawed. But before he could recover, Eli turned back to Jake and Robert. "Okay, guys, this looks as good a place as any. Let's stop here."

The two men came to a halt beside them.

"Hey, Connie," Jake asked, "you okay? You look like you've seen a ghost."

Conrad turned to him. He tried to nod, but wasn't sure he succeeded. He glanced about. It appeared that they'd reached the top of the mountain. They were in a small clearing, not more than fifteen feet by twenty. Through the spruce and pines, he caught glimpses of the valley stretching out below—mostly bluegrass and pastureland. A warm breeze crawled up the side of the mountain, barely brushing against them and having absolutely no effect upon the number of insects.

"I'm about to make an important decision," Eli said, throwing an amused glance at Conrad, "a very important *choice.* But I want to make certain it's my Father's will. I want to make certain I'm hearing Him correctly as we enter this last phase of my work."

"Last phase?" Robert asked.

Eli nodded. "The phase that will bridge the gap everyone is so concerned about, the gap between my Father's holiness and His mercy." Eli hesitated, perhaps hoping for some response. There was none . . . well, except for Jake, who could never endure any silence for too long.

"What's that got to do with us?" he asked.

Conrad saw disappointment flicker across Eli's eyes. Then, just as quickly, it disappeared. "I brought you up here because I'd like you to pray with me."

"That's it?" Robert asked. "We came all the way up here just to pray?"

"It's the most important thing you can do, Robert, and up here there will be no distractions."

"Sure." Jake shrugged. "We can do that."

Robert agreed. "No problem."

Eli nodded, a trace of the sadness returning. "How about over there?" he said, pointing to a fallen log resting near the edge of the clearing.

They strolled to it, then sat down, stretching out and making themselves comfortable on the thick carpet of pine needles. Well, all except for Eli. He seemed anything but comfortable. A little agitated, maybe. A little concerned, absolutely. But definitely not comfortable.

Once they had settled in, Eli waited a long moment. When no one volunteered to start, he began. He prayed on his knees. He usually did. It was a ritual of his that everyone had grown accustomed to. "Father . . . Father, we thank You for Your unfathomable goodness to us. Thank You for loving me, thank You for loving these friends You have given me . . . more than they even love themselves. And, Father, we thank You for Your faithfulness, that You can always be trusted, no matter what the . . ."

Conrad tried to pay attention and focus upon the prayer, but it was no use. His mind continued to swim with Eli's last words about parallel universes . . . and about his accident. The accident he'd nearly forgotten—and for good reason. Everything had returned to normal. Well, everything but Conrad's life. Thanks to Eli, that seemed to have changed radically.

He readjusted himself, leaning against the fallen log, waving off the droning bugs, and finally finding a comfortable spot in the needles. What had Suzanne said— *"Look where you are, look how far you've come?"* Dear, sweet Suzanne. She'd only been gone six days, but it felt like a month. They'd e-mailed several times, called almost as many. Michael had taken a turn for the worse. In fact, it was doubtful he'd make it through the night. Once again Suzanne had pleaded with Eli to come, and once again he had refused, always with the same explanation . . . "It has to be this way for God's glory. It's better that I don't come."

Conrad shook his head. It seemed so unfair. Eli was so quick to reach out and assist strangers, like that cat woman on the overpass. But when it came to those he was closest to, who loved him the deepest, he seemed to actually withhold that help. It reminded him of Coach Simmons back in high school, the track coach who, after sending the rest of the team to the showers, kept his star athletes and made them run one more lap. Even when they insisted they couldn't take another step, he ordered them to go one more. That's how it was with Eli ... one more lap, one more test, one more inch of growth. *"I don't want you crawling around like a baby the rest of your life ..."*

Conrad wasn't sure when he'd dozed off, but he knew when he awoke. For there, not fifteen feet in front of him, stood Eli. At least he thought it was Eli. It was hard to tell from the blinding whiteness of his clothes. They were as bright as the sun. So bright that it was nearly impossible to see his face. And standing there beside him were two others, clothed in equal brightness. At first Conrad thought they might be angels. But he saw no wings. Weren't angels supposed to have wings? He wasn't sure. But he was sure that they looked like men, like Eli except older. And, instead of jeans and T-shirts, they appeared to be wearing robes.

Neither of them noticed Conrad, Jake, or Robert. They were too deep in discussion with Eli—something about death and his fear of being "cut off from the Father." The two seemed to understand, and although it was impossible to tell who was speaking and to whom, the voices kept reassuring Eli that he was in "the center of the Father's will."

To his left, Conrad heard a disturbance. He turned and saw Jake staggering to his feet. The big man's eyes were as wide as saucers and he was shaking like a leaf. He was in such shock that he resorted to what he did best: Talk. "Eli ..." he stammered. "Eli, this is great. I mean, what's happening. I'd love to get a photo, you know, to remember this by. How 'bout a drink? Are your friends thirsty? I could run back to the camper, get a camera, grab a few sodas, it would only take a couple minutes."

Of course Jake didn't exactly make sense. What do glowing creatures drink? And were they really in the mood for a photo op? But it didn't make any difference to Jake, as long as he was talking. Unfortunately, all he succeeded in doing was disrupting their conversation. And with that disruption, came another phenomenon, even more frightening . . .

The air surrounding them began to sparkle, to glow like a bright fog. Only it wasn't just a fog of vapor, it was a fog of light—a light that grew brighter and brighter until it was so brilliant that Conrad could no longer make out any shapes or forms—no faces, no trees, not even the forest floor, only light. Terrible, frightening light. But it was more than light. It was a power, a majesty so intense, so terrifying that Conrad found it difficult to breathe. He opened his mouth, he started to cry out, but no sound would come. He tried rising to his feet, but he was too paralyzed to move. His heart pounded in his ears, loud and fast. Now there was only the pounding and the power and the horror—the paralyzing, terrifying horror.

And then, when he was certain he could stand no more . . . there was more. A voice exploded in his head. But it wasn't in his head, it was in his body, in the ground at his feet, in the light surrounding him. It filled everything inside of him and everything around him. It boomed like thunder, but a thousand times louder, and a thousand times more frightening:

THIS IS MY SON. LISTEN TO HIM!

Conrad's heart trip-hammered. The experience was too much. His head grew light, overloaded, he was passing out. And then, just before he lost consciousness, the light began to dim. The blazing cloud started to fade and dissolve. It dissipated rapidly, growing more and more faint until, finally, there were only a few wisps of vapor that blew and swirled about, lingering for just a moment until they, too, disappeared. Completely.

Conrad took several deep breaths, trying to clear his head, trying to shake off the paralyzing fear. He shot a look over at Jake and Robert. They were also breathing hard. He turned back to Eli and his visitors. But the visitors were gone. So was the glowing brightness of Eli's clothes. Now it was just Eli, looking back at them. He flashed a smile, then stuck his hands in his pockets and strolled toward them.

"Well, now," he said, breaking into his grin, "that was something, wasn't it?"

The men could only stare at him, speechless.

Eli's grin faded as he knelt down to join them. Suddenly he was very serious and very earnest. "You caught a glimpse of who I really am, of the glory I share with my Father. But it's important that you tell no one. Is that clear?"

They nodded numbly.

"Not yet. Not until I've made the sacrifice and come back from the dead."

CHAPTER ELEVEN

As Conrad drove Trevor's beat-up Toyota through the main street of Lebanon, Tennessee, population 25,000, he was surprised to see how little had changed since he'd visited Suzanne's parents so many years earlier. There was still the tree-lined streets of oak and maple, the big stately houses with their flower gardens of red, yellow, and white impatiens, and the pots overflowing like fountains with petunias. Then, of course, there were the magnolias (one of which had been transplanted to their home in Pasadena). In the town square, whose surrounding stores had mostly given way to antique shops and gift boutiques, older men sat off to the side not far from the gaze of the General Hatton statue, stewing over the latest gossip they'd heard down at Johnny's Barbershop or the Cardinal Cafe. And, as always, there was the heat and humidity. Plenty of both.

Once he'd passed through town, it was just a matter of minutes before he pulled the Toyota off the highway and turned down the lane leading to Suzanne's sister's farm. The crunching gravel and barking dog announced his arrival, and Suzanne was immediately on the porch, shading her eyes. He'd not even come to a stop before she was racing down the steps toward him. "Connie!"

He opened the door and climbed out just in time to catch her in his arms.

"Oh, Connie . . ."

He held her tight. How he'd missed her. She was his tent peg, the only constant in this ever-swirling, ever-changing world. But there was another reason he held her, and it had nothing to do with his needs. Instead, it had everything to do with hers. It had to do with her grief.

"I'm so sorry," he whispered. She nodded and tightened the embrace. He could feel her body shudder and he knew she was crying. It had been five days since her brother had died—one day since the funeral. The funeral Conrad had tried to attend so he could be by her side and offer support, but the one she had insisted he miss.

The dog quit barking. Now there were only the incessant cicadas and Suzanne's quiet sobs as she clung to him. He heard the screen door groan and looked over to see Cindy, his ex-sister-in-law, glaring down at them. She was a strong-willed woman who had seen no need to remarry after her divorce some thirty years earlier. She and Conrad had never been friends, even in the best of times. And once his affairs had started, Cindy was the primary force behind Suzanne's filing for divorce. Not that he blamed her. He would have probably given Suzanne the same counsel had he been asked. But now, for Cindy to see the two of them together, after all he'd put Suzanne through—well, he could only imagine what she was thinking.

They pulled back for a moment, just long enough for Suzanne to kiss him and for him to taste the saltiness of her tears, before they fell back into another embrace.

"I'm sorry I missed the service," he said.

She pulled back again, forcing a smile at him through her tears. "Liar."

"What do you mean?"

"My whole family was here, even Julia. You're tough, but facing all of them at the same time . . . I don't think so."

"I would have been here in a second if you hadn't insisted I stay."

She embraced him again. "I know."

"Is Julia . . ." He swallowed. "Is she still here?"

Suzanne shook her head. "She left right after the service."

Conrad nodded, feeling the familiar sadness. In the old days, he'd been able to avoid it with work or some other distraction. But not anymore. Not since Eli had begun stripping away his defenses, not since he was becoming more and more vulnerable.

"Where are the others?" Suzanne asked. "Where's Eli?"

"Right behind me. I wanted to get here just a little before them and—"

The dog resumed barking. They both looked out toward the road. A convoy of eight or nine vehicles began pulling into the lane with Will's camper in the lead. Conrad stole a glance at the porch and caught Cindy watching stoically. She was not going to like this. He turned back toward the convoy. He saw Eli sitting in the front vehicle, across the seat from Will.

A moment later Suzanne was racing toward him. "Eli . . . Eli!"

The camper pulled to a stop behind the Toyota. Eli opened the door to step out. And there was Suzanne to greet him, throwing her arms around him.

When they finally separated, he looked into her eyes. "How are you?" he quietly asked.

She nodded, glancing away, obviously trying not to cry.

"Suzanne?"

She continued looking away.

"Suzanne, look at me."

Her eyes faltered, then looked back to him.

Again he asked. "How are you?"

When she spoke her voice was thick. "It's just . . . If you had been here, I know you could have healed him. I know he wouldn't have died."

"Your brother will rise again."

"I know." She nodded, glancing away and wiping the tears. "On resurrection day, of course, but—"

"Suzanne. Suzanne, look at me." His voice was firm but growing in emotion. "Look at me."

She turned to face him.

"I *am* the resurrection, Suzanne. I *am* the life. Anyone who believes in me and dies will come back to life again. Anyone who lives and believes in me will never die but live forever. Do you believe that?"

She swallowed hard, blinking back the tears.

"Do you believe it?" he repeated.

"Yes," she choked, "I believe you are the Messiah, the Son of God—" But that was all she could say before emotion overtook her. Immediately, Conrad was at her side. When he looked at Eli, the young man's eyes were also brimming with tears. They spilled onto his cheeks and tracked down his face. Conrad had seen Eli moved with compassion before, but never quite like this. Maybe he finally realized his mistake. Maybe now he saw that he should have come earlier, before it was too late.

"Where have you buried him?" Eli asked, struggling to speak through his emotion.

"At Cedar Grove Cemetery," Suzanne answered. "The old part of town."

Eli nodded. Then, looking over to Conrad, he said, "Connie, I want you to get a permit."

"A permit? For what?"

"To exhume the body."

Conrad's jaw dropped. "Eli ... He's dead and buried."

"I know."

"But—"

"Didn't I say this would help you see the glory of God?" Eli wiped the tears from his eyes with the sleeve of his shirt.

"Well, yes, but ..." Conrad turned to Suzanne, hoping she would make Eli see reason. "Suzanne ..." But, even through her tears, she was looking at Eli with an expression of hope and expectancy. Was there nothing this woman could not believe? "Suzanne," he repeated.

Sniffing quietly, she turned to him and answered. "Do what he says, Connie. Whatever he says, do it."

Julia's drive between Pasadena and Thousand Oaks seemed even faster than the night before. And for good reason. Her mind churned with a dozen conflicting thoughts and emotions. Today would be the day. Granted, she could drag things out, turn it into a long and costly legal battle, keeping Roseanne and her all-too-eager spawn at bay while steadily draining their inheritance. But what would be the purpose, especially with the doctor's prognosis:

"It is my opinion your father's coma is irreversible."

Other words stewed and boiled in her mind, some spoken, some written:

I do not want life-sustaining treatment to be provided or continued if ...

"You would have declared him dead?"

"Jesus . . . Jesus Christ . . ."

". . . your father is already dead."

". . . if you are incapable of carrying out his order, then it is your responsibility to relinquish . . ."

"Jesus . . ."

"I'll never ever let anything bad happen to you."

"Pinkie swear?"

"I gave your Grandpa my word a long, long time ago. And you know what I always say?"

"I know, I know . . . you're only as good as your word."

The Janss Exit came so quickly that once again Julia nearly missed it. She veered to the right, barely catching the ramp, then took the same route through town as she'd taken the morning before—through the same sleepy neighborhood, the same abundance of trees, and the same faint aroma of horses and dry grass.

She turned into the hospital's driveway and was startled by the double row of speed bumps. They'd no doubt been there the day before; she just didn't remember them. She pulled in a few spots from where she had parked yesterday, and this time rolled down the windows an inch for the heat. Turning off the ignition, she opened the door and stepped into the morning sun. She closed her eyes and turned toward the brightness. Once again she let it bake into her face, hoping the heat would somehow melt away the tension.

But, of course, it didn't.

She thought of her mother. If she'd caught the same flight Julia had, and if she had successfully rented a car, she'd already be at the hospital grilling whatever physician was on duty. She was a determined lady, almost as determined as Julia . . . except for one fatal flaw. Her heart. Her mother was too soft, too full of mercy and grace. Much of that could be attributed to her fierce love for family—a love that had blinded her to her husband's betrayals. But there was another reason for her softness: her faith. A faith that, Julia had to admit, exceeded anything she or her father had ever understood.

Granted, she and Dad had kept the woman pacified—they said prayers at mealtime, went to church, participated in fund-raisers. There was even a time when her mother had managed to talk him into teaching first-grade Sunday school with her. But none of it stuck. At least not for Dad. And certainly not for Julia. On more than one occasion the two of them had conspired on ways to skip church. Sometimes their plans worked, like suggesting they take a drive up the coast (family drives were another one of Mom's weaknesses). Other times they weren't so successful. Like the Sunday morning Dad had an incredibly high fever, 107, Mom estimated by the way the mercury stuck to the top of the thermometer. And the scam might have worked if he had remembered to straighten the lampshade around the bulb after heating it up. Then there was that unfortunate incident with Binky the cocker spaniel. They just wanted him to appear sick enough for them to stay home and offer him some comfort. How did they know a single Alka Seltzer tablet could generate so much foam, and for so long?

In short, neither Julia nor her father were what you would call religious people. But that had never deterred her mother.

"Jules . . . Julia!"

She turned to see her mother quickly crossing the parking lot. Her shoulder-length, salt-and-pepper hair was pulled back. She wore her favorite calf-length summer dress and, of course, those clunky white tennis shoes. She always wore the tennis shoes.

"Hey, Mom," she called as she started forward to greet her. "You didn't have to come, you know."

"I know, I know."

"I mean it's not like he's a part of *your* life anymore."

"I know."

They met near the center of the lot and embraced. Julia had intended just a casual greeting; after all, they saw each other at least once a week—Mom made certain of that. But for a moment, Julia wouldn't let go. She *couldn't* let go. It was as if she was eight years old again, clinging to Mommy, wanting her to make everything all better.

Her mother must have sensed something, for she did not let go either . . . until Julia fought back the emotion and finally pulled away. But for some reason, she could not look directly into her mother's eyes. Instead, she directed her gaze toward the hospital.

"Are you okay, Sweetheart?"

Julia nodded. "Sure." But she knew her mother wasn't buying it, not for a moment. "We'd better go in and see what's happening."

Her mother nodded. And though she could still feel the woman's eyes searching her, Julia turned and they started for the hospital.

Conrad stood beside Suzanne as the backhoe rumbled and groaned, digging into the soft red earth. They were near the back of Cedar Grove Cemetery, the oldest of Lebanon's cemeteries. It was rich in history, with many of the tombstones dating as far back as the Civil War. In fact, General Hatton himself was buried beneath this hallowed sod. And unlike the newer cemetery across the street, this one still flew the Confederate flag. High above loomed ancient cedar boughs, protecting the crowd from the late morning sun, while at the same time steaming and dripping from an earlier downpour.

Two Wilson County deputies and two Lebanon police officers did their best to hold back the press and curious onlookers. And there were plenty of both. Conrad guessed about two hundred fifty. He recognized some of the reporters, though most of the networks used talent from their local affiliates . . . except in the case of Gerald McFarland. Lately, every time they turned around, McFarland was there with his crew. It had become clear to everyone, perhaps even to Eli, that EBN's interest was more than just news. It was now a personal vendetta—if not for McFarland, then at least for his boss, Dr. Kerston.

There were other onlookers . . . like the silver-gray Taurus with the government license plates. It was parked on one of the other lanes, windows rolled up, engine idling. The two men never bothered to get out. They didn't need to. They could make their observations and file their reports more easily from the comfort of the air-conditioned vehicle.

Then there were the locals. Disturbing the rest of the dead did not go down well in these parts—and it had given the citizens plenty of opportunity to work themselves into a frenzy. In fact, if Suzanne's family had not been such long-time and good friends with one of the county judges, it was doubtful a permit would have been issued. But it had been issued. It had taken three days, but it had been issued.

"Okay, hold it!" the head groundskeeper, a small stocky man, shouted. "We've hit the vault."

The backhoe driver dropped his machine into neutral and let it idle.

The groundskeeper motioned to another worker, a young Latino, who nodded and hopped into the narrow, four-foot-deep hole with a shovel. The backhoe operator climbed off his rig and joined him. They began scooping off dirt and digging around the lid of the concrete vault.

Even from where he stood, some twenty feet away, Conrad could smell the damp, musty earth. The odor concerned him. He knew nothing about embalming, had no idea how long its effects lasted, but he knew the body had now been in the ground four days. *Four days*. Surely, some decomposition had to have set in. And with that, most likely the smell. Conrad had smelled rotting flesh in hot, humid conditions once before—when he was just out of college and covering the last few months of Vietnam. It was not something he wanted to smell again ... or subject Suzanne to, especially if the source of that smell was her brother's body. But when he had confronted Eli earlier about the issue, his response was the same as it had always been. "Trust me, Connie—this will help you see the glory of God."

Of course, "seeing the glory of God" was not necessarily what the crowd had in mind. It certainly wasn't uppermost in the mind of Suzanne's sister. Initially, Cindy had opposed exhuming the body, threatened to use every option she had to stop it—until Eli had pulled her aside and they had talked, one-on-one—until, an hour later, she had emerged from the family room, unable to hide the tears in her eyes. But even that had not been enough to change her heart. Far from it. In fact, it was only after Suzanne had given her sister her word that she would quit following Eli should this little exhibition fail, that Cindy finally agreed to persuade Judge Whitman to issue the permit.

To see the glory of God.

A lot was riding on this morning. And for Conrad, it brought yet another question. Why had Eli suddenly agreed to start displaying his miracles? Surely he knew how fast word of this would spread. He'd even given in to Keith's persistent naggings about picking up another video camera (the last had been destroyed in Jake's camper) to get it all on tape. Why the sudden turnaround? What was Eli up to now?

Conrad was jarred back to the scene by the clanking of a chain. The workers were attaching it to the vault lid. A moment later, they were attaching it to the backhoe.

And that's when he saw her—Julia. It had been five years, but he recognized her instantly as she approached the group on the other side of the grave.

"Suzanne . . ."

"I see her."

Conrad started toward her, but Suzanne caught his hand. "No, Connie."

"What?"

"Let her come to you."

"But—"

"You'll scare her off. She sees us. If she wants to talk, she'll come over."

Conrad hesitated, unsure.

"It's got to be *her* choice."

There was that word again. *Choice.* He still didn't understand, not entirely. Then again, it wasn't the first time he'd failed to grasp their indefinable, female logic. He saw their eyes connect, didn't miss the quiet exchange of nods between them. Then, almost as an afterthought, Julia tossed a glance his way, giving him a nod as well, although exerting half the effort and far less enthusiasm.

"See," Suzanne said, "she's already coming around."

This was obviously a new definition of "coming around." Once again, Conrad started toward her. And once again, Suzanne gripped his hand. "No, Connie. Not yet."

He looked at Suzanne, still not understanding. The backhoe revved up again. Both turned as the chain tightened and the lid to the vault slowly rose. It dangled a moment before being lowered onto the wet lawn. Once again, the young Latino lowered himself into the hole, this time preparing to attach the chain to the coffin. But he'd barely entered before Eli stepped from the crowd and started toward the grave.

All eyes shot to him.

Obviously unsure what to do, one of the deputies moved toward Eli, indicating that he should come no closer. Eli slowed to a stop not ten feet from the hole. Everyone grew very still, the silence broken only by camera crews repositioning themselves.

Like everyone else, Conrad's eyes were glued to Eli. The young man was no longer wearing his trademark grin. In fact, he wasn't smiling at all. Instead he was a study of deep concentration . . . and compassion. He closed his eyes a moment. Then, after taking a deep breath and tilting his head toward the sky, he half shouted, half prayed:

"Father! Thank You for hearing me!"

Except for the idling backhoe, everything remained silent.

"I know You always hear me, but I am praying this so that they can finally believe it is *You* who have sent me!"

A longer pause this time. A few of the crowd fidgeted. Most remained unmoving, watching in silent anticipation.

Slowly Eli opened his eyes and lowered his head until he was staring down at the coffin in the grave. And then he shouted. They were only two words, but they were spoken with ringing clarity and absolute authority:

"Michael . . . arise!"

His voice barely finished echoing against the cedars when the worker in the grave cried in alarm and scrambled from the hole. The crowd pressed forward to see. But there was no movement. Nothing. Except a faint noise. A quiet scraping. Then muffled pounding.

"Get me a Phillips head!" the groundskeeper shouted to his assistants. "Somebody get me a screwdriver!"

One was produced, and instantly the man dropped to his stomach and reached down to the coffin lid. The pounding and scraping grew louder, more violent.

The crowd leaned forward, exchanging nervous glances with each other.

Conrad strained to listen. Were those muffled cries? Others appeared to hear them, too. So did Suzanne. Her grip tightened on Conrad's arm.

Suddenly, the coffin lid flew open. The groundskeeper leaped back with a scream as the crowd gasped. And for good reason. Because there, down in the casket with the top half of its lid thrown open, Suzanne's brother was struggling to sit up. Gasping for breath, filled with panic from being trapped inside, he looked around, wild-eyed, obviously disoriented.

"Somebody help him out," Eli ordered.

A handful of men moved to action. The rest of the crowd pressed in for a better look, breaking past the officers who were moving forward just as curious and open-mouthed as the rest. Suzanne released Conrad's arm and started pushing her way through the crowd to her brother. "Michael!" she cried, "Michael!"

But Conrad remained behind, unmoving. He vaguely took notice of the news crews pushing and shoving forward, of the shouts and cries. It was true. Just as Eli had predicted. He glanced down at his watch. It was only 11:45 A.M. In a matter of minutes, videotapes would be sent back to stations and beamed to networks where they would be edited in time to make every national and local news program of the evening. It was an amazing feat of publicity. Better than anything he or Keith could have dreamed up. In less than six hours, Eli Shepherd, who had been written off as an egotistical crackpot, would become the talk of an entire nation. Perhaps the world.

"That you might see the glory of God."

Conrad glanced around and spotted McFarland standing off to the side, watching his own cameraman fighting the fray for a better angle. Unable to resist the temptation, Conrad strolled over to him. "So." He cleared his throat, smiling mischievously. "What do you think of our boy now?"

But, when McFarland looked up, Conrad was surprised to see a face filled with sadness.

"Well?" Conrad continued to goad.

McFarland shook his head and quietly answered. "You have no idea what you've done, do you, Connie?"

The seriousness of his tone made Conrad uneasy. "Well, we've certainly raised the stakes, if that's what you mean."

But McFarland did not respond. Instead he looked back over toward the crowd, who were helping Michael out of the grave and onto his feet. Then, ever so quietly, almost indiscernibly, he repeated:

"You have no idea what you've done . . ."

PART THREE

CHAPTER TWELVE

July 4 had finally arrived, and opening celebrations for Dr. Kerston's City of God were in full swing. Every state dignitary who could be there was there. Every politician courting Dr. Kerston's sizable voting block who could show up, showed up. And so did the people. According to radio reports, by two o'clock over twelve thousand faithful, many of them prayer and financial partners, had passed through the twelve-foot-tall "Pearly Gates" and entered the grounds. Here they were greeted by high-school and college-aged "angels" only too helpful to pass out maps that directed them to the International Food Court (where they could "eat the food missionaries eat") or to the fitness gym ("to make that temple of God a heavenly body") or to the video arcade with games rewarding players for their godly deeds, or to God's Gifts and Goodies, or to the water park complete with all manner of giant slides as well as a dazzling Parting of the Red Sea attraction where, for a recommended donation of $7.50 (tax deductible), participants could actually experience the thrill of walking on the lake bottom with walls of water on both sides. Then, of course, there were the folks in animal costumes from the Noah's Ark exhibit who strolled the grounds only too happy to have their picture taken with Mom and Dad and the kiddies.

But the crowning glory was the Worship Center. Besides the fifty-two-bell carillon (one more bell than the Cathedral of God in Aurora, making it the largest carillon in the world), there was the actual sanctuary. When all three balconies were filled and the glass walls on either side rotated open to include the sitting area of the courtyards, the place could pack 12,750 people. Impressive. Everything about the City of God was grand and impressive, and Dr. Kerston had every reason to be proud.

Unfortunately, at this particular moment, the good doctor also had a reason to be upset. For, although the City of God's opening was a huge event, there appeared to be one event even larger . . . the arrival of Eli Shepherd.

Conrad had been right: the resurrection of Suzanne's brother had made national and world news. Despite the criticism by religious leaders, as well as by various doctors and scientists, the populace had once again turned their attention toward Eli. And the press, knowing a money-making story when they saw one, immediately got on board. In fact, for the past seventy-two hours since the resurrection, it had been impossible for Eli to appear anywhere without drawing a crowd.

His arrival here at the City of God was no exception. As their convoy arrived, word spread through the 120-acre site. Soon visitors and staff from every shop and exhibit were finding some excuse to drop what they were doing and swing on over to the park's entrance. Just helping him across the parking lot was proving to be an ordeal as media and visitors swarmed, as they shouted words of welcome and encouragement. In fact, it was all Conrad and the guys could do to clear a path ahead of him so he could walk.

"Hey, Connie!" Eli shouted as the crowd pushed and jostled them. "You and Keith really did your job this time. Nice work!"

Conrad frowned and yelled, "But we didn't do a thing!"

"Really?" Eli asked with just enough sparkle to make the irony obvious.

Conrad grinned back. He got the message loud and clear. This was neither his doing, nor Keith's. Somebody much bigger was in charge. And, at the moment, that Somebody was exceeding their wildest expectations. The thought brought more than a little satisfaction to Conrad. He hadn't been so wrong, after all. It was just a matter of the timing. When he'd wanted to push Eli to the forefront so many weeks earlier, Eli had declined. But now, suddenly, things had flipped. For whatever reason, the reluctant Messiah was no longer reluctant. At last he was doing things the right way—making his miracles public, going for the big events, seizing the day. Despite all of the backwards logic, despite all of Conrad's doubts (both in Eli and in himself), things were finally moving forward.

He glanced back at Eli as they continued to fight their way toward the entrance. But to his surprise, he saw the pleasure on Eli's face starting to fade. He leaned over and shouted, "Are you okay?"

Eli did not answer. Instead, the closer they drew to the complex, the heavier his countenance became. And Conrad wasn't the only one to notice. By the time they reached the white gates, the other guys were also exchanging uneasy glances and starting to question him.

From the swarming crowd, two men in navy-blue blazers emerged. Security, Conrad figured. They caught

Conrad's eye, flashed some kind of City of God I.D., and motioned for permission to talk with Eli. Conrad nodded and they moved in, only to be blocked by Will and Jake's commanding presence. "It's okay!" Conrad shouted. "They're with the park!"

They nodded and stepped aside.

"Mr. Shepherd!"

Eli turned toward them.

"We're with Security," the first hollered. "This thing is getting way out of hand! You've got to tell them to settle down. You've got to make them stop!"

Eli paused a moment and glanced across the crowd. Then he shook his head. "No!"

"What?" they yelled. "Why not?"

He leaned toward them and shouted, "If I were to tell them to be quiet, the very walls of your worship center would cry out over my arrival!" Before the guards could respond, Eli patted the first on the shoulder, smiled, and continued forward. Conrad gave the confused men a sympathetic shrug before following Eli through the Pearly Gates.

They headed across the red-tiled courtyard toward the central plaza just outside the worship center. The crowd grew thicker and pressed in harder.

"Please, Eli!" an unseen face shouted. "I've got leukemia! Just touch me and heal my leukemia!"

Another woman, much closer, caught the idea. "My diabetes!" she shouted. "Will you heal my diabetes?"

Others joined in. "Heal my back!" "My wife's got Alzheimer's!" Some of the folks Conrad could see, others he could not. "Will you lower my cholesterol!" a nearby father shouted. "I've got a sister with Parkinson's!" another cried. Amidst these demands grew others—some crying out for God's intervention: "Help me get a raise!" "Pray that my husband will come home!" Others shouting for riches. "Here!" a young woman yelled, shoving her pocketbook at him. "Just touch it, just lay your hands on my checkbook!" Many followed her lead, producing their checkbooks, their wallets; two or three even waved their Mastercards at him.

It was turning into quite a spectacle, and Trevor, Jake, Leon, and everyone else surrounding Eli traded amused looks. Everyone but Eli. For the deeper he entered the complex, the more he was overcome with emotion.

"Hey!" Once again, Conrad leaned closer and shouted over the noise. "You okay?"

"Get me to the fountain!" Eli yelled, motioning to the large fountain in the center of the plaza. "Get me to the fountain. I need to talk to them!"

Conrad nodded and passed the word on to the others. The group altered course and moved toward the fountain. It was a huge monstrosity of marble and concrete, some thirty feet in diameter, with multiple tiers of angels and biblical figures spouting water into the hazy afternoon sky. Once they arrived, Eli climbed onto the smooth, three-foot wall encircling it and turned to the crowd. Immediately they began to settle. As they did, Eli wiped his face and prepared to speak. Soon everything was quiet. Only the cascading water broke the silence.

"If you only knew what really brings fulfillment!" he shouted. His voice echoed through the plaza. "You can't find it in blessings! You can't find it in healings! You can't find it in wealth!" He let the phrase finish its reverberation before continuing. "And you certainly cannot find it in religion!"

The last sentence surprised them all. Eli said nothing, letting it sink in as he carefully surveyed their faces. From experience, Conrad knew he wasn't looking over a mass of people, but into individual hearts. After what seemed an excruciatingly long moment, he continued:

"Real joy—I mean deep, welling-up-inside-you joy—and real peace, they can only come from one thing . . . a relationship with God. They can only come when you are friends with God."

Once again he paused, letting the words echo through the plaza.

"What I'm offering you is friendship . . . friendship with the Creator of the Universe. That's what your soul yearns for. That's the thirst you've never been able to quench." Another pause. "Listen to me carefully. I am the living water." He motioned toward the fountain behind him and to the worship center behind that. "This water . . . it satisfies only for a moment. But if you drink from me—hear me now—if you drink of me, you will never be thirsty again! Never!"

The crowd stirred, sharing perplexed looks.

"How?" an older man in a Hawaiian shirt shouted. There was no malice in his face, only confusion.

Eli answered. "This water can only meet your temporary needs. It can only refresh a moment. It can never clean you. Nor can this park, or even this center." He turned to the rest of the crowd. "But if you come to me, I will refresh you, I will satisfy you, I will clean you like this worship center never can. And I will do it for eternity!" Again he paused letting the words echo and fade. "Through me you always have access to my Father; you will always be His friend."

A younger man in khaki shorts and far less friendly spoke up. "Are you saying that all of this—" He waved an arm toward the fountain and the center. "Are you saying that it's all useless?"

Eli turned to him. "All of the splendor that you see here, all of this glory, it is nothing but so much plaque upon the teeth of God!" The crowd stirred unhappily. "For without the Spirit of God, this center means nothing! It *is* nothing!"

Conrad watched the restlessness sweep across the faces. But Eli was not backing down.

"How can you say that?" a younger woman shouted. Others agreed. "Look at all the work and sacrifice that's gone into this place. And it's all for God's glory!" More people cried out, voicing their agreement.

Eli shook his head and did his best to shout over them. "God does not want your sacrifice! He wants your obedience! He does not want your works. He wants your faith." The group settled slightly, and he continued. "God does not want your religion of concrete and marble, your traditions of service and dead programs. He wants your living hearts! He cries out for your friendship!"

The restlessness grew.

"Are you saying this is all worthless?" an elderly woman yelled. Others joined in.

"I'm saying . . ." Eli took a breath. Once again he had to shout to be heard. "I'm saying that all of this will be destroyed!"

Conrad's head snapped toward Eli. What did he say?

"I'm telling you that this will be completely and utterly demolished!"

The crowd grew louder, more angry.

"It will be destroyed because you would rather worship the works of your hands than acknowledge the presence of Almighty God who, at this very moment, is standing before you!"

If the group had been worked up before, they were downright livid now. The shouting and yelling grew. Insults were hurled.

Conrad could only watch in amazement, marveling at how quickly Eli had pushed their buttons. But hadn't that always been his style—whether with crowds or individuals, hadn't Eli always moved his listeners beyond their comfort zone?

It was impossible now for Eli to make himself heard, so he sadly stepped down from the fountain wall. But instead of heading back toward the parking lot and the safety of their RVs, he turned and started toward the worship center.

Immediately Conrad was at his side. "Where are you going?" he yelled, barely hearing himself over the shouting crowd.

Eli yelled back. "Dr. Kerston invited us to his worship center, right?"

"Yes, but—"

"Then we're going to his worship center."

An angry man broke past Scott and Brent, lunging toward Eli. Fortunately, Jake moved in and, with the help of Will, managed to toss him back into the crowd. And still Eli continued forward. Despite the yelling, despite the outrage, despite the potential of being harmed, he continued toward the worship center.

"Any change with Conrad Davis?" Julia asked the nurse behind the counter.

The woman looked up. She was the one who had been there yesterday, who had caught Julia and helped her into a chair. "No, everything's pretty much the same."

"May we see him?"

"Certainly."

Julia felt the woman eyeing her, no doubt wondering whether there would be a repeat of yesterday's performance. "I had a chance to grab a little breakfast this time," Julia said, forcing a smile to reassure her.

The nurse nodded, then returned to her work.

Julia turned and escorted her mother toward room four. She had no more desire to see her father today than she'd had yesterday. But this time at least she was prepared. Or so she hoped. Still, even as they approached the sliding glass door to the room, she could feel her heart beginning to pound, a trace of perspiration breaking out across her forehead.

She glanced at her mother, who seemed to be taking it no better than she. How was that possible? After all he'd done to her . . . to them? After all the lying and cheating and destruction? After all these years since the divorce, how could she still be feeling something?

When the bed came into view, and her mother saw the swollen and bandaged head, she gasped. Instinctively, Julia reached out for her. "Are you all right?"

Her mother didn't answer.

"Mom?"

She gave Julia a slight nod but couldn't take her eyes from the bed. Julia looked for yesterday's chair and spotted it shoved against the wall. She reached for it, hanging onto her mother with one hand while stretching with the other. She grabbed it and dragged it across the linoleum.

"Here," she said, "sit down."

Her mother glanced around the room, asking, "Where will you sit?"

"I'll be fine."

"But—"

"I'll get another chair, Mom. Don't worry about me, just sit." Honestly, her mother could be such a mother sometimes.

Reluctantly, the woman eased herself into the yellow fiberglass chair. Julia could tell last night's flight had been a long one for her. Probably as long or longer than Julia's the night before.

Once her mother was seated, Julia crossed to the next room to look for another chair. But there was neither patient nor chair in it. She tried the next room, with no better results. The third time was the charm. She quietly slipped into the room so as not to wake the patient (though from the looks of things he would not be waking for a long time). She carefully picked up the chair and carried it out. But once she re-entered her father's room, she stopped short.

Her mother had pulled her chair closer to the bed. She was holding his hand and she had lowered her head. Julia knew exactly what she was doing. Just as she had not entirely given up her feelings for this man, neither had she given up on God. It was a tender, bittersweet moment— the first time Julia had seen her mother and father together in years. So many memories, so many—

Suddenly the alarm above the bed sounded. Her mother's head shot up, looking at it. Before Julia could react, the ICU nurse raced past her into the room. She glanced at the screen. "He's in V-fib," she said. She spun toward Julia, who could only stare. "He's in V-fib."

Julia's mind raced, trying to comprehend. What was she saying? Why was she telling her? "Does that . . . ," she stammered. "What does that mean?"

"He's arrested," the woman explained. "He's in V-fib. If we don't take appropriate measures he will die."

"Well—well, do something!" Julia demanded.

The nurse held her gaze, making it clear what she was asking. "Are you sure?"

"What?"

"Are you sure you want us to intervene?"

Suddenly, Julia understood. She was being asked the question. *The* question. She had the power of attorney, did she want measures taken to keep her father alive? The "heroic" measures that he had himself declined?

Without hesitation, she blurted, "Yes! Yes! Do what you have to do! But hurry! Yes, hurry!"

To enter the worship center, it was first necessary to pass through God's Gifts and Goodies. It was part foyer, part gift shop, and it encompassed a good ten thousand square feet, much of it enclosed by glass. As Conrad entered through the doors, he was not only impressed by Dr. Kerston's business savvy—the place was swarming with customers and long lines that stretched behind a dozen check-out counters—but he was also struck by the sheer genius of the merchandising. To his left was the sleepwear section with everything from King Solomon Slippers to Delilah negligées. Beside that was the office supplies section including Scripture-embossed pencils, message-from-God bulletin boards, and the ever-popular verse-of-the-day fax machines—"Share God's Word with your customers," the sign read. Up ahead stretched the home-video section with everything from God's Bods workout videos to various kid vids to *God's Divine Diet Plan*. And beside that, a music section throbbed with the latest sounds as a handful of teens gyrated to the glory of God.

Conrad looked on with mild amusement. No way could anyone say these people were backward or behind the times. In fact, as far as he could tell, this place had everything the world had to offer, maybe more. But, when he looked at Eli, he saw anything but pleasure. Instead, the man's face was growing so red that the veins on his neck had started to bulge. Others saw it too. Trevor, who was the closest to Eli, leaned over and asked something. But Eli did not hear. Instead, he suddenly broke past the men protecting him and headed toward the nearest check-out stand. With one giant sweep of his hands, he sent the merchandise and credit-card machine crashing to the floor!

People gasped. Some cried out. But Eli had barely begun. Turning toward the crowd, he shouted, "You may sell your goods anywhere you want, but not here! This is my Father's house!" He focused on specific shoppers and clerks, his chest heaving with anger. "This is not a place to satisfy your whims! This is not where you make profit! This is where you commune with God Almighty!" His eyes landed on the nearby Holy Hygiene display. He strode to it, grabbed the top of the cardboard sign, and brought the entire display tumbling down. Mouthwash, dental floss, toothpaste—everything crashed to the ground as bottles shattered, spilling their contents across the floor as people yelled and leaped back.

Eli turned to them and shouted. "You have made God's holy house a mall of merchandise!"

He crossed to the women's clothing department. Next to go was the display of "What Would God Do?" tube tops.

More panicked cries filled the air as people scrambled out of his way.

Conrad had never seen Eli so impassioned. But it was working. The gloves were definitely off, and he was definitely making a statement. Next he grabbed a belt from the scriptural ties and belts rack and began whirling it over his head, driving back anyone foolish enough to try and stop him.

He stormed over to the book section unopposed. Display after display came down. A hundred different versions of the Bible— *The Bible for Secretaries, The Bible for Athletes, The Bible for the Disabled, The Menopause Bible.* A moment later he was in the self-help section, clearing off shelves of *How to Make God Make You Rich,* and *Claiming Your Divine Health* as well as the best-selling classics, *How to Physically Please Your Godly Husband* and *Ten Steps to Raising Perfect Children.* Finally he hit the Messianic section, pushing over row after row of books with multicolored charts and transparencies explaining how each prophecy of the Messiah's coming would unfold.

Conrad heard more commotion and turned to see four security men hurrying through the crowd. He spun back to Eli, wanting to shout and warn him, but he knew that Eli couldn't hear. Even if he could, he wouldn't listen.

The crowd parted as the men pushed through.

Eli had entered the Holy Health Section and was working on the Spiritual Vitamin display (the one with a different Scripture reference printed on every tablet). And that's where they finally grabbed him. He put up no resistance, though the men might have worked a bit harder in restraining their force.

A moment later, sweating and breathing hard, Eli was escorted toward the back of the store. Conrad tried to follow, but there were too many people, and Eli was too far away. He could do nothing but stand and stare—and be impressed. For this was, indeed, a different Eli. This was an Eli of strength. A conquering Eli. Finally, the time had come. No more hiding of his miracles or of his powers or of his passions. At last, he was emerging as the leader Conrad knew him to be. At last he had become a force to reckon with. Yes, Eli knew exactly what he was doing. This arrest would only add fuel to his cause. And from what Conrad had seen over the past seventy-two hours, that cause had suddenly become very, very formidable. Finally, it was clear. Conrad really had backed the right horse.

Instantly, the serene ICU came alive. The ICU nurse had shut off the alarm and was already administering CPR as a female doctor appeared from nowhere. She was accompanied by a male nurse, who hustled Julia and her mother out of the room.

Now mother and daughter stood just on the other side of the glass door, numbly watching. Despite the flurry of activity, the staff maintained an eerie calm, a testimony to their professionalism . . . or to the number of life/death situations they faced every week. For Julia, it was like watching one of those medical TV shows, real but not real. As on television, the first thing the doctor did was raise her fist and smack the man hard in the center of his chest. Eyes darted to the monitor above the bed. The erratic readouts continued.

"Defib," the doctor ordered.

The word was barely uttered before a third nurse rolled a small portable machine toward the room, nearly colliding with Julia and her mother. "You need to leave!" she ordered as she pushed past them. Julia and her mother nodded, but they did not move. Maybe it was morbid curiosity, maybe it was sensing that this was her father's last few moments of life. Whatever the reason, Julia remained standing at the glass with her mother.

Covers were thrown back and her father's gown torn aside. How odd it was to see a man once so modest (she had seldom seen him with his shirt off) and so full of life, now lying there naked and pale and gray. She felt her mother leaning more heavily upon her.

The male nurse squirted gel across two electric paddles and placed them on her father's chest. Then, just as on TV, he yelled, "Clear!" The team stepped back. There was a brief click, and her father's entire body jerked grotesquely.

Julia heard her mother gasp and turned to her. Her knuckle was in her mouth as she watched in horror.

"Mom—do you want—"

Her mother shook her head. "We need to stay."

"Go to 300," the doctor ordered.

The ICU nurse resumed CPR as the second adjusted the settings on the machine. Once again the paddles were placed on his chest.

"Clear!"

This time Julia felt her mother turn her head. She wished she had as well. The body convulsed, causing the right arm to flop lifelessly off the table. Again the team turned to the monitor. Again there was no response.

"360," the doctor ordered.

The machine was reset. This time, when the paddles were placed on her father's chest, Julia did look away.

"Clear!"

Once again there was the dull click and the sound of his body jerking on the bed.

Julia turned back. The lines and numbers on the monitor made no sense to her, but the faces of those watching it did. They were not pleased. She noticed her own face growing wet, her head feeling a little light. She leaned against the glass door for support.

The doctor shouted out a number, followed by something that sounded like "epi" and the word, "push."

Immediately the male nurse produced a syringe and inserted it directly into one of the IVs leading to her father's arm. He emptied all of its contents. Seconds passed as the first nurse continued CPR, as all eyes remained fixed on the monitor.

After an eternity, the doctor reordered, "360."

Once again the paddles were placed on her father's bare skin and once again the command was given. "Clear!"

Another click. Another sickening convulsion.

Eyes turned to the monitor.

Nothing.

"Go to lidocaine," the doctor ordered.

Another syringe appeared in the nurse's hands. He injected it into the IV. More seconds passed as everyone stared at the monitor. How strange, Julia thought. They were no longer looking at her father, only the monitor. It was as if the man, the human, didn't exist. Only the machine.

Again the doctor ordered, "360."

"Clear!"

Another jolt, another body jerk.

How long will they keep this up? Julia wondered.

"Another epi!"

More syringes appeared. More drugs injected into the IV.

And more waiting.

"Okay," the doctor sighed, "let's juice him again." There was no missing the weariness in her voice.

"Clear!"

Another sickening click, and yet another convulsion.

How much more of this could her father's body take? How much more of this could *she* take? Besides the clammy dampness across her face, Julia noticed that the edges of her vision had started to grow bright, like an overexposed picture. And her mother? She turned to her. Her mother was as white as a sheet.

The doctor spoke again. This time too softly to hear. The ICU nurse looked over her shoulder at Julia. Others followed suit until the entire room was looking at her. What was going on? What did they want?

After another moment, the doctor spoke again, sounding even more drained. "All right, give me 375 milligrams of beryllium."

Another syringe appeared and was emptied into the IV.

Seconds ticked by. Julia glanced down at her mother's hand. It clutched her arm so tightly that it was leaving a bruise. How much longer? How much more of this would they have to endure?

The doctor stared at the monitor, her own face wet with perspiration.

Again the paddles were placed in position, and again the order was given.

"Clear!"

Another dull click. Another grotesque jerk.

By now, only the doctor and ICU nurse watched the monitor. The others simply stood, waiting. Until . . .

"What's that?" the ICU nurse asked.

The rest turned to the monitor.

"We've got something," the male nurse said.

The doctor reached for Julia's father's neck, carefully feeling for a pulse. She shook her head. "It's too weak, too slow. Give me a push of atropine." The male nurse nodded and prepared another syringe as the doctor, tendrils of damp hair dropping over her face, turned to the ICU nurse. "Attach the external pacemaker."

The nurse nodded and crossed toward another machine. She quickly attached it to Conrad's chest. As she did, the doctor finally stepped back from the bed and stood catching her breath, wiping her face with her sleeve. The episode had clearly taken a lot out of her. And when the machine was finally attached, she took another deep breath and simply said, "Call me if things change."

The ICU nurse nodded. Without further word, the doctor turned and headed for the door. As she stepped through, Julia knew she should say something but could only manage a raspy, "Thank you."

"For what?" the doctor asked as she briskly passed.

Julia turned. "For . . . bringing him back to life."

The woman slowed to a stop, then turned to face her. "That's the last thing in the world you should want to thank me for," she answered wearily. "Trust me." With that she turned and continued down the ICU corridor.

CHAPTER THIRTEEN

"You guys are missing the point," Conrad argued. "This is good news."

Brent frowned. "Eli lost it publicly, he's been thrown in jail for assault and destruction of private property . . . and you call that good news?"

"What exactly is your definition of *good*?" Leon asked.

"Look." Conrad rose from the edge of the bed and started to pace. The tiny motel room smelled of stale smoke, and there were far too many people crammed inside. It was another meeting, this time including Maggie, Suzanne, and everyone else in the group. Well, everyone except Eli, who was busy cooling his heels in the county jail. Conrad continued. "There isn't a person in this room who doesn't believe Eli is the Messiah, am I right? That he's the chosen one of God?"

The group nodded.

"We've all heard his claims. We've all seen his miracles. And not just us." He motioned toward Suzanne. "The entire world watched him raise your brother from the dead."

More agreement.

"Then do you honestly think, in your wildest dreams, can you honestly imagine that some jail cell is going to thwart his efforts?"

No one disagreed.

"Don't you see what's happening? It's unfolding exactly as he said."

"What's unfolding?" Keith asked.

"He's coming into power. The very thing you and I have been banging our heads against the wall trying to accomplish, he's accomplishing on his own."

"Run that past me again?" Will asked.

"He's finally rolled up his sleeves, Will. He's taken off his gloves and is finally going after the big boys." He turned to the rest of the group. "Isn't that what the Scriptures say the Messiah will do when he comes? Conquer and rule the world? Well, how do you conquer and rule the world without getting into the fray and getting your hands dirty?"

"So you're saying this is the beginning of him taking over?" Jake repeated.

"Exactly. You heard the crowd's excitement when he entered this morning. And what did he tell security when they wanted him to stop them?"

"That the very walls of the place would cry out," Keith answered.

"Precisely."

"And this is how he takes over the world?" Brent asked. "By getting arrested?"

Conrad answered. "Eli's ways have always been unconventional. There's no denying that, right?"

"'My ways are not your ways,'" Leon quoted.

"Exactly. And now he has finally quit playing the meek little lamb. Now he's getting down to becoming the warrior we always knew he could be. What did he say at the fountain about religion, about the City of God?"

"That it's all coming down."

"Right, the old system is coming down and it's about to be replaced."

"By what?" Maggie asked.

"By Eli!" Conrad answered impatiently. "He's been polite, he's been the gentlemen, and now finally he's going to start kicking butt!" He could tell some of the group was finally starting to come around. He reached into his pocket, making sure he still had the note. The one he'd just received. He wasn't sure whether he should mention it yet, or just hang onto it. He decided to wait.

"But how do you kick butt from a jail cell?" Leon demanded.

Jake answered, "Like Connie says, if death can't hold back Suzanne's brother, no jail cell's going to hold Eli."

Conrad added, "And even if it does, it suddenly makes him the underdog. The great, raise-people-from-the-dead prophet, being picked on by the big, bad, three-piece-suit and double-chinned establishment. Talk about becoming *the* rallying point. This is genius; it's absolutely perfect!"

More and more of the group were beginning to see his point.

"But . . ." Trevor coughed nervously. As the shyest member, he seldom spoke. When he did, it was always with difficulty. "What about everything Eli said about not returning evil for evil, and about turning the other cheek?"

"I don't know about you, son," Jake almost chuckled, "but I've about run out of cheeks. Wouldn't you agree, boys?" The group's agreement grew stronger. He continued. "I mean, I'm gettin' real tired of having to keep hangin' my head like some whopped dog. If what Connie's sayin' is right, then I say it's about time."

More agreement.

"Looks like the train is finally pulling out of the station, fellas," Will said. "And if that's the case, then I'm gonna be on board."

"That's right," others agreed.

"Guys . . ." It was Suzanne. Conrad was pleased to see she was participating as well. "Guys?"

They settled slightly.

"What Connie says makes a lot of sense . . . I mean, how can you be a conquering Messiah without conquering?"

They agreed. Conrad gave her a smile.

"But . . ." She hesitated, trying to find the right words. "What about all of his talk about dying to self? All these Kingdom of God principles he keeps insisting we live by."

"What about them?" Jake asked.

Suzanne frowned. "His upside-down logic of giving to receive, of serving to rule. Does this—what you're saying, Connie—does it really fit in with that?"

Conrad's smile faded.

"We can't lie down forever," Scott said.

"That's right," Brent agreed. "He expects us to do something."

"Does he?" Suzanne asked. "If he's the *physical* conquering king, I suppose you're right. But hasn't he always said he came to be the ruler of souls? Hasn't he always said his was a different kingdom?"

"What do you mean?" Conrad asked, doing his best to hide his irritation. It wasn't easy. After all the effort it had taken to sway the guys to his point of view, what was she doing trying to sway them back?

Suzanne shook her head. "I'm not sure. It's just this business of rolling up our sleeves and attacking the world . . . I don't think that's what he wants."

"Remember . . ." It was Trevor again. "Remember how he always told us that we should die? That we should turn everything we have over to him?"

The group grew more silent.

He continued. "Couldn't this be one of those times?"

"What are you talking about, Trev?"

"Shouldn't our desire for him to be this big deliverer, the conquering king—shouldn't we expect that to die as well?"

Jake shook his head gently. "Son, I appreciate what you're saying, but you don't want to take that type of thinking too far."

Will agreed. "That's like saying God has to die to be God. It don't work that way."

"It doesn't?" Suzanne asked. All eyes turned back to her. "Isn't that what Eli has always said, that he'd have to die? Remember?" She turned to Conrad. "At the prison with Ellen Perkins, remember all that talk about merging holiness with mercy? Remember how he said he'd have to shed his own blood to make that happen?"

"He said a lot of things," Conrad replied. "And not all of them make sense, at least literally. A dead king? I don't think so."

"He could have been talking in metaphor," Hector suggested, "or about some sort of spiritual death. I mean, who knows?"

"He also said, 'I am the resurrection *and the life*,'" Leon argued. "Doesn't sound like a dead king to me."

"I know," Suzanne sighed, "I know. But taking matters into our own hands right now just doesn't feel right."

A few more heads began to nod. If she didn't make complete sense, at least Suzanne's argument was enough to give the group some pause.

"So what do you suggest we do?" Jake asked. "Just sit around here, twiddling our thumbs?"

No one had an answer.

"I guess"—Suzanne cleared her throat—"we do what we've always done. What I did in Lebanon for all those days."

"What's that?" Will asked.

"We wait."

Looks were exchanged. A few heads nodded. No one could refute her argument.

Conrad sighed in exasperation. The group could be so dense sometimes—so timid and fearful. It couldn't be any clearer. Eli had shifted policy, had finally gone from invisible warrior to high-profile fighter. What were those statements at the City of God about, what was that violence in the gift store about, if it wasn't a declaration of war?

And still they didn't get it. Ever since Eli had gone public, ever since he'd raised Suzanne's brother from the dead, things had changed. But these people didn't see it. Yet, wasn't that how it always was with these guys? Seems like Eli had to say something a hundred times before they got it. Well, Conrad got it. Maybe the others hadn't, at least not yet, but that was okay—he had. Which would explain why he was the one who had received the message from Dr. Kerston. The message McFarland had passed on to him and that was now folded in his pocket.

The group may not understand the threat Eli was suddenly posing to Dr. Kerston and his establishment, but Dr. Kerston did. Why else would the man have requested a special meeting with Conrad, a meeting where he hoped to try and "work out their differences"? Yes, sir, things were changing. Swiftly. And from the looks of things, Conrad was going to be the man chosen to implement them.

"Dad, stop it! Stop it!"

Julia's father had grabbed her date and was literally dragging him out of the car by his neck.

"Dad!"

The kid didn't know what hit him. One minute he had unbuttoned Julia's shirt and was going for her jeans, the next the driver's door flew open, his head was slammed against the steering wheel, and he was being dragged out onto the pavement.

"Daddy!" Julia quickly covered herself, buttoning whatever buttons she could find, while scrambling out the other side of the car. *"Daddy, stop it!"*

But the man didn't stop. Her date may have been younger, but her father was stronger—and more importantly, fighting for her honor. Or so he thought. It was summer, between her sophomore and junior year in high school—those two months that she came out every year to visit him in California. And the kid? Some guy she'd met at a party. Good looking, sexy, and experienced . . . just the way she liked them.

Her father hit him hard in the gut, causing him to double over in a gasp.

"Daddy!"

He pulled the boy's head up by his hair and shoved him against the car.

"What'd I do?" the kid screamed, wild-eyed. *"What'd I do? What'd I do?"*

Julia raced around the car toward them. *"Daddy, don't!"*

"What'd I do?"

He held the boy against the car with his left hand, while clenching his right into a fist. Julia saw him lean back, preparing to smash the kid's face. *"Daddy, no!"* She lunged at him, throwing herself on his arm. *"Daddy!"*

He shook her off and grabbed the boy's collar with both hands, practically lifting him off the ground, their faces inches apart.

"That's my little girl!" He shouted, spittle flying into the boy's face.

"It was her idea!" the kid screamed. *"It was hers!"*

Her father hesitated, but only for a second. He lifted the kid even further off the ground, pulling his face even closer.

"It's true!" Julia shouted, tugging at his arm. *"It was my idea. It's what I wanted. Not him. Me! ME!"*

Again he hesitated.

"It's what I wanted!"

He turned to her, still not understanding.

"Me, it's what I wanted!"

"What?" He continued staring, eyes darting about her face in confusion. *"You're . . . sixteen years old."*

"And I was fifteen when I was doing it with Joey Palmer, and Truman Ardmore . . ."

She saw the understanding start to dawn.

"And fourteen with Scotty Johnson, oh, and some guy from summer camp I didn't even know . . ."

His gaze faltered, dropping to the ground, looking everywhere, anywhere, but at her.

"And let's not forget Jerry Hoover. You remember Jerry Hoover, don't you, Dad? That nice college kid who was interning with you?"

He kept staring at the ground, almost helplessly. Julia watched, basking in the victory and pain she'd inflicted. How dare he check up on her like that. How dare he! But even as she watched, she felt the victory starting to sour.

"I . . ." He continued looking down, beginning to shake his head. *"I didn't know."*

Julia swallowed, taking a breath, but could find nothing to say.

"I didn't . . ." At last he raised his eyes to hers. The expression stabbed her deep in the heart. He appeared so helpless, so . . . lost.

Though her rage was justified, she felt it slipping away. And that made her more angry. This was her victory and she wasn't about to let him ruin it. *"Why not, Dad?"* she said, holding her ground. *"Everybody always says we're cut from the same cloth. 'A chip off the ol' block,' isn't that how you brag about me?"* Again he looked at the ground. But she wasn't letting him off that easy. *"Well, take a good look, Dad. Take a good look at what we are."*

"I wanted . . ." His voice was hoarse, still searching. *"I wanted something better for you."* Slowly he raised his eyes. *"You deserve better than this, you are better . . . than this."*

His pain both tore at her and outraged her. But she didn't back down. *"What you see is what you get."*

He stood staring at her. She held his gaze until he was the one who finally turned. And then, without a word, he started back up the sidewalk toward the house.

Angry at his defeat and at the self-loathing welling up inside her, she shouted after him. *"A chip off the ol' block!"* He kept on walking. *"Like father, like daughter."* Her throat tightened, her body started to tremble. But she couldn't stop. *"Like father, like—"*

Suddenly she was back on her bicycle. Flying . . . sailing . . .

"Daddy, don't let go . . ."

"I'm right here."

"Don't let go!"

"Trust me, Sweetheart, I won't let go."

Then the silence.

"Daddy . . . Daddy, where are you? DADDY—"

"Julia . . ." It was her mother's voice. "Jules?"

She opened her eyes.

"Julia, Sweetheart?" She turned to see her mother standing at the sliding glass door to the ICU. "The lawyers are here."

Julia rubbed her eyes and nodded. "I guess I fell asleep. Who did you say was here?"

"A couple lawyers. And they brought along some doctors, too."

"We are merely proposing that he join forces with us, that's all." Dr. Kerston's assistant, a young man of nearly thirty in a neatly tailored Armani, grew more impassioned. "I mean, everyone in this room has seen the way he can work up and inspire a crowd."

"Both positively and negatively," Dr. Kerston added with a polite chuckle.

The others around the long table smiled knowingly. The conference room was large, mostly glass, and cheery with thick, intricately carved molding running along the ceiling. To the west, the sun hung low in the sky, and as it shown through the tinted windows it gave everyone in the room an odd, golden-gray glow.

Kerston's assistant continued. "And with that type of giftedness, plus his miracles . . . well, he would prove incredibly valuable."

"For whom?" Conrad asked.

"For the country, of course."

"Not to mention you," Keith said as he leveled his gaze at Dr. Kerston with the self-assuredness that can only come from the terribly young . . . or naive. For a moment Conrad wondered if he'd made a mistake bringing the kid along. Then again, such cockiness might be useful in stripping away the "civilities" of this group and getting to the real issues.

The assistant bristled at Keith's statement, but before he could respond, Dr. Kerston gave another chuckle, making it clear he was taking over. "No, son." He smiled at Keith. "What happens to me is of little consequence. To be frank, what happens to this complex of mine isn't all that important, either. And I think it would be fair to assume"— he leaned over the table to look down at his arch-rival from Aurora—"that Reverend Snyder here would say the same about himself and his organization. Am I right, Reverend?"

Snyder cleared his throat and nodded. "Yes, you are, Doctor."

Kerston continued, "And the same would go for any of these other esteemed clergy with us this afternoon."

The dozen or so distinguished gentlemen sitting around the table nodded in agreement.

"No," Dr. Kerston said, "we are talking about something far more important than one man or one particular ministry. What we're talking about is a movement, son, the turning of an entire country back to God, back to the very principles upon which we were founded."

More nods of agreement.

"That's what the City of God represents. That's what Reverend Snyder's Cathedral Hour represents. That's what we all represent. Wresting this country out of the hands of the heathen and putting it back into the hands of God."

"And we are coming very close to making that dream come true," Reverend Snyder interjected. "So close that it would be a shame to have division now. Especially when Eli's goals and ours are identical."

"Identical?" Conrad asked.

Dr. Kerston nodded. "Eli wants God to rule our nation; we want God to rule our nation."

"Exactly," Snyder agreed, making it clear he wasn't finished. "And with this charisma of his, as well as these . . . miracles, his partnership with us could become the very cornerstone on which to build our movement, on which to rebuild this nation."

"The cornerstone . . ." Conrad mused as he recalled Eli's parable back at the congregation in Texas.

"Pardon me?" Reverend Synder asked.

Conrad shook his head. "And Eli, what would he get out of this . . . partnership?"

Kerston's assistant answered. "Credibility. Power. With Dr. Kerston's sizable political clout—" Then, catching himself, he nodded to Snyder. "And with the good Reverend's reputation, as well as these other fine gentlemen, all Eli need do is say the word and he would instantly be endorsed by the entire religious community, both liberal and conservative."

"And," Kerston added, "if things were to work out and the timing was correct, your man could very well find himself holding some very high political office."

Conrad did his best not to show any expression. He hoped Keith was able to do the same.

"He could become our spokesperson," Snyder explained, "the galvanizing point for our entire movement. In many ways he could act as—"

"The Messiah?" Keith interrupted.

The group exchanged silent glances.

"That's . . . certainly a possibility," Dr. Kerston's assistant hedged. "But to be frank, he doesn't qualify, at least not yet."

"Qualify?" Keith asked incredulously. "He moves crowds, he changes lives, he raises people from the dead—and he doesn't qualify?"

Reverend Snyder answered. "The Scriptures clearly state that the Messiah will be a world leader, that the governments will rest upon his shoulder."

"And?" Keith asked.

"Well, no offense, my friend," Dr. Kerston smiled, "but as he is now, this behind-the-scenes teacher and healer of yours knows nothing about the ways of the world. Every time an opportunity arises to increase his support base, it almost appears as if he's set upon sabotaging it."

Conrad winced. That's exactly what they'd been fighting with Eli for so many weeks. At least until this new and improved Eli had emerged.

"And that's all right," Dr. Kerston continued. "He just needs a little . . . seasoning, some guidance along the way."

"Guidance from you guys?" Keith almost laughed. "The man raises people from the dead and you're going to give him guidance?"

Conrad appreciated Keith's candidness, but he also appreciated something else he saw. These men had an obvious desire, almost an urgency, to work with Eli. Could this have been Eli's plan all along? To wait, to hold back, and then to come in blazing with such overwhelming strength and power that they had to play ball with him? That certainly appeared to be the case now. Granted, they viewed him as a threat. Granted, they didn't see eye to eye on several issues, but wasn't their overarching goal the same? Didn't they both want to bring people to God? And if their goals were the same, shouldn't these men at least be listened to? Everyone knew Eli was not fond of the religious system, but if he were to align himself with them, even partially, wouldn't that give him enough clout to make them pay attention to his concerns, to allow him to begin changing the system from the inside out?

It was Reverend Snyder's turn to answer Keith. "I am afraid raising people from the dead is a far different skill than learning to survive in a political world."

"And often far more easy," Dr. Kerston chuckled.

The table responded in kind.

"Seriously though." Dr. Kerston leaned forward. "Eli Shepherd has tremendous gifts and power. We've all seen that. He's simply not yet learned to harness those strengths, that's all. The man is like a nuclear reaction. If channeled and properly directed, he will do great good. But if left unchanneled, he becomes a bomb, senselessly destroying himself and all those around him."

"And you think you can channel him?" Conrad asked skeptically.

"I think together we can counsel him," Reverend Snyder replied. "Assist him when he wants assistance. Be available to remind him of the big picture."

"Much as the two of you have tried," Dr. Kerston added.

Conrad tensed slightly at the camaraderie. "How do you know what we've tried?"

Dr. Kerston smiled. "Let's just say that the resources of those around this table can be quite extensive."

"And," Reverend Snyder added, "those resources, combined with the sizable influence wielded by the two of you should certainly be enough to make him see reason."

Keith muttered, "If only it were that easy."

Conrad shot him a look, but it was too late. Whatever suspicions these men had about his and Keith's frustrations with Eli were suddenly confirmed.

"Keith, it can be that easy." Dr. Kerston's smile broadened as he turned to Conrad. "With your influence and ours, I'm certain we can help Eli see reason. And once he does, I believe absolutely nothing can stop him."

Conrad was finding it harder to maintain his skepticism.

"If our goals are identical, why fight?" Dr. Kerston shrugged. "Why be enemies when we can become allies?"

"It might be a little easier to convince him of that if you hadn't thrown him in jail," Keith replied.

Kerston glanced at his assistant, who took the cue and cleared his throat. "In exactly ten minutes, Dr. Kerston will be holding a press conference," the young man said. "Since it's opening week for us and since the good Doctor agrees with much of what Eli has said, he is dropping all charges against Eli Shepherd."

When Conrad finally found his voice, it came out more ironic than he'd intended. "As a gesture of your good will and magnanimity."

"Call it what you like," Dr. Kerston answered as he started gathering his papers. "I'd prefer it to be a gesture of friendship, an opportunity for your man to reach his fullest potential. What you and Eli decide to do with that gesture is up to you. If you cooperate, everyone will win. Eli, the men around this table, you two, and, most important, the people of our beloved nation. And if you don't . . ." He let the phrase hang, then shrugged. "Well, as I said, it will be your decision."

Having gathered his papers, he rose. "Now, if you'll excuse me, gentlemen, I have a press conference to attend."

Those around the table rose and Conrad followed suit.

Hands were shaken and nods exchanged. The meeting had come to an end. In a matter of seconds Keith was on the other side of the table engaging Dr. Kerston's assistant in further dialogue. Conrad, on the other hand, was left with his notes and his thoughts. What he had expected to become a war of words had turned into a remarkable opportunity. If he'd heard clearly, the top religious leaders of the country were offering Eli a partnership in which all could benefit. In exchange for his cooperation, they would provide counsel (which he could accept or refuse) as well as a legitimate platform from which to speak. A platform that, if things played out correctly, could very well allow Eli to be accepted as who he claimed to be: the much awaited Messiah. No wonder Eli was so intent upon coming to the City of God. No wonder he—

His thoughts were interrupted by one of the secretaries, a petite woman in her mid-twenties who had been taking notes. She placed a brown leather briefcase on the table beside him.

"What's this?" he asked.

"Dr. Kerston is aware of how costly it's been for you and your group to travel all the way across the country to visit us. As a token of his appreciation, he wanted to donate this to your ministry to help defray expenses."

"Defray expenses?" Conrad asked. "You mean it's money?"

"Yes."

"How much?"

"Thirty."

"Thirty . . ." He searched her face for more information.

"Thirty thousand, Mr. Conrad."

He practically choked. "Thirty thousand dollars?"

She smiled tightly before turning and walking away.

The meeting with Roseanne, her children, the lawyers, and the additional doctors that had been brought in was even more brutal than the first. Although everything was conducted in a "civil and compassionate manner," the bottom line was always the same:

For all intents and purposes, Conrad Davis was dead.

The evaluation of the two new doctors was identical to that of yesterday's physician. There was little of Julia's father's brain that had not been damaged, and there was no chance of ever recovering its use. In fact, if it weren't for the machines forcing his other organs to remain functioning—"against their will," one of the doctors had pointed out—then Julia's father would have already experienced a more natural and certainly more humane "passing on."

Then, of course, there were the lawyers' arguments. Again and again, they pointed out that her father's wishes were for life support systems to be discontinued. And if, due to her emotional involvement, she could not execute his wishes, then she needed to relinquish her responsibility to someone who could.

But, as much as Julia wanted to give in, she knew that she had to carry out her duties. She could not give up her responsibility.

"It's not fair! All the other kids—"

"We're not talking about all the other kids."

"But—"

"If you refuse to take responsibility, you will stay in your room."

"Dad!"

"When you're ready to be responsible, we can talk."

The group meeting had ended over an hour ago, and Julia still felt like she'd been hit by a truck. Now, alone with her mother in the ICU lobby, she stared down at the paper. It was a single-page document, giving the hospital permission to remove her father from life supports.

"Daddy, will we always be best friends?"

"Yes, Jules."

"And you'll never let anything bad happen to me?"

"I'll never ever let anything bad happen to you."

"Good. And I'll never let anything bad happen to you."

She glanced at the pen she was holding. It was a Mont Blanc—a gift from her boss, Atlanta's District Attorney for—what had he said?—"unwavering devotion to justice." At the moment, she noticed that the pen was trembling violently.

"I do not want life-sustaining treatment to be provided or continued if I am in an irreversible coma or persistent vegetative—"

"In many ways, your father is already dead."

"You're only as good as your word."

"Julia . . ." Her mother spoke from the chair beside her, but Julia barely heard. Instead, she stared down at the document—at the single line across the bottom of the page that required her signature and the date.

"Your father's coma is irreversible."

"I gave your Grandpa my word a long, long time ago."

"Jules . . ."

"I do not want life-sustaining—"

"You're only as good as your—"

"Julia?"

She looked up. Her mother had walked over and was kneeling beside her. "You need to let him go, Sweetheart. You need to . . . let him go."

Julia turned to her, the woman's face blurry through her tears. "You agree with them?" she asked in surprise. It was the first time in a very long while that she'd asked her mother for advice. It felt good and frightening at the same time. Good to know she wasn't alone, frightening to realize how weak and vulnerable she'd become.

Slowly, almost imperceptibly, her mother nodded. "Yes, Sweetheart, I think they are right."

"What about the words?" Julia asked. "Mom, I heard them. It wasn't my imagination. What if he was praying? What if he was trying to do what you wanted him to do for so long? What if he was trying to ask Christ to be his, you know, his Lord and Savior?"

Her mother said nothing.

"What if by pulling the plug, I kill him before he has a chance to finish that prayer?"

The idea surprised her almost as much as her mother. So did the language. *Christ . . . Lord and Savior . . .* that was God talk, words her mother used. Not her. To be honest, she never said that name, unless it was during a particular moment of anger or she needed to impress the guys at the office. But what if she was right? What if he was crying out, trying to make some profession of faith, and she stepped in and cut him off before he could complete it?

"Jules . . . Sweetheart." Her mother reached out to take her hand. "I don't have the answer, I can't imagine anyone who does. But I know this: Jesus Christ paid an incredible price for your father's soul. He bought him with His life. He's not about to let him slip through His fingers by accident. He loves your father too much for that. He loves all of us too much for that."

Julia swallowed back the emotion and gave another swipe at her eyes. Her mother continued. "There's nothing you and I can do to change that. No second guessing, no decision, right or wrong. If there's any chance of your father being saved, he will be saved." Her voice grew husky and she had to pause before concluding. "No, Sweetheart, God's paid too great a price to let any of us slip through His fingers."

Julia closed her eyes. It was true. If Christ was who He said He was, He would not let her father fall through the cracks on some technicality. And if He wasn't . . . well, then it really didn't matter, did it?

She opened her eyes and looked back at the document, at the line running across the bottom of the page. She gripped the pen more firmly, trying to stop the trembling. Then with a deep breath, and while she still had the nerve, she lowered its point to the paper. She felt cold, detached, barely there. But, right or wrong, she was being responsible. Right or wrong, she was doing what she had to do.

It was over in five seconds: her signature, then the date. The death warrant for her father had been signed.

CHAPTER FOURTEEN

Julia felt she needed to be present as they removed the ventilator, the feeding tube, and the external pace-maker from her father. After all, the decision to let him die had been hers, she should at least be there to witness it. Of course, her mother had tried to change her mind, but Julia would not be swayed. It was only when the doctor had arrived, ordering that she leave and wait in the lobby, that she had finally given in. Although she'd put up a fight, she was secretly grateful for the doctor's resolve.

And yet, that was the only part of the process she missed. The moment the machines were removed she insisted upon returning to his side. That's where she would stay during his remaining moments on earth. That's where she would wait and watch. It was her decision. No, it was her *responsibility*.

As she took a seat beside him, she was struck by the silence—no machines hissing and clicking, no monitors beeping, no sound of the automatic blood pressure cuff tightening and releasing. Just silence. Natural, peaceful, silence … except for his raspy and sometimes irregular breathing.

She would only have a minute or so before Roseanne and her children arrived to pay their final respects—no doubt careful to display the perfect amount of bereavement before moving on. Her mother would also return, and would surely remain with Julia throughout the ordeal, staying at her side, staying at his side, until the very end. That's just how she was.

But until they arrived, these next few moments belonged to Julia . . . and her father. Though the tubes and hoses had been removed from his nose and mouth, she still could not look at his face. The swollen image was just too grotesque. Instead, she stared somewhere near the center of his chest, watching the uneven rise and fall of the covers as she tried to think what should be said.

No words came.

She wasn't sure what she felt, much less what she should say. Anger, sadness, loneliness, guilt—they were all there, but tied and twisted into a giant knot. She took a deep breath, trying to loosen that knot, but nothing worked.

Suddenly his body gave a shudder. Then another. Then he stopped breathing altogether. For a frightening moment, Julia feared that she'd lost the opportunity to say goodbye. But the breathing resumed—a little noisier, a little less even, but it resumed.

She looked down at his hand resting on the sheet. So strong, so masculine. Thick veins ran down the wrist and branched along its back. Rough knuckles sprinkled with black hair. She recognized some of the wrinkles and scars from childhood, when she would sit on his lap and he would read. But now the color was different. Instead of the calloused brown she'd always known, these hands showed blotches of purple. One patch stretched from his wrist, down the side of his hand, to the tip of his little finger.

His little finger . . .

"Pinkie swear?"

She remembered, so many years earlier, when he raised that very finger and crooked it the way she had taught him. And she remembered her giggling response. *"Pinkie swear."*

"I'll never let anything bad happen to you."

"And I'll never let anything bad happen to you."

The knot in her chest tightened. "I'm sorry, Dad," she whispered hoarsely. "I guess . . ." She took a moment trying to find the words. "I guess we're both failures."

It was the figure—*thirty*—that had so startled Conrad. That single word in the phrase Dr. Kerston's secretary had spoken when she handed him the briefcase. *"Thirty, Mr. Conrad. Thirty thousand."* Now Conrad was no Bible scholar, but there was something about that number—along with the offering of money, the meeting of top religious officials, and a lone spiritual hero who was threatening the religious establishment—that brought back a world of memories. A world that was not this world, but very similar. A world where a traitor had sold his own spiritual leader to the religious establishment . . . for *thirty* pieces of silver.

It had been a long time since Conrad had thought of the similarities between this world and his old one. A long time since he'd paid attention to the similarities between Eli Shepherd and Jesus Christ. But as he mulled over those similarities, the situation became more and more evident . . . the leader's entrance into a religious city, his clearing out the merchants, a meeting of his trusted follower with the religious officials . . . and the payment to that follower of *thirty* units of money.

It was more than coincidence. It had to be. And as he followed the events to their logical conclusion, he felt his insides tighten and grow cold. Was it possible? In his new world, in the unfolding of this reality, had *he* become the traitor?

The thought haunted him as he stepped out of the boardroom. It continued to gnaw and eat at him as he joined the others in welcoming Eli back from jail. And now, as they sat down at a celebration dinner in the banquet room of Mondovi's Italian Restaurant, it practically consumed him. How could it be? He'd not attended Dr. Kerston's meeting for his own gain; it had been for Eli. He'd not listened to the proposal for his benefit; it had been for Eli. Everything he'd done was to achieve Eli's objectives.

How then could such actions be considered traitorous?

To top it off, the plan Dr. Kerston had offered made perfect sense—combine forces, utilize resources, accomplish a common goal. All that plus getting Eli into the very center of the religious system so he could change it . . . it was the perfect situation, win/win logic all the way.

Unfortunately, it was the other logic that ate at him. Eli's logic.

"All of your life you've been taught to think with fleshly logic . . . and you're quite successful at it. But you're more than flesh, Connie . . ."

So what did that mean? Was he just expected to throw common sense to the wind? Ignore all of his God-given strengths and natural abilities?

". . . your very strength will become your weakness."

Conrad reached down to touch the leather briefcase sitting under the table between himself and Keith. They'd not spoken to Eli yet. Hadn't found the time. And at this particular moment, he wasn't sure what he would say even if they could. All he knew was that if a deal could be struck, it could very well make Eli one of the most powerful men in the nation, perhaps, someday, the world.

"If you want worldly treasures, fight with worldly weapons. If you want eternal treasures, fight with eternal weapons."

The teachings of all those weeks echoed inside his head. He felt Suzanne touch his arm and he turned to her. He forced a smile, but the look on her face said she knew something was wrong.

"Fame, power—these are the riches of this world, and they can be so terribly seductive."

Two tables over, Eli scooted back his chair and stood. It looked like he was about to make a toast. Conrad tried to focus on him, to drown out the conflicting thoughts raging in his head.

Finally Eli began. "I can't tell you how much I've wanted to eat this meal with you."

Several nodded as Jake quipped from a couple seats over, "Jailhouse food ain't that great, Eli?"

There were quiet chuckles, and Eli smiled. "No, Jake, it's more than that. This is the last meal we will eat together before I begin the sacrifice."

The humor in the room faded.

"Sacrifice?" Leon asked.

Eli nodded. "I will not eat it again until it is fulfilled in the Kingdom of God."

The group exchanged looks. But it was Trevor, who sat beside Eli, who asked the obvious question, "What are you talking about, Eli?"

Eli looked down at him. There was no missing the sadness in his eyes. But he did not say a word. Instead he reached for a loaf of bread sitting on the table before him. He picked it up, hesitated a moment, and then broke it in two, grimacing slightly as he tore it apart and crumbs fell onto the white tablecloth below. He took one half of the loaf and passed it to those sitting at his right; the other half he gave to those on his left.

"This is my body," he said quietly, his voice growing thick with emotion. "It is about to be broken for you. Take it and eat."

Except for the quiet hum of the air conditioner, the room was deathly silent. The bread began making its rounds, each member of the group quietly tearing off a chunk and passing it on to the next. Whatever was happening, whatever Eli was doing, they all sensed its terrible importance to him.

Conrad more than the others. For he knew exactly what was happening. He immediately recognized the ceremony. And if what Eli said was true, that he was about to be broken, then the chances were that somehow he, Conrad Davis, would be the one responsible. But how? By suggesting cooperation? By using a little common sense?

"All of your life you've been taught to think with fleshly logic . . ."

He watched numbly as the bread approached, each person tearing off a piece and solemnly putting it into his mouth before passing it on to the next. Soon Keith accepted the loaf, tore off his portion, and passed it on to Conrad.

Suddenly, everything grew still. Very, very still. As Conrad reached out to take the bread he could feel his heart pounding, hear himself breathing. It was like a movie. Like he was another person standing outside himself, watching and observing his actions. He'd never taken Communion. Not back in the other world. It was too sacred a ritual to practice if you didn't buy it. And Conrad was too honest, had too much integrity, to fake it.

But now . . . he did buy it, didn't he? Now, after all he'd seen. After all he'd heard. Didn't he?

He lifted his eyes and saw Eli gazing directly at him. He was paralyzed, unsure what to do. He needed encouragement, some assurance that it was okay to participate. With the money sitting under the table, with the terms of the meeting buzzing in his head, he needed to know. Some sort of sign. Something.

But Eli gave him no sign. He simply looked at him, waiting for his decision.

Conrad thought of passing the bread on and not eating it. How could he, with that money sitting under the table? How could he, if he was to become the betrayer?

But how could he not? Regardless of their differences, regardless of his struggles and quarrels, he still believed what Eli said about himself. More importantly, he believed who Eli was.

The pause lengthened. He could sense Suzanne's uneasiness, knew she was concerned.

"Choices . . . you're always forcing folks to make choices."

". . . to choose my way over your way, to choose my wisdom over the world's wisdom, to choose my Spirit over your flesh."

Choices . . . that had been it since the beginning. And hadn't he, step-by-step, excruciating decision after excruciating decision, made the choice to follow Eli? It wasn't easy—*I no sooner get a handle on one of those principles than you turn around and raise the stakes*—but isn't that exactly what he'd been doing? Following? Changing?

Still, there was another truth that surpassed all the others. One that he saw in Eli every time their eyes connected. His love. Regardless of the disagreements, regardless of the struggles, he knew Eli loved him. Eli would always love him. And he—he would always love Eli.

Before he had a chance to change his mind, Conrad quickly, almost impetuously, tore off a piece of the bread. He put it into his mouth and began to chew deliberately, thoughtfully. He had made his choice.

Still standing, Eli reached to an empty water glass on his table. Beside it was a freshly opened bottle of wine. The group watched in silence as he picked up the bottle and poured it into the glass. When it was full, he held it before them.

"This wine is my blood," he said. "It is a new agreement between God and man. And it is about to be poured out for the forgiveness of your sins."

He lowered the cup to Trevor, who took it in both hands.

"Each of you must drink it," Eli softly ordered.

Trevor looked back up questioningly. Eli gave him a quiet nod. Finally the young man raised the glass to his lips and took a small, hesitant sip. When he finished he looked back to Eli, who smiled and motioned for Jake to take it and do the same. Jake obeyed, scowling hard as he drank and then passed it on to Leon.

As with the bread, Conrad watched the cup slowly make its rounds.

"I won't be drinking from this glass," Eli said, "until you and I drink it together in the Kingdom of God."

At last the cup arrived and Conrad took it. *". . . my blood . . . a new agreement . . ."* He stared down at the crimson liquid, its thin patina clinging to the inside of the glass. *"My blood . . . poured out for the forgiveness of your sins."*

Forgiveness of sins . . .

Was it really that easy? No matter what he'd done, no matter whom he'd hurt? He stole a look over at Suzanne. No matter how many times he'd hurt them? The concept was staggering ... incomprehensible. As staggering and incomprehensible as everything else Eli had ever said and done. For him, for Conrad Davis to actually be forgiven, to be cleansed.

But of everything?

Even his betrayal of Eli?

The thought made his heart stop. It was too late, wasn't it? Hadn't he already taken the money? He looked back at Eli, who was again searching him with those deep, probing eyes. He felt his own eyes begin to burn with moisture. How much did Eli know? About the meeting? About the thirty thousand?

"Connie?" Suzanne whispered. "Are you all right?"

He barely heard. All he could do was stare at those eyes, those sad, loving eyes. And then, so slightly Conrad wasn't even sure he saw it, Eli nodded. He knew. Despite all that Conrad had done, it was okay. The blood still applied. Conrad had made his choice about following, and regardless of what he'd set into motion, despite the fact that he may have become his betrayer, Eli still forgave him. Tears spilled onto Conrad's cheeks. He had made his decision with the bread. And now, whether he had been the one to help shed it or not, he would drink Eli's blood.

With trembling hands, he raised the glass to his lips, all the time keeping his eyes locked onto Eli's—until finally, after so many years, after so many failures, Conrad Davis drank. He drank deeply, knowing if anyone needed forgiveness, he did. He took a breath and then he drank again, not one swallow but another, then another ... until Suzanne reached out and gently touched his arm indicating he should stop. Finally, almost reluctantly, he lowered the glass. A moment later he passed it on to her, his hands shaking with emotion. He knew she didn't understand. Not yet. Neither did he. Not entirely. But he had eaten the bread and he had drunk the cup.

How long the glass continued making the rounds, he wasn't sure. But the next time he heard Eli's voice he was startled by its grief.

"And now." Eli stopped and took a deep, heavy breath. "And now it begins. The time has come for one of you to betray me."

The room froze. Conrad's eyes darted to Eli, but Eli did not look at him. Instead, he sadly surveyed the group, letting the words sink in.

"What?" someone finally said.

"What did you say?" Keith asked.

"Who is it, Eli?" Jake called.

"You talking about one of us?" Leon asked.

"Eli? Mr. Shepherd." It was a new voice. The restaurant owner, a thin middle-aged Italian. He had just entered the room from his adjoining office. "You're on the news!"

"Again?" Jake sighed.

"No, this is different. Please, you must see this." The owner motioned for Eli to come. "Please, you must see this at once."

Slowly, almost woodenly, Eli started from his table and walked toward the office. Others followed. In moments the tiny room, which smelled of cheap aftershave and stale cigars, was crammed with people. Some stood inside, others at the door, straining to hear as the local news cast continued.

"... fifteen confirmed dead, at least twice that many injured."

At first Conrad thought he was looking at pictures of an earthquake—fallen walls, broken concrete, heaps of rubble with people digging ... until the reporter continued:

"Authorities are now certain it was a bomb. A large bomb placed right here in the baby stroller rental area of the City of God."

More images appeared—the shattered wall of the worship center, other people staring, standing in shock, some crying.

"Although the sheriff's office says there are no official suspects, authorities are currently looking for Mr. Eli Shepherd."

Eli's photo appeared on the screen.

"Less than twenty-four hours ago, near this very location, Mr. Shepherd was arrested for destruction of private property inside the worship center . . ."

The screen showed a video surveillance tape of Eli pulling down the displays and driving away panicked employees.

"And earlier, outside the center, he was reported as saying, and I quote: 'All of this will be destroyed. It will be completely and utterly destroyed.'"

The protests inside the office drowned out the rest of the report as Eli's photo reappeared on the screen along with a phone number for anyone to call having information.

"Mr. Shepherd . . ." It was the owner. "Mr. Shepherd, I am sorry, but I am afraid I must ask you to leave. You must not stay here. I am sorry."

Eli nodded. "I understand."

"Please understand—it is for your own good. I am sorry."

"It's okay, Mr. Mondovi, I understand. It's all right." Then, obviously numb from the report, Eli turned and made his way out of the office.

"What do we do now?" Scott asked.

"Where do we go?" Brent said.

But Eli gave no answer. Instead, he quietly started toward the tables. When he arrived, he turned to face the group. "Mr. Mondovi has been an excellent host, and I'm grateful he has opened this banquet room up to us."

"No, no, please, there is no need," the owner protested.

"But he's right, we need to move on. There's much more I want to tell you, so much more I have to say. And time is running out."

"If we go back to the motel they'll be waiting for you," Leon said.

"The same goes for our campers or cars," Hector added.

"What about that park down by the river?" Suzanne asked.

"Out in the open?" Brent said. "I don't think so."

"Why not?" his brother argued. "It's out of the way. I doubt many will see us."

A brief discussion followed, some of the group liking the idea, some of them not. But it seemed good enough for Eli. "The park will be fine," he said.

"Then we better go out by ones and twos," Leon suggested, "so we don't draw attention."

The group agreed. Moments later, Brent and Will were the first to head out the back door. Maggie and Trevor followed. It was only then that Conrad noticed that someone was missing. He'd not seen him since they'd risen from the table and headed to the owner's office. He looked over the group again. No, he wasn't there. Keith Anderson was gone. Instantly, Conrad's eyes shot to the suitcase under the table.

It, too, was missing.

"Honey, you've got to eat something."

"I'll be fine, Mom."

"If you want, I'll go down to the cafeteria and bring up something."

"Mom, I'm fine." Julia's voice was sharper than she'd intended. She knew her mother was only trying to help, to do her "mom thing," but still—

"You can't just sit here forever. You've got to take some breaks. What if he doesn't pass on until tonight?" she asked. "Or tomorrow? Are you going to just sit there until—"

"I'll stay here until it's over, Mom." This time she did intend the sharpness. "That's what I have to do. That's my ... responsibility."

Her mother said nothing, the silence broken only by the rasping, almost choking sounds of her father struggling to breathe. Over the hours his breathing had grown more labored, and louder.

The ICU nurse had called it a "death rattle," and assured them it was all part of the dying process. "About half the patients develop it," she had said. "But don't worry, he's not feeling a thing. He's not even aware he's doing it. It's just the muscles around his throat starting to relax."

"Are you sure?" her mother had asked skeptically. "It sounds like he's suffocating. Are you sure he doesn't feel it?"

"Absolutely," the nurse had insisted. "It's just his body shutting down."

And it was those words—"his body shutting down"— that had kept Julia at her father's side throughout the late morning and on into the afternoon. It was those words that, despite her mother's silent and sometimes not-so-silent concerns, would keep her at his side until the very end.

Another moment passed before her mother softly spoke. "You're so like your father." She shook her head. "So much like him."

Julia turned to her, knowing there was more. She was not disappointed.

"You two . . . always with your code of honor, always this sense of responsibility."

"Is that so wrong?" Julia asked.

Her mother looked at her sadly. "No, Sweetheart, it's not wrong, not wrong at all. Except . . ." She hesitated.

"Except what?"

Her mother shook her head. "No, it's not my place to—"

"Tell me," Julia insisted. "Except for what?"

Her mother took a deep breath and continued. "Except for when it makes you so . . . demanding. Of yourself and others."

"That was the way I was brought up, Mom. That's what he expected. 'You're only as good as—'"

"—your word," her mother finished the sentence. "I know, I've heard it a thousand times."

"It doesn't make it any less true," Julia insisted. Her mother did not respond, and Julia continued. "Look, just because he was a hypocrite and couldn't live by those standards doesn't mean I can't." Once again the outburst was louder than she'd intended. No doubt about it, her nerves were definitely frayed.

More silence followed, interrupted by another series of chokings and gaspings. Mother and daughter turned to watch with concern. Nearly a half minute passed before he started settling down and breathing easier.

"You've never forgiven him, have you?" her mother finally asked.

Julia turned to her. "Why should I? He destroyed our lives."

"No, Sweetheart, he didn't destroy our lives, at least not mine. I forgave him a long, long time ago."

"Well, maybe I don't think he should be let off that easily."

"Is that why you keep hating him?" her mother asked a little softer. "Is that why you keep letting him make you the victim—over and over again?"

Julia opened her mouth then closed it, setting her jaw. She would not be drawn into an argument. Not now, not when she didn't trust her emotions.

"Sweetheart," her mother continued, "everyone makes mistakes."

"Mistakes? *Mistakes?* The man cheated on you for years. He destroyed our family! Everything that was good and wonderful he threw away for his own selfish pleasures. Those weren't mistakes, Mother, those were betrayals!"

"And you'll never forgive him," her mother answered quietly.

Julia bit her lip, returning to her silence.

"What an awful world it would be if people weren't allowed to make mistakes. If they could never be forgiven." She reached out and set her hand on Julia's arm. "You've got to let go, Sweetheart. You've got to let go and move on."

Julia closed her eyes, fighting back the emotion.

"People can never be as good as they want. They need . . . *we all* need the grace to make mistakes. We all need to be forgiven."

Julia's own breathing grew heavier; she felt her body tighten. The words went against everything she'd been taught, everything she'd lived by.

"You've got to forgive him, Sweetheart. You've got to let go."

"There's so much to tell you folks, and so little time."

Even though the night was warm, Eli appeared cold as he sat huddled on the picnic table addressing the group. Some stood, others sat in front of him on the soft carpet of grass and pine needles. They'd selected a barbecue pit down by the river. Only a small knoll kept them out of sight from the main road.

Eli continued, "In just a few hours I'm going to be leaving you. You'll look everywhere, but you won't be able to find me."

"Where you going?" Jake asked.

Eli smiled, but it was that sad smile again. "Where I'm going you can't come, Jake. At least for now. Later, but not for now."

"No, sir." Jake shook his head. "I'll go with you wherever you go. I don't care what these yahoos say or do to you. I'm not leaving your side."

"You will leave my side, Jake. Before the bells at the courthouse chime tomorrow morning, you'll deny you even know me."

"No way."

"Not once"—Eli sadly noted—"but three times you'll deny me."

Jake protested until Eli held out his hand. "Please, listen to me carefully. I'm going to my Father. Once I'm there I'll fix up a place for you, for each of you." He paused a moment, carefully surveying the group. "Come on, don't look so sad. I'm not going to be gone forever. I'll come back for you, I promise."

"But . . ." It was Trevor. "Where are you going? How are you going to get there?"

"If you think over what I've been saying, you'll know the way."

The group remained silent. Brent gave a nervous cough. "I'm sorry, Eli, we don't know where you're going, so how are we supposed to know the way?"

Eli leveled his gaze at him. "I am the Way, Brent. I am the Truth and I am the Life. No one comes to the Father, but through me."

More silence. Then Scott spoke up. "Maybe if we saw the Father. You know, maybe if we caught a glimpse of Him or something, maybe that would help."

"Scotty . . ." Eli shook his head. "Have I been with you this long and you still don't recognize me? Listen carefully. If you have seen me, you have seen the Father." He looked around the stunned group and repeated, "If you have seen me, you have seen the Father."

Conrad, who sat on the bench beside Suzanne, looked at the others. Many were frowning. Some stared at the ground, trying to comprehend.

Eli tried again. "Everything I've said to you is what the Father has told me to say. Everything you've seen me do is what the Father has told me to do. I am in the Father and the Father is in me. Do you understand?"

Some nodded. Most did not.

Eli sighed. "If you can't believe because of my words, then believe because of the miracles you've seen me do. And I guarantee you, it won't stop there. If you believe in me, you're going to wind up doing even greater things than you've seen me do."

Eyes widened in surprise, and Eli appeared to almost laugh at their expressions. "Does that shock you? It shouldn't. I'm going to the Father, and you can ask anything along the lines of what I've been teaching and I'll do it for you. You got that? You can ask *anything* in my name and it will be done."

The group continued to listen in quiet shock.

"Pretty soon things are going to get real ugly. The ruler of this world is on the attack, and it's going to be rough. But try not to worry about that. It's all part of the Father's plan. A plan I intend to follow to the last detail."

He gave a nearly imperceptible shiver, then took a moment before continuing. "Even when things are at their worst, I don't want you to feel abandoned. I won't leave you alone; you have my word on that. When I go to the Father, I'll ask Him to send you His Holy Spirit. He'll be your friend. He'll be here to comfort you. Now, I know you've heard a lot of things. Some of them you understand, some of them you don't. But the Holy Spirit, the Spirit of Truth, He'll make everything clear to you. He'll remind you of everything I've said, while at the same time empowering you and giving you a supernatural peace, a calm assurance that defies understanding." Eli forced a smile that was almost his old twinkle. Almost. "The truth of the matter is, it's really better that I leave so He'll come down to help you."

He paused, looking over the group, letting the words sink in. Conrad looked down at his hands and stared hard. There was so much being said, so much to try and absorb.

But Eli wasn't done. Slowly, he rose from the picnic table and walked five maybe six paces to the nearest pine tree. An evening breeze had picked up, causing a faint whisper through its boughs. He turned to the group. "I am the tree. And you, my friends . . . you are the branches. When you live your life doing what I say, you stay connected to me. And when we're connected, the sap of the tree, my very life and power, will naturally flow into you, allowing you to bear fruit.

"But if you choose to disconnect from me . . ." He spotted a small dead branch on the ground and picked it up. "If you choose to disconnect from me"—he broke the twig with a startling crack—"then you will die. My Father will cut you off from His tree, and you will be good for nothing . . . except firewood."

The group remained silent, clinging to every word.

Eli approached them. In the moonlight Conrad could see moisture glistening in his eyes. "Love each other, my friends. It's the greatest command, and it is the surest sign that you and I are connected. Yes, rough times are going to come. People will hate you. They hated me, so why should it be any different with you? In fact, they'll actually throw you out of your congregations and kill you, thinking they're doing my Father a favor. Just as I have promised you power and love and incredible fruit, I'm also promising you hard times in this world. Count on it. But that's okay. I've beaten the world. So can you.

"It's going to be hard, but don't be discouraged. That's why I'm telling you everything now, so you won't be surprised by it. Pretty soon you won't see me for a few days. But then, a few days later, I'll be back."

He paused and quietly looked into their faces.

"Eli . . ." Suzanne tentatively asked. "I'm not sure about the others, but I still don't know where you're going or why we can't follow."

He smiled warmly at her and walked over. "In just a few hours you're going to start grieving like you've never grieved before." He knelt and took both of her hands. "Everything will seem completely dark for you, utterly hopeless. Your heart will be broken. The rest of the world will sing and celebrate, but you'll be filled with overwhelming sorrow. But only for a while. Because after that, your sadness will turn to joy."

He pulled her hands closer, resting his chin upon them. "Remember the pain you felt when giving birth to Julia?" He turned to Conrad, including him in the question. "Do you remember all of her suffering?"

Conrad nodded silently.

"That's what it will feel like." He turned back to Suzanne. "But only for a while. In childbirth, despite the incredible pain, when it was over, when you finally held little Julia in your arms, wasn't everything forgotten? Wasn't the pain replaced by joy?"

Suzanne nodded, tears forming in her eyes.

"I think we understand," Jake called from across the group. "And I can speak for all of us in saying that when this, whatever-it-is happens, we'll be right by your side. We'll help you through it, you can count on us."

Eli turned to Jake and slowly rose to his feet. "Do you think so?"

"You bet."

Sadly Eli shook his head. "No, Jake. Each of you will abandon me. To save your own skins, you'll run away. But that's okay. I'll still have my Father."

He took another breath and tried to smile. This time with far less success. His voice thickened. "The time is almost here, my friends. I'm going down by the river to pray. Those of you who want are welcome to join me. Because without prayer we won't get through this thing. Do you hear me? None of us will get through this thing unless we pray."

CHAPTER FIFTEEN

The past forty-eight hours had been exhausting for everyone including Conrad. From the entry into the City of God, to Eli's arrest, to a sleepless night of worrying and planning, to the meeting with Dr. Kerston's people, to Conrad's realization of who he had almost become, to the realization of who his protégé *had* become, to his struggle over accepting the bread and wine, and now this late-night prayer vigil in the park . . . it was a wonder he could concentrate on anything at all, let alone prayer.

Still, like the others in the group, he silently tried to obey. After such an impassioned speech by Eli, did he have any choice? The first hour had not been bad. Since prayer was basically foreign to Conrad, he did his best to remember the structure Eli had taught them: opening with worship, then praying for God's will to be accomplished, then for his own specific needs, then for forgiveness, and finally that he not get caught up in temptation but be freed from evil. It was a far cry from the "God is great, God is good" mealtime prayers little Julia used to rattle off, or her "Now I lay me down to sleep" at bedtimes. Still, he seemed to be getting the hang of it.

It was during the second hour that he ran into trouble. How long was a person expected to pray, anyway? And it wasn't just Conrad. Soon, others in the group also began stretching out and making themselves comfortable. Some even began dozing off. And who could blame them? The warm night, the soft carpet of grass and pine needles, the two days of emotional exhaustion . . .

"Guys."

Conrad woke with a start. There was Eli standing over them—hair disheveled, face coated in a light sheen of sweat. "Can't you stay awake with me and pray? Please, this is important."

Jake, Conrad, and a few others grunted apologies. They sat up and tried to focus. But as the minutes passed, Conrad's mind again started to drift. Maybe if he just thought of God's goodness. Maybe if he just lay down and pretended to be embraced by that goodness. It could still be considered prayer, a type of worship . . . just a little more comfortable, that's all.

As he drifted, he thought of Julia. He'd been doing that more and more lately, ever since he'd seen her in Lebanon at her uncle's resurrection. Actually, it had been longer than that. Much longer. Because somewhere, in the back of his mind, she was always there. At the moment it was a memory he couldn't place. He lay in a bed, stretched out with his eyes shut. And he sensed Julia sitting in a yellow chair beside him. She said nothing—just remained seated in complete silence. Yet, even then, he felt a deep sadness from her—a terrible, lonely anger. He'd always known she carried it. Just as importantly, he'd always known he was the one responsible for it. But, as he lay there, he could actually feel her anguish, deep down inside, throbbing in her gut, tightening around her chest. He tried to open his eyes, but they were sealed shut. He tried to talk, but his mouth would not move. Then he tried moving his hand. If he could just reach out his hand and offer her some solace, some sort of—

"Guys, please."

He started awake and saw Eli staring down at them. He looked worse than before. His face now dripping with perspiration that—was it Conrad's imagination, or was it pinkish red in color? It was hard to tell. Probably just a trick of the moonlight.

"Listen to me," Eli said, wiping his face with his sleeve. "The time is just about here. You've got to stay up and fight this with me."

Again apologies were made, and again the guys gathered themselves, sitting up, resolving to stay awake and pray. But for how long? Surely Eli didn't expect them to stay out here all night. Already a thin layer of fog was settling in the lower areas and a heavy dew had appeared. Conrad glanced around. Suzanne and Maggie had moved under the cover of the nearby picnic table. Others had left altogether, no doubt continuing their vigil in the comfort of their campers or motel rooms. And who could blame them? It was getting ridiculous. But Eli had already turned and was heading back to the river. So, with a heavy sigh, Conrad rolled down his shirtsleeves to fight off the dampness and scooted to the base of the nearby tree. Maybe if he just leaned against it. There, that was better. And maybe if he closed his eyes, just for a moment, to gather his thoughts, then maybe he'd be able to—

The blinding light startled him awake. He squinted toward the top of the knoll where patrol cars crept down the grassy incline toward them, their headlights on high, their flashers strobing blue-yellow-red, blue-yellow-red. Other members of the group also awoke, looking at one another in confusion, staggering to their feet.

There was a loud click followed by the brief squeal of feedback. "This is the Salem County Sheriff's Department," a voice rang through a P.A. "The park closed at sunset. You are in violation of county ordinance. Do not attempt to leave."

What had been concern in the group escalated to panic. "Connie?" It was Suzanne, searching for him in the glaring light.

"Over here," he called.

She spotted him and quickly moved to his side. "What's going on, what are they doing?"

He wrapped a protective arm around her. "I'm not sure." But he had a pretty good idea.

The cars eased to a stop thirty feet from them. Doors opened and slammed. The silhouetted forms of men approached in front of the light. Conrad's grip around Suzanne tightened. He looked back toward the river, hoping that Eli had had the good sense to slip away into the night. But, of course he hadn't. There he was, walking toward them . . . slowly, deliberately.

Conrad turned back to the blazing lights and the officers. He counted four cars in all, eight officers. As they approached, he caught glimpses of pale flesh against dark uniforms. Only one was dressed differently. He wore what looked like white shorts and a green polo shirt.

Leon was the first to recognize him. "Keith! What's happening, man?"

Keith did not answer.

"What's going on?" Jake demanded.

But Keith remained silent, heading directly for Eli. The two came to a stop facing each other not ten feet from Conrad and Suzanne.

Eli was the first to speak. "It's your hour now, Keith," he said softly, "the hour of darkness."

The words hit the young man hard, but he held his ground. Then he stepped up to Eli and, almost violently, threw his arms around him in an embrace. Eli did not resist. Then, ever so gently, Keith kissed him on the cheek. When they separated there was no missing the tears in both of their eyes.

"My friend," Eli whispered fiercely. "Do you betray me with a kiss?"

Keith tried to hold his gaze, but faltered, looking suddenly toward the ground.

"Eli Shepherd?" an approaching officer called.

Eli looked up to him. "Yes, sir."

"You're under arrest."

Eli nodded.

"For the bombing and murders at the City of God."

"I understand."

The officer arrived and reached to the back of his belt to pull out a pair of handcuffs. His bigger, burlier partner joined him. Conrad could only stare in disbelief. He felt Suzanne's body begin to tremble.

Jake's reaction was a little different. He lunged at the two men, landing a quick, powerful punch directly to the first officer's face—so hard that Conrad could actually hear the cartilage of the man's nose snap. But it was over before it began. The second officer's baton flashed from his belt and rammed, butt-first, into Jake's stomach, doubling him over. Next came the blow to his shoulders, a quick, hard chop that sent the big fellow crashing to the grass.

Leon and Will moved to his defense, but they were stopped by Eli. "No!" he shouted.

They froze.

"Don't you understand yet? After all this time, don't you get it? Those who live by violence will die by violence. If I wanted to, don't you think I could ask my Father in Heaven to send down thousands of angels?"

He looked at the first officer, who was bent over, holding his nose, groaning softly. Without a word, Eli knelt down and helped him straighten up. For just a second Conrad caught a glimpse of the man's nose—bleeding flesh and smashed bone. Eli reached for it. The second officer immediately prepared to wield his baton again until the first moaned, "No, don't." He waved off his partner, somehow sensing that Eli meant no harm. The partner hesitated.

Gently, Eli pulled the man's hands away from his nose. It was a mess. Carefully, he placed his own hands over the smashed cartilage and bleeding tissue. Everyone stood in silence as he whispered something Conrad was unable to hear. And then slowly he removed his hands. A quiet gasp rippled through the crowd. The nose was completely restored. Except for the smeared blood on the man's mouth and face it was as if the injury had never occurred.

The officer stared at Eli, then reached up to explore his face. As he did, Eli stooped beside Jake. "Everything is happening just the way I told you it would," he said, as he helped the big man to his feet, "just the way the Scriptures foretold." Then, turning back to the first officer, he said, "Please, let my friends go. You're not interested in them. I'm the one you want."

The officer didn't respond, still stunned at what had happened.

"Please," Eli repeated, "let my friends go."

He hesitated a moment, looking into Eli's eyes. Then he turned and gave the order. "All right, let the others go."

His partner started to protest. "But—"

"Let 'em go," he repeated. "He's the one we want."
Then, turning to the group, he ordered, "You have exactly
one minute to clear the area. Do you hear me? One minute."

The group traded nervous looks.

The officer repeated louder. "One minute or we start
making arrests."

There was uneasy shifting, more exchanged glances.
Finally, Brent and Scott, who were farthest away, started
backing up, slowly easing themselves out of the lights and
into the shadows.

But the others remained, at least at first.

The officer turned, trying to look as many in the eye
as possible. Some met his stare, others could not.

"Forty-five seconds!"

More shifting. More nervous glances. The tension built.

"Connie?" Suzanne whispered. "What do we do?"

Conrad weighed the possibilities. If they stayed, they
would be arrested with Eli, thereby proving their alle-
giance. But arrested for what? For trespassing? Not exactly
the same as being arrested for murder. What type of alle-
giance did that prove?

He saw another shadow moving against the lights. It
was Maggie. A moment later, Will turned and followed
her into the darkness.

Then Robert.

"Thirty seconds!"

Yes, he and Suzanne could stay at Eli's side. Yes, they
could be arrested, but what good would it do? Couldn't
they serve him better by avoiding arrest, by working for
him on the outside?

"Connie . . ."

And what about Suzanne? As far as he knew, the woman hadn't even had a traffic ticket. How could he subject her to jail—to the humiliation of being booked, searched, imprisoned? And for what? Trespassing?

He saw more movement: Leon was backing up, Then he turned and slouched off into the darkness. Others followed—Hector, Trevor—each turning and moving up the knoll toward the lights and into the shadows.

"Fifteen seconds!"

Conrad turned back toward Eli, who watched sadly as his friends continued to leave, deserting him one by one.

Then, without a word, Jake slowly turned. He took a step and hesitated. His internal struggle was fierce and obvious. So was Eli's. It was clear that he wanted to say something. But he didn't. Instead, he watched silently as Jake finally started again, lumbering off into the lights and into the darkness beyond.

Now there were only Conrad and Suzanne. Eli slowly turned to them. Once again his gaze locked onto Conrad's. What was he to do? Stay or leave? Be arrested and serve no use, or leave and be of help? What did Eli want? But as Conrad searched Eli's eyes, he saw no clues. As always, it would have to be his choice.

"Okay, folks," the first officer sighed heavily and motioned to his partner. The big man holstered his baton and reached for his pair of cuffs.

But he'd barely stepped toward them before Conrad heard himself cry out, "All right!"

The officer stopped.

"We're going," Conrad said. "We're . . . going." He glanced at Eli, but Eli no longer looked at him. Instead, he was staring at the ground. And it was that look, that expression of utter rejection that broke Conrad's heart.

Still, the decision had been made. Without a word he turned and, gently leading Suzanne, they started up the hill. He knew that part of her was desperate to remain behind, heard a muffled sob as she looked over her shoulder one final time. She could stay if she wanted. He was certain she knew that. Just as it was his choice to stay or leave, so it was hers. But she continued to walk by his side. And as they headed up the slope into the glaring lights, he said a silent prayer, asking that she not regret her decision as much as he was already despising his own.

Julia stepped out of the restroom. Although the knot in her stomach made it impossible to eat, she'd more than made up for it with the number of diet sodas she'd put down. As she reentered the hospital corridor, light from the late afternoon sun poured through the west windows, bringing out textures and shadows—the gurney against the wall with its cracked black vinyl and its stainless steel legs, the fire extinguisher behind the sleek, molded plastic cover, even the threads of the fabric wallpaper—everything was vivid and alive.

She headed back toward the ICU lounge, taking another deep breath. She'd been doing a lot of that lately, taking deep breaths. The ordeal was taking its toll. She glanced at her watch: 6:10 P.M. Seven hours had passed since they'd pulled the plug. Seven hours and he was still alive.

His breathing had grown louder and even more irregular, sometimes stopping for several seconds before starting up again with gasps and chokes. But it was the seizures that really took it out of her. They'd started three to four hours ago. The nurse assured her that, although it didn't happen with all patients, it was perfectly normal for others. Well, what was perfectly normal for others was not perfectly normal for Julia. To see her father's body suddenly jerk or contract did not make things easier.

She arrived at the white ICU phone, picked it up, and announced her presence. The door buzzed and she stepped inside. She passed the nurses' station. It was a new shift; the others had left at five. As she approached cubicle four she began to hear faint music. Someone was singing. The bed came into view, and she saw her mother sitting on the other side, near the window, looking down at her ex-husband and softly singing:

> *"Jesus loves me, this I know,*
> *For the Bible tells me so.*
> *Little ones to Him belong,*
> *They are weak but He is—"*

"Mom," Julia interrupted as she entered the room. "What are you doing?"

Her mother looked up, eyes slightly red and swollen. "It seems to calm him," she said. "It gives him some peace."

Julia looked down at her father's body. Her mother was right. There were no spasms, no jerkings, at least for the moment. Even his breathing seemed to come a little easier. She eased herself into the yellow chair beside him, directly across from her mother.

"Do you remember the year he taught Sunday school with me?" her mother asked. "With the first graders?"

Julia nodded, the memory almost making her smile.

"Oh, I know it was so he could duck out of church. You two were always good at dreaming up excuses."

"You knew that?" Julia asked.

"Of course. Anyway," her mother continued, "this was one of the songs we taught them. And they wanted to hear it every week, over and over again. So we sang it, over and over again. And your father, he never objected."

"No doubt hoping to use up the time so he wouldn't have to do all those arts and crafts."

Her mother laughed softly. "He did come home with a few glue-coated ties, didn't he?"

Julia nodded at the memory.

"But I think it was more than that," her mother said. "I think the singing gave him a certain comfort. I can't explain why, but he never said no." She glanced up to the bandaged head, staring at it for a long, tender moment. Then, quietly, she resumed the song.

"Jesus loves me, this I know,
For the Bible tells me so . . ."

Her mother was no singer, but there was something about her thin, wavery voice, about the simplicity of the song, that brought a tightness to Julia's throat.

"Little ones to Him belong,
They are weak but He is strong."

Her mother took a breath and without missing a beat said, "Sing with me, Jules."

"Yes, Jesus loves me.
Yes, Jesus loves me."

Julia opened her mouth, but no words would come.

"Yes, Jesus loves me."

Instead, her eyes suddenly brimmed with tears. She tried blinking them back, angrily swiping at them. But they kept coming. Something was happening, deep inside.

"The Bible tells me so."

It wasn't the singing, it wasn't the words. But whatever it was caused the tears to spill onto her cheeks and begin streaming down her face. Whatever had been unlocked inside of her made it impossible for her to stop.

Her mother continued:

"Jesus loves me, this I know,
For the Bible tells me so."

Suddenly a sob escaped from Julia's throat. Then another.

Her mother looked up in surprise and came to a stop. "Jules, what's wrong?"

Embarrassed, Julia took another swipe at her tears, but it was no use.

"Julia . . ."

"I don't know." She tried to laugh. "I, uh . . ." She swallowed hard, trying to regain control. "I can't, uh . . ." Another sob escaped, which she covered with a cough.

"Are you okay?"

She shook her head. "I don't know." After another gulp she continued. "What's wrong with me? Why can't I sing that? It's just a stupid little . . ." She swallowed again. "Just a stupid little song."

Her mother said nothing, watching as the tears continued to fall.

Another sob slipped out. Again Julia shook her head. "I don't know . . ." She looked away, trying to get out the words. "I mean, I'd give anything to have that kind of faith."

After a moment her mother answered softly. "You can."

Julia shook her head, wiping her face. "No."

"Yes, you can, Sweetheart, all you have to do is ask."

"No . . ." More tears came. "It's not that simple."

"Yes, it is, Jules, it's just that simple. It's just a matter of choice."

Julia tried to answer but could no longer speak. Instead, she lowered her head and quietly wept. She was grateful that her mother said nothing more, that she no longer had to answer questions. A full minute passed before her mother started singing again. Softly, gently. And although the song had unleashed powerful unknown emotions within her, and although she couldn't join in, Julia still found a peace as her mother continued.

> *"Yes, Jesus loves me,*
> *Yes, Jesus loves me.*
> *Yes, Jesus loves me.*
> *The Bible tells me so."*

As the number of deaths from the bombing rose, so did the public outrage. As early as 8:30 A.M., a small crowd had started gathering outside the Salem County Courthouse where Eli was held. They were not happy. In fact, as far as Conrad could tell, they had all the earmarks of a mob in the making, a mob growing more and more hungry for justice. And, true to form, the media was also arriving—stirring up things, poking cameras into faces, asking people what they felt—not, of course, before telling them about the latest tally of deaths. Nineteen was the current count, nearly a third of them infants.

Conrad had seen this type of unrest before—as a student reporter back in Chicago, during the '68 Democratic Convention, just before the riots broke out. And he was nervous. Even though there were only forty or fifty people, and even though somebody had had the good sense to station a guard at the top of the courthouse steps as a reminder that no disorder would be tolerated, those things did little to ease Conrad's fears. This gathering was a tinderbox of outrage that, if not defused, would eventually ignite.

Earlier he'd tried contacting the sheriff's department, using his press credentials to get more information. But as soon as he'd mentioned his name, their attitude seemed to change—almost as if they'd been alerted that he might call.

"Excuse me . . . excuse me, aren't you one of Eli's followers?"

Conrad recognized the voice and turned to see Gerald McFarland shoving a microphone into Jake's face. Of the group only he, Jake, and Trevor had shown up outside the courthouse.

"I . . . uh . . ." Jake looked at the camera, startled, then at the small group gathering around it. He coughed slightly. "I've heard him speak, if that's what you mean. At the City of God, when he was at the fountain." He swallowed.

"No, no," McFarland insisted, "haven't you been on the road with him?"

More people turned in his direction. A few exchanged hushed words.

Jake shook his head. "No, you got me mixed up with somebody else."

But McFarland was ruthless. He knew that Jake was part of the group, had seen him a number of times. "No, I'm sure you were with him."

Other people began to approach, straining to listen. Jake's eyes darted to Conrad, then to Trevor.

McFarland continued, "In fact, I think we've got footage, back in Texas when you—"

"I said I don't know him, so I don't know him, all right?" He swore to further make his point. "I'm here to see what's going on, just like the rest of you." He pushed past McFarland and the camera. "Now, if you'll excuse me ..." He entered the crowd of onlookers, which parted slightly for him to exit. He'd only taken a half-dozen steps before the courthouse clock began to chime. Conrad glanced up. It was nine o'clock. He turned back to Jake. Instead of slowing or even turning, the big man had lowered his head and picked up his pace.

Conrad watched sadly. He knew exactly what the big guy was feeling—had felt it himself. Was still feeling it. Hadn't he also betrayed Eli? Maybe not here, but what about the night of the arrest? How was he any different from Jake? Or Keith, for that matter. Granted, he'd not sold Eli for cash, but he'd still denied him. Like Jake, like Keith, like the rest of the group, he'd still betrayed him. Would it ever stop? This waffling weakness? This cowardliness of giving in to the world's ways and refusing Eli's? Would he ever—

His thoughts froze. What on earth? There, at the foot of the courthouse steps, he saw Julia. She was sitting, but not on the steps. Instead, she sat in a yellow molded chair. And beside her ... was a bed. A hospital bed with someone in it. What was going on? What was she doing here? He closed his eyes and reopened them, but she was still there. Her head was bowed slightly and, although he couldn't be sure, it looked as if she was crying.

Confused and concerned, he started toward her. But he'd barely taken a step before another voice called to him.

"Connie . . . Hey, Conrad?"

He turned to see Leo Singer, his rival from *Up Front* magazine. And there, trailing behind him, were Ned Burton and a soundman. They were obviously here to cover the story. After his initial surprise came the resentment . . . and the realization. Burton had always been Conrad's cameraman. Not Singer's. But now, here the two of them were, a team. Leo was in, Conrad was out. It was as simple as that. Funny, he'd almost forgotten how expendable he was.

He turned back toward Julia, but she was no longer there. Neither was her chair. Nor the bed. He frowned and turned to search the courtyard.

"You okay, buddy?" Singer asked.

Conrad continued to look, but saw nothing.

"Connie?"

He turned back to them. "Yeah, uh . . ." He caught Burton's eyes and they exchanged nods.

"So how you been?" Singer asked. "Getting all that rest you so desperately needed?"

A sizable portion of Conrad wanted to punch him in the face, but he managed to exercise restraint.

"Did you hear the news?" Singer continued.

Conrad scanned the courtyard one last time for Julia but with no success. "What news is that?" he asked.

"It just came in a minute ago. Preliminary results indicate that the same materials used to make the bomb at the City of God were used in the bomb that blew up your guy's trailer in Montana."

Conrad turned to Singer. He now had his full attention. "What?"

Singer nodded. "That's right."

Conrad felt a wave of relief wash over him. "So we've got proof that it's some sort of conspiracy, then."

"What do you mean?"

"If they're the same materials, then whoever blew up the RV also planted the bomb at the City of God."

"Uh, not exactly."

"What do you mean?'"

"Actually, the theory being floated is that the bomb that blew up that RV was in your boy's possession."

"Meaning . . ."

"Meaning it was an accidental explosion from the bombs that he and his followers were making."

Conrad felt himself growing cold. "What?"

Singer shrugged. "That's the story. Of course there's no confirmation yet, but—"

"So you haven't reported it?" Conrad couldn't hide the urgency in his voice.

"Of course not. Not till we get it confirmed."

Conrad looked uneasily at the people milling about the courtyard. There were a dozen more since the last time he'd checked. "Good," he said, "because if word got out . . ."

"I know, I know," Singer nodded, also looking over the group. "Unfortunately, just because we're not in the business of reporting rumors"—he threw a glance toward McFarland—"doesn't mean others aren't."

Conrad spun toward McFarland. He got the message. Loud and clear. He pushed past Singer—"Excuse me"—and started across the courtyard toward McFarland. "Gerry! Gerry!"

If Singer had received word, chances are that McFarland had too. And, knowing his style, let alone his agenda, it was doubtful that he would be quite as discerning in separating fact from fiction. "Gerry!"

A crowd was gathering around him, listening intently as he interviewed a black mother holding her child.

"What?" she practically shouted at McFarland as Conrad approached. "Are you sure?"

McFarland nodded. "The report was released moments ago. So as a mother, tell us—how does that make you feel?" He shoved the mike back into the angry woman's face. The expressions of those listening showed equal outrage. Murmuring and unrest swept through the crowd. Immediately, Conrad knew. McFarland had already struck.

The match inside the tinderbox had just been lit.

CHAPTER SIXTEEN

K eith!" Conrad banged on the peeling door of the motel room. "Keith, open up!"

No answer.

"Keith!" He knocked again. The kid's car was in the parking lot. He had to be there. "Keith!"

Going to see him had been a last-minute decision, when Conrad couldn't get through to Dr. Kerston's people, when suddenly all ties had been severed. But they would listen to Keith. They'd have to. And they'd have to realize how dangerous it was for Eli to remain in the courthouse. Any minute, that crowd could go off. And when they did, no solitary guard stationed up on the steps could stop them. Reinforcements had to be brought in. And quickly.

"Keith!" More banging. More silence . . . except for the strange ditty going around inside Conrad's head. It had started on the drive over. A nursery rhyme. One that he hadn't heard in years.

> *Jesus loves me, this I know,*
> *For the Bible tells me so.*

It was the weirdest thing. And even weirder was the fact that he couldn't seem to shake it.

> *Little ones to Him belong,*
> *They are weak but He is strong.*

He stole a look over his shoulder. No one was in the parking lot—just Keith's car and the battered Toyota Travis had loaned him. Without hesitation he crossed to the window, slipped off his shoe, and bashed it through one of the panes. The brittle glass shattered effortlessly, one of the advantages of a cheap motel. He reached in, unlatched the lock, and pushed up the window.

"Keith?"

He shoved aside the sun-rotted drapes and stuck in his head.

The boy was on the bed, slumped against the back wall. His chest was soaked in blood.

"Keith!" Conrad lifted himself into the window, trying to avoid the shards of glass. He wasn't entirely successful; something caught his Dockers and he heard them rip as he crawled through.

"Keith!" He started toward the bed—then stopped, suddenly seeing the splattered blood on the wall and the open wound in the back of the young man's head. In his hand he held a .32 caliber Beretta. But he was still breathing. Conrad could see his chest moving, hear little gurgling sounds from his throat. He headed for the phone on the nightstand, scooped it up, and quickly punched in 911. The first two tries were unsuccessful; then he remembered to dial 8 for an outside line.

"911," a voice answered.

"I need an ambulance at Twin Pines Motel on Cumberland Road. There's been a shooting. Severe head wound, lots of blood."

"You say there was a shooting?"

"Yes, at Twin Pines Motel. Hurry, he's still breathing, but barely."

"Can you see him from where you are?" the voice asked.

"Yes."

"Is he in the room with you?"

"Yes," Conrad answered impatiently.

"Now, by shooting, what exactly do you—"

"Just get out here!" Conrad slammed down the phone.

"Connie . . ." It was Keith's voice, barely audible.

He scrambled onto the bed. "I'm right here, buddy, I'm right here."

"Tell him—" Keith coughed a moment, wracking his entire body.

"Shhh." Conrad wanted to hold him, but was unsure how. "Take it easy, you'll be okay."

"Tell him . . ." He coughed again. "It wasn't supposed to be like this."

"Save your strength, don't talk."

"No." Keith tried to shake his head. "They're moving him."

"Eli?"

He tried to nod.

"Where?"

The gurgling grew louder. It was more difficult for him to speak. Yet he forced out the word. "Atlanta."

"Good—that's good, then."

Keith shook his head. "It's a setup. He'll never make it." More coughing, then a deep, unsettling breath that brought gagging and the vomiting of blood. Conrad recoiled, but the blood splashed onto his pants anyway, immediately soaking through. He felt his stomach turning, but did his best to ignore it.

With great effort, Keith wheezed out the word, "hijacking . . ." He took a shuddering, gasping breath, underwent another set of wracking coughs, and ended with the whispered word, ". . . lynching."

Before Conrad could react, Keith's hand rose, reaching out for something, anything. Conrad gave him his own hand. The boy clung to it desperately. "Tell him . . ." He pulled Conrad's hand closer to his face. "Tell him I'm sorry."

"He knows," Conrad whispered, his throat aching with emotion. "He knows."

The fact seemed to give Keith comfort. He released his grip, then lowered his hand back to the bed. Conrad stared down at it, his vision blurring from tears. The kid took a deep, ragged breath. And then another.

"Keith?"

The boy did not respond.

"Keith, hang in there, buddy!"

But there was no answer—just a long, slow exhale that ended in a faint, gurgling wheeze. He did not breathe again.

"Why won't he let go?" Julia asked as she stared down at her father. His breathing had grown louder, more uneven—sometimes choking, sometimes gasping, sometimes stopping altogether. Then there were the muscle spasms and convulsions. "Why does he keep hanging on?"

"I don't know," her mother whispered hoarsely from across the bed. "He's always been a fighter."

Julia looked up at her. The woman's face was streaked with tears, her hair disheveled. These hours were definitely taking their toll upon her as well. Outside, Julia noticed that the sun was just setting, filling the ICU cubicle with a tranquil, pink glow. It reminded her of the beautiful sunsets that had filled their living room, back in Pasadena.

"Mom?" She cleared her throat.

Her mother looked up.

"Do you remember on my birthday, do you remember when he was teaching me to ride my bicycle? Over at the park on Devonshire?"

Her mother nodded.

Suddenly Julia felt embarrassed. "I know it's stupid to bring this up, but ... do you remember when he let go of the bike and I crashed so hard?"

"Yes."

"Did he ever ... did he ever tell you why he let go?" Suddenly she felt emotion welling up deep inside her again. She did her best to keep it under control. "I mean, one minute he's beside me, promising he'll never let go ...the next, he's broken his promise and I'm crashing into the ground." She looked back down at the bed. "It's just a little thing, but I never, I never understood why he let go. I mean, after he made such a big deal and promising and all."

"He didn't let go."

Julia looked to her. "What?"

Her mother shook her head. "No. At least not on purpose. He fell, Julia. He twisted his ankle, and he fell."

Julia's mouth opened.

"You didn't know that?"

She shook her head in silence.

"He was running beside you then stepped into a hole. He twisted his ankle and fell. He felt terrible about it. I remember him telling me in bed." She mused quietly. "Had a hard time getting to sleep that night, if I recall."

"I thought . . ." Julia's voice grew husky. She looked down at the bed, again struggling for control. She blinked, saw a tear blur her vision, then fall onto the sheet. "I thought . . . he let go . . . on purpose."

"Oh, no, Sweetheart. He fell. He stumbled and he fell."

Julia kept staring at the sheet, suddenly very lost, unable to get her bearings. It was a little thing. Not even worth mentioning. And yet, after all this time, after all these years . . .

Her mother continued quietly. "He stumbled, Jules. We all stumble." Then softer. "The trick is being able to forgive ourselves and get back up. To forgive ourselves, and others . . ."

Conrad barely held his panic in check as he raced back across town to the courthouse. If what Keith said was accurate, and he saw no reason to doubt him, then every second counted. The paramedics had cleaned him up some, but he took no time to change his pants or shirt. He had to get back to the courthouse. This thing had to be stopped.

Parking was impossible. The courtyard was now flooded with people. He pulled the Toyota into a loading zone across from the building and turned on the flashers, hoping that would slow down the ticketing and tow-away process. He scrambled out of the car, dashed across the street, and entered the angry crowd.

He pushed and weaved his way toward the steps. But when he looked up, he saw people at the top being denied entrance by the guard. He might be able to bluff his way in, but he didn't have the time to waste if he failed. He veered to the left, working his way to the side of the building, where the crowd thinned, and then to the back where there was virtually no one. He spotted a loading bay at the far end and headed for it. The steel cargo door had been rolled down, and a guard was posted next to the adjacent doorway. A guard who Conrad soon discovered had been given the same orders as the one in front.

"But I have valuable information," Conrad pleaded. "I need to speak to someone in charge."

"I'm sorry." The balding young man shook his head. "The building is sealed."

"But . . ." Conrad fumbled for his wallet and produced his press card. "I'm with the media."

"You and half the people here," he answered.

Conrad sighed wearily. In the distance he heard the rumbling of thunder. A storm was approaching. He tried another tack. "Listen, I'm a personal friend of his. And I have every reason to believe his life is in danger. Serious danger."

The guard looked at him, obviously nonplussed. He'd have to do better than that.

"Please, just let me—"

Suddenly the door behind them groaned open and two women stepped out.

"Suzanne!" Conrad called.

She looked up, startled. "Oh, Connie . . ." She moved past the guard, and the two embraced.

"I'm so scared," she whispered.

"Me too."

"What's going to happen?"

"I don't know."

When they separated, she turned to the woman behind her. "This is Eli's mother, Mrs. Shepherd. And this"—she motioned toward Conrad—"is Conrad Davis."

The woman looked up at him and forced a faint smile. There was something familiar about her. Something about her eyes—their startling blueness. And their compassion. She hesitated, as if sensing something familiar about him as well.

"It's an honor to meet you," Conrad said.

She nodded, holding his gaze. "Have we met?" she asked.

And then he knew. "Yes," he answered, "just once. A long, long time ago . . . in a laundry room in Santa Monica."

She stared at him, in quiet wonder. "You were there?"

He smiled. "Just briefly."

She nodded, ever so gently.

Then, pulling his eyes from hers, he turned to Suzanne. "Is he okay?"

She shook her head. "They wouldn't let us see him."

"But she's his mother."

"They said he fell down the stairs and injured his head. He got pretty banged up, and he's in the infirmary now where they're working on him."

"Infirmary?" the guard asked.

They turned to him. "That's right," Suzanne said. "They suggested we come back in an hour or two. Why?"

"Nothing, I just, uh . . ." It was obvious the guard had something on his mind.

"What?" Conrad asked.

He ignored Conrad and spoke directly to Mrs. Shepherd. "So you're Eli's mother?"

She nodded.

"My momma, in Oklahoma, she attended one of Eli's services. Had a bunch of cancer eating up her inside female parts."

"Was my son able to help her?" she asked.

He broke into a grin. "Next day when she went to the doctor, it's all gone. As good as new, they said. Never had to bother with no operation. Never needed it."

Eli's mother reached out and touched his hand. "I'm glad."

But he wasn't done. "And the thing where he raised that guy from the dead in Tennessee. We must of seen that on TV a dozen times."

"That was my brother," Suzanne answered.

"No kidding?"

She nodded.

A relationship was starting to form, and Conrad quickly took advantage of it. "What were you saying about the infirmary?" he asked.

The guard looked back at him, the spell almost broken.

Conrad pressed in. "You said something about an infirmary."

The man hesitated, then answered, "We don't have one."

"What?" Suzanne asked.

The guard shook his head. "No, ma'am. Not here."

"Then where is he?" she asked.

The guard shifted slightly, glancing away.

"Do you know?" Mrs. Shepherd asked.

The guard said nothing.

"Please. If he's not in the infirmary, where is he?" Once again she touched his arm. "Please, tell me what they've done with my son."

The man looked away. It was obvious that he knew something, but equally as obvious that he could not tell.

Conrad took another stab. "So he's not in the building."

The guard's eyes shot toward Conrad's in betrayal. "I didn't say that."

But Conrad had his information and there was little time to waste. "How long ago?"

"What?"

"How long ago did they leave?"

"I didn't say he—"

"Please, we don't have much time! How long?"

The guard hesitated.

Conrad pursued. "I'm not asking you to tell me where they took him. Just tell me how long ago he left."

The guard glanced back toward Eli's mother.

"Please," she whispered.

"About ten minutes ago." He took a breath and continued. "I'm not saying it was him. But a guard and a driver, they come out with somebody pretty badly beaten. They got in one of our vans over there and took off. 'Bout eight, ten minutes ago."

That was all Conrad needed. "Thank you." He reached out to take Suzanne's arm. "Come on."

She resisted. "But—"

"We haven't much time!"

Suzanne turned to the guard. "Thank you."

"I'm not sayin' it was him," he repeated.

"I understand."

"Thank you," Mrs. Shepherd said softly. "Thank you."

The guard nodded quietly, then looked away.

Suzanne took Mrs. Shepherd's arm and the three of them started back to the car. There was more thunder.

Louder. Closer. They skirted around the crowd. Eight to ten minutes. The van had an eight- to ten-minute jump on them. There was not a moment to waste.

"Where to now?" Conrad shouted.

"Stay on 212 till you get to the 16!" Suzanne yelled back. She peered at the map on her knees. "When we hit the 75, it's a straight shot north to Atlanta."

"He'll never get that far," Conrad called, as he glanced out to another of the dozens of side roads leading into the Oconee National Forest. "If they intercept him, it'll be out here somewhere in the sticks, under cover of the woods."

He wiped his face. It was practically noon, and the heat was sweltering. The air conditioner in Trevor's car had given up the ghost long ago, and even with both windows down there was little escape from the July heat. Only the thick thunderheads moving in offered promise of relief. "You sure that's not too windy back there?" he shouted to Eli's mother.

"Don't worry about me," she called.

Any other time the drive would have been peaceful. Thick canopies of pine and hardwoods lined the road. A dozen different smells and fragrances blew in. From time to time the pristine white wisteria caught their eye, and of course the kudzu, always the kudzu—the thick green vine from Japan that was slowly taking over the state of Georgia.

They'd been on the road fifteen minutes. Conrad pushed the Toyota a good twenty to thirty miles per hour over the speed limit. There had been no sign of the van. There might never be—particularly if Dr. Kerston or whoever he'd hired was doing his job correctly. It didn't take a rocket scientist to figure out the scenario: If Kerston and his little group wanted Eli moved, they certainly had enough political clout to get Eli moved. And if there just happened to be a bunch of vigilante types who got word of the move and took matters into their own hands by hijacking the van ... well, it would certainly be a tragedy, but one that the good Dr. Kerston had no control over. And why an old-fashioned lynching? Maybe the good ol' boys just liked the symbolism.

"There!" Suzanne pointed. "Back there!"

Conrad hit the brakes, quickly slowing the car. "Are you sure?"

She shook her head. "I didn't see a van, but there were a bunch of cars moving down a dirt road."

Conrad nodded, slowing the car enough to make a U-turn. The worn tires squealed on the hot asphalt as they turned and doubled back.

"There!" Suzanne pointed down the dirt road. "See, down there."

To their left, three or four hundred yards away, a group of cars was moving under the trees through the mottled sunlight.

It was a long shot, but the best they had. Conrad turned sharply off the highway and sped down the road— not fast enough to draw attention, but fast enough to catch up. They were practically there when the group reached the top of a small ridge and began turning to the right. Dropping in behind, he followed. They pulled into a large overgrown field, apparently the remains of a forgotten farm. And there, under a grove of hickory, sat a gray county van.

Conrad brought the car to a quick stop, threw open the door, and climbed out. Suzanne and Eli's mother followed.

"No." He turned back to them. "You two stay here."

"He's my son," his mother insisted.

"Mrs. Shepherd—"

"Please. He's my son."

Conrad turned to Suzanne, but she was already nodding in solidarity with the woman. Resigning himself, he motioned for them to hurry.

The wind had picked up, blowing the tall grass against their thighs as they waded through it. In the distance there was a flash of lightning. The storm was much closer. Conrad counted about a dozen cars, some newer models, some older. He spotted a circle of shouting men just beyond the van and picked up his pace.

As he approached, he caught glimpses of someone on the ground inside the circle. Between the legs he saw boots kicking him, hard. It looked like a game. One man would step into the circle, deliver a powerful kick or two with the appropriate oaths, then step back, making room for the next assailant who would enter and repeat the process.

Conrad finally arrived at the fringe of the circle and began pushing some of the men aside, pulling others out of the way. "What are you doing!" he shouted. "What's going on!" Some resisted, others pushed back. But most were too absorbed in the proceeding to notice.

Breathing heavily, he finally forced himself to the front . . . where a flash of lightning forever froze the scene in his mind. There on the ground, bleeding and gasping, was what had once been Eli Shepherd. Only now he was a beaten pulp—his face so bloody, so swollen he was nearly impossible to recognize. Coughing blood and choking, he flew first in one direction, then another as the men's boots landed merciless blows, kicking him in his chest, his gut, his groin, his face.

Another flash of lightning lit the scene, and suddenly Conrad was no longer staring down at Eli. Suddenly, he was staring down at himself! Suddenly, *he* was the one on the ground, *he* was the one being beaten, *he* was the one coughing blood.

The image lasted only a moment, just through the flicker of the lightning, and then it was gone. But there was no denying what he'd seen. He closed his eyes and opened them. Now it was Eli again—wearing his favorite jeans, his favorite T-shirt, both covered in blood and mud and clay.

Conrad broke from the group and staggered into the circle, pushing the current attacker aside. Someone grabbed his shoulder. He tried to break free, but the man's grip was strong. Instinctively, he spun around and swung for the man's face, landing a blow. The pain in his hand was instant. It felt like he'd broken it, but he'd worry about that later. As he turned back toward Eli, someone caught him around the waist and flung him hard to the ground—so hard that the air was knocked from his lungs. Then, before he could catch his breath, a boot landed square in his gut. And then another. They continued—three, four, a half dozen—he lost track. Most were to his stomach and chest, one caught his face, another his left temple. He began losing consciousness.

"All right," a distant voice shouted, "get him to his feet."

At first Conrad thought they meant him. He opened a swollen eye and saw Eli on the ground beside him. They were less than a yard apart. A rope had been tied around Eli's neck. "What's happening?" Conrad gasped.

Eli's face was hamburger, too swollen to show an expression. Conrad wasn't even sure he saw the mouth move, but he heard the words: "Justice ... mercy ..." That was all Eli spoke before the rope jerked and yanked him up and out of sight.

Legs strobed past as Conrad fought to get to his knees. He almost made it until another foot landed hard in his left side, sending him sprawling back into the red clay.

Justice ... mercy? What was he talking about? There was no justice here. And certainly no mercy.

"Connie!" He heard Suzanne's voice, saw her kneeling at his side. Eli's mother was behind her. "Connie," Suzanne cried, "are you okay?"

"Yes," he lied as she helped him to his knees. There was another flash of lightning. It had started to rain.

He struggled to stand, but Suzanne protested, "No, stay down."

At first he refused—until he tried to stand, and realized he had no choice in the matter. He couldn't get up. Not without her help. Still on his hands and knees, he looked up and spotted the crowd moving toward the edge of the forest, pulling the stumbling Eli by the rope. Ahead of them, a rusting green Bronco was being directed under the large bough of an oak tree.

"NO!" Conrad shouted, trying to rise.

"Connie, don't!"

But he didn't listen. Using all of his strength, he finally made it to his feet. But the move was too abrupt, and once again consciousness began to slip away. He leaned against Suzanne so he would not fall.

Another flash of lightning—and it happened again. It wasn't Eli they were dragging by the rope. It was himself!

Those were *his* ripped Dockers, *his* bloody shirt, and that was *his* swollen, beaten face. Conrad stared in astonishment. As he did, memories poured in. Memories of his failures. Memories of the first time he'd cheated on Suzanne—that production assistant in Baltimore. Then the young intern, right there in his office, right there in their home. And Julia's voice when she'd caught them. *"Daddy, Daddy, what are you doing?"*

"Connie . . ." He turned. Suzanne was speaking, but she sounded far, far away.

He looked back at the crowd. The vision continued as he watched himself being dragged by the rope. In some strange way it made sense—watching himself being beaten, watching himself being mocked. After all, that's what *he* deserved. Not Eli, but Conrad. Look at all his failures, look at all he'd done to the only woman he'd ever loved.

"Connie . . ."

Again he turned to Suzanne. So much pain he'd caused, so much misery. And not just to her. What about Julia? Look how he'd ruined her life. How he'd turned her into someone incapable of having a relationship, into someone who according to Suzanne didn't even consider herself worthy to be a mother.

He looked back at the angry mob dragging him toward the Bronco. Of course. Of course, of course, of course. That's what he deserved. That and more. That was the justice Eli was talking about. But how did that—

"Connie, are you all right?"

He glanced back to Suzanne and nodded. But when he looked back at the scene, it had changed again. He was no longer there. He was no longer the one being dragged by the rope. It was Eli. Now they were cinching *Eli's* hands behind his back. Yanking the cord so hard that it was *Eli* who flinched in pain.

Another flash of lightning. The storm had arrived. The rain came hard as the wind whipped and snapped their clothes.

The mob forced Eli to climb onto the hood of the Bronco. But it was wet, and with hands tied he slipped to his knees, nearly falling off. The crowd laughed and shouted. There was another flash of lightning, closer yet, followed by a tremendous crash. Some looked up in concern. Most didn't notice.

"Here!" A no-neck bulldog of a man grabbed the loose end of the rope. "Let me help!" With a grunt, he flung it over the oak limb.

More lightning, followed by a ringing clap that echoed through the trees. Bulldog Man pulled the slack until there was none, until he was literally hoisting the coughing and choking Eli to his feet by the rope around his neck.

"Hey, miracle boy!" someone yelled. "Let's see you get out of this!"

Conrad turned to Suzanne and shouted over the wind. "Get me over there! I've got to help him!"

"There's nothing we can do!" she shouted back.

"Suzanne—"

"There's nothing we can do!"

He broke free from her and staggered forward, taking a step or two before his legs gave out and he sprawled into the clay.

"Connie!"

He struggled to his knees, not taking his eyes from the scene. The rain blew harder, stinging his eyes, making it difficult to see. But it looked as if Eli was stuck. Part of his pants leg was hung up on a custom-made chrome ornament welded to the hood. More lightning. The ornament was a sharp, jagged cobra, poised to look like it was striking.

Bulldog pulled harder, but in vain. Eli's pants leg was firmly stuck. It became a contest over which would give out first, Eli's pants or his neck.

"Here!" another shouted. "Let me help!" He leaped onto the front bumper of the Bronco, unsnapped Eli's jeans, and pulled them down over his knees to his feet. The group laughed and mocked as the man yanked the jeans off one foot, then the other. To complete the effect, another reached up to Eli's underwear and pulled it down to his ankles, then off his feet as well.

"Try it now!" the first shouted to Bulldog.

He nodded and pulled on the rope. Suddenly Eli was stretched to the limit, standing on his toes, coughing, gagging, gasping for breath. Bulldog crossed to a lower branch and quickly tied off his end. Another man scrambled up onto the hood. He produced a large knife and in two neat slices, completely removed Eli's T-shirt and peeled it off his back.

Now the spectacle was complete, and the crowd voiced their approval.

Another flash of lightning. Another deafening boom. And, once again, Conrad was staring up at himself. *He* was the one naked. *He* was the one humiliated and being choked.

Justice and mercy, justice and mercy. The words resonated in his head. *Justice and mercy . . .* More memories rushed in. More failures. From childhood, from adolescence, from his adult life. But always ending with his cheating on Suzanne. *You're only as good as your word.* How many times had he said that, quoted that, made it his motto? And how many times had he failed? If you're only as good as your word, and if your word was useless, doesn't that make you—

"Connie . . ."

He'd failed. Failed miserably. Inexcusably.

"Daddy . . ."

He spun around. What was Julia doing there? Why was she holding him? Where was Suzanne? He looked frantically about, then turned back to her. Tears burned his eyes. He tried to speak. It took forever for the words to come. "I'm sorry," he finally choked, "I'm so sorry."

"What?" It was Suzanne again.

He turned back to the Bronco. Now it was Eli on the hood. Not Conrad, not as it should be. But Eli.

Justice and mercy, justice and mercy . . . The words continued to echo in his head, forming on his lips. *Justice and mercy . . .*

"What?" Suzanne asked. "Connie, what are you saying?"

He shook his head.

The Bronco's driver hopped behind the wheel and revved the engine. The crowd hooted and hollered.

Justice and mercy, justice and mercy . . . weren't those the words Eli had used in Texas when they were visiting the convicted murderer, Ellen Perkins?

There was another flash of lightning, so close Conrad felt the hair on his arms rise.

The driver popped the clutch, giving the Bronco a jerk to scare Eli. It did the trick. Laughter and jeering followed as he fought to keep his balance.

Justice and mercy . . . that was the paradox that had troubled McFarland. The two concepts that he insisted were contradictory, that could not coexist . . . God's holy justice, and His loving mercy. Yet those were the two opposites that Eli had promised he would bring together.

Justice and mercy . . .

Suddenly the realization roared into place, so powerful that it left Conrad staggering under another wave of dizziness. Was it possible? Could it be? Here? Here, at this very moment? Could it be that the two were finally being united?

Justice for every one of Conrad's failures? Punishment for all he'd ever done wrong? But a punishment poured out onto someone else? Yes, Conrad should be up there. Yes, Conrad was the one who should be punished. But another person was taking that punishment for him. Justice was still being accomplished, holiness was still being preserved, but through the suffering of someone else instead of Conrad. Through the suffering of Eli.

And that—*that* was the mercy.

Justice and mercy. Two opposite truths coming together in one man, in one act of unfathomable love.

The Bronco revved again.

"Father!" Eli shouted into the raging wind. "Forgive them! They don't understand what they're doing!"

More taunts and jeers. The Bronco revved. The crowd shouted in anticipation. This would be it. The time had come.

Suddenly Eli searched the group, looking for someone, until his gaze landed upon Conrad. Through the rain, through the wind, their eyes connected. And if Conrad had any doubts about his theory, they were silenced by the love he saw in those eyes. Despite the unimaginable terror, the humiliation, there was no missing the love. And the mercy.

The engine revved louder. The crowd grew impatient. Then, with the last of his strength, shouting one final time into the wind, Eli cried, "Everything . . . is . . . accomplished!"

The driver popped the clutch, sending his vehicle into reverse, causing Eli to drop from the hood. A lightning bolt seared through the air, splitting a hickory not ten feet away. But the frightened cries of the men could not be heard over the deafening boom of the thunder. They stared in horror and astonishment. But Eli's neck had not broken. Instead he dangled, kicking and squirming, his eyes bulging wildly, while slowly, in excruciating agony, he began to suffocate.

Suzanne turned her head. So did Eli's mother. But Conrad did not. He could not. This was his. What Eli was undergoing was the punishment for Conrad's own failures. Failures for which he would never have to suffer. Justice was being served. Pure, undefiled, holy justice . . . and with it, infinite, loving mercy.

Together. At the same time. In one man.

Nearly two minutes passed before Eli quit twitching. Soon his body hung lifeless, swaying back and forth in the wind, his face purple-black, his eyes protruding from their sockets. The sight had become so hideous that even the most jaded spectator had grown silent. And yet, just as Eli had cried, everything was finished. Just as he had promised, it had all come to pass.

Justice and mercy. The union was complete.

CHAPTER SEVENTEEN

J ules . . ."

"I see." Julia rose to her feet.

"On his face."

"I see it. I see." At first she thought it was a trick of light, some game the last rays of sun were playing. But it wasn't. A tiny drop of moisture was slowly inching its way down his crinkled face, escaping from the corner of her father's eye.

"Connie . . ." Her mother rose. "Connie, can you hear me?"

"Dad. It's me, Julia."

"Connie, can you hear us?" Her mother's voice grew more hopeful. "Connie. Connie!"

Julia strained, listening, watching. Amidst the ragged breathing she searched for some indication, for any sign that he was trying to communicate.

"Dad. Dad!" It was all she could do not to touch him, to try and shake him awake. "Dad, can you hear me?" She leaned closer to his face, shouting. "Dad, are you there!" Desperation took hold; she could barely keep it in check. "Dad! *Dad!*"

"Please . . ." She spun around to see the ICU nurse standing at the door. "Lower your voices. The other patients—"

"He's crying!" Julia exclaimed. "He's—" Catching herself, she dropped her voice. "Look at his face, see for yourself. He's crying."

The nurse appeared skeptical, then walked toward the bed.

"See!" Julia pointed. "Right there. Look at his eye. Look at his eye!"

The nurse leaned closer and took a careful look.

Julia held her breath, waiting. She glanced over at her mother, who was biting her knuckle in equal anticipation.

At last the woman pulled back. "I'm sorry."

"What?" Julia said. "It's right there, you can see for yourself!"

"I'm sorry."

"But—he's feeling something. He must be. See for yourself."

The nurse shook her head. "It's merely a reflex action. I am sorry."

"A reflex action? A reflex action to what?"

"Julia," her mother called softly from across the bed.

Julia turned to her. "You see it! We all see it!"

The nurse reached for a tissue from the unused packet on the steel tray beside the bed. "It's just a watering eye," she said.

"But . . ." Julia knew she was on the verge of losing it; she could hear it in her quivering voice. She took a breath, fighting for control, then tried again. "Couldn't it be? Couldn't it be some sort of emotion?"

The nurse gently shook her head as she reached over and carefully dabbed up the moisture. "I'm afraid not. Not in his condition. It's just more of the body shutting down."

Resentment grew as Julia watched the tear disappear. This woman was wiping away her last hope. But, exercising that iron will of hers, she remained silent. Grieving, aching, wanting the nurse to stop, she said nothing.

The nurse finished and turned back to Julia. "I am sorry," she repeated softly.

Julia glanced away, not wanting the moisture in her own eyes to be seen. Her father's body gave another rattling, nerve-wracking gasp and another long exhale.

"It shouldn't be much longer," the nurse quietly said. "Not much longer at all."

Julia nodded.

"Connie!" Someone was banging on the motel door. "Connie, open up!"

Face buried in his pillow, Conrad exerted all of his effort to lift his head high enough to catch a glimpse of the radio alarm: 7:12 A.M.

More pounding. "Connie!" It was Suzanne.

As consciousness filtered in, so did memories of the past two days—Friday's lynching and inconsolable grief, followed by Saturday's absolute hopelessness.

"Connie, open up!"

He pulled aside the covers and cried out in pain. Two ribs had been bruised and one cracked during the beating he'd received Friday. But with determination, he swung his feet over the edge of the bed to the threadbare carpeting.

More pounding. "Connie!"

Something had to be wrong. Maybe the arrests they'd feared and talked about yesterday were finally happening. After all, if Eli was considered guilty of the bombing, didn't that make them all accessories? If Eli was arrested, wasn't it logical for their arrests to be next?

"Connie!'

He rose and limped to the door, running his hand through hair that stuck out in all directions. He fumbled with the chain lock, slid it aside, and opened the door. The morning sun glared behind Suzanne so brilliantly that he winced.

"He's gone!" she cried.

"Who's gone?"

"Eli!"

"What are you talking—"

"I just heard it on the news. There was some sort of break-in at the morgue. They took him, Connie." She sniffed loudly, fighting back the tears. "They stole his body!"

The information was like cold water in his face. "Are you sure?"

She nodded and swallowed. "It's not enough that they kill him, now they steal his body!"

Conrad's mind spun, trying to understand, trying to devise a strategy. "All right," he finally said. "Let me get some clothes on and we'll head down there." He reentered the room, painfully slipped into some pants and a shirt, then stumbled back out into the sunlight. Three others had also emerged from their rooms—Jake, Maggie, and Trevor, who was in his car motioning for them to hurry and climb in.

With some difficulty Conrad crawled into the back-seat; Suzanne and Maggie climbed in on either side of him. The door barely shut before Trevor ground the car into gear and it lurched forward.

Despite the sense of urgency, few words were spoken. The dull numbness from the past two days remained. Up front, Jake produced a map from the glove compartment. He gave short, terse directions. The rest of the car remained silent. This latest news was just one more weight added to their overwhelming burden of grief. Grief in losing a great friend. Grief in seeing evil triumph over good. And, on a more selfish note, grief in realizing how much of their life had been wasted for nothing. Nothing except humiliation, ridicule, and now a complete lack of purpose. What do you do when your God has been killed?

And if they weren't consumed by the grief, there was their sense of personal failure. True, they may not have been the ones to lynch Eli, but that didn't stop them from feeling responsible. Over and over again, Conrad wondered if he should have done more, been more persistent, stood firmer, refused to desert him at the park. And yet, what he felt was nothing compared to what he was sure Jake was going through.

The big man sat in the front seat, sullen. And devastated. Since denying Eli at the courthouse, no one had seen or talked to him in nearly twenty-four hours . . . until he had showed up at the motel last night—drunk, face swollen from crying, clothes and hair a mess. Whatever torture he'd been through must have been excruciating. And it had not left him unchanged. In many ways he was a different man. Silent, full of remorse, and broken. Very, very broken.

Conrad felt Suzanne shudder and knew that she was crying again. Was there no end to the indignity, to the suffering?

As he looked out the window into the early morning, his mind drifted back to Friday afternoon—and to the thoughts he'd reflected on ever since the killing. He couldn't share those thoughts with the others, not yet, but that union he understood to have happened, that bringing together of justice and mercy, was still very much on his mind.

In the old world, the one before the accident, when he heard of Christ dying for his sins, he simply chalked it up to being part of his culture—a lathering televangelist, a dangling necklace, a peeling fresco. But what he'd seen was the slaughter of a real human being, a loving, giving person, the greatest person he'd ever met. The slaughter of a love that had looked him directly in the eyes and said, "I'm doing this for you—it's all for you."

The memory still gave him chills.

Trevor pulled the car onto Cumberland Avenue and after about a mile took a left. As he did, Conrad began to experience that sensation again—the one of Julia being present. Suzanne sat at his left, and he could have sworn Julia was sitting at his right. The feeling was so strong that he actually caught himself stealing a peek over at Maggie, just to make sure. But of course it was Maggie. There was no Julia. How could there be?

Trevor turned left again at the 1400 block and a moment later, they saw it. Although it was 7:30 on a Sunday morning, the place was bustling. Yellow police tape had been stretched from one corner of a two-story brick building out to the nearest parking meter, where it ran along the other meters until it reached the opposite corner and stretched back to the building. It blocked off not only the entrance but the entire front sidewalk. It didn't, however, discourage the media from setting up. One or two reporters had already begun filming their stories from the edge of the tape.

And there, in the midst of it all, stood McFarland, scouting with his cameraman for the best place to make his report.

As they slowed, Conrad leaned past Maggie and rolled down the window. "Gerry?" he called. "Gerry!"

McFarland turned and spotted him. "Hey, Connie!" He motioned for him to join them. "You won't believe this."

"Stop the car," Conrad ordered.

Trevor obeyed.

Maggie opened the door and stepped out, allowing Conrad to do the same. But his feet had barely hit the pavement before an officer banged on the hood of the car, motioning for Trevor to move on.

"They're with me," McFarland called out.

"I don't care who they're with, they're not stopping here. There's parking over the next block."

"He's media." McFarland jabbed a thumb at Conrad.

"Move it!" the officer barked.

A baffled Maggie looked unsure whether to get in or stay out.

"I said move it!"

Reluctantly, she ducked back into the car. Conrad leaned down and shouted into the window. "I'll meet you across the street. Just give me a couple minutes."

Trevor nodded and the Toyota lurched forward.

"Find out what you can!" Suzanne called as they pulled off.

Conrad gave a nod and immediately heard McFarland say, "So, your boy keeps making the news even when he's dead."

Conrad turned. He was cool and matter-of-fact. "You knew about the lynching, didn't you?"

McFarland blinked at his candor.

Conrad repeated himself, this time feeling his anger rise. "You knew they were going to kill him, didn't you?"

The big fellow shook his head. "No," he said almost sadly. "I did not know that. I knew about the deal with Keith Anderson, I knew the arrest was coming. But the lynching, I hadn't a clue."

Conrad stared a moment, unsure whether to believe him. Not that it made much difference.

"Take a look at this, Connie." McFarland turned and started toward the building. "You won't believe it." With some effort the big man ducked under the police tape. Conrad followed. They crossed the sidewalk and climbed the six steps to the entrance. When they arrived at the open double doors, McFarland came to a stop.

"When the police got here, these doors were just like you see them now. Both standing wide open. And the funny thing is, there are no marks showing forced entry."

"What about other doors?" Conrad asked. "The back? Maybe a window?"

McFarland shook his head. "Nothing." He motioned for Conrad to follow, and they entered the building. "Because of your man's disturbing habit of raising folks from the dead, and those nasty rumors that he would do the same for himself, they posted not one but two guards over at that desk the last couple nights." He motioned toward a mahogany receptionist counter to their left.

"And what did they see?" Conrad asked.

"Nothing."

"What?"

McFarland cleared his throat. "They said they were asleep."

Conrad threw him a look. "Both of them?"

"That's what they say."

"While on duty?"

"That's the story."

"And they're saying it publicly?"

McFarland looked at him a moment, then answered. "They are now." He motioned for Conrad to follow. "Come on."

Beyond the mahogany counter were a handful of windowed offices, each with yellowed venetian blinds. To the right was an old elevator and a set of stairs. They headed right and took the stairs down into the basement. Conrad felt the air cool as they descended. When they hit the landing and turned, he saw glass doors leading to a moderate-sized room. Though the walls, ceiling, and tile were dingy, the doors were much newer. Through them he saw two officers and a photographer drinking coffee and talking.

McFarland pushed open the doors and they entered. The place looked like some sort of laboratory. Each wall had a counter and at least one stainless-steel sink and set of faucets. In the center sat an old-fashioned operating table, complete with a surgical lamp hovering above it. To their right was the only wall without a counter. It contained what looked like a half-dozen stainless-steel freezer doors—each four feet high and two and a half feet wide. Nothing unusual for a morgue. However, the second door from the left was slightly different. It had been blown off its hinges and lay on the floor below. And the brushed, stainless-steel surface around the opening had been melted to a smooth glass finish. It was as if some great energy had erupted from inside the vault. An energy so intense that it had melted the surrounding steel.

At the moment a lab technician was kneeling beside the opening, carefully scraping samples. Directly behind her, against the far wall, rested a steel table that had obviously been rolled out from inside the vault.

"What happened?" Conrad asked.

"You tell me," McFarland said. "That was the freezer his body was in. And that"—he motioned to the table—"was the gurney it was on."

Conrad started toward the freezer, but McFarland held out his hand. "I wouldn't get too close if I were you. We're not sure what happened in there."

Conrad nodded, then turned back to the table. At one end sat a neatly folded sheet. It was a blotchy beige and brown, its edges slightly singed. "Where'd that come from?" he asked.

"It covered the body."

Conrad stared silently, trying to piece it together.

"Any ideas?" McFarland asked.

He shook his head. "You?"

The big man sighed. "The official theory is somebody broke into the building and stole the body."

"That's absurd," Conrad scoffed. "You said yourself there was no forced entry. And both guards falling asleep, then openly admitting it? Come on, who are you kidding? And this . . ." He motioned toward the destroyed freezer compartment. "I don't know what happened here, but it sure doesn't look like someone just rolled out the body and took it."

McFarland nodded. "And that half-baked cloth over there. To take the time to neatly fold it before leaving?" He shook his head. "I know what you're saying, but what other story—"

"Connie."

Conrad turned to see Suzanne barging through the glass doors, an officer catching up from behind, grabbing her arm. "Ma'am, I told you this is a restricted—"

"I saw him!" she shouted breathlessly.

Conrad's mouth dropped. "What?"

The officer tightened his grip and began pulling. "You're going to have to come with—"

"Eli!" she cried. "I saw Eli!"

Julia continued to watch her father. The episode with the tear had been nearly thirty minutes ago—already a distant memory. Now her mind reeled again with the words her mother had spoken earlier. *"He stumbled, Jules. We all stumble."* And the realization still left her stunned. All this time, all of these years she'd thought he'd purposely let go, that he'd purposely hurt her. But that wasn't true at all. He'd tried to save her, but he had failed. It was as simple as that.

"You're only as good as your word."

It had been his life's motto. And hers. The truth he had taught her to live by. But maybe, just maybe it wasn't the entire truth. Maybe there was more.

"The trick is being able to forgive ourselves and get back up."

Maybe failure is to be expected. Not condoned, but considered part of the process. The human process. She scowled hard at the body, trying to understand. That's not to say we don't strive to be good, that we don't strain with every fiber of our body to do right. But when we fail, when we stumble and fall, we don't lie there in defeat. And we don't despise others who have also fallen.

"The trick is to forgive ourselves, and to forgive others . . ."

It seemed to be a two-part process. Striving for perfection, yes, but there was more. Striving for perfection, while relying upon ... she searched for the phrase. Striving for ... And then it fell into place: *Striving for perfection, while relying upon ... grace.* That was the word, the missing ingredient ... grace.

"Mom!"

She turned to see little Cody racing around the sliding door towards her. She barely had time to rise from the chair before he threw himself at her, hugging her waist with all of his might.

"Sweetheart, how ... what are you ..." And then she saw Ken round the corner.

"Hey, Jules." He smiled softly, then glanced at her mother. "Suzanne."

Julia gave him a nod while at the same time indicating her displeasure. Then she knelt beside her son.

"Mom, it was the coolest thing. They gave us some chicken and chocolate cake and some headphones and we got to watch a movie and they gave me this lame pin." He pretended to roll his eyes as he displayed the plastic airplane fastened to his shirt. "And Dad said maybe we can go to Disneyland or Universal Studios and ... is that Grandpa?"

Julia looked tenderly at her son and brushed the hair from his eyes. Even though she was irritated that her request had been ignored, she was still moved to see her baby boy. She always was. "Yes, that's your grandpa, Sweetheart." She had a sudden impulse to pull him back into an embrace, but knew better. Even now he was starting past her toward the bed. She quietly watched as he arrived and stared at the bandaged head.

"You sure that's him?" he asked.

"Yes, I'm sure."

"Hi, Cody."

He looked up at Suzanne across the bed. "How 'bout coming over and giving your grandma a big hug?"

The boy grinned and scampered around to her.

Julia turned back to Ken who had entered the room, already raising his hands. "I know, I know you said you didn't need us. But I figured . . . you know, maybe Cody should see his grandfather at least once before he passes on."

Julia shook her head, almost amused.

"What?"

"You never could lie, could you?"

He gave a shrug. "It was the best excuse I could find."

"So you flew all the way out here just to hold my hand," she said. It was a touching gesture, even though it did annoy her.

"He's your father, Jules. We're . . . your family."

She looked at him. Despite her irritation, she was grateful to be surrounded by people who loved her, people whom she loved . . . well, as best as she knew how.

"How'd you get him past the nurse?" she asked. "He's under twelve."

Ken grinned. "Just turned on some of that ol' Preston charm."

Julia nodded. He did have charm, no doubt about that. And love. At least for her. Funny, despite all the things she had done to him, all the ways she'd failed him, he was always there for her. Always ready to understand and to forgive. As far as she could tell, the guy loved her more than she loved herself. He certainly forgave her more, she knew that. Forgiveness. There it was again. What had her mother said? *"The key is in being able to forgive."*

"Look!"

She turned to Cody, who stood at the head of the bed, pointing. Her father was breathing heavily again—deep, uneven breaths.

"Is he going to die now?"

Suzanne knelt beside the boy and wrapped her arms around him. "Soon," she said softly, leaning her head on his shoulder. "Very soon."

"Does it hurt?" he asked. "It looks like it hurts."

"No, they gave him medicine to take away the pain."

"All of it?"

She nodded. "All of it."

The breaths came harder, more desperate. Julia stared down at the heaving chest. She sensed Ken moving to her side.

"Has he been doing that long?" he asked.

Julia nodded. "But not like this."

The head rolled slightly on the pillow, then the entire body gave a jerk.

"Mom?" Cody looked up at her.

"He's okay, Sweetheart. He's just getting ready to leave us."

"Now?" Cody asked.

"I think so."

The head moved again. There was another desperate, gasping breath. And another, even more urgent. Then, ever so softly, Julia heard her mother begin to sing:

> *"Jesus loves me, this I know,*
> *For the Bible tells me so."*

As she sang his body seemed to relax. The breathing grew less frantic.

"Little ones to Him belong,
They are weak but He is strong."

She paused a minute to explain to Cody. "It makes him feel better. I think it makes it easier for him. You want to sing with me? You know the words, don't you?"

The little boy nodded. She resumed:

"Yes, Jesus loves me.
Yes, Jesus loves me.
Yes, Jesus loves me."

Softly, he joined in on the last line.

"The Bible tells me so."

The two took a breath and repeated the verse a little louder.

"Jesus loves me, this I know,
For the Bible tells me so."

Julia looked on, moved by the earnestness in her son's voice, by his unquestioning faith.

"Little ones to Him belong."

He looked up to his parents. "Come on, we're supposed to sing."

"They are weak but He is strong.
Yes, Jesus loves me."

Ken joined in. Quietly, hesitantly.

"Yes, Jesus loves me.

Yes, Jesus loves me.
The Bible tells me so."

Her father's body shuddered again. He made another effort to breathe, but it came out more as a grating, wheezing gasp.

"Come on, Mom!" Cody looked up at her, his eyes full of concern. "We've got to sing. For Grandpa."

They began again:

"Jesus loves me, this I know."

Julia opened her mouth. At first there was nothing.

"For the Bible tells me so."

Then, ever so faintly, words began to form.

"Little ones to Him belong,
They are weak but He is strong."

And with the words came the tears. Tears spilling over and tracing down her face.

There was another wheezing gasp, worst than the last. He was trying to breathe, but no air would come. Urgency filled Cody's voice. It filled all of their voices. Urgency mixed with hope ... and faith. The time had finally arrived.

"Yes, Jesus loves me."

With each word, Julia's voice grew louder. More because she willed it than felt it. But if willing it was the place to start, then willing it was where she would begin.

"Yes, Jesus loves me.
Yes, Jesus loves me.
The Bible tells me so."

Her father gave one more gasp, more desperate than all of the others. And still Julia sang.

> *"Jesus loves me, this I know,*
> *For the Bible tells me so."*

Her throat ached. The tears continued. And still she sang.

> *"Little ones to Him belong,*
> *They are weak but He is strong."*

She felt Ken wrap his arm around her shoulders. She moved in closer to him—to this man who had flown across the country to be by her side, to this man who could love her and forgive her, warts and all.

Her father's entire body convulsed. Suddenly his breathing stopped as if he was holding his breath. And then, ever so gradually it relaxed, slowly exhaling as all air slipped from his lungs.

Julia watched, her throat constricting. But she continued to sing. She had to. She sang for her father, she sang for her family, and mostly, for the first time in a very long time, she sang for herself.

> *"Yes, Jesus loves me*
> *Yes, Jesus loves me.*
> *Yes, Jesus loves me.*
> *The Bible tells me so."*

Leon Brewster swung hard, and to his amazement he actually connected with the ball. It was a hot grounder that scooted between Maggie at third and Scott, who was playing shortstop.

"Atta boy!" Conrad shouted. "Run, Leon, run!"

Leon, who hadn't swung a bat since a police raid at his porn studio eight years earlier, took off for first. His gait was not as smooth as it could be, mostly because of his designer shoes, but somehow, someway, he made it to the base before the ball.

"All right, Leon!" Conrad clapped and laughed. "Way to go!"

They were at another softball field. It was similar to the one on the West Coast where Conrad had first met the group—although this one was a bit higher class, with bleachers rising some thirty to forty feet into the air. Suspecting that he might be too old to play and maintain any sense of dignity, Conrad opted for standing behind the backstop and rooting. At the moment Leon's side was down by three, but things were looking up. With Leon on first, Brent on second, and Trevor on third, things were definitely looking up.

He glanced at Suzanne, who was clapping and cheering beside him. She was always beside him now. And he was always beside her. Just like old times. No, better than old times. Because now, at long last, he had finally found what he'd been looking for. He had finally found that "something" to fill up his emptiness. And it had nothing to do with women, or fame, or work.

Lately, the group had been teasing the two of them about setting a wedding date. And a date would come; there was no doubt about it. But neither of them was in any hurry. After all, she was already a part of him, and he was already a part of her. It had been that way since they'd first exchanged vows nearly thirty years ago. It had simply taken Conrad a few decades longer to finally grasp it.

Over five weeks had passed since Eli's lynching and since he had first appeared to Suzanne. Initially, even Conrad had found it difficult to believe her claims, thinking they had to be some sort of hysterical fantasy. But after Eli had appeared to the guys down at Kentucky Fried Chicken, where he insisted upon eating a wing (extra crispy) and cole slaw to prove he wasn't some vision or ghost, then appeared to Scott and Hector and gave them an afternoon Bible study, pointing to over three hundred prophecies he had fulfilled during his stay on earth, and later when he'd appeared to those hundreds of people at the local mall ... well, word was quickly spreading that Eli's resurrection was more than somebody's wishful thinking or overactive imagination.

Of course, Dr. Kerston and his associates were going out of their way to dispel what they insisted to be rumor and fabrication. On at least two separate occasions, the guards at the morgue were featured guests on his TV talk show, where they carefully explained how they had fallen asleep on duty, and how Eli's followers must have broken in and stolen the body. Interestingly enough, they were never discharged from their services as security guards, and, according to a little investigative reporting by Gerald McFarland, the new religious correspondent for *Up Front* magazine, both of them had received lifetime memberships to visit the City of God.

Earlier, Eli had given strict orders to the group that they were not to leave Salem County. He'd said they were to stay put until he sent some sort of "Helper," the one he'd promised them the night of his arrest. Where and when that would happen was anybody's guess. But it didn't matter to Conrad. Not anymore. Conrad was done setting agendas. If Eli wanted them to wait, they would wait. If Eli wanted him to stand on his head whistling the national anthem, he would stand on his head and whistle the national anthem. It may not make sense, it may be totally absurd, but if there was one thing Conrad had learned, it was that Eli Shepherd could be trusted. Not only in the predictions he'd made about himself, but in that upside-down, Kingdom of God living he was so fond of describing.

"Uh-oh." Suzanne lowered her head and chuckled.

"What?" Conrad asked. He looked over and saw Jake approaching the plate. Uh-oh was right. The big man's batting average had not improved since the first time Conrad had seen him at the plate. It still hovered around .000. With two outs and the bases loaded, this was not a good sign.

"Come on," Suzanne shouted encouragingly. "You can do it, Jake. You can do it."

"Oh, brother," Conrad muttered—and then received an elbow in his side, with her admonition.

"Be nice."

Reluctantly, he joined in the clapping. "Come on, Jake, let her rip."

The big guy took a couple practice swings.

Out on the mound, his brother, Robert, went through his prepitching ritual, rolling his head, squinting at the plate, until finally he lobbed the ball . . . right across the strike zone. Jake's swing came a moment or two later.

"That's okay," Suzanne shouted. "You're doing great, you're doing great!"

"Anybody ever accuse you of being an optimist?" Conrad teased.

She continued clapping while flashing him a smile. "Guess I've always believed in the long shots."

Conrad caught her drift and grinned back. How glad he was for that to be the case.

Robert went through his wind-up routine and lobbed the second pitch. It was just as perfect as the first. Once again Jake swung, and once again he missed.

"Shake it off!" Suzanne shouted. "Shake it off! This one's got your name on it now. This one is all yours!"

Jake nodded, wiped the sweat from his face with his big, meaty hand, and took a couple more practice swings.

"Keep your eye open for the high lob, outside corner."

The voice came from behind them, up in the stands. Conrad turned, shielding his eyes from the sun. Someone was standing on the very top bleacher.

Jake heard him too. He gave a half glance before directing his attention back to the mound and taking another practice swing.

"Watch for the outside corner pitch," the stranger repeated.

Now it was Suzanne's turn to look, the sun also causing her to squint.

Conrad looked back at the mound. Robert stared up into the stands, a little miffed. The stranger had created a problem. If he threw an outside corner lob, would his brother be expecting it? Or would Jake expect just the opposite since it had just been broadcast from the stands? It was an interesting dilemma, a choice both would have to make.

Back at the plate Jake crouched, preparing for the pitch. Beads of sweat reappeared on his face.

Robert started his wind-up ritual—rolling his head and squinting at the plate. The runners on their bases prepared to take off. This was it. Two strikes, bases loaded. It was now or never.

Jake took one more practice swing, focused, and waited.

At last Robert pitched the ball. As it came toward the plate, Jake stepped forward, preparing for an outside corner lob. He guessed correctly.

CRACK!

The ball flew off the bat, sailing high into the air. Everyone froze. No one believed their eyes—most of all, Jake. It was a home run, a grand slam!

"Atta boy, Jake!" Suzanne shouted. "Run, Jake, run!"

But Jake barely heard. Instead, he turned toward the stands and looked up at the stranger standing in the sun. A grin spread across his face. Then, still holding the bat, he started to run. But not toward first. Instead, he started around the backstop toward the stands.

"Jake!" Suzanne shouted.

But the man didn't stop, he didn't even slow. "Eli!" he cried, and continued to lumber forward.

Conrad whirled around and stared up into the stands. Of course. Why hadn't he recognized him before? His heart began to pound. It had been six days since Eli's last appearance. For Conrad, each visit was more meaningful than the last. And for good reason. That was his life standing up there, his purpose for living. Still holding Suzanne's hand, he also started toward the bleachers, at least a dozen steps ahead of Jake.

They reached the bottom of the steps and started up. Eli remained standing in the sun, some thirty, forty feet above them. As they ran, that same children's song started to ring in Conrad's ears, the one he and Suzanne used to sing to their Sunday school class so many years before. He wasn't sure where it came from or why he was hearing it now, but it was definitely there.

Jesus loves me, this I know,
For the Bible tells me so.

The steps were steep, and Conrad could already feel the strain in his legs. Apparently so did Suzanne. That's why after only a dozen or so she let go of his hand. "You go on," she panted. "I'll catch up."

Conrad nodded and continued. His heart beat harder now; he could hear it pounding in his ears.

Little ones to Him belong,
They are weak but He is strong.

His breathing grew more difficult. He definitely wasn't as young as he used to be. But he wouldn't stop. After all, that was Eli standing up there in the sun, stretching out his arms to him.

Yes, Jesus loves me.

Conrad's legs became more and more unsure. The pounding in his ears grew louder. And his breathing became more difficult. He could feel the burn in the back of his throat. Felt his lungs crying for more air. But still he ran.

Eli was just ahead. In the blinding glare of the light Conrad could see him opening his mouth. He was saying something, but they were still too far apart for Conrad to hear.

Yes, Jesus loves me.

His legs started to lose feeling. Again Eli spoke, and again Conrad strained to listen. But there was only the song and the pounding in his ears. The thunderous, rapid pounding. And it was no longer a steady rhythm. Now it had become erratic, out of sync.

He breathed harder, gasping for air, trying in vain to fill his lungs.

Yes, Jesus loves me.

His legs turned to rubber, becoming foreign objects. And still he ran. He was less than ten feet away now. Ten feet from Eli, who stood arms outstretched. Even in the sunlight, Conrad could see him grinning. And Conrad grinned back. Despite the exhaustion, despite the lack of air, he couldn't help grinning.

The pounding grew wild, deafening. Out of control.

Again Eli spoke, and again Conrad strained to hear. But he could not. Not yet.

Yes, Jesus loves me.

They were six feet apart.

Suddenly his legs were gone, no feeling, no control. His right one almost buckled, nearly throwing him into the steps. But he kept pushing. His lungs burned like fire, screaming for air, but he continued.

Four feet.

Eli stretched his arms wider, preparing for the embrace.

The Bible tells me so.

One step to go. Conrad stumbled, began to fall. But he was close enough that it didn't matter. He was close enough for Eli to catch him. And he did. He fell into Eli's arms and they embraced. Conrad clenched his eyes against the tears. It was so good to hold him, so good to be held.

And then, suddenly, the erratic pounding in his ears stopped. Now there was only silence. Lovely, tranquil silence. His lungs no longer burned. They no longer needed air—as if being in Eli's arms gave him all the air he needed. He tightened his embrace, burying his face in Eli's neck. Nothing else mattered. Not his hopes, not his desires, not even his breath. Only Eli.

After a long moment, he opened his eyes. The light behind Eli now surrounded him, surrounded *them*. It had wrapped its brilliance about them. Blinding, overpowering, yet full of love—full of the same love as Eli's embrace. In fact . . . it *was* Eli's embrace. Part of Eli held him in his arms, while another part enveloped both of them in his light. Eli was both the light and the embrace.

He was also the motion. Conrad was not sure when it had started, but they were moving. It could be a thousand miles per second, it could be gentle drifting, he wasn't sure, but they were definitely moving. He looked about, caught up in the splendor and wonder of what he saw. Finally, he whispered, "Where are we going?"

Eli smiled warmly. And then in that tender, loving voice of his, he answered, *"We're going home, my friend. We're going home."*

It had been ten minutes since Conrad Davis had stopped breathing. Ten minutes of tears, quiet reflection, and, just moments ago, a little prayer that Julia had asked Ken to say. The request for a prayer had surprised her almost as much as it had surprised Ken. But the past forty-eight hours had brought many surprises.

The ICU nurse entered and silently placed a rolled-up towel under her father's chin to keep his mouth from sagging open. Then she turned and quietly exited, letting them have the time to themselves. A moment later, Ken prepared to slip out. Sensing her need to be alone, he encouraged Cody to say his goodbyes, then turned to Julia and said, "We'll wait for you in the lobby." He gave her a slight embrace, and she patted his hand in thanks.

Now it was just mother and daughter standing in the room. Neither said a word. After a long moment, Julia's mother slowly bent down and kissed his cheek. The words she spoke were quiet, so soft that Julia nearly missed them. "Sleep well, my love. Sleep well." And then, with quiet dignity, she rose, looked down upon him one last time, and turned to walk out of the room.

Now Julia stood all alone. There wasn't even the ragged breathing to disturb the silence. Her mind churned with a thousand conflicting thoughts and emotions. So much had happened in such a short time. It would take weeks—months—to sort it out, but something had changed. Inside her. Something deep. And although there was intense sadness, there was also a lightness. A weight had been removed. A weight heavier than anything she had ever imagined.

She stepped closer to the bed, unsure what to do. After a moment she reached out and gently stroked his exposed arm with the back of her hand. It was already growing cold. "Goodbye, Daddy," she whispered. She looked down at the bandaged face. "I guess I'll see you a little later." It was a simple statement, but the only one she could think of. She took another breath, let it out, then turned and started for the door.

But she stopped in the doorway. Another thought had come to mind. Something closer to her heart. She turned back and spoke. "I know you're not perfect. I guess none of us are. But . . . I love you, Dad." She swallowed hard and continued. "I will always love you." Then, slowly raising her hand, she crooked her little finger. And, smiling through brimming tears, she added, "Pinkie swear."

With that, she turned and headed out of the room to join her family. The family that had been waiting for her all these many years.

Now
Available

THE FACE OF GOD

BILL MYERS

Best-Selling Author of *Eli* and *Fire of Heaven Trilogy*

Softcover 0-310-22755-0

CHAPTER ONE

"Jill ..."

She gave him a brief nod, indicating that she'd heard.

"Come on," he urged, "the rest of the group is waiting."

Her brief nod was followed by a brief smile, indicating that she'd heard but was in no particular rush to do anything about it.

"Jill ..."

Another nod, another smile.

He shook his head, frustrated and amused. After twenty-three years of marriage he knew the futility of trying to hurry his wife when she wasn't interested in being hurried. He sighed and glanced around the tiny shop, one of a hundred stalls squeezed next to each other inside Istanbul's Spice Bazaar. Every inch of floor space was covered and every shelf was filled with spilling bags and open barrels of nuts, candies, fruit, seeds, pods, stems, leaves — some fresh, some dried; some ground, some whole — more spices and herbs than he'd ever seen or smelled in his life.

The aromas were dizzying, as were the bazaar's sounds and colors. A menagerie of vendors beckoning the passing crowd to "come, see my jewelry ... perfume for your lady friend ... a souvenir for your children ... beautiful key chain to ward off evil eye ... finest gold in all Turkey ... natural *pirinc*, good for much romance ... Visa, Mastercard accepted ... come, just to talk, we have some tea, my friend, just to talk."

It was that last phrase that did them in yesterday. They'd barely left the hotel lobby before a merchant was escorting them into one of the city's thousands of oriental rug shops. They'd made it clear they were not buying. The rugs were beautiful but there was no

15

room in their house nor their budget. The owner nodded in sympathetic understanding. But after two hours of chitchat, pictures of a brother who lived in America, and more than one glass of hot tea, they found themselves viewing his wares and feeling obligated to at least purchase something — which they did.

Seven hundred and fifty dollars' worth of something!

But today was another day — he hoped.

"Jill . . ."

She nodded. She smiled. And she continued talking to the leather-faced shopkeeper. The bartering was good-natured. Jill had purchased a quarter kilo of *halvah* — a deadly rich concoction of ground sesame seed and honey. She'd already paid for it, but before passing the bag to her, the old-timer tried to persuade her to buy more.

"I'm afraid it will make me even fatter," she said, pretending to pat an imaginary belly.

"A woman of your beauty, she could eat a hundred kilo and it would make no difference."

Jill laughed and the man threw Daniel a wink with his good eye, making it clear the flirting was all in fun.

Daniel smiled back. It was obvious the fellow liked Jill. Then again, everyone liked Jill. The reason was simple. Everyone liked Jill because she liked everyone. From the crankiest congregation member to the most obnoxious telemarketer, his wife always found something to like. And it wasn't a put-on. The sparkle in her eyes and delight in her voice was always genuine. Unlike Daniel, who had to work harder at his smiles and often thought his social skills were clunky, Jill was blessed with a spontaneous joy. And that joy was the light of his life. A day didn't go by that he didn't thank God for it — even as high school sweethearts, she a cheerleader, he a tall, gangly second-stringer for the basketball team. He could never figure out what she saw in him, then . . . or now. But he never stopped being grateful that she did.

As the years of marriage deepened their love, she had moved from someone who always touched his heart to someone who had become his heart. In many ways she had become his center, a constant point around which much of his life revolved. He cherished this woman. And though he seldom said it, her heart and love for others was a quiet challenge and model that he never ceased striving to emulate.

Yes, her love for people was a great gift—except when they were on a tight schedule, as they were now, as they always seemed to be. Because no matter how friendly you are, it takes more than a sincere smile to keep a forty-five-hundred-member church afloat.

"Jill . . ." He motioned to his watch, a Rolex. It had been presented to him by the elders for twenty years of faithful service. Twenty hard-fought years of sweating and building the church out of nothing. Originally he'd hated the watch. Felt it was too flashy for a pastor. But because of the politics involved, he'd forced himself to wear it. You don't keep a forty-five-hundred-member church afloat without understanding politics.

"This I do for you," the shopkeeper was saying. His good eye briefly darted to someone or something behind them. "I sell you one-quarter kilo and give you an extra quarter for free."

"No, no, no . . ." Jill laughed, suspecting another ploy. "Just one-quarter kilogram, that's all we need."

"No." The man's voice grew firm. "I have made up my mind."

"But we only have enough to buy one-quarter."

"This I have heard." The shopkeeper spoke faster. He turned his back to them, momentarily blocking their view. "But for you, I give a most special gift." When he turned to them, he was already wrapping it in the same slick, brown paper he had used before.

"Please," Jill said, laughing, "you don't understand."

Again the man's eye flickered to somewhere behind them. "I understand everything," he said, forcing a chuckle. "It is free. I make no joke." He dropped the item into the bag and handed it to her.

"But I can't. I mean, that is very generous, but I can't accept—"

"You must," he said, smiling. "It is the Turkish way." He glanced behind them and spoke even faster. "It is an old Islamic custom."

Jill frowned. "An old Islamic cust—"

He cut her off with growing impatience. "It is good for your soul. It will help you hear the voice of God. Go now." He waved his hands at her. "Leave my shop now. Go."

Jill glanced at Daniel, unsure what to do.

He hadn't a clue.

She turned back to the shopkeeper, making one last attempt. "Listen, I don't think you understand. We are only paying for—"

"Leave my shop now!" His impatience had turned to anger. "Do you not hear? Leave! Leave or I shall call the authorities!"

Jill frowned. Had she inadvertently offended him? Had she—

"Leave! *Allah Issalmak.* God keep you safe!" He turned his back on them and set to work organizing a nearby barrel of pistachios.

Again the couple exchanged glances, when suddenly two uniformed men jostled past them. In one swift move they grabbed the shopkeeper by the arms. He looked up, startled. He shouted at them but they gave no answer. He squirmed to get free but it did no good.

"Excuse me!" Jill reached toward them. "Excuse—"

Daniel grabbed her arm. "No . . ."

She turned to him. "What?"

Although he wanted to help, he shook his head.

"Dan—"

"We don't know him. We don't know what he's done."

The shopkeeper shouted louder. He pleaded to the crowd but no one moved to help. The two men dragged him from the stall and out into the cobblestone street, where his shouts turned to panicked screams as he kicked and squirmed, trying desperately to escape.

Again Jill started toward him, and Daniel squeezed her arm more firmly. She came to a stop, not liking it but understanding. Off to the side someone caught Daniel's attention. He was a tall man dressed in a dark suit and a brown sweater vest. But it wasn't the clothing that attracted Daniel's attention. It was the man's focus. Instead of watching the shopkeeper, like the rest of the crowd, he was scrutinizing the two of them.

The look unnerved Daniel but he held the gaze—not challenging it but not backing down, either. The man gave a slight nod of greeting. Daniel hesitated, then returned it until his line of sight was broken by more uniformed men rushing in. They shouted at the crowd, forcing the people to step back as they began scouring the premises, rifling through the bags and barrels, tipping them over, spilling them to the ground.

When Daniel glanced back to the man in the suit, he was gone. But Daniel had an uncanny sense that they were still being watched. He leaned toward Jill and half whispered, "We need to go."

"What are they doing?" she demanded.

"I don't know but we shouldn't be here." He wrapped a protective arm about her shoulder, easing her forward.

"What are they doing?" she repeated. "What's going on?"

"I don't know." He guided her through the crowd.

"Where are they taking him?"

Daniel did not answer. Instead he continued moving them forward. He didn't look back for the man in the suit. He didn't have to. He knew he was still there. And he knew he was still watching.

✳

"But, Ibrahim, with the greatest respect, the Qur'an calls for only 2.5 percent of our profit to go to the poor."

"That is correct. And now I wish for us to double that."

A palpable silence stole over the *Shura*, the council of ten men, most of whom were under the age of thirty-five. They came from various countries — Egypt, Iraq, Libya, Afghanistan, Syria, Jordan, Lebanon, Azerbaijan, and of course right there in Sudan. Each was well trained; many held degrees from universities in the West. Each was responsible for a specific operation within the organization. And now as Ibrahim el-Magd spoke, he knew each was quietly calculating the financial impact his imposed charity would have upon each of their divisions.

Abdullah Muhammad Fadi, in charge of the organization's European and American businesses, continued speaking as he reached for his laptop computer. "So by doubling it, we are changing it to . . ."

Ibrahim el-Magd already knew the figure. "Five percent of 1.8 billion increases our *zakat*, our charitable gifts, to ninety million dollars."

The silence grew heavier. Only the rhythmic beating of the overhead fan could be heard. With quiet resolve Ibrahim surveyed the *mujihadeen* sitting about the table, his dark, penetrating eyes peering into each of their souls. They were good men, devoted to Allah with all of their hearts and minds. Despite their devotion to family, they had left behind wives and children for this greatest and most holy of wars. They had given up all for this, the most final *jihad* that Muhammad himself, may his name be praised, spoke of.

Across the table, young Mustafa Muhammad Dahab cleared his throat. "May I ask ... may I ask why this sudden increase in charity?"

Ibrahim turned to the youngest member of the group. Mustafa was a handsome fellow who had not yet taken a wife and who, according to sources, was still a virgin, Allah be praised. He would make a great father, a great husband. More importantly, he was becoming a mighty man of God. At the moment he was in charge of managing and laundering drug money for the Russian Mafia — a one-billion-dollar operation for which their organization received twelve percent. Ibrahim did not begrudge the boy his question. He knew he merely asked what the others were thinking.

For the briefest moment he thought of sharing his vision of the night — the dream that had returned to him on three separate occasions. The dream of a face. A terrifying, blood-covered face. A face twisted with rage and fury. A face so covered in its opponent's blood that it was nearly unrecognizable. Nearly, but not quite. Because Ibrahim knew whose face it represented; he sensed it, felt it to the depth of his soul. It represented the face of God — the face of Allah as he poured out his great and final wrath upon all humankind.

Ibrahim stole a glance at Sheikh Salad Habib, his chief holy adviser. Although every man in the room had memorized the Qur'an as a boy, it was Sheikh Habib who helped interpret it in terms of the jihad. Knowing Ibrahim's thoughts, the old man closed his eyes and shook his head almost imperceptibly. Such truth as the dream was too holy to share; it would be considered blasphemy, at least for now.

Ibrahim understood and quietly raised his hand toward the table. "It is no small honor to be chosen as Allah's great and final winnowing fork. And for such honor we must all increase our devotion and our commitment. Time and time again the Western infidels have proved how power and money corrupt." He leaned forward, growing more intense. "This shall not, it *must not*, happen to us." He looked about the table. "This small gesture — what is it but merely a reminder that it is Allah and Allah alone whom we serve. Not ourselves. And if necessary, if we need another reminder, I shall raise the percentage again, to ten percent or forty percent or, if Allah wills, to one hundred percent." He lowered his voice until it was barely above a whisper. "This is the time, my friends, above all other in history. This is the time to purify ourselves. For our families. Our world. This is the time to take charge of every thought and deed, to remove every unclean desire — ensuring that all we say and think and do is of the absolute and highest holiness."

Ibrahim looked back to Mustafa. The young man nodded slowly in agreement. So did the others. He knew they would understand.

After a suitable pause Yussuf Fazil, his brother-in-law, coughed slightly. Ibrahim turned to him. They had been best friends since childhood. They had grown up together in a tiny village on the Nile. Together they had studied the Qur'an, attended Al-Azhar University in Cairo. And though Yussuf had chosen Ibrahim's sister for his younger, second wife, it did little to bring them closer — for they were already family, brothers in the deepest sense of the word.

"What about the remaining stones?" Yussuf asked. "What progress is being made?"

Ibrahim was careful to hide his irritation. His insistence that they wait until the stones were retrieved had created a schism within the council, an ever widening impatience lead by Yussuf Fazil himself. Yet despite the group's frustration, Ibrahim remained adamant. They already had four stones. They would not begin the Day of Wrath until the remaining eight were found and consulted. He turned to the group and gave his answer. "Another has been sighted in Turkey."

"Only one?" Yussuf asked.

Refusing to be dragged into yet another discussion on the issue, Ibrahim glanced at Sheikh Habib. The old man took his cue. His voice was thin and reedy from lack of use, from his many days of silent study and prayer. "It is our belief — " He cleared his throat. "It is our belief that the remaining stones will surface very, very quickly."

Ibrahim watched the group. He knew many considered this action superstitious, even silly. And because of Yussuf, he knew that number was increasing. But he also knew the absolute importance of consulting with Allah before unleashing his greatest and most final fury. Still, how long could he hold them off? Plans for the Day of Wrath had been under way for nearly four years. And now as the day finally approached, they were supposed to stop and wait? How long could he hold them at bay? A few weeks? A month? Every aspect of the plan was on schedule. They were nearly ready to begin . . .

Except for the stones.

Sensing the unrest, Sheikh Habib resumed. "There have been several rumored sightings, all of which we are pursuing. Europe, Palestine, here in Africa. It should not be long."

Mustafa Muhammad Dahab asked respectfully, "And we are certain they will enable us to hear his voice?"

The sheikh nodded. "According to the Holy Scriptures, just as they had for Moses, the twelve stones, with the two, will enable the inquirer to hear and understand Allah's most holy commands."

"And yet the additional two stones you speak of, are they not — "

The rising wail of an air-raid siren began. Tension swept across the table. Some of the Shura leaped to their feet, collecting papers; others moved less urgently. But all had the same goal — to reach the underground shelter as quickly as possible.

The compound, like many others of Ibrahim el-Magd's, was well protected by armored vehicles, tanks, antiaircraft guns. At this particular base in northern Sudan there were even Stinger missiles. Since the vowed retaliation for the World Trade Center, such precautions were necessary for any organization such as theirs.

Ibrahim rose to his feet and gathered his robes. Although he was anxious to join his wife, Sarah, and his little Muhammad in the shelter, he was careful to watch each of the Shura as they exited. He owned a half dozen camps scattered throughout the Middle East. Less than twenty people knew this was the compound where they would be meeting. In fact, to increase security, the location had been changed twenty-four hours earlier. The odds of the enemy choosing this particular time and this particular location to launch a strike were improbably high — unless there was an informant. And by watching each of the men's behavior, Ibrahim hoped to discover if any was the betrayer.

The first explosion rocked the ground, knocking out power and causing the white plaster ceiling to crack and give way. Pieces fell, shattering onto the table before him.

"Ibrahim!" Yussuf Fazil stood at the doorway, motioning in the darkness. "Hur—"

The second explosion knocked them to the ground. Dust belched and poured into the room.

"Hurry!" Yussuf staggered to his feet, coughing. He raced to Ibrahim, then used his own body as a shield to cover him as they rose. Supporting one another, they picked their way across the cluttered floor. The explosions came more rapidly as they stumbled into the dark hallway, as they joined office personnel racing toward the tunnel with its open steel door ten meters ahead. Ibrahim could see the people's mouths opening in shouts and screams, but he could not hear them over the thundering explosions.

He arrived at the tunnel and started down the steep concrete steps. The reinforced shelter lay twenty-five meters below — a shelter that security assured him could never be penetrated, even by the West's powerful Daisy Cutter bomb. The earthshaking explosions grew closer, throwing Ibrahim against one side of the tunnel, then the other. They continued mercilessly, lasting nearly a minute before they finally stopped.

Now there was only silence — and the cries of people down in the shelter. Ibrahim emerged from the stairway and joined them just as the emergency generator kicked on. Nearly forty faces stared at him, their fear and concern illuminated by the flickering blue-green fluorescents. Two tunnels entered the shelter — one from the living quarters, one from the office area. His wife and little boy had no doubt entered through the living quarters.

"Sarah!" he shouted. "Muhammad!"

He scanned the group but did not see them.

"Sarah!"

Still no answer. People started to stir, looking about.

"They were outside," a voice coughed.

Ibrahim turned to see a secretary. Her veil had fallen, revealing black hair covered in plaster dust, and a face streaked with tears. "They were outside playing when the . . ." She swallowed. "They were outside playing."

Ibrahim shoved past her. He began searching the group, holding his panic in check. "Sarah!" The people parted for him to pass. "Muhammad!"

There was still no answer. He turned and started toward the office tunnel.

"Ibrahim!" It was Yussuf's voice. "Don't go up! Not yet! It is not safe!"

He paid no attention as he arrived at the tunnel and started up the steps two at a time. Bare lightbulbs in wire cages lit his way.

"Ibrahim!"

His heart began pounding. Up above he could see the dull, hazy glow of daylight.

"Ibrahim!" The shouting persisted but he did not answer.

The higher he climbed, the thicker the dust grew. But it was not the dust of his beloved desert. No. This dust tasted of plaster and concrete and destruction. He arrived at the top of the steps and saw the steel door half twisted off its hinges. He stepped through the opening, crawling over a jagged piece of concrete as he entered the hallway. It was illuminated by dust-choked shafts of sunlight. He looked up and saw that much of the roof was missing.

"Sarah!" The dust burned his throat. He coughed violently and staggered forward. To his left was the collapsed wall of the communication center. And beyond that more daylight. He choked and gagged as he climbed over another concrete slab, slipping in the debris, splitting his shin on the broken cement. "Muhammad!" He entered the room, side-stepping fallen desks and shattered computers until he reached the gaping hole where a wall had been. "Sarah!" More coughing. He could barely breathe.

He climbed through the opening and jumped to the ground, hitting so hard that he heard his ankle snap. But he barely noticed as he continued forward, coughing, choking, limping. "Muhammad!"

Everything was eerily still except for the desert wind and ... He strained to listen. Was that a voice? "Sarah?" he called.

There it was again. A woman. Crying.

He started toward it. "Sarah ..." Limping, squinting through the dust, he continued forward until ... There! Thirty meters ahead. The color of dirt. The form of a woman kneeling with her back to him.

"Sarah?" He limped toward her.

She was weeping.

"Sarah?"

At last she raised her head and looked over her shoulder. His heart sank. It was just as he feared. Though the face was coated in blood and dust, he instantly recognized her. "Sarah!"

He hobbled toward her.

She held something in her arms. A form—much smaller, covered with the same blood, coated in the same dust. Then he saw the face. It was not crying. And though its eyes were open, it did not move.

The anguish leaped from Ibrahim's heart before he could stop it. "*Muhammad . . .*"

*

"These caves, were they not excavated first in . . . what was it?" The stooped old man from the Israeli Department of Antiquities and Museums turned to his two colleagues—one a heavyset middle-ager, the other a frail thirtysomethinger.

Before either man could answer, Helen Zimmerman spoke up. She didn't mean to interrupt, but it had always been difficult for her to remain silent amid ineptness and ignorance—both apparent strong suits among these three. "It was in 1885," she answered. "And later, in the 1970s, the area was surveyed by Barkay and Kloner for Tel Aviv University's Institute of Archaeology."

The old man eyed her suspiciously. "No . . . I believe the later date was 1968."

Of course he was wrong, dead wrong; it couldn't have possibly been 1968. But Helen knew she had to play the game. Though it killed her, she managed to choke out the words, "Yes, 1968 . . . I believe you are right."

The old duffer nodded, pleased with his superiority.

Helen led the officials behind the altar of the Church of St. Etienne, just a stone's throw from Jerusalem's Garden Tomb and only two blocks from Damascus Gate. As she moved down the worn limestone steps into the cave's musty, cooler temperatures, she could feel their eyes watching her. At least that's what she'd anticipated. That's why she'd worn the tailor-fitted slacks and snug-fitting shirt—neither immodest enough to offend their Orthodox sensibilities but definitely enough to hold their interest. All part of the game.

They arrived at the cave's entrance hall, a fifteen-by-twenty-foot room surrounded by six burial chambers—two in the north wall, two in the east, and two in the west. She removed her baseball

25

cap and shook back her hair, allowing the thick auburn curls to fall suggestively to her shoulders.

"And you think . . ." The middle-ager coughed. It could have been from the sudden change in temperature or out of self-consciousness. Helen hoped the latter. "And you think your group can find more artifacts here?"

"I know we can," she said with a smile, holding his eyes a moment — not long enough to be flirtatious but long enough to fluster and cause him to look away.

Good, she had him. One down and two to go.

"And why exactly is that, Dr. Zimmerman?"

She turned to the old-timer. "Our resistivity meters, as well as ground-penetrating radar, indicate there are at least three more hollow spaces underneath this floor, perhaps four."

"Burial vaults?" Thirtysomethinger asked.

"Perhaps . . ." She reached to the scented handkerchief about her throat, slowly working it loose. At least that was her intention. Unfortunately, she'd tied the knot just a little too tight. She pulled harder. Still nothing. *Great,* she thought. *Just great.* But that's okay, she'd improvise. She'd simply dab the perspiration at the nape of her bare neck with her long, slender fingers.

Thirtysomethinger swallowed, causing his Adam's apple to bob up and down.

She continued, pretending not to notice. "But regardless of what it may or may not be, the chances of it belonging to the First Temple Era are high — and each of us knows the rarity of such finds." She lowered her fingers to the top of her open blouse, gently wiping away the dampness. "Do we not?"

Again Thirtysomethinger swallowed.

The old-timer cleared his throat. "We can appreciate your interest in this area, Dr. Zimmerman, and your expertise. But the committee's decision to grant permission to dig here — well, it would be much easier if you . . . that is to say . . ."

"If I were to embrace your literal interpretations of the Scriptures?"

The old man shrugged. "There are many groups interested in the First Temple Era, and if word of your theory were to spread . . ."

Helen had been expecting this move and knew it was time for the speech. The one she'd given a dozen times in a dozen such situations. "Gentlemen, as a child of Orthodox parents, I can appreciate your devotion to the Holy Word. But as I have proved in my research of Mizpah as well as my assistance at Megiddo as well as numerous other locations, there is no archaeologist more qualified, none more committed to finding truth, than myself. I am a woman of science, gentlemen, of cold, hard facts."

She gave a dramatic pause before driving in the stake.

"I have no bias. I have no agenda to prove or disprove. I am only interested in truth. That is why my work is so frequently published and why you have agreed to meet with me today. If the Scriptures are truth, then you having nothing to fear. My care and exactness will only validate their authenticity."

That was it, short and sweet. She had finished — well, except for holding the eyes of Thirtysomethinger a bit longer than necessary to make her point. Well, a bit longer than necessary to make *that* particular point. He swallowed again, giving his Adam's apple the workout of its life, then glanced away.

Two down.

Again she reached to her handkerchief, giving the knot another tug. And then another, somewhat harder — until it finally gave way, but with such force that her elbow shot out and nailed Thirtysomethinger directly below the left eye.

"Augh!" he yelled, doubling over and grabbing his face.

"I'm sorry!" she cried. "Are you all right? I'm terribly sorry. Here, let me see."

He shook his head.

"No, please. I'm so sorry. That's ... Really, I'm so sorry." And she was. More than they could imagine. Because it always happened. Whenever the stakes were raised, whenever she got nervous, she'd inevitably come down with a severe case of ... well, there was no other word to describe it but clumsiness. Severe, incredible clumsiness.

Of course Thirtysomethinger assured her that everything was fine. But when he was finally persuaded to remove his hand, she saw the large red mark on his cheek. She could only imagine what stories would be flying around the office about how he had acquired his shiner. It was an unfortunate setback but not the end of the world. She'd just have to work doubly hard to reestablish the mood. She had to. Because once she mended fences with Thirtysomethinger, there was still the old-timer to work on.

She stole a look over at him. The old codger would take a bit longer but that was okay. She had been playing the game for nearly a decade, ever since grad school. She knew the rules. She knew what men were like. And she knew the disadvantages of being a woman in their world. But she also knew how to use those disadvantages to her favor — even if it meant utilizing these somewhat demeaning tactics.

Now they would move deeper into the cave. In its intimacy she would share with the old-timer her deep respect for the Scriptures — and eventually confess how she looked forward to someday embracing their inerrancy as he did. Yet for now, as a scientist, she must force herself to simply look at the facts. It was all true. She never lied ... unless she had to. But it would take time. Still, the old guy would eventually join his colleagues in supporting her proposal. That's how it worked. Dr. Helen Zimmerman, University of Washington professor of archaeology, sighed wearily, almost audibly. Like it or not, that's how it always worked.

*

Daniel Lawson sat in the tour bus parked outside their hotel and endured another verbal barrage from Linda Grossman. Boy, could that gal talk. Nine times out of ten it involved issues she thought the church needed to address. And what made it even worse was that nine times out of ten she was usually right. She was definitely a woman on a mission, which explained her going back to college for her master's degree in education. It would also explain why on two separate occasions she had applied to be their director of Christian education. Unfortunately, she was a woman, and though the position didn't involve the actual teaching of men, as the Scriptures prohibit — well, she was still a woman.

At the moment she had attached herself to one of the elderly ladies, Darlene Matthews, and was sitting with her behind him, doing her best to increase the old woman's self-esteem.

"You should see the lovely scarf she purchased, Pastor. And at such a low price. She's become quite the bargain hunter on this trip. Haven't you, Darlene?"

Darlene shrugged, the crinkled skin of her face glowing from the attention.

"Don't be so modest. Tell Pastor what the shopkeeper started off asking."

"Really, Linda," the old lady murmured, too embarrassed to speak.

But not Linda. "One and a half million lira. Can you imagine that, Pastor? They wanted one and a half million lira for one little scarf."

Daniel shook his head. "That seems a little steep." As he spoke, he noticed movement through the bus window behind them. One, then two, blue-and-white cars with *"Polis"* written across their doors slid to a stop in front of the hotel.

Linda rattled on. "That's what she thought. So she — well, go ahead, Darlene, tell Pastor what you did."

Darlene looked up nervously.

He smiled. "Please, tell me what happened."

She took a timid breath, then finally began sharing the trials and triumphs of buying a scarf in downtown Istanbul. Daniel continued to smile and tried his best to stay interested, particularly after Jill's criticism of him earlier that morning. *Not loving his congregation?* What was she talking about? After all he'd done? After all he'd sacrificed?

Still, even now as he listened to Linda and Darlene, he caught himself dropping into autopilot, uh-huhing and you-don't-saying whenever appropriate. Of course he rebuked himself. After all, he was their pastor; these details should be interesting to him. They certainly were to Darlene. And as a pastor, wasn't it his responsibility to "rejoice with those who rejoice" and "mourn with those who mourn"? Even if it was over a scarf? So why during the past few years had it become so difficult? When the congregation was one or two hundred members, his interest and compassion had come easily. But now — now that they were up to forty-five hundred, now that he had in essence moved from senior pastor to CEO — it had become next to impossible. Yet impossible or not, it was still a requirement, a command. And despite the difficulty, despite his failure, he would strive to obey it. That was Daniel Lawson's trademark. Regardless of the cost, he always obeyed.

"So I told him that the scarf was far too expensive and then I turned and I started walking away, and then he called back to me and said he would make an exception and sell it to me for only one million lira, and I said ..."

Daniel glanced at his watch, then out the window. What was taking Jill so long? Again he tried to focus.

"... it was still too expensive and that I really meant it. Then he said ..."

And again he failed.

Initially Jill had been opposed to going back into the hotel. This morning the group was only going to visit the palace museum, Topkapi Sarayi. Why did she need to cover her shoulders for a museum? But Daniel was gently insistent and explained, as he often had to, that a pastor's wife needed to go out of her way to appear modest. As usual, Jill didn't see his logic and had dug in — good-naturedly, but dug in nonetheless. And it wasn't until he offered to go back to the room himself that she told him to stay put and headed off the bus to the hotel.

But that had been — he glanced at his watch — twelve minutes ago.

"... and then he dropped the price once again to eight hundred thousand lira. Can you believe that, Pastor — eight hundred thousand lira?"

Daniel gave another nod of interest and glanced about the bus. There were forty-two of them on this year's tour. The same tour he and Jill led church members on every year — six days in Israel, one in Ephesus, yesterday and today in Istanbul, tomorrow Athens, then Rome. It was always the same, and though he knew he should be enthusiastic, though he tried to be enthusiastic, he had grown bone weary of the routine. But not Jill. No sir, she thrived on mixing with the people and getting to know them as they traveled together. She always had a great time on these things. Until last night ...

Until the incident with the shopkeeper. Until they arrived in their hotel room, unwrapped the halvah, and discovered it wasn't exactly an extra piece of candy that he'd slipped into their bag. Instead it was a strange, rectangular-shaped stone. It was about the size of one of those complimentary bars of soap they give you in hotels. Yet it was anything but soap. By its green color, Daniel guessed that it was some type of emerald. It appeared very old and was worn smooth — so smooth that the written inscription on the front, which looked Arabic or Hebrew, had nearly disappeared.

"... and so I told him it was still too expensive and that I really didn't want to waste any more of his time, and then he said to me ..."

Daniel nodded as he reached for the stone in his pocket. Silently he ran his fingers over its smooth edges. It was obviously stolen. The cagey old merchant had simply passed it on to them to get rid of the evidence. Both he and Jill had agreed to turn it over to the authorities first thing that morning, once they got the group up and going through the museum. But the fact that it was illegal didn't bother them as much as did the dream. Jill's dream. The one that had led to her criticism about his lack of love for the congregation. The one that had caused her to cry out in her sleep, waking both of them earlier that morning ...

"It's nothing," she had said somewhat sheepishly as they lay together in the small hotel bed.

But her voice betrayed her and he persisted. "Please, tell me ..."

"It's just the excitement from that stone and the old man's arrest, that's all."

There it was again, the uneasiness. He reached over and snapped on the bedside lamp. "What was it, Hon? Tell me, what's wrong?"

She shook her head.

"Tell me," he softly persisted. "What is it?" He waited. Finally she turned to face him. That's when he saw the tears. And that's when he reached out and took her hand. Was it his imagination or was she trembling? Gently he repeated, "What's wrong ..."

She took an uneven breath. He said nothing but waited until she was ready, until she finally spoke. "It was about you."

"Me?"

She tried to smile but didn't quite succeed. "You were all decked out in some sort of holy man's garb — you know, with the robes and everything."

"Like a priest, a Catholic priest?"

"No ... fancier than that. Like one of those paintings from the Old Testament. You know, the high priest with all those robes and a turban and that vest thing in the front. And there was the stone, our stone, right near the center of the vest."

"And that was scary?"

She shook her head.

"What, then?"

She took another breath. "You were weeping. It was the weirdest thing. You couldn't stop crying. And when I asked you why, you tried to answer but couldn't. You were too overcome."

"With what?"

She wiped her face and looked at him. "With love. God's love. You were overwhelmed with his love for your congregation. It was incredible. I've never seen anything like it ... especially from you."

The last phrase surprised him. "Especially from me?"

She said nothing but glanced away. He could see that he'd stumbled upon something, and tried again. "I'm not sure what you mean. Are you saying I don't love the congregation?"

She looked down at his hand.

"What is it?" he asked.

She shook her head.

"No ... please, tell me."

She sighed, then with quiet resolve answered. "You used to love them like that, Danny ... but that was a long time ago."

"What?" He tried to hide his incredulity. "What does that mean?"

"I think ..." She paused, constructing her thoughts. "I think you love *serving* God ... and I think you love serving his people. But I don't think you really love either of them, sweetheart ... not like you used to."

The words were a shock. If he didn't love God and his people, why was he killing himself serving them all these years?

"But it's okay," she said, reaching up to his face and gently pushing the hair out of his eyes. "Because you'll get that love back, Danny Boy. He told me."

"Who?"

She smiled.

"Who, Jill?"

"The face."

"Face?"

"Of God."

Daniel blinked. "I thought you were dreaming about me as a high priest."

"I was. You were a high priest and you were wearing that stone and then it started to glow. And the brighter it glowed, the more your face ..." — she swallowed — "the more your face started to twist up and contort, like you were being tortured or something. And then suddenly …" — she took another breath — "suddenly it was covered in blood … so much blood that I couldn't even recognize you, until at that instant I somehow knew. I was no longer looking at your face, but at … at the face of …"

"God?" Daniel asked.

She nodded, then answered hoarsely, "Yes. I've never seen such pain and passion. But it had also become yours — your pain and your passion. And then he spoke. And then you spoke. It was you but it wasn't you. It was like the two of you were the same … sharing the same face … the same passion. And then you spoke …"

Daniel hesitated, almost afraid to ask. "What did I say?"

"You said … you said, 'I hear his voice, Jill. I finally hear his voice.'"

"And then?"

She swallowed again. "And then I woke up."

The conversation had been nearly six hours ago, yet it continued to haunt him. The images were so strange and eerie. And the accusation. Of all she had said, it was the accusation that ate at him the most. Not love God? Not love his congregation? How could she possibly mean that?

He ran his fingers over the stone again. *"It will help you hear the voice of God,"* the old man had said. Yeah, right. More likely to give you spooky dreams and send you to a Turkish prison for possession of stolen goods. He sighed. Yes sir, the sooner they got it into the hands of the authorities —

"Pastor Lawson!"

Daniel glanced up to the front of the bus. The hotel's young desk clerk stood at the door. "Pastor Lawson …"

Darlene stopped her story.

"You must come!" the desk clerk shouted. "Come at once!"

Daniel rose to his feet. "What is it? What's wrong?"

"Your wife."

A cold knot gripped his stomach. "Jill?"

"Come!"

Daniel raced up the aisle to the bus door, then down the steps. "What's wrong?" he demanded. They started running along the sidewalk to the hotel. "Tell me what's wrong!"

The young man did not answer. He didn't have to — it was written all over his face. They entered the hotel and rushed through the carpeted lobby, jostling more than one patron, until they reached the brass doors of the elevator. But Daniel didn't stop. He headed straight for the stairway, throwing the door open so hard that he nearly shattered its glass window. Trim and still athletic, he took the worn marble steps two at a time. He flew around the second-floor landing, grabbing the iron railing to make the turn, and sailed up to the third floor. He burst through the door, barely winded — until he saw the other door, the open one at the end of the hall. *Their* door. Her clothes were strewn across the carpeted floor inside the room. Two or three police stood about. Suddenly it felt as if someone had punched him in the gut.

He sprinted down the hall. As he arrived, a roly-poly official with a mustache turned to block his entrance, but Daniel easily pushed past him and into the room. That's when he saw her — sprawled on the carpet between the doorway and the bed, her chest heaving, her white blouse soaked in blood.

"Jill!"

He shoved through two more officials and dropped to his knees at her side. He wanted desperately to pick her up, to hold her, but knew better.

She heard his voice and opened her eyes. They twinkled slightly in recognition.

"Get a doctor!" Daniel turned to the police. "Someone get a doctor!"

"He is on his way," the mustached man answered.

"Danny Boy . . ." Her voice was a faint whisper.

"Shh. Don't move. They'll be here. They're getting some help. Don't move. You'll be okay."

She tried to shake her head but broke out coughing, wincing in pain.

"Don't move, don't move." He reached down to her belly, to the soaked, slashed shirt. A wave of nausea swept over him when he saw her stomach. He looked back to her face and forced out the words. "You'll be . . ." His voice constricted. "Hang on, you'll be okay." Turning, he shouted over his shoulder, "Where's the doctor? How long's she been this way? Get a doctor!"

The men shuffled, trading glances, examining the tops of their shoes.

"I see him," she whispered.

Daniel looked back to her. "What?"

"His face." She was looking directly at him. "That awful, passion-filled face."

"Shh," he croaked. "Don't talk. Will someone get a doctor!"

"I'm going to leave now, Danny Boy." Her voice grew fainter.

He lowered his face closer. Hot tears sprang to his eyes. "No," he fiercely whispered. "You can't . . ."

"It's going to be okay."

"You can't!"

"I have to." Her voice was mostly breath now. "It's the only way."

"No. We're supposed to grow old together, remember? We're supposed to laugh at each other's wrinkles. That's the deal, remember?" He angrily swiped at his tears. "You can't leave . . . not now, not like this."

"He loves you, Danny." The words were nothing but air.

"No!" Tears splattered from his face onto hers. He tried wiping them away but only smeared the blood from his hands across her cheek.

"And you'll love him . . ."

"Stop . . . be quiet. You need your strength. Be quiet now."

"He promised. You'll hear his voice and you'll love him."

"No . . . You can't go. You're all . . . You're all I have."

"You'll have him . . ." — the words were barely audible — "soon . . ."

"No, you can't . . . You can't go . . ."

She gave him the faintest trace of a smile, part sad, part understanding.

"Listen to me . . . Listen!"

She did not respond.

"No, you can't . . . Listen to me. Listen to me!"

But she no longer looked at him. She no longer looked at anything.

"No! No . . ."

He felt hands taking his shoulders. They tried pulling him away.

He fought them. "She'll be okay. She's just . . . She'll be all right . . ."

The hands continued to pull.

"She's okay." He looked up at them, images blurred by tears. "She's just . . . Where's the doctor! Somebody get a doctor!" He turned back to her. "Jill!" And still they pulled, beginning to drag him away. *"Jill . . ."*

WHEN THE LAST LEAF FALLS

A NOVELLA

BILL MYERS

When everything seems lost, God's love has a way of turning life around.

This retelling of O. Henry's classic short story *The Last Leaf* begins with an adolescent girl, Ally, who is deathly ill and angry at God. Her grief-stricken father, a pastor on the verge of losing his faith, narrates the story as it unfolds.

Ally's grandpa lives with the family and has become Ally's best friend. He is an artist who has attempted—but never been able—to capture in a painting the essence of God's love. One day, in stubborn despair, Ally declares that she will die when the last leaf falls from the tree outside her bedroom window. Her doctor fears that her negative attitude will hinder her recovery and her words will become a self-fulfilling prophecy.

This stirring story of anger and love, of doubt and hope, speaks about the pain of living in this world, and the reality of the Other world that is not easily seen, but can be deeply felt. Talented storyteller Bill Myers enhances and updates a storyline from one of the masters and brings to light the awesome power of love and sacrifice.

Hardcover 0-310-23091-8
Audio Pages®, *When the Last Leaf Falls/The Faded Flower* 0-310-24046-8

Pick up a copy today at your favorite bookstore!

ZONDERVAN™

GRAND RAPIDS, MICHIGAN 49530 USA

WWW.ZONDERVAN.COM

THRESHOLD

BILL MYERS

Some say Brandon Martus has a mysterious ability to see into the future, to experience what scientists refer to as a "higher dimension." Others insist he is simply a troubled Generation-X member plagued by the accidental death of his little sister. It isn't until he teams up with Sarah Weintraub, the ambitious neurologist, that a far deeper secret unfolds.

Utilizing the latest discoveries in brain research and quantum physics, the two carefully wind their way through a treacherous maze of human greed and supernatural encounters that are both legitimate and counterfeit—until they finally discover the astonishing truth about Brandon Martus.

This book takes you from the mountains of Nepal to the heartland of America, through the deceptions of hell and into the hands of Jesus Christ, in a carefully researched, thought-provoking, and thoroughly electrifying journey.

Softcover 0-310-20120-9
Mass Market 0-310-25111-7

Pick up a copy today at your favorite bookstore!

ZONDERVAN™

GRAND RAPIDS, MICHIGAN 49530 USA

WWW.ZONDERVAN.COM

FIRE OF HEAVEN

BILL MYERS

In this riveting sequel to *Blood of Heaven* and *Threshold*, Brandon Martus and Sarah Weintraub follow God's calling—right into danger.

This is not another end-times thriller, but one of the most intense and thought-provoking pieces of Christian fiction to come along in years. As the couple prepare for the final showdown against Satan himself, they must live and proclaim the truths Christ has given his end-times church. From America to Jerusalem, Brandon and Sarah battle the forces of man and hell while learning the true cost of following Christ.

Follow Brandon and Sarah as they learn the importance of their God-given calling and struggle to fulfill what they are to do, all the while battling supernatural evil and forces beyond their control.

"I couldn't put Fire of Heaven *down. Bill Myers's writing is crisp, fast-paced, provocative, and laced headily with Scripture. A very compelling story."*

—Francine Rivers

Softcover 0-310-21738-5
Mass Market 0-310-25113-3
Abridged Audio Pages® Cassette 0-310-23002-0

Pick up a copy today at your favorite bookstore!

ZONDERVAN™

GRAND RAPIDS, MICHIGAN 49530 USA

WWW.ZONDERVAN.COM

We want to hear from you. Please send your comments about
this book to us in care of the address below. Thank you.

ZONDERVAN™

GRAND RAPIDS, MICHIGAN 49530 USA

WWW.ZONDERVAN.COM